My Best Friend's Wedding

BOOKS BY TILLY TENNANT

The Summer of Secrets
The Summer Getaway
The Christmas Wish
The Mill on Magnolia Lane
Hattie's Home for Broken Hearts
The Garden on Sparrow Street
The Break Up
The Waffle House on the Pier
Worth Waiting For
Cathy's Christmas Kitchen
Once Upon a Winter
The Spring of Second Chances
The Time of My Life
The Little Orchard on the Lane
The Hotel at Honeymoon Station

AN UNFORGETTABLE CHRISTMAS SERIES
A Very Vintage Christmas
A Cosy Candlelit Christmas

FROM ITALY WITH LOVE SERIES
Rome Is Where the Heart Is
A Wedding in Italy

HONEYBOURNE SERIES
The Little Village Bakery
Christmas at the Little Village Bakery

Tilly Tennant

My Best Friend's Wedding

Bookouture

Published by Bookouture in 2021

An imprint of Storyfire Ltd.
Carmelite House
50 Victoria Embankment
London EC4Y 0DZ

www.bookouture.com

ISBN: 978-1-80019-915-6
eBook ISBN: 978-1-80019-914-9

To my girls, who make me proud every day

Chapter One

It was hard to think of winter when summer was so gloriously in evidence outside the window of Libby's tiny attic office. It was always a bit too warm up here, but with the skylight open, birds singing as they hopped about on the roof and a gentle breeze tickling the back of her neck, Libby didn't mind.

Occasionally she'd catch the cry of a market-stall vendor from the street below, and the cars up and down the high street were a constant accompaniment. In a short while she'd run to fetch her lunch and eat it out on the grass of the park that sat in the centre of the town and admire the rectangle of fragrant roses, now at their finest, maybe slip off her shoes and dangle her feet in the brook that ran through it. She might see someone she knew who would stop for a chat if she was lucky, and if the ice-cream cart was out, she'd treat herself to one before heading back to work. Libby was a woman who didn't want or need much in life; she was happy with the simplest of pleasures, and her home town offered plenty of those.

But right now she had to concentrate, and thoughts of the glorious sun outside weren't helping. It was Libby's job to run the old tailoring shop that had graced the high street of Wrenwick for over a hundred years, a place of oak panelling and Minton-tiled floors that had withstood many attempts to modernise, and where the staff were still expected to address customers as sir and madam. Libby had a wonderful team of workers there with decades of experience between them and the kindest souls, so it was no hardship to manage them at all.

She also had duties that included payroll and buying, which meant choosing and ordering the stock they would be selling season to season. Not that the suits they sold in the summer were hugely different from the ones they sold in the winter, except that more of what they sold in the summer would be worn at weddings, and – apart from the sun outside – this fact was proving to be Libby's second stumbling block.

She'd have to run her choices by the owner of the shop, of course, the great-great-grandson of the founder of Swift's Formalwear, but as she usually played it safe and traditional – pinstripe, plain, the occasional houndstooth or tweed – the owner would have no qualms releasing the budget for her to put her order in. She loved old Mr Swift and she loved running his store, which was just as well, because he loved the golf course a lot more than he did the shop that paid for his membership there. He was perfectly content to sit back and let Libby organise it for him and didn't really care how it was done. And if she was perfectly honest, Libby appreciated the trust he placed in her and was conscientious enough to repay it handsomely.

It wasn't the golf course, or Eric Swift's lack of interest in his shop, or even the weather outside that had Libby currently staring into space. It was the fabulous yet totally different to Swift's Formalwear's standard aesthetic suit she'd just seen in one of their trendier (largely unused) supplier catalogues. It was electric blue, slim-cut and very much consuming her current thoughts. Or rather, what was consuming her thoughts was what her own Prince Charming would look like in it. With only three weeks to go until her own wedding, she found herself imagining what Rufus might look like in rather a lot of the suits she saw.

She'd always been a sucker for a man in a well-tailored garment, which was rather serendipitous considering the job she'd ended up in, and the catalogues she was expected to trawl through as part of her duties were proving to be like catnip to the bedraggled moggy that often sat by the back door of the shop waiting for her to sneak a saucer of milk out there. This particular suit was very fitted, meaning it would show off his toned physique perfectly, and the shade would accentuate the blue of his eyes to such an extent they might pierce the very soul of anyone who happened to gaze into them (and Libby hoped very much that would only be her).

It hadn't all been plain sailing with her and Rufus, and the previous few months had been especially traumatic as they'd lost… well, she didn't want to dwell on that now. They both knew what they'd lost and the pain didn't need saying. The point was, Libby hoped, above all else, that their wedding would signal they'd finally come through it and that they'd finally be able to move on to the next phase of their lives together. She was forced to admit they still had a long way to go to full healing, but she was happily optimistic that married life would hurry that along nicely.

The wedding ceremony was due to take place at the prettiest church in a nearby village. In fact, it was the village where Libby's grandma had grown up, the same church where she'd been christened, where she'd married Libby's granddad and where Libby's great-grandparents were both buried. It was more of a chapel really, built from the same grey stone that characterised much of the Peak District, surrounded by rolling hills and majestic crags, with a churchyard shaded by oaks and horse chestnut trees, where bluebells grew in secret corners and poppies and marguerites lined the paths.

Libby's grandma had been blessed with the happiest marriage, and it was only the untimely death of her husband that had cut it short.

Libby had hoped, in having her ceremony at the same church, she and Rufus would be blessed with a marriage that happy too. Libby's grandma had been thrilled with the choice, and Rufus hadn't minded where the wedding took place as long as they were getting hitched, so she'd eagerly arranged for the traditional reading of the banns which he'd attended without complaint and then the date had been set.

There would be ups and downs and trials in their future – there had already been enough – but their marriage would be a fresh start, Libby was convinced of that. They could look forward, build a life together, maybe even try for another baby... though the last part was a discussion they hadn't been able to have yet and Libby realised Rufus was going to take some convincing. She had to admit to being nervous herself, but if they wanted to start a family they were going to have to deal with the loss of their first child or they'd never do it.

Whenever Libby thought of that event, the sky seemed to darken a little. The fact that the accident which had caused it had happened here in Swift's sometimes threw a shadow over her working life too, but her job was so important to her, so much a part of who she was, that she'd fought hard not to let that drive her out. It could have happened anywhere, she'd told herself, on any set of stairs. And, at the end of the day, she was convinced there were no colleagues anywhere who would have looked after her the way hers had in the weeks afterwards. If ever there was a reason to rail against her instincts to leave, it was that.

Libby tried not to dwell on that now. What mattered was that she and Rufus were finally making a promise to each other. For a while, when their grieving was new and raw and things were at their darkest, Libby had been afraid she was going to lose him. But now they were getting married and everything was going to be good again. She had to believe that, and holding on to that hope was the thing that had ultimately got her through the heartbreak she'd been forced to endure.

Libby's mobile was on the desk, and it pinged a message. She looked and smiled – talk of the devil… her grandma.

Are you still coming for tea after work?

Libby's smile grew. Her grandma was no dinosaur when it came to using her phone and she had the very latest model, but she'd still take a voice on the line over a text any day. She was only texting Libby now instead of calling because she knew her granddaughter would be at work and possibly not available to chat. So, instead of replying by text, Libby picked up her phone and dialled her grandma's number.

'I was just thinking about you,' she said as her grandma answered.

'I thought my ears were burning. I hope it was good.'

'It was. Actually, I was just thinking about St Dom's.'

Her grandma chuckled. 'So you weren't thinking about me really; you were thinking about your wedding.'

'Yes, but I was thinking about how lovely it is that you got married there and soon I will too. So in a way it was about you.'

'I'll believe you, though thousands wouldn't. So, are you still coming to tea or not?'

'Will Mum be there?'

'No, it's just us.'

'Try and stop me then!'

'You're terrible,' her grandma chastised, but there was humour in her tone. 'It's lucky I don't tell her what you say about her.'

'Aww, Grandma, you know we just clash,' Libby sighed. 'She's been at it again, trying to lecture me, telling me I should be doing this for the wedding and that for the wedding and how perfect and so much better hers was to my dad. I mean, I'm sure it was lovely at that big church in town but it's just not for me and Rufus. Your little chapel is way cuter and far more romantic.'

'I know, my love. She tries to lecture me and I'm her mother. I don't know how she turned out so uptight because she certainly doesn't get it from me or your granddad.'

'That I can vouch for – you're a sweetie and so was Granddad. So yes, count me in for tea but please don't wear yourself out – you know you have to take it steady.'

'Ever since I was diagnosed with this bloody disease everyone treats me like I'm made of glass. I can still make a cup of tea and put some sandwiches out… as long as I take my time doing it.'

'Well, I'm sure that's true but I'd hate to think of my visit wearing you out. It's not just any bloody disease, it's Parkinson's and it's a big deal. It's no wonder we treat you like you're made of glass… you kind of are now whether you like it or not.'

'Don't remind me. Every time I hear that name I feel like punching a wall. I can't tell you how frustrating it is to struggle with things you used to find easy.'

'I'm sure it is, but that's your reality now and we all just want to know that you're taking care of yourself.'

'Well, I am. So you can come for tea and I won't be a bit worn out. If I can't make a sandwich and get some cake out of a pack for my granddaughter then I can't see that life is worth living anyway.'

'Don't say that.'

'It's true. So I'll see you at six thirty and you can tell me all about how the wedding plans are going.'

'Well, I can but there's not much more to tell you than last time we caught up. Everything is more or less organised – has been for months. I'm just doing a few last-minute things now…'

Her gaze went back to the open catalogue on her desk. They'd already purchased Rufus's morning suit, of course, and that was now hanging in his wardrobe ready for the big day. In fact, as she'd told her grandma, they'd purchased everything they'd need, including Libby's gown and a dress for her best friend and bridesmaid, Willow. Libby had decided she was going to wear her dress for the entire day, and they certainly didn't need the expense of another suit for Rufus, but the idea kept on coming to her of another, less formal, edgier version for him to wear to the evening reception. Her eyes returned to the blue suit in the catalogue. Not only would Rufus look amazing in it, but he'd probably be more comfortable in it too, and Mr Swift was bound to be OK with her ordering it – in fact, he'd probably gift it to her if he learnt it was for the wedding.

'If you're busy I'll let you get on,' her grandma said into the pause.

'OK, I'll see you later. Want me to bring anything?'

'Just yourself.'

'Right.' Libby smiled. She always asked her grandma if she ought to bring anything and her grandma always replied in the same way. Libby had no doubt it was how things would always be. 'See you then. Love you.'

'Love you too.'

Libby ended the call and stretched, sending her gaze up to the skylight. It really was a glorious day, a sky of the deepest, clearest blue, the sort of day on which jobs ought to be banned so the whole country could sit in a park or on a beach somewhere soaking up their vitamin D while they sucked on an ice lolly. Maybe she could finish her ordering after lunch; the temptation to sneak out early was definitely hard to resist right now.

No sooner had this thought occurred to her than the old Bakelite phone on the desk rang with a strangely melancholy tinkle. It was an original, maybe made in the forties or fifties. It had been in use when Libby had first taken her job at the shop (over twelve years ago), and as long as it continued to work, Libby suspected it would be in use for a good many years to come. That it worked at all in the age of 4G and Wi-Fi was a minor miracle in any case, though the only calls it really dealt with now was the shop floor contacting Libby in the office when they needed her or the odd supplier with a direct line to the beating heart of Swift's admin. Libby picked it up.

'Oh, you haven't gone for lunch yet then…'

Melanie, one of Swift's sales assistants, was on the other end of the line.

'I thought I hadn't seen you go out,' she continued, 'but I wasn't sure.'

'No, I'm still working through these catalogues. Everything alright down on the shop floor? Not getting too rushed off your feet?'

'No, it's fine here. So you're up there getting distracted by suits for Rufus again?'

Libby couldn't help a light laugh. 'Why do you have to know me so well?'

'Because you've pretty much talked about nothing else since the new season catalogues arrived,' Melanie said with a tone that suggested she was wearing a cheeky grin at the other end of the line. 'Anyone would think you were excited about this wedding or something.'

'Really? How on earth would anyone get that impression?'

'I can't imagine,' Melanie said wryly.

'So, is there something you need me for, or have you just phoned to take the piss?'

'Actually, there's someone asking for you in the shop. Your cousin, I think. Says she needs a quick word.'

'Kylie?'

Libby frowned. As cousins, she and Kylie were reasonably close, both in age and in personality, and they got along as well as any cousins did, but Kylie had never come to the shop asking for her before. For a start, she worked at the snooker hall at the other side of town and it was quite a trek to come over to see Libby during work hours. And secondly, if it was a social call, surely she'd wait until Libby had finished work to see her. Rufus wouldn't have minded her coming to the flat – he quite liked Kylie and they always had a laugh whenever they ran into each other. In fact, he'd taken up snooker since meeting her and they had regular chats at the snooker hall when he went to practise with his friends, so there was no reason at all for her to worry about seeing Libby at home.

'I think that's her name. You only have the one, don't you? A very pretty blonde girl, softly spoken.'

'That sounds like Kylie. It's definitely not Craig and he's my only other cousin. He's not blonde or pretty and he's as gruff as they come.'

Melanie laughed lightly. 'Shall I bring her up to the office?'

'That's OK – I'll come down. You're right, I am due to get lunch so I might as well see her on my break.'

A couple of minutes later Libby was on the shop floor. She fully expected to see her usually gregarious cousin chatting away to Melanie, but instead she found Kylie standing in a corner looking at her phone with an anxious expression. Libby's cousin had blonde hair far lighter than Libby's auburn, and she was much slighter too, petite and slender with wide blue eyes that were clearer and gentler than Libby's own. But they shared the same heart-shaped face and the same full lips. As Libby greeted her, she rushed to stash her phone in her handbag.

'Kylie…?'

Straight away Libby could see her cousin's eyes were red and swollen.

'Hey.' Kylie tried to smile but it only made her look more pained. 'Sorry to bother you at work but… well, it just couldn't wait any longer.'

'It's alright, I'm due on lunch. I'm going to get a toastie and a drink from the coffee shop on the corner. I may be paying a king's ransom on a wedding but I'm sure I can manage to treat my favourite cousin to a coffee too if you want to join me. I thought I might sit in the park to eat if you fancy it.'

'No, I couldn't, I—'

'Kylie…' Libby said gently. 'You look as if you need one… and perhaps a friendly ear too. Something's happened, hasn't it? I did wonder when Melanie called me but now… Is it a family thing? Has something happened with your mum or dad?'

'No, Mum and Dad are fine. It's…' Kylie glanced uneasily at the counter, but Melanie was chatting to Ernie, one of their oldest and most regular customers. 'Could we go somewhere just to talk?'

'But not the coffee shop?'

'I mean, if you need to get your lunch I guess I could talk to you on the way.'

'If you're sure you don't want to hang around and grab a drink with me then I suppose we could do that.'

Kylie gave a grateful nod and was already on her way to the shop's exit door before Libby could suggest they leave. Libby followed her out onto a street so bright it caused her to squint until her eyes adjusted to the glare.

'God, it's gorgeous today, isn't it?' she said. 'The sort of day where you wish you could give yourself instant time off.'

'You're the boss,' Kylie said vaguely.

Libby smiled. 'Not quite – at least, I don't have that much power.' She was about to make some more small talk – at least enough to see them the few hundred yards to the coffee shop – when Kylie spoke into the silence.

'I can't even begin to figure out how I tell you this,' she said. 'So I'm wondering if I should just come out with it.'

'Tell me what? Kylie, what on earth is going on with you?'

'I think I'm pregnant—'

'Oh! Kylie… you don't have to worry about telling me that! Just because I lost… well, I'm not going to be angry with you for being pregnant, despite whatever else has happened! Although I get the feeling you're not happy about it… is that why you were so worried about telling me? Because it was an accident? I didn't even know you were seeing anyone—'

'The father is Rufus.'

Libby stopped dead on the pavement, and it took Kylie a full three seconds to realise before she stopped too and turned back.

'What?'

'We… we, um… We've kind of been seeing each other…'

'Don't be ridiculous. Rufus and me… we're getting married – why would he be seeing you?'

Why was Libby suddenly feeling strangely detached? The street was real enough, and yet it felt as if she were standing on a hologram. She knew her cousin was telling her something monumental, something horrible, but she could barely take it in. Kylie was seeing Rufus? This couldn't be real. This had to be some terrible nightmare. Surely Libby would wake in a moment, safe in her bed, shaken but with the memory of her dream already fading.

'I know…' Kylie began to cry. 'I'm so sorry! I don't know why I couldn't stop myself, but he's so… and I was lonely and he kept telling me how he needed some comfort because you… and I wanted to put a stop to it, I really did, and I tried and I told him he needed to concentrate on you and the wedding and… but I love him, Libby. I'm sorry but I love him and the wedding is almost here and I don't know what to do. He says he doesn't want to go through with the wedding but he doesn't know how to tell you. He says he wants to be with me but the day keeps getting closer and he does nothing and I couldn't stand it any longer and I just snapped and I'm sorry to tell you like this but you have to know because you're my cousin and I can't let you marry Rufus when he wants to be with me.'

Libby stared at Kylie as her words tumbled over one another like rapids over rocks, but nothing was going in.

'I don't understand.'

'I'm sorry,' Kylie said. 'I'm so, so sorry… and I know you can never forgive me and I'm sorry for that too, because even if you never forgive me, I can't give him up.'

'*My* Rufus?' Libby said slowly. 'You're talking about my Rufus?'

Kylie nodded. 'Yes,' she whispered.

'I don't understand.'

'I know. I'm not sure I understand either.'

'Rufus is in love with you? *My* Rufus?'

'He says he is. He didn't know how to break it up with you.'

'And you're having a baby? His baby? Are you sure it's his?'

'Yes… I mean… well, yes.'

'*Rufus's* baby? *My* Rufus?'

'It couldn't be anyone else.'

Libby looked at Kylie, barely able to form a coherent thought. The words were hitting her ears but their meaning was getting lost somewhere en route to her brain. 'Why would you say this? I'm getting married in three weeks.'

'He doesn't want to get married.'

'But we have to – everything's booked and the invites have gone out and—'

'Are you even listening to me?' Kylie cried, causing several passers-by to stare. 'He doesn't want to marry you, and even if you went ahead it would be a terrible mistake!'

Libby shook her head. 'We *have* to get married – everything's ready.'

Kylie grabbed Libby by both hands and held her in a strong but tear-filled gaze. But she winced as Libby snatched her hands away.

'Please, Libby… don't make this harder than it is already. I'm trying to save you. I watched everything progressing and I thought I could ignore it, that things would work out, that Rufus would do something to stop it, but now that the day is so close and I can see that he's not, I have to. This is the worst conversation I've ever had with anyone in my life, but now I'm pregnant, it's one I can't avoid any longer. Hate me if you want, and you'd have every right to, but if I can do one thing for you, it's this, so let me do it.'

'But you're my cousin!'

'I know.'

'And he's my… my Rufus!'

'I know that too.'

'I was supposed to spend forever with him!'

'I'm so sorry. Believe me, if I could change what's happened I would, but I can't and I can't change that I love him too.'

Libby turned to walk back to the shop, numb, blank, unable to compute anything she'd heard. How could a day of such ordinary contentment suddenly turn into this?

'Libby!' Kylie called after her. 'Please… talk to me. Slap me, cry, react… say something!'

But Libby carried on walking. The sun was shining and the town was buzzing with shoppers, cars speeding up and down the main road, market traders calling, children squealing and laughing, the scents from the florist catching the breeze as she passed it. Everything was good in the town of Wrenwick and life carried on as it always did.

But not for Libby.

What was Libby supposed to do now?

Chapter Two

Libby frowned at her phone as she stood outside the door of the coffee shop, the very same coffee shop she'd been on her way to when Kylie had given her the news that had turned her life upside down almost six months before. Today there was no sun, only freezing rain beating at her umbrella as she stood at the door, poised to go in. Lunch breaks were brief and, sometimes, as manager, Libby didn't get one at all, but today, she made certain to take the half hour she was entitled to. Something had been on her mind from the moment she'd gone to bed the night before, had kept her awake for a large part of it, and had still been troubling her when she'd woken this morning. It wasn't a conversation she wanted to have with her best friend and certainly not one she could have in earshot of her colleagues in the shop, but, in the end, she'd felt there was no other choice so had ducked out to have a quiet word at the same time as she grabbed a sandwich.

She read the text that had come through that morning once more with a heavy sigh. She might have known it wouldn't last, given the nature of its beginning, but she couldn't help but be annoyed that her entire life had been turned upside down for what had amounted to a brief summer fling between two people she ought to have been able to trust. Somehow, the fact it hadn't lasted made things worse. If it had been true love, if it had ended up standing the test of time, at least her own heartache wouldn't have been in vain. Now, it all seemed like such a waste. She'd cut ties with a cousin she'd been very fond of and lost a man she'd loved and all for nothing. In the end, there hadn't even been a baby – Kylie's pregnancy, the thing that had forced her hand and made her reveal the affair to Libby, had been a false alarm. Libby had to suppose, in light of Rufus and Kylie splitting up, that was probably for the best, but it hardly helped.

Please, we need to talk. Kylie's gone for good, and I swear I'll never do anything like that again if you'll only give me one more chance to prove it.

It wasn't the first text or phone call from him since the one from Kylie breaking the news that she'd left Rufus. She'd read that one so many times it was indelibly etched into her memory:

I'm so sorry, Libby. I've left Rufus; I thought you ought to hear it from me before anyone else told you. It wasn't working, and I realise you may be angry with me about how we went through all that heartache for nothing, but I hope one day you can forgive me. X

Phone calls from Rufus were easy to ignore, of course, but his texts lingered, the temptation to open the messages too great and then, once opened, the words right in front of her and more difficult to shut out. While Kylie had expressed hope for forgiveness but hadn't really expected any and seemed full of remorse, wanting only for Libby to hear the news from her before she learnt it from the family gossips, Rufus was telling a slightly different story. He said he'd done the leaving because he wanted her back, and though Libby wanted to believe him, she was inclined to trust Kylie's word a little more.

In the end, however, she really had nothing to go on but one word against another. As neither Kylie nor Rufus had exactly given her anything to trust over the recent past, she didn't know what to think. Her logical brain was telling her to stay well away from it, but there was a little corner of her heart that was still broken, still pining for what she'd lost, wondering what it might be like to try again with the man she would have been married to by now had her cousin not had different ideas.

But right now, it wasn't her own lost wedding that was on her mind, but another imminent set of nuptials. The wedding of her best friend, Willow, was less than two weeks away, and the notion that Rufus might turn up had occurred to her in a sudden and panic-filled flash shortly after his latest text. She'd ignored his calls, refused to answer the door when he'd called at the flat and wasn't replying to his texts. But where was the one place he knew she was guaranteed to be? The wedding he'd been invited to as her plus-one, way back when everything between them had been rosy.

This morning Libby had phoned her grandma to ask what she ought to do, and her grandma had wasted no time in advising her to tackle it. What she ought to do was call Rufus and ask him directly if he was planning to go. And even though Libby's grandma gave the best advice, and even though Libby knew she was absolutely right, she couldn't bring herself to do it. A telephone conversation with Rufus was just asking for trouble in so many ways, and that was without factoring in the possibility that hearing his voice might just reduce her to tears. And if he said yes, he was planning to go to Willow and

Tomas's wedding – what then? She could tell him not to, but what power did she actually have to prevent it?

There had to be another way to deal with it, and that was what Libby was planning to try now. Without another thought, she dialled Willow's number.

'Libby… What's up?'

'Can you talk?' Libby asked, though she assumed that as Willow had answered the phone she was between classes at the school where she taught and free for a few minutes.

'I'm just finishing lunch,' Willow said. 'But I have time if it's quick.'

Libby drew a steadying breath. 'Rufus is still trying to meet up so we can talk.'

'Keep telling him to get lost – he'll get the message in the end.'

'Yes, but it's not that simple, is it?'

Libby heard a sigh at the other end. Of course they'd already discussed this, almost every day since Kylie had dumped Rufus or Rufus had dumped Kylie or whatever. Willow knew all about Libby's resolve not to give him the second chance he kept pestering for, but the problem was, both she and Libby also knew – without having to say it – that Libby's resolve might not be quite as strong as she would have everyone believe. She'd blocked him out so far, but it hadn't been easy. She could be as angry, hurt and betrayed as she liked, but suddenly switching off her feelings for him? Well, as everyone knew, love didn't work like that.

'Lib… please tell me you're not thinking of taking him back?'

'Of course not.'

'Then what's this about?'

'The wedding.'

'Yours?'

'No, yours. I think he might turn up. I mean, he was my plus-one when you originally sent out the invites.'

'Yes, but your plus-one means it could be anyone. Bring somebody else.'

'Actually, you put his name on the invite.'

'But things have changed.'

'I know that and you know that… but Rufus… I just have this horrible feeling he might turn up, just because he knows I'd be a captive audience there.'

'You're going to be far too busy as my chief bridesmaid to be giving any kind of audience. I think you're worrying over nothing – nobody's that obtuse.'

'We're talking about the man who decided the best person to have an affair with was my cousin.'

'You said yourself you can't help who you fall in love with.'

'Yes, but that was before… I was trying to get my head around him and Kylie.'

'Lib… I know you've said you're not, but could this worry be because you're still a little in love with Rufus? You can ignore him, right, even if he is stupid enough to turn up at the wedding? Unless there's something that would make it difficult to ignore him…'

'How could I be in love with a man who treated me as he's done?' Libby said with a tight laugh, though it was the laugh that perhaps gave it away.

'Oh, Libby…' Willow said, her voice filled with pity. 'Why didn't you tell me this before?'

'Because there's no point, is there? Even if I did still have feelings for Rufus I'd be an idiot to take him back, wouldn't I? So the best thing to do is not to think about it, which I have been trying to do. It's easier not to think about it when I can ignore his texts and the doorbell and everything else, but harder when he's sitting in front of me.'

'The thing is,' Willow continued patiently, 'if we sent an invite with his actual name on then we've sort of already invited him, haven't we? Maybe this can be your ultimate test. Say the worst happened and he did turn up, I'd help you to get through it and avoid temptation. You'd go home at the end of the night and you'd have passed, and perhaps then, knowing you *can* resist, you can really start to get over him.'

Libby heard the school bell ring in the background. Time was tight to sort this out now before Willow had to go back to teaching her class, but Libby had been feeling increasingly stressed about this issue and she needed a reassuring answer.

'But what if I can't resist? And you'll be busy – it's your wedding, you can hardly babysit me.'

'You're going to have to face him sooner or later. I'd say a room full of people is perhaps the best place to do it.'

'A room full of people who know what happened between us.'

'It's hardly a room full who know that. A handful at best – me, you, Tomas, my mum and dad… there's hardly anyone else who knows. In the end, I'm not sure how we're supposed to get out of it? I don't want him there any more than you do but I can hardly call and say, "Sorry, Rufus, you have to stay away because we prefer Libby to you."'

'I'm your bridesmaid – I have to be there! And he's the one in the wrong. And you do, don't you?'

'Prefer you? Of course we do! Well, I do. But Tom is friends with Rufus, don't forget. Indirectly, admittedly, but they do know each other quite well, and they always got along.'

'I know that, of course I do! I'm really not saying this to be obstructive or to make life difficult or embarrassing for you or Tomas, and

I know he sort of likes Rufus, but even he must be able to see how awkward having him there would be.'

'He does, but it's still not a phone call either of us would want to make.'

'Yes,' Libby said flatly, the wind now well and truly out of the sails of an argument that had never really been made with much hope to begin with. She'd known it was a big ask, and perhaps unfair too, but she'd had to check just the same. 'I get that, it's just…'

'You know what,' Willow said brightly, 'I really think we're worrying about nothing. I would think Rufus would have enough sense to realise he won't be welcome, even if he does still want to take up an invitation that was issued when you were together. And if he comes, I honestly don't think it will be as bad as you imagine. You're sensible and strong – you know getting back together with him is a very bad idea, and when push comes to shove, I think your resolve will hold.'

'I don't know about all that, but I don't really want to risk leaving it to chance.'

'I suppose I'll have to talk to Tom about it then,' Willow said with a weary sigh. 'He might see a way to have a word with him about it that doesn't sound rude.'

'You know I wouldn't make a fuss about this unless it was really important, Will, and I hate to ask you, but surely you can see how horrible it would be if he came?'

It was only because Willow was Willow, and the person who probably understood Libby best in the world, that Libby could be so frank about her feelings on the matter, but even so she couldn't deny a pang of guilt for what probably sounded whiny and selfish. This was Willow's big day and part of Libby, desperate as she was to ensure Rufus didn't turn up, realised she might be taking the shine off it. She could only hope her friend understood that she didn't mean to at all, and that she wouldn't ask this of her unless she felt she had no alternative.

'Yes, yes of course I can. I'm so sorry, Libby, I should have realised; I don't want anything to cause a bad atmosphere. I'll ask Tom what we should do.'

Willow's wedding day was just a week away. While others had been rushing around buying gifts and turkey and crackers and generally getting ready for Christmas, Libby's best friend had been nagging caterers and florists and the dress shop, where the alterations they'd asked for were going down to the wire. She'd told Libby on many occasions that a Christmas Eve wedding had seemed like such a fun idea when they'd first planned it and would fit well with the school holidays so she'd have plenty of time off to enjoy it, but if she'd known back then how much more difficult getting married at Christmas would make things she'd have thought twice.

As for their current dilemma, it hadn't really occurred to Libby that she'd need to have this conversation with her friend until this point, although, on reflection, perhaps it ought to have. Willow knew only too well how devastated Libby had been after her split from Rufus – Libby had spent enough evenings at her house crying since the summer when it had all happened. Libby hadn't said anything to Willow about his invite before because she hadn't realised she'd need to, but, in fairness to her friend, Libby hadn't considered that he might come either.

But she'd woken that morning to see the text from Rufus, and then a post on social media (and yes, she knew she ought to block his account, but some morbid curiosity wouldn't let her) that had set alarm bells ringing – he was out buying a new formal suit (and, thank God, not at the store where she worked). Was it for this wedding?

Was it a not-so-subtle warning to Libby that he planned to have that talk with her no matter what she did to avoid it? He was pally with the groom, but only because Libby and Willow were friends and they'd had couples' nights out. He was also friends with a few of the groom's mates, but that was just because he knew Tom through Willow and Libby. They were tenuous links – at least they were in Libby's eyes. Surely Rufus hadn't imagined that friendship with Tom could continue? And even if it did, surely he didn't really think it was OK to take up a wedding invitation that had been extended to both of them long before they'd split?

'Honestly,' Libby said, suddenly feeling a bit helpless about the whole thing, 'if I know Rufus at all, perhaps Tom talking to him is a waste of time. Someone telling him not to be there is probably a sure-fire way of making sure he goes.'

'He wouldn't,' Willow said doubtfully. 'Would he? If we asked him not to and he knew he wasn't welcome? And he'd have to turn up alone – that would be miserable for a start.'

'He's friends with some of Tom's friends now though, isn't he? And I think there might even be one or two other mutual friends – he probably wouldn't have to sit alone.'

'I didn't think of that,' Willow said. 'God, I'm so sorry, Libby. I never even thought this might happen.'

'No, I'm sorry. My pathetic behaviour has caused all this stress for you… You're right, if I had anything about me I'd only have to think about what he did and I'd close my ears to anything he had to say, no matter how persuasive he was…'

Libby paused. She felt mean now about complaining. It wasn't Willow's fault and she didn't want this to cast a shadow over her friend's big day.

'Do you know what?' she rallied. 'Screw him! If he wants to come, if he's stupid enough to come, then he's going to have to deal with watching me flirt with every man in the place.'

'And you're going to look amazing,' Willow agreed warmly. 'There's no better revenge than walking in there looking like a goddess so he can see what he threw away. Even better if you remain completely unattainable. Perhaps next time he'll think twice about going off with someone's cousin.'

Libby gave a small smile, but she wasn't altogether certain that swooshing around in a huge ball of claret silk was quite what the person who'd invented that theory had had in mind.

'All this worry and he probably won't come,' she said.

'Please don't be stressed about it – Tom will sort it out; he's really good at things like that. If it means you're happy he'll make sure Rufus gets the message – after all, you're far more important to us than he is.'

'I'm sorry if I seem as if I'm making a fuss,' Libby said. 'I know it sounds unreasonable, but I really don't know what I'd do if he were there.'

'Of course, I understand. I suppose I'd feel the same if Tom did something awful like that to me.'

'Yes, but he's never going to because he worships you – lucky cow.'

'I am lucky, aren't I?' Willow said, and Libby had to smile because she could hear the adoration in her friend's voice. If she hadn't known such a thing couldn't exist, Libby would have thought Tom was the perfect man. And even if he wasn't perfect, he was certainly perfect for Willow.

She was thrilled for her friend that she'd found her soul mate, but sometimes it made her a little sad that she hadn't yet managed to find her own, and that the man she'd thought might be it had betrayed her so readily. From what she'd gathered from those in the know, it had taken hurtfully little temptation to lead him astray.

What hurt even more than the betrayal with her own cousin was that he'd done it when Libby was at one of the lowest points in her life. It could have been so much worse, she'd tried to tell herself, when it had transpired that Kylie hadn't been pregnant with his baby after all, but he'd still chosen to stay with her for four months afterwards. In the end though, none of that had mattered. What had really mattered was that when the chips were down, when she'd needed Rufus more than ever, he'd decided it was all too much effort. Rather than tackle their problems as a couple, he'd gone off to find fun elsewhere, leaving Libby to face the darkness alone.

It just went to show that you never really knew anyone at all, no matter how much you thought you did.

'Lib, I'm so sorry, but I really have to go back to class. Shall I come round to see you later?'

'You're busy, it's OK. I'm making a fuss about nothing.'

'Do you really think that?'

'No,' Libby said ruefully. 'But you're right – you can't very well phone Rufus and tell him not to come. It's mean and it's rude and it's not fair to expect you to.'

'You could do it. You'd have my blessing if it helps.'

'That would involve me having a conversation with him and I'd rather rip out my own tongue. No,' Libby said flatly, 'I'm going to have to hope that Rufus has enough common sense to realise that coming to your wedding is the worst idea since Eve decided to chomp on that apple. Leave it – I'm sure there's no need to call him.'

'He's not stupid,' Willow said, her tone encouraging. 'He'll see sense no matter how tempted he might be to come.'

'Yes.' Libby folded her umbrella and stepped into the coffee shop. She took a breath, painted on a smile and decided that maybe she ought to try and be as positive as Willow about it. 'Of course he will.'

Chapter Three

Libby was worn out and the wedding cars hadn't even arrived yet to take the bridal party to the venue. In fact, they had ages until they were due to leave, but with three hyperactive bridesmaids wreaking havoc on her patience, along with a start that was earlier than even her usual work day, if someone had suggested Libby retire for a nice nap in a dark room, she'd have jumped at the chance. Not that there would have been much peace anywhere with Tomas's three nieces in the building.

'I don't know how you cope,' she said as Willow's mum, Adrienne, handed her a mug of tea. Willow was sitting on a kitchen chair while the mobile hairdresser wound her hair into rollers. Adrienne's were already in, while Libby's were already out, and she was currently floating around in a hairnet so her curls wouldn't drop too much before it was time to get dressed.

'I think we're very much guaranteed to get granddaughters and not grandsons when your time comes, Willow,' Adrienne said.

'Tomas is a boy,' Willow said with a light laugh. 'So his mum didn't just have girls.'

'Yes, but then he had three sisters and they've all had little girls so far, so…'

Libby took a sip of her tea. 'Let's hope yours are a bit calmer than these three,' she said.

'They're just excited,' Adrienne said sagely.

'Well I'm frazzled just being in the same house as them for a couple of hours – God knows how their mums cope.' Libby looked up as the kitchen door flew open. 'Speak of the devil,' she added in a low voice. 'Actually, make that three little devils…'

'Can we have our dresses on now, Willow?' the oldest girl, Scarlet, asked. She had dark hair so thick it was almost impossible to tame, with heavy eyebrows and dark eyes and a fiery temperament, which made Libby think that when she was older she'd be a sultry heartbreaker with no mercy for anyone who dared fall for her. But at eight, thankfully, all that was well in the future, so no heartbreak to deal with today, although there was plenty of headache.

'Not yet,' Willow said patiently.

'When?'

'A bit closer to when we leave.'

'Why do we have to wait until then?'

'We already talked about this, darling,' Adrienne said. 'We don't want them to get messed up.'

'But we wouldn't mess them up!' India said, looking faintly offended at the notion. India was the second oldest, but though there was only a few months between them, she seemed far younger than Scarlet. She was also the niece who looked most like Tomas – still dark-haired but with softer brown eyes than Scarlet and a gentler tone to her voice.

'You might not mean to,' Willow said. 'But accidents do happen. Look, even Libby doesn't have her dress on yet.' She gestured to her own dressing gown. 'And I don't have mine on either. Because we're trying to keep them safe until the big moment – see?'

Scarlet didn't seem to see at all. She just folded her arms and pouted to make it known that she thought Willow's plan was stupid. The other two hovered uncertainly at the kitchen door, clearly torn by the need for Willow's approval of their behaviour and their desire for Scarlet's approval as their more forthright peer.

Libby had thought many times during the morning that having the girls get ready at Willow's house without the supervision of their parents was a mistake, and right now she was absolutely convinced. But Scarlet, India and Olivia had been desperate to be a part of the process, and though there really wasn't enough room in Willow's tiny house for everyone to be there, it did mean that Willow could see how they looked and make sure it was exactly as she had envisaged when she'd chosen the dresses and hairstyles. Once they were at the venue, she'd told Libby, it would be impossible to change if anything wasn't right.

At first, Libby had agreed readily to help keep an eye on things – she was the only adult bridesmaid, after all. But that was before she'd met them and discovered just what a handful three girls between the ages of seven and eight could be – especially when they were all together with a ringleader like the formidable Scarlet. But despite her reservations now, she had to step up to the plate. She was the manager of a city-centre shop, for goodness' sake – how much more difficult could it be to keep track of three little girls?

'At least wait until all our hair is done and then I'll help you to get into your dresses,' she said. 'It's fine...' she added in reply to Willow's doubtful glance her way. 'I'll watch like a hawk to make sure there are no mishaps. I'm sure we can stay clean if we stick the telly on and stay in one place until the cars arrive.'

'Thank you!' India raced over to throw her arms around Libby's waist, knocking her mug and throwing tea all down her dressing gown in the process.

'Hey!' Libby squeaked.

'Oh… sorry…' India said, looking suitably shamefaced.

'It was an accident,' Libby said, trying not to look as flustered and hassled as she felt. 'But you see now how easily it happens? That's why we're not putting our dresses on until we absolutely have to.'

All three girls nodded, and Libby forced a smile that told everyone she had things under control when really, inside, she felt she'd have more control over the tide than these three.

'OK, so why don't we all have juice while we wait?' Adrienne said brightly. 'Come to the fridge and choose what you'd like.'

The girls followed Willow's mum across the kitchen – Scarlet first, followed by India and Olivia together, who were so similar to each other they looked more like twins than cousins. Willow smiled up at Libby.

'Nicely done,' she said in a low voice.

'Sure…' Libby looked down at her tea-stained dressing gown. 'Handled like a pro.'

'It'll be fine once they calm down.'

'I don't think there's any danger of them calming down any time soon – that's the problem!'

'They're jittery right now – it's natural. We all are.'

'You're not,' Libby said. 'And you're the one who really ought to be.'

'I'm just excited. Jittery inside, but in a good way. I mean, I get to marry the most gorgeous man in the world in a few hours' time.'

'Yeah. Lucky cow.'

Willow grinned. 'Aren't I just?'

*

Libby was making last-minute checks on her appearance when her phone rang. She picked it up with a fond smile.

'Hey, Grandma. How are you?'

'I'm as well as can be expected. I'm more interested in how you are right now.'

Libby's smile grew. Her grandma had suffered over the last few years, more than anyone ought to – first in the loss of her beloved husband and then with the diagnosis of Parkinson's, a condition which had severely impacted her life and the walks in the Peaks that she'd previously loved – but she rarely complained and was always more concerned about how everyone else was doing. It was just like her to call today, and Libby had a good idea what the motivation behind it was.

'You mean the wedding?' she asked.

'Well, I don't want to dredge up old feelings, but I was just sitting here thinking about how brave you're being, and then I wondered if you were really feeling as brave as you look. I wanted you to know I'm thinking of you.'

'I'm alright, Grandma. What's done is done – no point in dwelling on it.'

'Are you sure about that?'

'Well, no…' Libby's grandma would see through her white lie, so what was the point? Libby could be honest with her – that she had been thinking a lot about Rufus and the wedding she'd never had. 'But it doesn't mean I can't still enjoy my best friend's wedding, does it?'

'It's such a shame what happened. Two young girls ruined by one man. All those plans undone.'

'We weren't ruined. He just pissed us off.'

'It's quite right to put a brave face on it for everyone else, but you don't have to for me.'

'I know, Grandma. But if I don't then I might cry instead, and that's not really an option today.'

'That's my girl. Courageous and strong.'

'Well, I learnt it from you, Grandma.'

There was a chuckle at the other end of the line. 'Oh, I wish! But thank you, Libby.'

'So… I don't mean to throw you off the line but was there anything else? It's kind of hectic here and I think the cars are due to arrive soon.'

'Oh, no… I just wanted to check on you and wish you luck for the day. Give my best to the bride and groom too, won't you? My gift arrived?'

'I think so – they've all been taken to the venue for opening later.'

'Let me know, won't you? And if they don't like it, I have the receipt—'

'Grandma, of course they'll like it! It's a flipping Wedgwood tea service! What's not to like? It must have cost you a fortune!'

'Well, I don't have much else to spend my money on and Willow is a special girl. She deserves it.'

'She does.' Libby smiled. 'But she'll tell you it's too much when she opens it.'

'Probably. It won't make any difference. All I ask is that they get years of use from it and it will have been worth every penny.'

'I'm sure they will,' Libby said.

'Well, I'll let you get on. I want to see lots of photos and I want to hear all about it when I see you tomorrow.'

'You definitely will,' Libby said. 'You'll be there in time for lunch with us?'

'I'm going in the morning and staying all day.'

'Good, I'll be a little later because...'

'Yes, I know, you'll have a hangover. Might as well make the most of the opportunity to get one – I do miss a good night of debauchery myself.'

Libby laughed. 'I can imagine! So I'll see you tomorrow around lunchtime then.'

'Who is cooking lunch tomorrow?' her grandma asked.

'I'm not sure but I think it's Dad's turn.'

'Oh, thank goodness for that!'

'I shouldn't say it, but I agree,' Libby replied, her laughter growing. 'But don't tell my mum for God's sake!'

'Don't worry; I wouldn't want to be on the wrong end of her wrath either. We can be each other's allies tomorrow.'

'So you'll back me up when she starts lecturing?'

'As long as you back me up too.'

'Done!' Libby said.

The door to the bedroom opened a crack, and Libby heard Willow calling something downstairs before she saw her.

'Grandma... I'd better go. I'll see you tomorrow.'

'Have a lovely day today, won't you? And have a few drinks for me.'

'I'm going to do my very best! Love you, Grandma.'

'Love you too.'

Libby ended the call just in time to see Willow walk in. 'Oh my God! You look incredible!'

Willow smiled nervously. Her hair and make-up were all done and she had got into her wedding gown with the help of her mum while Libby had taken care of the young bridesmaids.

'You don't think it's too much?' She looked down at her dress and then back again at her friend.

Libby had seen Willow wearing the dress before – she'd gone with her for fittings, and then they'd had to ask the shop assistant to fetch the sample to admire it once more when they went for Libby's own dress fittings – but somehow, though she'd thought it lovely, she'd failed to see the full glory of it. As Willow stood in it now, her honey-blonde hair pinned into an elegant but effortless updo, her make-up natural and glowing, her excitement and happiness shining from within her, Libby was blown away.

On the face of it, the dress was simple enough. There were no jewels, no huge underskirts; there was no plunging neckline – it was a modest, high-necked, long-sleeved design, the fitted bodice an ivory antique lace with a skirt that fell around her with layers of tulle like waterfalls. It was a dress that needed to be worn to bring it to life, and if Libby had seen it on a hanger in the shop for her own wedding she would have passed it by without a second look. But Willow had seen the potential, the uniqueness of it, and, wearing it now, she brought it to life, turned it into something exquisite and wondrous. Libby had never seen her friend look more radiant, as if made from pure, beautiful joy. She sniffed her tears back – it wouldn't do to ruin her make-up now, not with less than half an hour until the cars were due to pick them up.

'God no! You're perfect! If you were any more perfect you wouldn't be allowed to exist!'

Willow's smile was more certain now. And then it spread. 'Silly,' she said, though she was now beaming.

'Tomas is not going to know what hit him.'

'I hope so,' Willow said.

'Trust me – he's going to love it. He's going to think you're the most beautiful girl in the world – and let me tell you, you are!'

Willow blushed, but she was clearly thrilled to hear Libby's warm words.

'Are the little ones ready?' she asked.

Libby raised her eyebrows. 'You mean the trio of torment? Just about. I had to bribe India to hand over her comfort blanket – I mean, I'm not one to judge and I don't have kids, but a blanket, at her age? She's got to be, like, eight, right? Scarlet decided to sneeze down her dress – don't worry,' she added quickly in reply to Willow's sudden look of consternation, 'it wasn't too bad and we got it out. Olivia said she felt sick but as soon as we mentioned her not being able to raid the sweet stall at the reception she was miraculously cured. I'm guessing it was just nerves.'

'I know how that feels,' Willow said with heartfelt sincerity.

'They're downstairs with adults more responsible than me – i.e. your mum and dad – waiting for the car. Good luck to the people who have to keep them focused at the venue until you arrive... hang on, wait a minute... that's me!'

Willow grinned. 'Yeah, sorry about that but it's sort of how chief bridesmaid works.'

'If you'd told me that was the deal I might have said no – I can't even communicate with kids, let alone keep them in line. It's like trying to give instructions to cats.'

'Isn't the saying *herding cats*?'

'God, if I had to herd them as well I would be screwed! I don't know how you do it every day at work.'

'The age range in my class is a little older. I'm more likely to have to deal with raging hormones and stealth Snapchatting than comfort blankets.'

'They all seem the same to me,' Libby said. 'Confusing, slightly scary, not-quite-formed people.'

Willow laughed lightly. 'If you can keep them all clean and stop them from eating the cake before the service starts I'll consider you a childcare genius. I know they're not the easiest kids, but they *are* Tomas's nieces, so…'

'I know, you had to ask them to be bridesmaids. Don't worry, I'm just messing around – I knew what I was getting into when I said yes to you. I'm sure we'll get by, and I can have my breakdown tomorrow when they've gone home.'

'You'll be a hundred per cent allowed too.'

There was a squeal from downstairs. Had it been any higher in pitch there was no way either woman's ears would have picked up the frequency. Willow grinned and Libby rolled her eyes as a second squeal answered it, which was then followed by the sound of childish wailing.

'Oh God,' Libby said. 'I have a feeling it's going to be a long day.'

'Hopefully they'll be so in awe of the occasion when the service begins they'll be stunned into silence,' Willow said.

'We can certainly hope for that,' Libby replied, 'but…'

She gave a comical frown of deepest scepticism and Willow laughed.

'If anyone can manage them, you can,' she said. 'Go for the oldest – that's Scarlet – win her over and the rest should follow. Easy as pie.'

Libby laughed. 'Your trust is touching but sadly misplaced.'

Just then the bedroom door opened and a man peered round it.

'The car will be here any minute,' he said.

Willow smiled. 'Thanks, Dad.'

Willow's dad, Gene, was a slight man with a permanent expression of brewing mischief. He and his wife had been blessed with Willow far later in life than they'd intended and were much older than Libby's own parents, but somehow still seemed more youthful in their outlook. He now opened the door wider and gazed with affection at his daughter.

'You look absolutely beautiful,' he said.

Willow laughed. 'You said that twenty times already, Dad.'

'And I'm going to say it twenty times more.' He looked at Libby. 'You too, Libby. You look lovely.'

'Thanks, Gene.' Libby smiled broadly, though she suspected he was just being courteous, because no father was going to have eyes for anyone but his own daughter on her wedding day, and that was really OK.

'Right,' he said briskly, shaking himself into action. 'I'd better go and check your mum is ready. Last time I checked she was swearing at her curling irons so I made a hasty exit in case she turned her ire on me. I don't even know why the curling irons were out... she'd already had her hair done by the professional and for some reason she was doing it again.'

'I think it's stress,' Willow said. 'She just wants things to be perfect. Honestly, she was all kinds of twitchy when she was helping me to dress earlier – I swear she's more nervous about today than I am.'

'Always been the same.' Gene shook his head sagely. 'I know she wants everything to be perfect for you – we all do, but we'd rather not have a nervous breakdown while we're at it.' His gaze turned to the window, where the clouds were billowing heavy white. 'No snow yet, at least.'

'Perhaps we won't get it after all.'

'Could do with it staying away.'

'I think it might have been romantic to have a bit,' Willow said.

'A bit,' Gene agreed. 'It's the forecast for more than a bit that worries me.'

'The papers always make a fuss,' Libby said. 'Snow is forecast and suddenly it's Snowmageddon – it's going to be the worst snow mankind has ever seen. We all make a fuss and end up getting a very disappointing flake or two.'

'True enough,' Gene said. 'Spoken like the voice of reason.'

'Libby's always the voice of reason,' Willow said. 'That's why she's such a good person to have around.'

'I'm not so sure about that but thank you for saying so.' Libby looked at the window again and Willow followed her gaze.

'As long as it doesn't stop us getting to the venue, that's all I care about,' Willow said. 'Once I've got that ring on my finger, it can do whatever it likes.'

'Lovage Hall is quite cut off,' Gene said.

'We're in England, not Siberia,' Willow said. 'No matter how much it snows, it can't be that bad.'

Gene raised his eyebrows, as if he had a different opinion on the matter, but said nothing as he left them to make the final touches to their preparations.

'I love your dad,' Libby said. 'Such a cutie.'

'I think he quite loves you too,' Willow said as she checked her teeth in the mirror. 'In fact, when we were teenagers, I think on more than one occasion he wished he could swap us and adopt you instead.'

'Your dad always adored you.'

'Yes, but I'm sure I wasn't always rainbows and candyfloss.'

'None of us were.'

Libby allowed her gaze to take in Willow's bedroom. Willow and Tomas had their own place, but they hadn't fully moved in yet. Willow had quite liked the idea of being able to start her wedding day here, in a way that was very traditional and very her. She gave the impression that she was a thoroughly modern miss, but Libby knew her friend was big on family and family traditions, and she loved the old ways.

The posters of defunct boy bands had come down, and at the last redecoration Willow had swapped them for art prints instead. Libby recognised a Van Gogh, a Klimt and a couple of other images she knew well, though she wasn't sure who'd painted them. The single bed had been swapped for a double that was undoubtedly nicer to sleep in but swamped the space so there was very little room for anything else. The walls had been painted a calming green – the colour was actually called Willow Haze, which had decided Willow's choice on the spot. It was all very nice but a bit too grown-up for Libby's tastes – she'd liked it better when it had been covered in posters of boy bands with a tatty single bed and soft furnishings that didn't match the pink walls at all.

'We've spent some mad hours in here, haven't we?' she said.

'A lot certainly got discussed within these walls,' Willow agreed. 'I hope to God my parents never bugged the place.'

'They'd have been horrified,' Libby agreed. 'And definitely wouldn't have wanted to adopt me then!'

'I lost my virginity in this room,' Willow said.

'I know,' Libby said, laughing. 'And not to Tomas. I hope you've kept that one to yourself.'

'I might trot it out one day when I want to make him jealous. Anyway, he's not daft – he knows there were other boys before him.'

'Didn't you ever discuss it?'

'Once, but it made him all weird and jealous so I didn't go into detail. You know what's funnier?'

'What?'

'You lost your virginity in this room too!'

'Shh!' Libby hissed. 'I don't want your dad to hear that!'

'Oh, I think he has a pretty good idea some wild stuff went on at that party. My parents never went away and left me for the weekend ever again after that.'

'You should have done a better job of hiding all those empties and they'd never have known you'd even had a house party.'

'Oh, like you've never told me that before, *Mum*...'

'I still can't believe I let that guy anywhere near me. What an absolute loser and what an awful first shag.'

'First shags aren't all they're cracked up to be for anyone, are they? I wish I could have some conversations with my teenagers in class about it – might save them all some horrible mistakes.'

'What would you tell them? I seem to recall pretty much nothing will put you off at that age.'

'I'd tell them it's basically ten minutes on your back hoping you're getting it right and making noises you've heard on porn films. That ought to do it.'

Libby giggled. 'Thank God we don't have to go through all that again.'

'Amen to that. Still, we did have some fun, didn't we?'

'We sure did. And just because you're going to be a smug married it doesn't mean the fun has to stop, right?'

'Right. Starting with the wedding. Later, I'm going to get Tomas to line up his friends for you to—'

'Car's here!' Gene yelled up the stairs. 'Action stations!'

Willow took a deep breath and then gave Libby a manic grin. 'OK, let's go!'

On a road like this, Libby's Citroën would have rattled the very bones out of her body, but the Rolls-Royce she was currently sitting in dealt with it effortlessly, gliding regally along as if hovering above the ice and grit and potholes of country lanes that must have been so infrequently used that whoever was supposed to take care of them had clearly forgotten that they existed at all. The only thing stopping Libby from actually falling asleep (apart from her obvious excitement for the wedding that they were speeding towards) were the little girls she'd dubbed the trio of torment, sitting in the car with her – alternately bickering and giggling raucously together, but noisy whatever state of interaction they were in.

'Ow! You're squishing me!' India cried as Olivia leant across her to play with the button that controlled the car sound system. There was no music on, and Olivia probably had no idea what the button actually did but seemed determined to tinker anyway.

'I'm not!' Olivia snapped, though she moved back to her own seat anyway.

'Scarlet's taken her seat belt off!' Olivia then announced in an attempt to take the heat off herself.

'I haven't!' Scarlet said. 'It's under my arm!'

'You're not supposed to wear it there,' India said. 'You might die.'

'I'm not going to die,' Scarlet scoffed.

'It will cut you in half if we crash – my dad says so,' India replied with an imperious air of superior knowledge.

'Your dad's stupid,' Scarlet returned, though she hurriedly rear-ranged her seat belt so the strap was now across her body again.

'*Your* dad's stupid,' India said.

'He's not.'

'My mum says he is. She always says she doesn't know why Auntie Rachel married such a useless lump.'

'Well my mum says your dad's punching!' Scarlet cried.

'What does that mean?' Olivia asked.

'It means he punches everyone in the face,' Scarlet said, while the others looked at her in horror and Libby couldn't help but smirk. Having seen India's parents, she could, indeed, confirm that India's dad was punching, though clearly not quite in the way Scarlet meant.

Though Libby was stuck in the same car as the little bridesmaids, alone and in an advanced state of terror at the thought of having to keep them in line from now until the wedding ceremony was over, she was doing her best to keep it bottled up and sometimes, like the punching comment, she was even finding it a little amusing. Their conversations veered from bewildered to desperately misinformed, and she half wondered whether she had sounded that funny at the same age. Still, there was no denying they were hard work.

Don't show them fear, India's mother had laughingly said as she'd dropped her off at Willow's house that morning – *they'll smell it and they'll go for the kill.* Olivia's mother had commented that Libby would've been calmer had she known what having children was like. (Libby had smiled graciously, but, as she had so many times before, wished people would think for a moment before saying things like that.)

Libby had decided on a policy of laissez-faire, which meant doing her best not to get involved with the politics of a trio of tweenie girls unless she really had to. If any of them looked like they might kill one of the others – or, worse still, mess up her dress – then Libby would spring into action. Otherwise, the little darlings could get on with it.

As these and other thoughts ran through her mind, she gazed out of the window. The hedgerows were high and thick with the glossy leaves of berry-studded holly bushes, and when there was a flash of field beyond, it was dappled with the dusting of snow that had fallen throughout the morning. The sky was as thick and heavy as an eiderdown, the odd flurry of fresh snow coming now and again as if someone had shaken feathers from it. The forecast had warned of a much heavier covering, but so far there was nothing to suggest the inexact science of weather forecasting would be any more accurate than it usually was.

'Are we there yet?' Scarlet tugged at Libby's dress so forcefully Libby's heart skipped a beat; she was convinced the little girl was going to rip it.

'Almost,' she said, trying not to let her panic show.

And then, to her utmost relief, Lovage Hall came into view – first the rooftops of grey slate and tall chimneys, which Libby pointed out to great excitement amongst her young charges, and then the rest. It was set back in what looked like miles and miles of grounds, the drive up to it almost as long as the one they'd taken to get to the gates, with its own woodland and lake and humungous gardens and huge sandstone pillars along its frontage. If Mr Darcy on horseback had galloped across her line of sight, Libby wouldn't have been a bit surprised.

'Oooh!' Olivia cried. 'Look at that! Is that it, Libby? Is it? Is that the wedding, Libby? Where are all the people? I can't see the... Oooh! Look at all the cars! Scarlet, India... look at all the cars! I've never seen so many cars! And there are the people! How many are there, Libby? Scarlet, India... look at all the people!'

Libby smiled as the girls' chatter went supernova, and she was still smiling when the car eventually pulled up on the sweeping gravel drive that led to the main house. She was relieved to see the cars containing the families of the trio of torment were already there, the occupants standing shivering on the steps of the house as they waited. Chatting amiably to them were Tomas's parents – who Libby had only met once, though they seemed very nice – and Willow's mother, Adrienne, whom Libby adored as much as her own mum. (Sometimes more, because Adrienne didn't have a judgemental bone in her body, which was more than Libby could say about her own mother.) Willow's dad was in the bridal car with Willow, of course, and Libby assumed that Tomas was inside with his best man in the ceremony room. Lots of other guests were waiting too – some of them Libby recognised, though many she didn't.

Her anxiety levels suddenly at maximum, she scanned the gathering to see if Rufus was amongst them. She'd eventually agreed with Willow that he'd be pretty obtuse to come in the circumstances and they'd decided not to make the phone call to ask him explicitly to stay away, but that didn't mean she'd completely discounted the possibility that he might turn up. He hadn't RSVP'd to say he was going to be there but, if he had a mind for mischief, Libby was sure her ex wouldn't let a small thing like formality stop him. She'd done her best to put the idea out of her mind today, and had even enjoyed the morning so far, but she wouldn't be able to completely relax until she'd seen for herself that he wasn't there.

She'd told herself that even if he was stupid enough to turn up, there was no reason why she had to take any notice. She could simply rise serenely above it and bask in the glory of having such an important role in the day's proceedings – but saying it and believing it were very different matters. The hurt Rufus had caused was something she'd find hard to forgive for a long time, the temptation to give him that second chance he kept asking for even harder to resist. But resist she had to, at least if she was ever going to look in the mirror and view herself with a modicum of respect again. He'd caused trouble and heartache in ways she could never have imagined possible, and to invite him back into her life would be a huge mistake. She'd never forget the look on Kylie's face as she'd broken the news of their affair to Libby, how wretched she'd clearly felt about it, but then how different Rufus's had been when Libby had confronted him, having given up a precious afternoon having tea with her grandma to tackle something so awful.

'I'm sorry,' he'd said simply. 'I've been a shit, I know. I didn't want this to happen, but it has.'

'That's all I get?' she'd yelled, unable to prevent what he would say were hysterics. She'd managed to stay calm for Kylie because she'd been in shock, but Rufus was a different matter. She'd had time to process and think about what she was going to say, although most of her carefully prepared speech had gone out of the window when she'd come to deliver it. 'You ruin my life and that's all you can say?'

'What else do you want me to say?'

'And you want to be with Kylie?'

'Yes.'

'Unbelievable! I don't think you're even sorry at all, are you? Admit it!'

'OK,' he'd said with infuriating calmness. 'If it makes you feel better then I will.'

Libby had raged at this. She couldn't recall anything else she'd said, and she hadn't known what else she'd wanted Rufus to say, but even an attempt at denial would have been better than what she'd got. He'd expressed regret that his face just hadn't backed up. It was like he'd been on autopilot, like he'd known he had to apologise but he hadn't really meant it at all. In the end, Libby didn't know who to feel most sorry for – herself for the betrayal, or Kylie, who was about as desperate and guilt-stricken as anyone could be. Of course, Libby hadn't been able to face her since, especially when she'd thought her cousin might be pregnant, but she'd heard plenty from family members who, of course, had soon found out. At least it had given them all something to gossip about.

There was no sign of him amongst the faces here now, and Libby gave a silent sigh of relief, thankful for small mercies. It looked as if he'd made the smart choice after all.

Their chauffeur opened the car doors and the younger bridesmaids tumbled out before Libby had even gathered up her skirts. Two of them had left their posies in the car and Libby had to call them back to retrieve them, while one had left the wrapper to a sweet (that Libby hadn't even noticed her eating) on the floor.

'Settle down… stick with me… straighten your skirt there, India… Scarlet, leave those petals alone – there's hardly any left on those roses… Olivia… your nose is running – let me see if I can get a handkerchief…'

Standing expectantly, waiting for Willow's car to arrive, Libby did her best with the trio of torment, feeling like a weird cross between Mary Poppins and Miss Trunchbull. Thank goodness help was at hand though, and now, when things went a bit awry, someone related to the culprit would step forward and have a quiet word.

Libby glanced across to where the parents stood as a pack. Olivia and India's mums were laughing at something on a phone, while Scarlet's mother simply looked on as her little darling absently pulled at the petals in her posy with an expression that spoke of her deep gratitude that someone else would have to wrangle her daughter for a while. None of them seemed very keen to assume any parental responsibility any time soon. So perhaps not...

As Willow had yet to arrive, it gave Libby a few moments to take in her surroundings in more detail. The pillars at the entrance to Lovage Hall had been garlanded in flowers, and there was a chalkboard standing next to the doors with a message welcoming Willow and Tomas and their guests and running down the order of the day's events. Snow had collected at the base of the vast pillars and it dusted the steps, despite someone having very obviously cleared them that morning – Libby could tell because it lay a lot thicker on the gardens and driveway. It was obvious everyone was very cold but nobody seemed to mind, and the covering of snow made everything look even more magical and romantic than it already did.

Adrienne came tottering over to Libby on candy-pink heels that were hugely unsuited to the current weather. They matched the pink hat she was wearing and the pink-and-white dress that was paired with a white blazer. Libby considered for a moment that her ensemble would have been far better suited to a summer – or even spring – wedding, but Willow's poor mum must have been freezing today in it. She didn't seem to mind, and though she looked to be dithering a bit as she said hello, she was also in such a state of excitement that Libby mused she probably hadn't noticed her teeth were chattering at all.

'Oh, don't you all look beautiful!' she cried as her gaze ran over the bridesmaids in their claret silk and tulle. 'I must get a photo before we go in with the house in the background... Isn't it just the most gorgeous place?'

'Mine itches!' Scarlet said, pulling at the neckline of her dress.

'Bridesmaid dresses aren't meant to be comfortable,' Libby said, her mind very much on how tight the waistband of her own was right now. How she was going to eat more than a crumb at the wedding breakfast she had no idea. 'If they were comfortable we'd be wandering around in them every day, wouldn't we?'

'Yes,' India said, though she looked quite doubtful that she ought to be agreeing with Libby's logic at all.

'I would,' Olivia said. 'Mine's not itching – I love it. I'm going to wear it for the school disco next term.'

'You can't do that!' Scarlet said.

'My mum says I can so there!' Olivia replied tartly.

'You'll look stupid.'

'No I won't! You look stupid all the time!'

'Now, girls… a bit of harmony for my photos please,' Adrienne said.

As she pulled a digital camera from her clutch bag (Libby had to wonder how on earth she'd fitted it in there), she continued to wax lyrical about the venue as she took her own photographs of Libby and her charges. There was a professional photographer taking his own, and they would undoubtedly be better, but Libby couldn't blame Adrienne for snapping away in her own excitement. In a strange way, those photos, though they might not be good quality, would probably feel more authentic too.

'I'm cold,' Scarlet moaned. Libby had some sympathy – she was getting pretty chilly now too, despite the faux-fur wrap that had come with the dress and was currently draped around her shoulders.

'Oh, please smile for me, Scarlet,' Adrienne said, lowering her camera for a moment. 'You're ruining the picture.'

'I can't smile – I'm just too perishing!'

Olivia turned to her. 'What's perishing?'

'Cold,' Scarlet replied with a withering look that suggested she thought Olivia supremely stupid for not knowing.

'Can't you manage a little one?' Adrienne asked. 'We'll be going inside soon.'

'Can we go inside now?' India reached round to scratch at her bottom through her dress, leaving half the fabric up there. Libby hastily pulled it free before anyone noticed.

'We have to wait for Willow,' Scarlet said imperiously. 'That's how you do bridesmaiding. You have to hold her dress.'

'Yes, if it goes on the floor, it will get dirty,' Olivia agreed. 'We have to stop it going on the floor.'

'Or sometimes you walk behind and look pretty while the grown-up bridesmaid takes care of the bride's dress,' Libby said, deciding it would be infinitely better for her to take care of any kind of contact with Willow's gown.

'Oh,' Olivia said, looking crestfallen at the suggestion that they wouldn't be the most important people at the wedding after all.

'I mean, you'd have to assist me,' Libby added, backtracking now, as all three girls seemed deeply disappointed. 'But I'd take care of most of it because I'm bigger and I can hold more fabric.'

'Oh, yes.' Scarlet nodded as if that was the most obvious thing in the world. 'I see.'

'And we do need all you pretty flowers walking with the beautiful bride,' Libby continued. 'Just like in your posies – Willow's the big roses, and you're the little white... whatever those lovely little white flowers are. They make the roses look extra special. See?'

'What about you?' India asked, scratching her bottom again. Libby frowned, itching to slap her hand away, but she had to be content with a quick check to make sure the little girl's dress wasn't sticking up there this time.

'What about me?' Libby asked.

'Which flower are you?'

'Well, I'm one of the white ones too.'

'But you're not small and pretty.'

It had taken less than a second to dismantle the analogy that Libby had thought so clever – it served her right for thinking she might be able to take control of this situation.

'I guess…' Libby looked over the posy India was holding. 'The berries!' she said after a moment. 'I'm the berries… I add interest!'

'Yes, you add drama,' Adrienne agreed, and though she was probably talking about their flower arrangements, Libby couldn't help but detect a subtext. Was she talking about her split with Rufus? Had Willow been filling her in on *all* the events of the last few months, not just the ones in the public sphere? Had she told her mother any of their private conversations? About Libby's panic at the thought of Rufus attending the wedding?

She was spared any further musings on the subject by the arrival of arguably the most important car of the day – certainly the most anticipated. Willow had been given the opportunity to arrive early at Lovage Hall and take a suite to get ready in, but she'd wanted to get dressed at home and drive in – not only had she wanted to keep things traditional, but she'd undoubtedly relished the chance to arrive in a suitably dramatic style like this.

Libby beamed as she spotted her best friend in the back of the car. Every time she saw her, Libby felt she couldn't look more beautiful, but then she did. The trio of torment were silent now, eyes like saucers as they watched the car pull to a sedate halt and the chauffeur hop out to open the door for the bride. As Willow emerged there was an audible gasp from the guests who had braved the cold to wait for her, but it didn't last long as someone came from inside the building to usher the stragglers in so that proceedings could begin.

Libby could understand perfectly well why everyone was gasping because no gown had ever suited a woman as perfectly as Willow's did. Libby allowed her thoughts, for just a second, to stray to the dress she'd planned to wear for her own wedding. It was far sleeker and more classic than Willow's – ivory satin with a wide skirt and a neckline that swept across her breastbone and bare shoulders. She'd planned to wear her auburn hair pinned at the sides but cascading down her back with a pearl tiara and classic roses in her bouquet. Would people have stared and gasped as she'd emerged from her own wedding car? Would they have looked and thought how beautiful and perfect her gown was?

Before she started to cry (and not for the right reasons), she drove the memories out. There was no point in dwelling on what would never be, and even if by some miracle the chance to marry Rufus came around again, she'd never have him now, not in a million years. In her more pragmatic moments, she thanked her lucky stars that the dream had fallen apart when it did – if he was capable of betraying her in her hour of need and with someone so close to her, there was no reason why he'd have seen marriage as a barrier either. If he hadn't done it before they were married, it was fair to assume he'd have done it at some point afterwards. If there was no other reason to resist his pleas for a second chance, there was that one.

Willow smiled at her mum, who was standing with Libby and the girls, gazing at her daughter and obviously bursting with pride. Gene strode round from the other side of the car to take Willow's arm, ready to walk inside with her.

'Get the dress!' Libby heard Olivia cry in a sudden panic. 'Quick…
it's going on the floor!'

'Don't worry,' Libby said, holding her back. 'It's only the hem on
the snow. There's nothing to worry about; it won't get dirty on snow.'

It might get wet, she added in a private thought, but it might end
up dirtier if India got her hands on it, given they'd been up her bottom
all morning. Perhaps a damp hem would be preferable.

'Let's get into position,' Libby said, herding the girls around her.

'I'll go and get my seat,' Adrienne said, hurrying away and leaving
Libby with her charges. Willow and her dad came towards them.

'Ready?' Libby asked.

Willow gave an enthusiastic nod. 'I'm more than ready. I'm not
nervous at all, you know, I just can't wait to be married to Tomas. Is
that weird? Aren't brides supposed to be nervous?'

'I wouldn't know,' Libby said, and then instantly regretted her
choice of phrase as she noted Willow's smile slip. She hadn't meant
to make her friend feel guilty that her big day had arrived while the
wedding Libby was supposed to have was now nothing but a discarded
hope. 'I mean, it's probably what people say who aren't sure they ought
to be getting married at all,' she added hastily. 'But you're absolutely
sure – more sure than anyone I've ever seen. I completely get why –
Tomas is an absolute gem.'

'He is, isn't he? Sometimes I can't believe my luck.'

'And I think sometimes he can't believe his,' Libby said.

'As it should be!' Willow said with a little laugh, before she faced
the doors. 'Last few minutes as a single woman.'

'Yep. Sad about that?'

'No…' Willow shook her head and beamed at Libby. 'I'm very,
very happy.'

'Good. If you were anything else I'd slap you silly.'

'Ready?' Gene asked his daughter.

Willow nodded. 'Yep.'

'Right then…' he replied with a broad smile. 'Let's go and get you married!'

Chapter Four

Libby had seen the grand ballroom of Lovage Hall twice before – once when she'd been for a snoop round with Willow on a day Tomas hadn't been able to make it for a meeting with the manager, and once again when they'd had the wedding rehearsal, but she'd never seen it look like this.

Chairs had been placed at either side of a temporary aisle. They were wrapped in white netting tied with blood-red satin bows interlaced with sprigs of spruce and berries, and they led the eye all the way down to the altar, which was decorated in the same manner and framed by a towering Christmas tree. Stout candles set in arrangements of silver pine cones and more berries had been placed along the route, marking out the aisle, while more of the spruce garlands traversed the ceiling in low-hanging rows.

Breathtaking didn't begin to cover it, and for Willow and Tomas, a couple who were as crazy about Christmas as they were about each other, it was the perfect place to make their vows.

The decision to marry on Christmas Eve had been an easy one. Willow had put the idea to Tomas and, as she'd expected, he'd agreed with no hesitation. It had meant some grumbling from family members who were stuck in their ways and didn't want Christmas to be about anything but Christmas, but in the end most of them had come round to the idea that this year would be a little different.

Libby's eyes misted as she took it all in, barely able to bear the emotion, the drama of the occasion and the knowledge of what it meant to her best friend. And buried beneath that, though she didn't want to recognise it, was a little sorrow too. A day like this would never be hers – at least it felt that way. She'd planned her own wedding, but it had been snatched away, and the manner in which it had happened had left her feeling that even if the chance ever did present itself again, she would probably find it difficult to trust anyone enough to make that sort of commitment.

The sweet strings of a quartet brought her back to the room, and as they began to play, Willow started to make her slow and steady way down the aisle, just like they'd practised in their rehearsal. Libby silently and reverently followed, prompting her little charges to do the same, and awed silence descended over the congregation.

Libby allowed herself a tiny smile for those faces she recognised as she walked, gaining bigger smiles in return, though every gaze always went back to Willow soon after.

Except for one. Libby had never seen him before, and yet, as his eyes unexpectedly locked onto hers they gave her such a jolt that she almost let out an involuntary squeak of surprise. He was sitting with the groom's friends and family, and although Libby was certain they'd never met, there was something about the way they connected so instantly, it was like she already knew him, like she'd always known him. It was the strangest feeling. Perhaps not love at first sight – she didn't even know if she believed such a thing could exist in the real, sensible world – but if it wasn't love, she didn't know what it was. Lust?

No, not even as simple as lust – this was a connection that couldn't be explained, that defied any kind of description and certainly didn't resemble anything she'd felt before.

Dragging her gaze forward again, she tried to order her thoughts once more, though something had shaken her that she couldn't get rid of, and she had to wonder what the hell had just happened. She wanted to look back and see him again, but, of course, in the current circumstances that was impossible.

Concentrate, she told herself, *don't be so ridiculous*. And it *was* ridiculous. She could only imagine it was some strange side effect of the heightened drama of the occasion, and she decided right there and then to put it out of her mind. Whatever her emotions were telling her, they were mistaken. And even if they weren't, something that started this way could only be unhealthy. She'd just got out of one toxic relationship and she wasn't about to rush into another. Besides, she had no idea who this man was; nor did she know anything about him.

Then her thoughts were pulled back to the room as she felt a tug on her arm. She looked down to see India trying to get her attention.

'Libby… Libby…' she whispered, though loud enough that it might as well have been a shout.

'Not now,' Libby hissed back.

'But, Libby, I need—'

'India, please… this is a very important moment. We're the pretty flowers – remember?'

'But I need the toilet!'

Libby tried not to roll her eyes as she turned to face the front again. They'd almost reached the altar, where a beaming Tomas waited, and India would just have to hang on now whether she liked it or not.

'Libby, I need the toilet!' India repeated.

'Could you just hold it for half an hour?' Libby returned in a whisper that was louder than she would have liked but necessary to communicate with India over the strains of the quartet.

'No, I really can't!'

'You'll have to – just for a little while. Surely—'

'I can't! It's coming down my leg!'

Inwardly cursing, unable to ignore the problem now, Libby desperately scanned the gathering for India's mum. She found her easily – one of the few people watching the bridesmaids rather than the bride, and one in particular. Which was lucky, because she seemed to realise quickly that something was amiss and signalled it to Libby, who returned it with the subtlest look to indicate she was right to think so and they needed her help. Thankfully, she understood and made her way over to them as discreetly as possible.

'I need the toilet, Mummy!' India wailed now, careless of the fuss she was making and dancing around, just to make it obvious. 'I can't hold it at all, really, not even for one more second!'

India's mum looked as mortified as Libby and slightly furious as well, but she was left with no choice but to whisk the little girl away. Libby was sure that in years to come, India would be annoyed that she'd missed the most important and prestigious bit of her very first wedding having a pee, but she supposed those memories might have been a whole lot worse if she'd actually peed herself in front of the altar.

The bridal procession came to a halt just as India and her mum left the hall and the registrar began his speech, meaning Libby had no more time to worry about it.

'Good morning, everyone. We're here today to celebrate the wedding of Willow and Tomas...'

It was informal, sincere and, as the registrar continued with the preamble, Libby quickly decided she liked it more than a lot of the fussy scripts she'd heard read out in church. Not that she didn't love a good church wedding with all the trimmings – who didn't? – but this was far better suited to Willow and Tomas, who were informal, sincere and without affectation of any kind. As a couple, they were devoted to each other and to their friends and family, and it was plain for anyone to see, and they didn't need fancy words to tell you that, because it was in every one of their actions.

Libby felt the tears come to her eyes once more, tears of joy for her friend and for the occasion, but also a little in pity again. If she and Rufus had got this far, if they'd made it, would they have been the sort of couple you could bet on like Willow and Tomas? She'd once thought so, but now she wasn't so sure. Perhaps it was better they'd never made it to the altar, and that fact alone troubled her, especially when she'd been so willing to marry him, right up until the moment he'd betrayed her.

But then, she couldn't even blame Kylie, as much as she wanted to. Rufus had gone looking elsewhere, and there was a reason for that. Kylie, in the end, had been caught in the crossfire, probably on the rebound after breaking up from her own long-term boyfriend, charmed by Rufus's good looks and interest in her. Much as Libby hated to think it, she had to assume it wouldn't have taken much effort on his part to get Kylie to fall for him.

She was shaken from her musings by the return of India to her side and, as she smiled vaguely down at the little girl, decided it was probably for the best she hadn't been allowed to dwell on her maudlin memories. This wasn't her day and it wasn't her time to be sad about things she couldn't have – it was the day to celebrate Willow's happiness.

No sooner had she decided this than Willow and Tomas were taking their vows and then the registrar was winding up his speech and they were all proceeding out towards another room set up for the wedding breakfast. A long blink would have seen anyone miss it: the registrar had started to talk, Libby's attention had wandered for the shortest time and then Willow and Tomas were husband and wife at last.

In between the ceremony and the wedding breakfast was photos and champagne. Of course, when the time came for the bulk of the official wedding pictures to be taken, parental responsibility for the trio of torment was nowhere to be seen. It was possible they'd dashed to the hotel bar to grab a drink or taken the opportunity of a quiet moment to catch up with friends and family while their little darlings were otherwise engaged and, if she was honest, Libby could hardly blame them for that. It did mean, however, that she was lumbered with the task of keeping them in line, and she couldn't help but feel that a little moral support from mum or dad in this regard would have been very helpful.

After a couple of group photos before everyone wandered off, followed by tons of shots of Willow and Tomas together, Willow by herself, Tomas with his best man and with their parents, the photographer beckoned Libby over.

'Could I have the bride and bridesmaids?'

Most of what he'd taken so far had been in the great hall, and while Willow had mentioned to Libby how lovely the snow would look against the claret of their dresses, Libby had very much been hoping that the idea of going outside for their pictures would be shelved. It had started to snow again, and although it was hardly the blizzard conditions Gene had feared earlier that morning, it was enough to make going out there in a silk and tulle dress less than pleasant.

'Where do you want us?' she asked. 'Perhaps by the windows? Or the fireplace?'

'I thought we were going to have some outside,' Willow said. 'We haven't done any in the gardens yet.'

The Italian-inspired gardens were fast disappearing under the snow, but Willow didn't seem worried about that. And Libby had to suppose that it would look quite magical as a feature of the wedding album, so she quickly decided not to quibble about it, even if she didn't exactly fancy standing around in it.

'Yes, let's go out!' Scarlet shouted, and before anyone could call her back she was tugging at the handle of the emergency exit.

'Not that door!' Libby cried, but too late. Scarlet managed to yank it open and a high-pitched whine that was the alarm to alert staff the door had been opened was already filling the air. Added to that was a freezing blast of air that had Libby rushing over to close it again.

'I was going to suggest the patio outside the orangery,' the photographer said in a voice tinged with barely disguised weariness that suggested he'd had to contend with plenty of overenthusiastic children over the years.

'You can't go that way!' India said, marching over and pulling Scarlet away from the door with such force Libby thought she might do some serious damage.

Scarlet shook her off and glared at her. 'The man said we had to go outside!' She pointed to the gardens. 'I was going outside because he said so!'

Libby took a deep breath. 'This way…' She beckoned the girls to follow her. Willow brought up the rear, fighting with the length of her dress alone now that none of her bridesmaids seemed to care about helping her with it quite as much as they had at the start of the day.

'Are you sure you want shots outside?' Libby asked as they opened the French doors of the orangery out onto an arctic patio.

'Yes.' Willow stepped out. 'They'll be lovely. We shan't be long.'

'Well, we won't have to worry about the girls standing still long enough to get cold,' Libby said wryly. 'Us, on the other hand, we might soon be frozen to the spot.'

'I'll try to make it quick,' the photographer said cheerfully from behind them. It was alright for him to be cheerful, Libby thought, because from somewhere he'd managed to produce a coat and a hat, though how he'd managed to get them so quickly was a mystery. And if he really didn't think they'd need to be out there a long time, he was probably going to be sadly mistaken if the trio of torment had anything to do with it. He might have experience of photographing children, but these children? And in this snow…

Dutifully, Libby put aside her complaints and they filed out into the cold. Luckily there was a pergola that was fairly sheltered so they could stay dry while the photographer got his tripod set up. And then came the challenging bit.

'Just stand a bit closer… not that close… now I can't see that little girl's face… Turn this way… no, towards me… not that much… oh, now that's not enough again… a smidge… it means a little bit… Let's all try to look as if we're happy, shall we?… No, come back, I'm not done yet… That little girl, can you lift your flowers? No, not that high… Can you all face me?… I know it's cold; we'll be done shortly…'

In the end they were out in the cold for longer than Libby or anyone else was happy about. Even Willow, who'd been adamant they did the al fresco shoot, looked fed up.

'I think we must have enough now,' she said finally in a firm voice that suggested she had no intentions of doing a single photo more.

'Great,' the photographer said. 'So you little ones can go inside and warm up. Grown-up bridesmaid... I don't suppose you can go and ask the groom and the parents to pop out to us for some external shots with the bride, could you?'

Libby glanced at Willow with a barely disguised grin. She'd said she'd wanted magical snow-filled photos, but she didn't look quite so sure now. But Libby wasn't going to be the one to remind her of the old saying – that people ought to be careful what they wished for...

The tables for the sit-down meal were set with the same theme as the room the ceremony had taken place in, with branches and garlands of spruce and berries, silver pine cones and stout, parchment-coloured candles. There were rows and rows of fairy lights strung across the ceiling – they were lit now and they looked pretty enough, but it was still daylight; the full, magical effect wouldn't be seen until night fell and the room was transformed for the evening reception.

Libby had barely settled in her seat when the champagne started to flow and the first course of pâté, smoked salmon or vegan cheese tartlet arrived in front of the guests. Libby recalled lots of conversations about food with Willow, during which she'd pondered all sorts from a fish supper to Christmas lunch, but in the end she'd settled on a more traditional wedding breakfast menu, and Tomas was happy to go along with anything she wanted. So there was a choice of turkey (for anyone feeling prematurely Christmassy), beef or monkfish, or another vegan option to follow this one, then the sweet trolley, then cheese, then a dessert wine with chocolates, and all the while the champagne would be keeping everyone topped up. The little ones had plates that more resembled those in a fast-food pit stop than a lavish wedding celebration, but they all seemed delighted they hadn't been subjected to the yukky-looking concoctions their parents were wolfing down.

Before the food came the speeches. Tomas and Willow's were both short and incredibly sweet, thanking everyone they knew and declaring their happiness that they'd found their soul mates.

The best man, Solly, stood up next. Solomon – or Solly as everyone called him – was six foot four (or maybe more) with a voice as big as his presence and a laugh that shook the room, and pretty soon he had the rest of the room laughing with him.

'Tomas was a ridiculous boy,' he began. For a moment the guests looked shocked, but then smiled as he continued. 'Ridiculous in that he was so tiny and cute – even by year nine he still looked like a prepubescent girl – that everyone thought he'd escaped from the nursery next door. It also meant he had this weird effect on all the girls in our class, who wanted to mother him. Then he suddenly got huge and good-looking in year ten, and from that point we didn't know whether to be glad for him or hate him because he was nabbing all the girls – and not for mothering at all. But the thing about Tomas is, it never went to his head. He was always a good bloke who would do anything to help a mate, and whenever he broke up with a girl, she always wanted to be friends afterwards. Except for Lauren Shingle who knocked one of his teeth out... but then, she *was* Lauren Shingle.'

There was a ripple of laughter, while Tomas put his head in his hands and shook it theatrically, and then Solly continued. 'But even though he had all those girlfriends and they were all so fond of him, there was only ever one girl truly capable of stealing his heart, one true soul mate he was destined to be with… and that would be Lauren Shingle.'

Solly grinned while Willow laughed and Tomas mimed that he was going to kill him later.

'Of course, there was also Willow,' Solly added. 'And lucky for her, Lauren turned out to be a sociopath with shares in a local dental practice. But when Tomas first mentioned he'd had an incredible date with an incredible girl, I knew us lads had lost him. I could tell she was special, and when I met her I could see why. And I was right… we have lost him, as today goes to prove. But I couldn't imagine losing him to someone more perfect and I couldn't be happier about being here today to complain about it. So I'd like everyone to raise their glasses. To Willow and Tomas!'

'Willow and Tomas!' everyone cried, and when Libby glanced over, she could see that both Willow and Tomas had tears in their eyes.

And then it was Willow's dad, Gene's, turn.

He stood up with a nervous smile at the room, smoothed his suit jacket with a shaky hand, and turned to a set of hastily scribbled notes.

'I don't do a lot of public speaking,' he began. 'Mostly because I wouldn't want to put anyone through it, but today I'm happy to put you all through it…'

There was a ripple of polite laughter around the room. Libby smiled. She knew a lot about Willow's remarkable dad – mostly from Willow herself – and one of the things she knew that not many others did was that he'd overcome the most debilitating childhood stammer. Every social situation caused him some anxiety and he still had to concentrate on every conversation to get the words out first time in a way others could understand. Libby knew just what strength it was taking to make this speech now, how hard he was working to get every sentence out. She glanced at Willow, who was watching closely as he spoke, and saw the pride in her eyes but also the held breath at every pause, the anxiety at every point where he might stumble, and Libby felt it all too.

'So I'll keep it brief,' he continued. 'My beautiful daughter, Willow, is the child Adrienne and I never thought we'd have. We met later than I would have liked and took too long to marry, and by the time we'd got all that out of the way we thought it was too late to have children. But then Willow came along. She was our little miracle. We'd already been happier than we thought any couple could be, but she made us happier still, and she lit up our lives in a way we'd never thought possible. We felt spoilt, our lives more perfect than we deserved. But today the impossible has happened. Today we get the best son-in-law we could have hoped for. As all fathers do, I never imagined that any man would be good enough for my little angel, and when we first met Tomas I have to say I was afraid I'd been proved right...'

He grinned down at Tomas, who nodded. 'I don't think blocking your toilet was the best introduction...'

Everyone laughed and, when it died down, Gene continued. 'I'm sure there are better ways to meet your girlfriend's parents,' he acknowledged. 'Willow's whole life has been building up to this moment and I don't mind admitting I've often thought it would be one of sadness for me when it came. At the very least I wouldn't want to lose my little girl, but my worst nightmares saw her marrying a man I didn't think was right for her one bit. Today she marries Tomas, and I'm not sad at all. I know Tomas will love and care for her and I know she'll be happy as his wife, and I'll be happy knowing she'll be happy, loved and safe for the rest of her life. So I want to say thank you to Tomas for being a man I can trust with the care of my little miracle, and I want us all to toast…' He raised his glass, and Libby could almost see the relief in his face; he'd got through possibly the most stressful day of his life – another few seconds and he would never have to do it again. 'To Willow and Tomas. May their lives be filled with joy, health and comfort.'

'To Willow and Tomas!' everyone repeated, raising their glasses once more. Libby wiped away more tears and, as Gene sat down, she gestured a little round of applause at him, and he gave her a knowing smile. His hadn't necessarily been the funniest, the most entertaining or eloquent speech of the day, but, knowing what Libby knew, for her it had certainly been the most moving. She was really going to have to get a grip on her emotions though. Much more of this crying and her mascara was going to be completely off and she'd have to go begging for a top-up from someone, not to mention that her nose would be the size of a Christmas satsuma. Feeling vaguely embarrassed as she dried her eyes, she swept the room, hoping she wasn't the only softy.

That was when she saw him again, the man she'd been so entranced by as she'd followed Willow down the aisle earlier that day. He was talking to an old couple seated at his table. Libby searched her memory and seemed to recall they were relatives of Tomas. As the man hadn't yet noticed her watching, she took the opportunity to get a better look. There was no denying that she liked what she saw too. He was toned, but not a muscle-bound meathead, his dark hair was cropped but not short enough to look intimidating, there was a dimple in both cheeks when he smiled and his eyes were the colour of a clear winter sky… striking… mesmerising almost… like that guy who played James Bond in the films…

She almost laughed out loud at the absurdity of her imaginings and then realised she'd actually been staring in a way that might have been considered inappropriate had he noticed. With his suit and tie though, he did look a little James Bond-ish. If there was one thing Libby liked to see on a handsome man it was a well-cut suit, and in her line of work she'd seen plenty. None had ever had quite the effect on her this guy was having though. James Bond or ordinary guy on the street, she wouldn't mind seeing his licence to thrill, she thought wryly, and as she glanced again she had to stifle another grin lest she look like a total lunatic to the casual observer.

But then he happened to look straight at her and, like a schoolgirl with a crush on the teacher, she blushed and hurriedly shifted her gaze, suddenly fascinated with her napkin. When she dared to raise her head he'd gone back to his conversation with Tomas's elderly relatives.

Willow's voice reminded her that today wasn't about her at all, though Libby did wonder if she might get a nice little bonus out of it for herself. Was it impossible to imagine that her best friend's happy ending might signal the beginning of her own story after all?

'Have you seen it now?'

Libby homed in on Willow's conversation with her dad.

'I'm so glad we're not trying to get to Lovage Hall right now,' she continued. 'It's really coming down – I don't think we'd have made it.'

'I think it's thinning though,' Gene said, though he sounded less confident than his words suggested. 'It keeps stopping and starting. The snowploughs will be out too.'

'I hope so,' Willow said, sounding just as doubtful. 'It wouldn't be a very good end to the day if our guests were stranded in the snow trying to leave here. Even worse if anyone trying to get here is stuck.'

'You're worrying too much,' Gene said. 'It'll be fine.'

Libby's gaze went to the vast windows that ran along the outside wall of the great hall where they were currently eating. The snow looked lovely, of course, as fresh snow always did – and especially romantic on an occasion like this – but as large flakes continued to fall, Libby could understand why Willow might worry.

Libby tried not to worry, however. It was bound to stop soon, no matter how heavy it looked right now. Heavy snowfall never lasted long in England; by the time the taxis arrived to take people home she'd bet it would be all over. Just as Gene had said, the snowploughs were probably out already to clear the country lanes and all that would be left for later would be a glittering moonlit wonderland, just in time for people to wake to a gorgeous white Christmas morning.

Of course, it might still put off some guests trying to get in for the evening reception. It was a shame and Willow would be disappointed if that happened, but a small part of Libby – to her shame – was also relieved. It meant no Rufus. Every hour that passed without him showing up allowed her to relax a little more, the hope building in her that he wouldn't come. She'd enjoy her day a lot more if she knew for sure, of course, but as things stood it was looking promising. She'd be able to let her hair down at the evening reception, just like every other guest, without the anxiety that having him there would cause her.

The other thing that would allow her to relax was the discharging of her duties as chief bridesmaid, and thank goodness for that, she thought dryly as she noticed a commotion across the room and quickly surmised that Scarlet had managed to tip her lemonade all over her mum's lap. They were sweet girls, the three little bridesmaids, but being able to hand them back to the care of their parents was one aspect of the day Libby was particularly appreciative of. She wouldn't miss trying to keep the trio of torment in line.

'More champagne, madam?'

Libby looked back to see a waiter close by with a fresh bottle. She held up her glass.

'Lovely, thanks.'

'You are welcome,' he said in a dreamy accent. Spanish perhaps? He was maybe mid-twenties, handsome too – worth a fling in anyone's book. The thought gave her an inward smile; it was almost a shame Rufus wasn't here. It might have been fun to flirt with a handsome waiter in front of him, just to see the look on his face, and certainly satisfying. It was one thing for Rufus to cheat on her, but she'd bet it would be quite another for her to exact any kind of revenge for it.

'What's your name?' she asked him.

'Santiago.'

'Hmm...'

She was tempted to try a corny line, something about what time his shift finished and whether he had staff quarters at the hotel, what his plans for after work might be and how he felt about women in huge claret dresses when, from the corner of her eye, she noticed Willow suddenly stiffen. Something about the alarm in her movement now had Libby's full attention, and she looked closer to see her friend's eyes widen in shock. In the instant Libby had stopped talking to him, the waiter had moved on with his champagne, but he was already forgotten as Libby followed the direction of Willow's panicked gaze and her heart almost stopped.

'You've got to be kidding me!'

Libby had spoken out loud without even realising. Gene turned to her.

'Are you alright?'

His words were full of concern, as anyone's would be had they seen Libby's desperate expression. She felt suddenly sick, the ground falling away from her. Willow tapped Tomas on the arm and tried to point discreetly at the doors to the hall, and then Tomas sprung from his seat and raced across.

Willow leant over to Libby. 'I'm so sorry... We really didn't think he'd come so we... and then he didn't come to the service... I thought it would be alright. I didn't imagine he'd be so...'

'Blatant?' Libby eyed Rufus cagily as Tomas remonstrated with him, clearly doing his best to keep it discreet and probably trying to explain with as much tact as possible that he wasn't welcome at the wedding. But Rufus was calmly shaking his head and pointing at the windows, and then Tomas led him to a waitress and had a word, who then found him a seat at a table across the room. Libby continued to watch, as if her eyes were magnetised to his figure, as Rufus made himself comfortable and introduced himself to everyone else already seated there.

As much as Libby wanted to stop staring at him, she couldn't. Incredibly, he was wearing a suit very much like the electric-blue one she'd been salivating over the day Kylie had come to Swift's to tell her about the affair, and he looked so good in it Libby felt her heart squeeze with regret. He glanced up and gave her a small, brief, uncertain smile, and she wanted to scowl at him in return, but she couldn't. She could only stare in mute shock.

Please don't let him come over, please don't let him come over...

But then a man sitting at his table started to talk to him, and Libby finally managed to look away to see Tomas stride back to his own seat next to Willow. As he sat down he gave Libby a helpless and apologetic shrug.

'What did he say?' Libby asked in a low voice. 'Why has he come?'

'He says he came to wish us well.'

'Seriously?' Libby asked incredulously. 'I think we all know why he's come. And even if it's true and he *has* just come to wish you well, what made him think it was a good idea?'

'He says he got halfway here and thought the same thing himself,' Tomas said. 'But then he thought, as he was dressed up, he might as well come to the wedding anyway. I've just told him that while I appreciate the sentiment, it wasn't exactly his most brilliant idea. I think he gets that now, but he's stuck, whether anyone likes it or not. He'll have to stay now.'

'Stuck? What do you mean?'

'Have you seen the weather?' Tomas angled his head at the windows. 'He says the lanes are impassable.'

'He would say that.'

'I think he's telling the truth, Libby. He says his car is stuck and he had to walk the last half mile. Looking outside, I can believe that much at least.'

Libby glanced over as discreetly as she could. She had to admit that Rufus was a bit soggy, though it hardly detracted from the fact that he looked good – the kind of good that could be very bad for her.

He seemed sad and quiet as he watched a waiter set a place for him. *Good*, she thought. He deserved to sit with people he didn't know and he deserved to feel lost and alone.

But did she really think that? Did she really think it was good? Was she truly happy to see him sad?

'Are you alright?' Willow asked.

Libby forced a smile for her. She might be annoyed at this turn of events, even upset, but it wasn't fair to make Willow suffer for it.

'I'm fine – it doesn't matter.'

'It does. I'm so sorry, Libby, we—'

'Willow, it's fine. I don't have to talk to him just because he's here. I'm sure once the snow clears and the roads are freed up again he'll be on his way. I bet he'll be gone before the evening reception begins. Tomas just said he's already realised it was a bad idea to come. Please… don't worry about it – it's just one of those things.'

Willow looked unconvinced but she nodded. Libby hated that her own drama was clearly impacting on her friend's day. Just to show how OK she was, Libby picked up her champagne and took a long drink.

'Now,' she said as she put the empty glass down and searched the room, 'where's that fit waiter with my refill…?'

Willow smiled a little, and as Libby made a show of trying to locate more booze, she suddenly connected with someone else. Not the waiter, or even Rufus, but that man again, the one she kept on locking eyes with, the one who'd shaken her so completely as she'd followed Willow down the aisle that morning. Despite everything else going on at that moment, Libby was hit by that same jolt of strange, inexplicable connection, the same sudden and desperate need to know him better.

Talk about terrible timing, she told herself as she dragged her gaze away, but even then his presence lingered in her thoughts. What was going on in her brain right now? Whatever it was, there was no common sense involved, she knew that for sure. Her ex was sitting feet away looking fine and intent on trying to win her back, there was a whole wedding going on around her and she was being distracted beyond reason by a total stranger.

'Tomas,' she whispered, leaning across to tap him on the arm. He looked over.

'I'm sorry, Libby,' he began, 'I know it's not ideal but—'

'No, I know,' she said, 'it can't be helped now. It's not that, it's…'

She paused. She'd been about to ask him who the man she kept staring at was but suddenly realised it would look very much like she was only interested because Rufus had just arrived. After all, wasn't that exactly what she'd thought about doing with their waiter – hoping that someone would report back to Rufus to make him jealous? Maybe it was for the best that it hadn't happened; maybe it wouldn't have shown her in a good light. And maybe the same could be said for asking Tomas about the mystery man – at the very least it might make her look petty to Tomas, and she didn't want that because she was too fond of him to want to lose an ounce of his respect. No, flirting deliberately with someone else in front of Rufus might be satisfying but it probably wasn't the best idea she'd ever had.

That wasn't to say she wasn't still interested though.

'It's nothing,' she said finally.

Tomas waited another second to make sure she'd finished before turning to answer something his mum had asked him, leaving Libby to glance at the man and Rufus in turn, unable to make up her mind who was causing her more distraction. Then she directed her gaze to the windows and hoped fervently that her prediction about the snow would prove to be right. If not, it promised to be a very interesting evening – and not necessarily in a good way.

Chapter Five

The speeches had ended and the mood became less formal as everyone continued with the wedding breakfast. And then less formal developed into a little rowdy. The places that Willow and Tomas had so painstakingly planned for the sit-down meal quickly meant nothing as the guests began to shuffle themselves around to sit with people they'd rather, flirt with someone they'd just met or simply to keep an eye on unruly little bridesmaids.

Libby watched the migration gradually and stealthily unfold as she occupied her own very static place at the top table with Willow, Tomas, the best man and the couple's parents. Though Rufus had thrown plenty of loaded glances Libby's way and she'd done her best to look as if she hadn't noticed, the meal had passed without real incident. He had obviously decided it wasn't a good idea to try and talk to her during it, and Libby had to appreciate it might be the first sensible thing he'd done since their split.

Santiago, the hot Spanish waiter, had returned with more champagne, more than once and Libby thought more than was necessary. She felt a lot less like indulging his attention now than she had earlier that day, especially in light of the new complications that had arisen. As for the mystery guy, she hadn't needed to ask Tomas about him in the end. He'd come to the table to offer his congratulations to Tomas and Willow as the formal part of the meal had wound up and guests had started to drift off to the bar or to freshen up before the evening reception if they were staying, or even to optimistically try and get home through the snow. As the room became quieter, Libby overheard their brief conversation.

'You look stunning,' he said to Willow. 'Beautiful. Far too good for this loser.'

Tomas laughed. 'Oh, I know I'm punching above my weight. I won't apologise for it.'

'I wouldn't either,' he said.

'It's good to see you,' Tomas replied. 'We're both chuffed you made it.'

'Well, I was coming back to England anyway to see the folks for Christmas; I didn't really have an excuse. Not that I needed one – I wouldn't have missed it for anything. It's been great catching up with the guys from our class too.'

'You've probably had more time to chat to them than I have,' Tomas replied. 'I'll have to grab them all later at the evening do.'

'You should, though I'm pretty sure you're forgiven for not having much time, today of all days.'

Tomas shook his head slowly as he smiled at his friend. 'I still can't believe you ended up with a job in California. How long is it since you went? Must be…'

'Four years now.'

'I'll bet life is incredible there,' Willow said, joining the conversation now as her mum and dad went off to get a drink.

'Well, the weather's certainly more reliable,' he said.

'It's reliable here,' Tomas said. 'Reliably unreliable. You know for certain every day will surprise you and be nothing like the forecast.'

'That's true,' Tomas's friend said. 'Looking at it now I'm really glad I decided to get a room here for tonight. Wouldn't have fancied trying to get back to my parents' house in this.'

'God, no!' Willow agreed warmly. 'Though a lot of our guests don't have rooms.' She turned to Libby, who quickly looked down at her nails to make certain nobody could accuse her of listening in. She realised she probably wasn't very convincing as she glanced up again.

'You're going to try and get home tonight, aren't you?' Willow said.

Libby nodded. 'I was hoping so. I'm supposed to be having lunch with my parents tomorrow. Besides, the prices here…'

Tomas grinned. 'They are a bit, aren't they? Obviously our suite is in with the wedding package or we wouldn't have shelled out either. No such problem for a big-shot Hollywood special effects whiz, eh, Noah?'

His friend grinned. 'I wouldn't say big shot, but I'll take whiz.' He shrugged. 'I don't get home much these days, so I thought I'd splash out, plus I get to have a good drink and a proper catch-up with my old buddies. I don't splash out like that often, trust me.'

'I don't suppose you need to splash out on hotels abroad with all that sunshine and glamour on your doorstep,' Willow said with a smile.

'I promise you – I don't see as much of that as I'd like to either,' he said. 'Too busy working.' He smiled at Libby, his gaze resting on her for just a little longer than it needed to, that strange connection jolting her again. She hadn't imagined it – no way. Something in his look now told her he felt it too. Close up he was even more attractive, obviously intelligent now that she'd heard him speak, and very interesting. She had a name at last now too – Noah.

If the day had panned out any differently maybe she'd have tried to get to know him a lot better, but there was a fly in the ointment in the form of Rufus that wasn't going to be exactly helpful in that department. Despite what Willow had said to the contrary, trying to reassure Libby, plenty of people in that room knew Rufus was Libby's ex, and no matter how interested she was in Noah it would look like a deliberate ploy to get back at Rufus. Not that Rufus didn't deserve it, but then, it wouldn't be fair to Noah either, and to use him like that certainly wasn't a good start to anything they might have... which was probably nothing anyway now she'd discovered he lived in California. A fling would have been fun, but a fling would absolutely have been all she'd got, even if she'd wanted more.

He turned back to Willow and Tomas again. 'Can I buy either of you a drink?'

'Oh, I've had far too many already,' Willow said, laughing lightly. 'I really need to think about pacing myself if I'm going to last the night.'

'Me too,' Tomas said.

Noah grinned and then turned to Libby. 'I don't think we've met before... I'm Noah, old friend of Tomas.'

'Libby,' she said, offering her hand for him to shake. 'Old friend of Willow...'

'I was very impressed with your herding skills this morning.'

'Herding?' Libby frowned slightly.

'The little bridesmaids,' he said. 'You showed admirable control. It could have turned into a full-scale riot from what I saw.'

She laughed. 'God, I had no control whatsoever! If anyone was in charge it was definitely one of them.'

'Well, at least you all looked cute.'

Libby wasn't sure how to take his comment so she simply smiled. They *all* looked cute? The idea that he'd lumped all the bridesmaids and their poofy dresses in the same category didn't fill her with hope that he might think she at least looked a little bit more interesting than merely *cute*. He could have said beautiful, pretty, or even just lovely. But then, when she considered the swathes of claret tulle currently drowning her figure, it was hardly surprising – cute was probably about the best she could hope for.

Willow leant into Tomas, who wound his fingers between hers and gazed down at her.

'I think I'm a bit drunk already,' she said. 'I could probably do with a lie-down about now.'

Tomas kissed her tenderly on the forehead. 'Lightweight.'

She gave him a woozy grin.

'Tomas…' They all turned to see his mother marching over to them. 'Uncle Pieter is asking for you…' She lowered her voice. 'I think he wants to give you money because he forgot your wedding gift…'

Tomas raised his eyebrows. 'Well, there's an offer I can't refuse, though he really needn't worry about it. I'll go and have a word with him.'

'Should I come too?' Willow asked.

'I think it would be polite,' Tomas's mum said. 'As the money is for both of you.'

Willow nodded and then turned to Libby. 'You'll be alright if we disappear for a while to talk to Pieter?'

'Of course!' Libby said brightly. 'I'll go and pester your mum and dad for a bit so I won't be lonely.'

'I'm here on my own too,' Noah put in. 'Well, more or less,' he added in answer to a questioning look from Tomas. 'I mean, the guys are here too but they have girlfriends and wives with them and they don't want me hanging around all day.' He smiled at Libby. 'How about we pester each other for a while? That offer of a drink is open to you too.'

'I should…' For a moment Libby thought about turning him down. Rufus would be stalking the place, and though he vaguely knew some of Tomas's friends and would probably grab them for a quick chat, she was still worried he might seek her out with the intention of having that very unwelcome talk about them getting back together.

Now that she thought about it, she was wondering what had taken him so long, because she'd been expecting to have had to fend him off by now. Perhaps, in the cold light of day, he'd decided it wasn't a good idea after all. It was an encouraging thought, but it still might be far safer to be talking to Gene and Adrienne because that would most definitely put Rufus off approaching her. Then again… She looked at Noah. A drink with him was too tempting to turn down. And if Rufus had seen sense at last, then there was no reason to turn Noah down at all.

'That actually sounds good,' she said. 'I'd love to.'

'Right then.' Willow gave Libby a swift kiss on the cheek. 'We'll see you in a bit.'

'Don't rush on our account,' Libby said.

'Yes, I'm sure we'll be just fine,' Noah agreed.

Willow was giggling loudly at something Tomas was saying as they walked away.

'She does sound a bit tipsy,' Libby said as she and Noah watched them go.

'You're good friends?' Noah asked as he gestured for them to go to the bar.

'Oh, yes, I've known her for years. We met when we were sixteen – worked at the same clothes shop as Saturday girls.' Libby smiled at the memory. 'It was the only time in my life I actually liked going to work on a Saturday.'

'You have to work Saturdays now?'

'God yes, and every week I long for a proper weekend!'

'I can imagine. My job's a bit all over the place – I sort of work whenever I'm needed really. Doesn't make for a spectacular social life, or for much time in that Californian sunshine. So you and Willow stayed close all these years? How long is it since you worked in the shop?'

'It's been twelve years since I started there.'

'You still work there?'

She couldn't help a wry smile at the surprise in his expression. It probably did make her sound very unambitious. 'I'm the manager now actually. It's a nice job really – I didn't see the point in leaving when I was content there. I suppose that makes me sound quite dull, doesn't it?'

'No. It makes you sound like someone who is... well, like you said, content. Willow's a teacher, isn't she?'

'Yes – she got onto her course while we worked at the shop. That's why she ended up leaving; though she was always going to leave really.'

'I'll bet she's a great teacher.'

'She is,' Libby said fondly. 'Amazing. And high-schoolers too – I always think she must have the patience of Job for that.'

'So what kind of clothes does your shop sell?'

'Formalwear. If you ever get the urge to own a cummerbund, I'm your woman.'

'Interesting,' he said with a slight grin. 'If I ever make it to the Oscars I'll be sure to look you up for mine. I mean, not sure what one is but I'll bet it looks the bomb.'

Libby smiled, but even as she did a memory flashed into her brain, one that certainly wasn't welcome. The first time she'd laid eyes on Rufus he'd come into the store to buy a suit for a corporate function. He was good-looking and well spoken, with that kind of floppy-haired, easy charm that came with a public-school education, and she'd been surprised to learn that he had, in fact, attended a neighbouring state school and was more or less working class like her. He'd joked throughout the fitting, and she'd learnt that he'd recently graduated with a law degree and was now working at his first job. As he'd settled the bill for his new suit he'd asked her for a drink and she'd said yes without hesitation. She'd been so excited... she was sure she'd found the one.

Their first date had been as perfect as could be and they'd gone from strength to strength – at least, she'd thought so. Her family and friends had all loved him, and even Willow, who was usually so astute when it came to seeing right through a fraud, had been taken in. She'd encouraged a friendship between him and Tomas; they'd gone on double dates and days out together. Tomas had helped Libby and Rufus move into their flat. She and Rufus had set a date for their wedding, and then Libby had fallen pregnant in a happy and welcome accident. It had all been utterly, sickeningly, dreamily right. Until that one dreadful day when she'd lost their baby.

After that, things had just gone from bad to worse, until it had all been utterly, sickeningly, horribly wrong. Nothing had been right since that day, and at times it had felt as if nothing would ever be right again. But she'd taken comfort in the knowledge that Rufus would be there by her side, helping her through her grief, helping her to heal from her loss. How wrong could a woman be?

It just went to show that you couldn't trust life, you couldn't trust anyone, and you couldn't predict how either might betray you one day.

Libby shook the memories and smiled up at Noah. She'd have to get used to trusting men again and there was nothing much she could do about that. But for now, maybe a bit of short-term fun wasn't such a bad prospect? At least there was no real scope to get hurt having a pleasant evening with a handsome man at a wedding reception, a man who would be flying back to the other side of the world in a few days.

'So you work in California? And Tomas said special effects… seriously?'

'Seriously.'

'Oh my God!' Libby laughed. 'I didn't actually expect you to say yes! You've got to tell me all about it!'

'Are you sure? It's actually kind of boring to talk about – much more fun to see on the screen once they're done.'

'I don't care – it's got to be more interesting than what I do.'

'Well… hold that thought…' He gestured to the bartender, who was now waiting expectantly for their order. 'Let's get drinks so at least you'll have something to do while your eyes glaze over.'

Libby ordered a spritzer and Noah had a whisky soda, and they were about to settle at a quiet table when Rufus walked in with a friend of Tomas he and Willow had introduced him to back when Libby and Rufus were still together. All four of them, knowing the situation, suddenly looked on edge. Libby had to feel sorry for the friend – Marcus – who must have felt super awkward. She managed to contain the groan in her throat and tried to give them both a carefree smile – to reassure Marcus that she didn't mind him talking to Rufus and to show Rufus that she didn't care about him being there.

In reality, however, the incident only went to show her that it was perhaps going to be much harder than she'd imagined staying out of Rufus's way today. Why he'd made such a stupid and irritating decision to come here was a mystery. He was educated and smart – smart enough, surely, to realise there was no way she was going to give him a single moment of her time on today of all days. And then he had to go and get stuck! Why couldn't he have stayed home like any normal person would?

'Do you mind if we...?'

Libby looked up at Noah, trying not to let her gaze stray back to Rufus, even though she knew he was watching her.

'I mean,' she continued, 'I don't suppose we could take our drinks somewhere quieter? I thought the orangery looked nice – big windows, comfy chairs...'

'Sure,' he said. She liked the way he let slip the hint of an American accent on the word. Mostly his accent was the same as hers, but every so often there'd be a funny stress on a word that would give away the fact he no longer lived in the UK. It was cute. 'I don't mind – happy to sit wherever you like.'

Being very careful to maintain the don't-look-at-the-ex rule, Libby hurried from the bar so fast she almost lost Noah, hoping he wouldn't guess there was anything untoward going on here. She could have told him, of course, played it straight, and more than likely he would have been perfectly understanding. And why did it matter anyway? It wasn't like there was going to be anything between her and Noah – nothing permanent anyway. But it felt like a weird and off-putting obstacle to a pleasant afternoon with a handsome, interesting man that she just didn't need to introduce into the mix. And despite all she'd told herself about quick flings and no future, if there was any interest from him she didn't want to destroy it before they'd begun.

The orangery was a beautiful, bright, high-ceilinged, glass-walled room. The woodwork was painted a delicate sage green and the plasterwork a complementary cream that gave it a lovely, calm period feel, and the huge windows had wonderful views of Lovage Hall's Italian gardens. The floor was tiled in a classic monochrome design, and dotted around the space were plump and inviting sofas and chairs in soothing tones of green and biscuit. If there was a perfect spot to appreciate the snowy scene outside Lovage Hall right now, this was probably it. Although twilight was moving in fast and the pearly light of the afternoon was now dove grey, the snow fell soft and heavy like blossom petals shaken from a cherry tree. As Libby and Noah settled into a couple of armchairs, she could see it collecting at the corners of the window frames. Outside, it was so deep that the fountains, statues and shrubs were nothing more than woolly shapes.

A Christmas tree twinkled in the corner of the room, almost tall enough to touch the ceiling and decked in ruby bows and baubles. There were even more of the stout, parchment-coloured candles sitting in pine-cone-and-spruce arrangements on tables around the room.

'They've spared no expense with the tree,' Noah said. 'You've got to wonder how they got that monster in.'

'Hmm…' Libby sipped at her drink. 'Anyone would think it was Christmas or something, the state of this place.'

He grinned. 'Are you warm enough in here?' he asked.

Libby nodded. The room was cosy enough, but now that he'd put the idea in her head, and with the view outside so frosty, she suddenly shivered.

'No you're not,' he said. 'Here…'

He took off his jacket and offered it.

'Honestly, I'm fine,' she said. 'I left my wrap somewhere, but if I'm honest, I have no idea where – Willow will kill me if she finds out!'

'Your secret is safe with me. But please, take my jacket... missing wrap or not, I'd feel less guilty if you borrowed it.'

'There's no need to feel guilty.'

'There's also no need for you to be cold when I have the cure for it right here.'

With a smile she took the jacket and wrapped it around her shoulders, trying not to let the scent clinging to it go to her head, though that was proving easier said than done.

'So,' she said, 'tell me about life in Hollywood. Is it like the films? Are there famous people on every corner?'

'I don't actually live in Hollywood,' he said with a sheepish smile. 'I know Tomas likes to rib me about it but my life in California is nowhere near as exciting as he likes to think it is. In fact, I'll bet your suit shop is far more interesting.'

'It's not *my* suit shop and it's not – it's seriously dull.'

'Ah, come on, it can't be. I bet you get loads of interesting customers with mad requests. You do made-to-measure?'

'We can, but we mostly sell off the peg. There's not much call for custom-made these days; it's quite expensive and most people just don't need anything that formal in their day-to-day lives.'

'Still, you must get some interesting customers. Politicians? Celebrities? Local dignitaries?'

She shook her head with a smile. 'I wish I could say we do but most of our customers come in for a wedding suit or a day at the races, corporate awards, that sort of thing. I think you might be confusing us with a proper Savile Row tailor.'

'It's an odd job for a woman to do... oh God, that sounds proper sexist, doesn't it! I'm so sorry, I mean...'

'It is a strange job for a teenage girl to take up,' Libby said. 'Don't worry – your comment is nowhere near as sexist as some I've had in the shop. And most of the other staff members are male so I'm used to a few raised eyebrows by now.'

'So how did you get into it?'

'It was just a passing comment made by my uncle one day actually. He knows the owner – sort of; they used to play squash at the same club – and one day he was saying that the shop wanted a part-time assistant. My cousin Craig – who was my uncle's first thought – wasn't really interested, but I was looking for a job too so I went into the shop the following day and persuaded them that I could do it as well as any boy.

'Obviously, there were things I didn't do – measuring inside legs and things... most of the customers wouldn't have wanted me to anyway – but we had plenty of people to do that and what they wanted me for was mostly fetching and carrying, pressing the suits and filling in order paperwork, that sort of thing. Well, I could do anything like that well enough. The owner decided I was more reliable than any of the lads they'd had before so when they needed another part-timer they got another girl – Willow – which is how we met.

'Willow never cared for it much, and she'd say that herself now; she just did it for the extra pocket money. I loved my job there though. I know it sounds weird but I really enjoyed helping customers. Some of the blokes who come in might never have bought a formal suit in their life and it will often be for something very special, where they really want to look their best. Now I have a lot more experience I can help them choose, and I get a lot of satisfaction from seeing the look on their face when we find the right one.'

'Sounds a bit like a dating site,' Noah said. 'You find men their perfect match.'

'It's funny but I suppose it is a bit like that. And, just like dating, if he finds the right one, he'll keep it forever.'

'So how did you end up manager?'

She shrugged. 'It just came up. I'd been working there full-time for a few years after college – didn't really think that going off to uni was for me – and when the old manager retired the owner asked me if I'd take the job.'

'He must really value you then.'

'I like to think so. I like to think we're good friends now too.'

'So who's minding the store today then?'

'Jake, my part-timer, and Clarence, one of the old guard; he's been there from an apprenticeship; he was working there when I started and he's almost sixty now. It won't be busy today as it's early close and Christmas Eve. In fact, they'll be closed by now, I expect – I told them to shut the place up if they didn't get any customers for a good long stretch. No point in them hanging around on Christmas Eve, especially if the snow there is as bad as it is here.'

'I don't think the snow in Greenland is as bad as it is here right now,' he said, looking at the windows.

'You might be right about that.' Libby followed his gaze to take a look herself. The flakes were heavier than ever, coming down so fast it was hard to make out anything more than a couple of feet beyond the windows. 'So, that's all there is to know about me—'

'Your job is all there is to know?' he said with a smile. 'I don't believe that for one minute.'

'It's true – trust me. I want to know about your job. It must be exciting, working in films. What exactly do you do then?'

'Hmm, it's really not exciting to anyone not in the industry. It's not like directing or cinematography or any of those other really cool jobs that people think of when they think of the movies.'

'Even if you make cups of tea for the cast I'll still think it's cooler than what I do. Come on… you said you'd tell me about it.'

'OK… you asked for it. You know when you watch a sci-fi film and the spaceship explodes at the end of the film?'

'Yeah?'

'Well, that's what I do. I blow up pretend spaceships.'

'That's an actual job?'

'Yep, and it's my job.'

'Wow, who knew? You literally blow up spaceships for a living?'

'Well, I do blow up other things too. And sometimes I help create pretend disasters by doing the pyrotechnics for exploding buildings and cars and stuff.'

'That is without doubt the most impressive thing I've ever heard!'

'Aww, most people think it's nerdy.'

'Seriously? Surely they don't! I think that's so cool; people must tell you it's cool!'

He grinned. 'Tomas doesn't.'

'Well, Tomas wouldn't,' she replied with a grin of her own. 'He's a proper tease – can't help himself, can he? I'm sure he thinks you're cool, even if he'd never say it.'

'Well, he never could give anyone a compliment without giving them a ribbing at the same time.'

'Except for Willow.'

'Oh, except for Willow. He wouldn't dare – she definitely holds all the aces in that relationship.'

'As it should be,' Libby said, smiling. 'The women should always hold the aces.'

'Well, we'd probably be lost without you,' he agreed.

'It's funny how you're such an old friend of Tomas's and yet you and I have never met before.'

'I don't get home much. I don't think I've been home apart from the odd flying visit for about three years or more. My family prefer to come to me if the truth be told – better weather.'

'Can't say I blame them for that. Do they get to see you work?'

'It's difficult for them to visit sets when the pyrotechnics are being set up and filmed, but I have got them in at other times. They've met a few actors too.'

Libby's eyes widened. 'Who?'

'Ah...' he said with a sly smile now. 'That would be telling, wouldn't it?'

'Ah, come on, who?'

'I'll give you some clues. One is an Irish guy who once played a lion...'

Libby shook her head. 'Not a clue. Tell me!'

'No, you have to guess. How about this one: man of many faces. Captain Jack...'

'Johnny Depp!'

He grinned. 'Mum nearly passed out when she met him.'

'Who's the other one?'

'Goes after his daughter when she's *Taken*...'

'Huh?'

'If you can't guess, I'm not going to tell you.'

'Oh, please...'

'No, you're going to have to work it out.'

'But I can't! Now who's the tease? I'm going to ask Tomas later.'

'You'll think of it before then.'

'Have you worked with tons of famous people then?'

'I'm often on set when they're not – safety and all that. And some of the effects I create aren't even done on set – we do them in miniature and make them look much bigger with camerawork and sound effects. So, yeah, I've worked on films with famous people in them, but not necessarily *with* those famous people – if that makes sense.'

'Oh, see, now I'm less interested…'

He grinned. 'I told you it wasn't cool.'

It was, and the look on his face told Libby that secretly he knew it was.

'It's nice in here, isn't it?' he added, giving the room a once-over. 'Good views, quiet, comfy…'

'I'll bet it's even nicer in the summer.'

'Oh, I don't know… I'm finding it pretty perfect right now.'

He gave her such a look that she wondered whether he was talking about the orangery or his present company, and she found herself hoping it was the latter.

'Same again?' he asked after a moment of charged silence. Libby gave an absent glance at her glass, surprised to discover she'd finished her drink without even realising it.

'That sounds good,' she said. 'Thank you.'

He took their empties to the bar with him, leaving Libby to settle back in her chair, thoughtful as she mused on the snow outside. For the first time that day she was slightly concerned for her chances of getting home after the wedding, though not actually worried yet. There was still time for it to stop and the snowploughs were bound to be out by now. At least, she had to have faith that they would be, although she also had to recognise that it was Christmas Eve, and did the local authority even send things like snowploughs out on Christmas Eve?

Still, she thought as she took another look at the sumptuous orangery, there were worse places to be stuck. She didn't want to hire a room at Lovage Hall's hotel if she didn't have to – it was an expense she could do without – but, she supposed, she could find a comfy armchair to sit and nap in if it really came to it. It might even be an adventure, an amusing memory from the day to look back on with fondness in years to come – how she'd had to spend the night on a chair in her bridesmaid frock, snowed in at Lovage Hall.

An involuntary shiver suddenly raced over her and she pulled Noah's jacket closer around her. It was funny, it smelt almost how she'd imagine California to smell, like ocean and tall trees and snowy mountains. Silly, of course, because how could an aftershave smell like a place? She smiled to herself as she took another sniff and decided it really did smell how she imagined California might.

A movement in the doorway caught her eye and she looked up with an absent smile, expecting it to be Noah with their drinks. But the smile faded as she saw Rufus come in. Hurriedly, she shrugged off Noah's jacket and put it onto the arm of his chair. She didn't even know why she felt the need to – it wasn't like she had to explain what she did to Rufus, but suddenly she felt guilty about wearing it.

'Hey,' he said, walking towards her table.

'Not now,' she said wearily.

'But you don't know—'

'I do, and I don't want to—'

'I just want to talk,' he said, ignoring her plea and taking Noah's seat.

'You can't sit there,' she said.

'Because that flash mate of Tomas's will come back?'

Libby narrowed her eyes. 'Flash? That's rich coming from you. And I don't see what it has to do with you anyway.'

'You're having drinks with him.'

'Still nothing to do with you.'

'But do you… are you having drinks with him because you fancy him or…?'

'I don't see why I owe you of all people any kind of answer to that question. I know why you're here, Rufus – and you can forget it.'

'Won't you at least hear me out?'

'No, I won't. Now can you please leave?'

'Not until you've heard what I have to say.'

'I don't care what you have to say. I don't want to hear it and I don't want to see your stupid face! I've heard what you have to say enough to last me a lifetime already – I don't know what you could possibly add to any of it that would make our situation better.'

'OK,' he said slowly. 'Well, if you won't listen to anything I have to say about us, at least let me give you some advice, as a friend.'

'What advice? What could you possibly give me that I'd need?'

'It's about that guy.'

Libby shook her head impatiently. 'What guy?'

'The one you're getting very pally with today.'

Her mouth fell open. 'Seriously? I mean, *seriously*, Rufus? We're actually having this conversation? You're unbelievable! You have no right to comment on anything I do now – you shouldn't even be here!'

'I was invited,' he said stubbornly.

'You know what I mean!'

'I had an invite,' he repeated. 'Tomas and Willow are my friends too.'

'Only because of me! They're *my* friends; you only got them by default and you lost any right to keep them when you decided to have an affair with my cousin.'

'Don't be like that, Lib.'

'My name is Libby, not Lib, and maybe I feel like being "like that" right now. You don't get to have an opinion anyway. Where I'm concerned, you don't get to have any kind of opinion on anything – you gave up that right when you had your fling.'

'I know that, but I still care about you.'

'That's rich!'

'I know you don't want to believe it but it's true. I know I'm yelling into the abyss trying to talk to you but I've seen you with that guy and I wouldn't be able to rest if I didn't tell you—'

'Whatever you're going to say, please don't. I'm having a nice, uncomplicated time with a man who happens to be good-looking and entertaining, and I don't want it to be ruined by you – God knows you've ruined enough for me. Please, just leave me alone.'

'But he's—'

Libby leapt to her feet. 'If you don't leave me alone I'm going to find a member of staff and tell them you're harassing me and I'll get you thrown out.'

He stared at her, clearly torn and desperate to say what he'd come to say, but she stared right back, challenging him to dare try it. Neither of them even blinked, until another voice made her spin round, a mixture of relief, dread and inexplicable guilt on her face.

'Noah!'

'Everything alright?' he asked carefully, glancing between the two of them. Rufus was still in the seat he'd recently vacated while Libby was standing up, and she realised it must have been very obvious something intense was going on between them. 'Do you need me to come back later?'

'Rufus is going now,' Libby said with forced brightness. 'He just came to say a quick hello – didn't you, Rufus?'

Libby's heart was in her mouth for the ten seconds it took Rufus to answer – a blink of an eye in the real world, but to her it felt like an excruciating eternity. She thought he was going to blow it, and he so easily could have if he'd wanted to. It might have been the sight of Noah, drinks in his hands, bigger, more confident, more assured than him, that put Rufus off, or it could have been the thought of Libby's predictable wrath, or it could even have been a last courtesy to her, a recognition of the fact they had once loved each other that stopped him. Whatever the reason, he simply gave a tight smile and stood up.

'That's right. I just thought I'd say hello. Libby and I go way back – wouldn't have been right not to.'

Rufus started walking towards the doors. Then he turned back.

'Noah, isn't it?' he asked.

'Yes.'

'Old uni friend of Tomas – I have got the right guy, haven't I?'

'You have, but—'

'Oh, you don't know me; we haven't met before. I've heard a lot about you today, that's all.'

'Oh,' Noah said, and if he'd wanted to know more about what exactly Rufus had heard, he didn't get the chance to ask. Rufus simply gave a last nod to him and then to Libby before he left them.

'That was a bit weird,' Noah said, more to himself than to Libby as he draped his jacket over the back of his seat with a vague frown.

'Sorry, it's just… he's a bit like that.'

'He's always that intense?' Noah asked.

'That's one way to describe him.'

'You know him well?'

'Quite well, but we haven't seen each other in a while.'

'You and he weren't…?'

'It was nothing – it didn't mean anything,' Libby lied. She didn't know why she felt she had to lie, but she didn't want to think about Rufus or his ill-timed attempt at reconciliation at all, and starting a truthful conversation with Noah about their past would force her to do just that. She was having a great time with Noah – it was fun and uncomplicated and it was making her feel good about herself for once. It wasn't fair for Rufus to spoil that – like she'd told him, he'd spoilt enough for her already. It wasn't fair to come here now with that handsome face in that gorgeous suit reminding her of a past and a love she was trying so hard to put behind her. If he had one ounce of affection left for her, as he said he did, then the kindest thing he could do was to leave her alone to get on with her life without him.

'I expect he'll be leaving soon – before the evening reception starts. He only popped in to wish Tomas and Willow well.'

Noah glanced at the windows. 'I wouldn't be so sure of that. If this snow carries on, no one will be going anywhere tonight.'

Chapter Six

'Libby!'

She and Noah had just finished their second drink when India and Scarlet came racing across the orangery towards them.

Only two-thirds of the trio of torment, Libby thought. As they usually hunted in a pack, she had to wonder where the other third was.

'Libby! Will you come outside with us?'

'What?' Libby laughed lightly, angling her head at the windows. 'It's nearly dark and it's snowing!'

'Please!' Scarlet and India begged in unison. 'Only for a little while.'

'A little while is enough to get pneumonia,' Libby replied. 'I'm sure your mums wouldn't thank me for taking you out there. And we're hardly dressed for it.'

India shrugged. 'My mum says if I want to catch my death then go ahead.'

Libby was fairly sure that didn't mean she had her mum's blessing to go out and catch her death, and she was just about to say so when they were interrupted by someone else arriving.

'Hey. Noah!'

Noah stood up to shake the man's hand. 'I meant to come and say hello earlier but I got a bit waylaid…'

'No worries…' the man said. Libby tried to place him. She thought she'd seen him at a table with some of Tomas's old university friends and so guessed he was a part of that same circle Noah had been part of too. 'Come and meet Daisy; I've been telling her all about you!'

'Daisy…?'

'My girlfriend.'

'I didn't know you were seeing someone.'

'We met last month. I like her a lot.'

'You must do if she's lasted a month,' Noah said with a laugh. He looked at Libby.

'You go ahead,' she said. 'You must have a lot of catching up to do.'

'Maybe we can pick up our conversation again later?'

Libby nodded and smiled, and then Noah and his old friend walked out of the orangery towards the great hall.

'There's a spare seat now.' Libby patted Noah's recently vacated chair. 'Why don't we stay here in the warm and chat.'

Both girls looked disappointed.

'But our mums said we could go outside,' India said.

'Are you sure they actually meant that?' Libby asked.

Scarlet nodded.

'What about Olivia's mum?'

'Olivia's not coming,' Scarlet said testily.

'She said Scarlet was bossy,' India put in. 'So we're not friends with her now.'

'Seems a bit harsh,' Libby said. 'Couldn't you make it up? Won't she be lonely with nobody to hang out with?'

Scarlet folded her arms and shook her head vigorously. 'She's with her dad, so she's not lonely.'

'Hmm…' Libby said. 'OK…'

The thing about girls of that age (and even Libby could vaguely recall it) was that dramas rarely lasted long and were forgotten in a heartbeat. Before the end of the day she was sure the three would be reunited, like the witches from Macbeth once again. Perhaps she was worrying too much about it.

'So can we go out?' India asked.

'You seriously want to go outside in this?'

'But there's so much snow!' Scarlet cried. 'We could have the most awesome snowball fight!'

'OK…' Libby put her hands up. 'Absolutely no snowball fights. For a start, you'd pummel me. And we don't have any way to get dry afterwards.'

'But, Libby… our mums said—'

'How about we go out on the patio for a few minutes to have a good look? You can have snowball fights tomorrow at home, can't you?'

'It'll be gone by then.'

'I'm sure it won't – it's too deep to melt that quickly,' Libby said. 'It's my final offer.'

Scarlet and India looked at each other, and then back at Libby, before Scarlet gave a sullen nod.

'I suppose so.'

'OK, I have a plan for this,' Libby said practically. 'Stay there for a second.'

She dashed to the bar.

'I don't suppose I could borrow three trays for a few minutes?' she said. The bartender raised his eyebrows slightly but handed them over anyway.

'Thanks,' she said, smiling. 'It's for a very good cause and I'll bring them straight back.'

'What are those for?' Scarlet asked as Libby returned with her equipment. Then her eyes widened. 'Are we going sledging?'

'Oooh!' India cried. 'Can we?'

Libby laughed. 'No. We couldn't sled on these – they're far too small… for my bottom at least. No, they're to go over our heads so we don't get soaked.'

Both girls took their trays, seemingly content enough that they were being escorted out, and then they undid the French doors and stepped out onto the patio, Libby immediately shivering and wishing she still had Noah's jacket. If either of the girls were cold they certainly didn't show it.

It didn't take long until their trays were abandoned anyway, so that the snow could cover them as they giggled and kicked it about, flattening the floral arrangements decorating their hair and soaking satin shoes that Libby was fairly certain would never recover from the onslaught. She wasn't about to stop them: firstly, they weren't her children and, now that the service was over, she had decided they weren't her responsibility either (though she did feel a little responsible still); and secondly, they were simply having too much fun. And if she was being totally honest, so was she, despite her initial reservations about going out. It wasn't until she was so cold her teeth were actually chattering like a cartoon character's and both the girls had glowing, dripping noses that she decided enough was enough.

'OK, girls, I really think we need to go inside.'

'But we've only just come out,' India said, grabbing a tray and immediately holding it over her head, probably in a pre-emptive attempt to head off any arguments about them getting wet and cold.

'We've been out long enough for me to be freezing, and you must be as cold as I am,' Libby said.

'I'm not one bit perishing,' Scarlet said.

'Me neither,' India agreed, lowering the tray again to let the snow fall into her already soaked hair. 'See... not a bit cold!'

'Well, I'm not saying I don't believe you,' Libby said, 'but I'm definitely a lot perishing and I need to go in. I'd prefer it if you came back with me too. The dancing will be starting soon anyway, and we want to be dry for that, right?'

'The disco?' Scarlet asked.

'Yes.' Libby smiled, already edging towards the French doors.

'OK,' Scarlet said, sounding simultaneously disappointed about curtailing their snowy activities but excited at the prospect of the dancing.

'Come on then...' Libby held open the doors for them. 'Let's go and make ourselves beautiful again.'

They went into the toilets to dry themselves off as best they could under the hand dryers, and by the time they'd done that and Libby had fixed her hair and make-up, they returned to the rest of the guests to find Willow and Tomas were mingling once more. At some point Tomas had changed out of his morning suit into something just as snappy: a slim-fitting snazzy claret houndstooth check to go with the colour theme of the wedding with a matching waistcoat – a set Libby had sold to him, naturally. It was a lot more relaxed and informal but he looked devilishly handsome and stylish in it.

Willow had opted to stay in her wedding dress. It was comfortable enough for the evening reception, she'd told Libby as she'd planned out her day, and if she was spending all that money on a gown then she wanted to wear it for as long as she could. She'd let her honey hair loose now and that, with the bohemian style of her dress, gave her the look of a goddess from a pre-Raphaelite painting. She looked every bit as beautiful as she had that morning, but in a way that was more recognisable as the old Willow Libby knew so well.

Willow smiled as she found Libby again. 'Have you been alright?' she asked.

'Yes, fine. I had plenty of company.'

'Only…' Willow faltered as she glanced at Tomas, the ease in her expression suddenly gone. 'We've just bumped into Rufus… he was trying to leave actually.'

'Well, that's good, isn't it?' Libby asked. It was going to be difficult for Rufus to succeed, but she wasn't going to stand in the way of his attempt because it would certainly make her life less stressful if he was gone.

'Yes, I suppose it is, though I'm not convinced it's safe for him to leave,' Tomas said. 'I did just say that to him, told him he might be better off giving it an hour to see if the snow stopped.'

'But he said…' Willow paused uncertainly again. 'He said he wasn't going to stay here and watch you make an idiot of yourself. What's been happening between you?'

'Nothing,' Libby replied. 'I spoke to him for a couple of minutes but after that, thankfully, he stayed out of my way.'

'I just thought it was a weird thing to say,' Willow added.

Libby shrugged. 'It's Rufus, isn't it? Who knows what he means.'

'So you don't know… Nothing's happened that *we* ought to know about?' Willow pressed.

'No,' Libby said firmly. 'And if he wants to go home right now then who are we to stop him?'

Willow looked as if she might disagree, but she did seem to relax a little.

'Willow, it's not your job to referee us anyway.' Libby tried to give her a reassuring smile. 'We're two adults who ought to manage some civility for at least one afternoon. I know I said I didn't want him to come and I can't deny I was pissed off when he arrived, but I was never going to start a fight with him, not on your wedding day, and whatever I think of Rufus, I'm pretty sure he wouldn't either. We had a quick word, yes, and he said some things I didn't want to hear and I told him not to waste his breath, but that's really it. He went off and left me alone, then I was busy with India and Scarlet... actually, we went out to play in the snow.'

At this Willow grinned. 'Did anyone ever tell you you're weird?'

Libby laughed. 'I think you just did! It was their idea, I can assure you.'

'But I bet you enjoyed it.'

'I did a bit... It was bloody cold though.'

'Really?' Tomas asked with mock surprise. 'Who'd have thought snow might be cold?'

'Very funny.' Libby prodded him in the chest. 'Shut up, you.'

'You love kids really,' Willow said, 'even when you're complaining. That's how come I knew you'd be a great chief bridesmaid. One day you'll be the most perfect mum—'

A sudden look of mortification crossed Willow's features as she clapped a hand to her mouth.

'God, Libby, I'm so sorry! I didn't think, I—'

'It's alright,' Libby said gently. 'We can't pretend that it never happened.'

'I know, but...'

Willow glanced helplessly at Tomas, who looked as pained as she did, and then back at Libby.

'Really,' Libby said. 'Stop stressing. I know you didn't mean anything by it and people are going to talk about babies in front of me from time to time; I'm not going to lose my shit every time they do.'

Willow seemed far from happy, but was distracted by Tomas, who checked his watch and then gave her a meaningful look.

'Is it that time already?' she asked.

'Yep.'

'What time's that?' Libby asked.

'We need to start greeting the evening guests,' Willow said. 'At least, the ones who've managed to make it. Coming? We could do with you there if you fancy a bit of handshaking.'

With Rufus gone Libby could relax and enjoy the evening as a VIP guest. 'Of course.' She smiled. 'I am the chief bridesmaid, after all, and someone's got to flirt with all the attractive single men.'

'Oh dear,' Willow said as they began to walk to the main doors of the great hall where the reception was due to begin. 'I hope the selection won't be too disappointing then.'

'Oh,' Libby said, having already decided she might just search out Noah for another round of drinks, 'I'm sure the selection will be just fine.'

There was a lull in arrivals. There had been quite a lot of lulls – almost more lulls than periods of activity. As Tomas, Willow, Libby and Olivia (who'd been invited to help as Scarlet and India were probably up to mischief somewhere) waited to greet their evening guests, Willow was visibly more disappointed with every passing minute. Many of the people who'd been there at the morning service and wedding breakfast had stayed on and were in the great hall waiting for the evening reception to start. That was something, at least, Willow had said. So far, however, very few of those who'd been invited only to the evening reception had managed to get there.

'I expected a few no-shows,' Willow said glumly. 'It's Christmas Eve and people have traditions – I understand that. I had thought some people would put those aside, just for this year, and come anyway. I mean, I understand the weather's bad too but…'

'It can't be helped,' Libby said. 'You weren't to know it would snow like this… nobody could have known it would snow like this, not even the forecasters. They gave out snow but nowhere near this bad.'

'Don't be sad…' Tomas pulled Willow into his arms. 'Not today. The people who wouldn't come – it's their loss; they'll miss a great night. We'll still have a great time, and, on the upside, there'll be more space on the dance floor.'

She looked up at him. 'What about the people who wanted to come but couldn't get here?'

'Well, we really can't do much about that, I suppose,' he said lamely, his attempts to cheer her up backfiring.

'The atmosphere will be rubbish,' Willow said. 'We've all been to those parties – flat as old lemonade because there's nobody there. I don't want our wedding to be one of those parties.'

'It won't be,' Tomas soothed. 'The most important people are here already; everyone wants to make it a night to remember and they're up for a good time. You worry too much.'

'You do,' Libby agreed. 'Tomas is right – the people who really matter are here.'

'Not all of them,' Willow insisted.

'Most of them,' Tomas said. 'Enough for you to stop dwelling on what you can't change. We'll catch up with the others after Christmas perhaps. If it makes you happy, maybe we can even put on another night, something a bit belated and more low-key but where they can still celebrate with us. How does that sound to you?'

'It won't be the same.'

'No, it won't – there's no dressing that up – but it's the best we have. What we don't want to do is ruin our night tonight worrying about who we don't have here and in the process spoiling it for those people we do have here. See?'

Willow reached to kiss him. 'I suppose you're right. Do you think everyone who's going to come will have arrived by now then?'

'Even if they're not, I'm sure any latecomers won't be expecting us to stand here all night waiting to greet them. They'll come and find us if they manage to get through, I'm sure. Why don't we go and join the party?'

Libby rubbed Willow's arm. 'Sounds like a good idea to me,' she said. She turned to Olivia. 'What do you think? Party time?'

'Will you dance with me?' Olivia asked shyly.

'Girl! I'm going to dance you into next week!'

Olivia let out a snorting giggle and Libby glanced up to catch Willow smile fondly at her.

'Thanks,' she said quietly.

Libby frowned. 'For what?'

'For being the best friend I could ever have wished for!'

Chapter Seven

Libby sniffed back a tear as Willow and Tomas took to the floor for their first dance as husband and wife. They had the space to themselves, and although Libby didn't actually recognise the song they'd chosen, she knew it held huge significance for them. If her memory served her correctly, Willow had told her it was the song she'd been listening to when she and Tomas had made up after their very first argument, while Tomas had told her he was sorry for hurting her and vowed to do everything in his power never to hurt her again. As far as Libby knew, he'd kept his word, and no tiff they'd had since had been as big or as damaging as that first one. So this song, she supposed, was symbolic of that promise, and perhaps that was why they'd chosen it. Not to mention that it was achingly beautiful and very fitting.

Willow had her head resting on Tomas's shoulder and looked as perfectly happy and content as it was possible for a woman to look, while Tomas was proud and protective and had eyes for no one else. The lights were low, the candles now lit around the room, and the warm glow enveloping the couple as they swept around the floor to their special song revealed a scene of sheer joy.

The song came to an end and everyone clapped, then other couples were invited to join them. Libby sat at her spot on a table at the edge of the dance floor, watching as Gene led Adrienne out to dance. She was alone but she didn't mind so much because if Rufus had been here he might foolishly have looked for her to dance and that would have been about as awkward as it got. She allowed herself to scan the room briefly for Noah, whom she hadn't seen for an hour or so, but she couldn't pick him out amongst the faces in the partial gloom. Perhaps he was catching up with old friends, and perhaps that was a good thing really, because while she would have enjoyed him asking her, this dance was maybe a bit too intimate for two people who'd just met.

'Canapé, madam?'

She looked round to see Santiago, the hot waiter who'd quite taken her fancy earlier that day. It was funny, it seemed like a lifetime ago now, before Rufus had come to mix everything up and before she'd got to know Noah better. While she could appreciate that Santiago was handsome, the attraction just wasn't there in the same way now. She supposed it had only ever been an idle distraction, devoid of enough substance to sustain anything more meaningful.

'You are not dancing?' Santiago asked as Libby declined the tray of nibbles he'd offered.

'No, I'll let the couples have their fun.'

'Ah… of course…'

He gave her a last smile before taking the tray to weave through the other guests again. Libby cast a glance at the bar and saw a rare gap. Quickly deciding to take advantage, she jumped up to get herself a refill.

As she waited to get served there was a tap on her shoulder, and she turned to see Noah smiling at her.

'I thought you'd gone,' she said.

He laughed. 'Where on earth would I have gone? It's like Siberia out there. I've been catching up with a few old friends. Quite a lot of old friends actually.'

'Ah. Had fun?'

'Depends on what you think is fun. It was definitely lively.'

'It's getting a bit livelier in here too,' she said, glancing at the dance floor, which was now full of couples slow dancing.

'You're not dancing?' he asked.

'Well, as I'm standing here with you, I'd say probably not.'

He grinned. 'It's just with you being the chief bridesmaid and all I thought you'd have guys queuing up to ask you. Isn't it tradition that the chief bridesmaid and the best man get it on?'

'It might be, but as he's here with his wife, maybe not in this case.'

'Ah, you could be right; might be as well to steer clear of that tradition tonight.'

She gave another smile, but this one was a little harder to form. She had no idea why, but Noah's well-meaning banter was sort of disappointing to hear. He'd thought she'd be inundated with offers of a dance because she was the only adult bridesmaid and not because he thought she was attractive?

'Clearly the bridesmaid thing isn't working for me,' she said with a shrug.

'Can I get you a drink?' he asked.

She shook her head. 'That's kind but you bought me drinks earlier. If anything, I ought to be buying one for you.'

'That wouldn't be very chivalrous of me, would it? Mine's a whisky soda.'

She laughed lightly. 'Right then…'

'I'm joking,' he said. 'I wouldn't hear of it. Please, let me get you something.'

She was about to refuse him again but then she thought, what the hell? If he wasn't going to ask her to dance – and it looked very much as if he had no intention – then she could share a drink with him instead.

'Thanks,' she said. 'I'll have a white wine spritzer.'

'Your drink of choice?' he asked. 'I seem to recall you were drinking them earlier.'

'Helps me to pace myself so I'm not steaming drunk as soon as the disco kicks in.'

'Ah.'

'I'm sure I'll be on the neat gin by eleven.'

He smiled and was then distracted from further comment by the bartender coming to take his order. Libby watched him. She was beginning to realise that something had changed since earlier that day. She couldn't put her finger on what it was, but something was different, like a distance that hadn't been there before, as if he'd put some sort of barrier up. She wondered if it was deliberate, whether he knew he was doing it, whether he'd decided she wasn't worth the effort after all. Perhaps he had his eye on someone else now. He was still friendly, but he wasn't holding her gaze in the same way, and she didn't detect that obvious interest now. Perhaps seeing her with Rufus earlier was the cause. Maybe he'd worked out that things in that regard might be complicated – too complicated for him to want to get involved. But then, Rufus was gone now, so...

Figures, she thought. She tried not to let it bother her – she could still enjoy Noah's company – but she couldn't shake the disappointment. She'd been convinced there was a real connection there, something more than idle flirting, but she must have been mistaken. If he was so easily able to switch it off, it couldn't have been worth anything after all.

He paid for their drinks and leant on the bar, glass in hand as he turned to her again.

'So you're still determined to go home after the party?'

'I don't know what else I can do. I don't have a room booked… I just hope the snow stops soon. I promised my grandma I'd be over for Christmas lunch too… We're eating with my parents and she's kind of relying on me as a human shield.'

Noah laughed. 'That sounds bad.'

'It is. Anyone would think she was a teenager, she gets so many lectures from my mum. So I have to get home by hook or by crook. The snow's bound to thin, even if it doesn't stop – right?'

'For your sake I hope so too, though even if it does, I'm not sure what cab companies will fancy coming all the way out here if the roads are bad. Especially at Christmas.'

'Well, there's a little nugget of optimism for me to treasure,' she said.

He grinned. 'Sorry, I didn't mean it to sound like that. I only meant it's not looking so great. Perhaps you ought to think about a plan B just in case. Could you call your grandma and warn her she might need to take body armour if you don't make it?' He took a sip of his drink and then nodded towards the doors of the hall. 'Isn't that your friend? Looks like he had a go at getting home and changed his mind.'

Libby followed Noah's gaze to see Rufus walk in. His hair was wet as he peeled off a snow-covered coat that suggested he'd walked quite a way in the blizzard that was now raging outside.

'Bloody hell,' she groaned under her breath.

Did the appearance of Rufus mean the roads were impassable? Maybe he'd just changed his mind and had wanted to come back to the party, or maybe he'd never really intended to leave at all – though if it was some kind of ruse for her benefit it was a strange and pointless one. She really needed to stop thinking that everything was about her, she reflected wryly. There was probably a perfectly innocent explanation – though she couldn't deny it was about to put a serious damper on her night. Perhaps the story had just been mixed up and he'd only gone out to secure his car for the night, fully realising that there was no way he was going to make it home through the snow. She was fairly sure he wouldn't have had a room booked but, with more ready cash than her, he wouldn't think twice about getting one now if he needed to, leaving her stuck with him hanging around all night.

There was a tug on her arm. Libby looked down to see Olivia there.

'Will you dance with me now? You said you would.'

Libby searched for her brightest smile. 'I did, didn't I?' The reappearance of Rufus had well and truly rattled her – a lot more than she was happy about – but that wasn't Olivia's fault. Why did Libby have to let him get to her anyway? She'd made it clear she wanted him to leave her alone, so she ought to be able to ignore him well enough as long as he honoured her request. Rufus was many things but he wasn't a pest – she had every reason to hope he'd recognise boundaries when they'd been put in place.

'Go on.' Noah's voice cut into her thoughts. 'I'll keep your drink safe for you – I'd like to see your moves.'

'I'll bet you would,' she replied dryly as she handed him her glass. 'I have a feeling you'll be sadly disappointed though – I have nothing that's going to get me on *Strictly*.'

'I think I'll be the judge of that.' He looked down at Olivia and smiled. 'I bet you're an amazing dancer – am I right?'

'I do ballet and jazz,' she replied brightly.

'I knew it! I could tell you'd be a good dancer.'

Libby offered her hand to Olivia. 'In that case, you can show me some moves.' With a last look at a grinning Noah, she went with her new best friend to the dance floor.

The music had changed tempo and was now more upbeat, and the swaying couples had been replaced by groups of laughing revellers, flinging themselves about with drunken abandon. Libby and Olivia's own dance consisted of an odd and sporadic mix of shoulder shakes, bunny hops, jiving, twirling, waving hands and general messing about. There was a definite absence of any ballet or jazz or any kind of formal dance whatsoever, but there was something quite liberating about the fact that Libby could dance like this, and because it was with Olivia, nobody judged. She and the little bridesmaid giggled and whirled, and Libby found joy knowing that these were the sorts of moments that carried a young girl into adulthood. Libby still treasured plenty of them herself: glorious, perfect evenings with her mum and dad or a favourite aunt and uncle where their world, just for a moment, had revolved completely and utterly around making her happy.

The song faded into a new one, and then, from nowhere, India and Scarlet appeared.

'Can we dance too?' India asked.

Olivia looked less than happy about having to share Libby now, but neither she nor Libby could very well say no, despite the other girls having been quite happy to ditch Olivia earlier that day. Another growing-up memory and a tougher lesson, Libby reflected, this one not quite so fondly remembered but probably just as important.

It seemed Olivia had already learnt it and realised it wouldn't do her any favours to be churlish about it. She glanced up at Libby and then smiled at the other girls.

So all four of them began to mess about to a new song and, as she leapt about, Libby chanced a look across to the bar and saw Noah was grinning as he watched them. That was good, wasn't it? It meant he found her funny? Entertaining? Sweet and kind? Or maybe he thought she looked ridiculous? Did it mean he was interested or not?

Aside from the obvious first connection of that moment walking down the aisle that morning, she really hadn't been able to figure him out at all. More to the point, she couldn't work out why it mattered so much. In any other situation she'd have shrugged it off and moved on – why not this time? What was so special about this guy? He was good-looking, charming and all those other things, of course, but she'd met men like that before and they hadn't affected her like he seemed to.

She was still pondering the question when she saw Rufus go to the bar, the snow now melted from his hair, and his coat probably hung up again in Lovage Hall's cloakrooms, and after he'd ordered a drink he turned to Noah and started to talk to him.

It was inexplicable, the way Libby's heart started to race, but she couldn't help it. What was Rufus up to? Why was he so fixated on Noah? They didn't know each other and Libby could think of other people present who did know Rufus, so if it was company he needed, surely he'd go and find them? He'd wanted to say something earlier... in a bid to nip in the bud any potential hook-up between her and Noah, of that she was sure. She'd told him to back off, yet here he was now, talking to Noah, a man he barely knew, like they were old friends. What was he up to? So much for recognising boundaries...

For a second Libby considered going over there to break up the conversation, but would that only make things worse? What reason could she give? Would it arouse suspicion where there would have been none had she left well alone? And suspicion of what exactly?

This was getting out of hand, she decided. For all she knew Rufus was just having a friendly chat with another man on his own at the bar, passing the time, commenting on the weather, nothing more. Maybe there was really nothing to worry about after all.

Forget it, she told herself. *Get a grip*. Noah didn't seem all that interested anyway; he was listening politely, but with one eye on the dance floor he hardly looked engaged. Besides, even if Rufus was trying to make her look bad, Noah would be an idiot to take anything Rufus told him seriously – they didn't know each other at all and Noah barely knew Libby any better. And if that were the case, and if Noah did prove to be that idiotic, then Libby would have had a lucky escape and Rufus would have done her an unwitting favour.

She turned her attention back to her little friends, who were having so much fun they'd been quite oblivious to her distraction. They grinned up at her and then at each other, and then Libby happened to look across the dance floor again, this time her gaze settling on Willow – who had her head resting on Tomas's shoulder as they sat together at an abandoned table.

Willow looked across and caught Libby's eye and smiled fondly at her. Libby summoned a smile to send back, and the mere act of forcing herself to do it made her feel better, so it became a proper genuine one. Tomas noticed her now too and offered a thumbs-up. He was starting to mouth something when the music suddenly stopped and the room was plunged into darkness.

There was a collective gasp and then a brief, charged silence, followed by everyone beginning to talk again at once.

'What's going on?'

'The power's gone?'

'Someone call the manager!'

'It'll be back on in a minute…'

'Must be the weather!'

Libby felt the girls close around her and she gathered them in.

'Don't worry,' she said, 'I'm sure it'll be back on in a minute.'

'I don't like it,' India said in a small voice.

'It's just the dark,' Scarlet said.

'I don't like the dark,' India replied.

'It won't hurt you,' Olivia said.

'No,' Libby agreed, 'it won't. And it's not completely dark.'

'Yes it is,' India said. 'I can't see anything – not even my mum.'

There was no arguing that it was *very* dark, if not quite totally thanks to the few candles that remained burning on the tables. It was true every light in the building had gone off, along with all the ones in the grounds outside, and with heavy clouds obscuring the night sky there wasn't even moonlight to ease their minds. Libby didn't often fret in situations like this, but even she was now gripped by a creeping sense of vague panic, something that seemed to be spreading through the room, though she tried not to let the young bridesmaids see that.

Time passed, and the conversations became slightly more frantic. Libby could sense people starting to move around the room, perhaps trying to make their way back to tables or loved ones. Libby kept up the positive charade for the girls, but the longer the power stayed off, the harder her own unease was to hide. In most cases a loss of electricity would last seconds at most, but, as this went on, until more than two minutes had passed, Libby was beginning to wonder if they were going to get it back at all.

'Ladies and gentlemen…'

Libby turned in the direction of the voice and saw Lovage Hall's manager, his face lit from below by a lamp he was carrying. In any other situation she'd laugh out loud, because he looked like he was in a cheesy eighties horror flick. He was followed by two other staff members who now went round the room lighting more candles as he spoke.

'I'm sure it hasn't escaped your attention that we seem to be having a temporary issue with the power. I've been told this is affecting the entirety of the local area but the power company are working hard to get us back up and running as quickly as possible. We do still have heating and we're trying to get some lighting arranged as we speak… As for everything else, I'm afraid we'll have to sit tight and wait, but hopefully it shouldn't be too long before we can get your entertainment started up again.'

Barely had he finished than guests started to swarm over to ask more questions. Libby had plenty of her own but she didn't see the point in hassling the poor man – he could no more get the power back on than stop the snow and she was certain his ability to answer questions about it would be quite limited. The electricity company would have been inundated with calls and would have given the sparest information – probably because that was all they would have until they could locate the problem and begin to work on it.

At least the room grew a little lighter with every candle that was lit and she had to admit that it looked a lot prettier than the disco lights had. She looked down to see Scarlet, India and Olivia all seemed a lot less anxious now – in fact, they all looked a little bit excited. Libby supposed that now the initial panic was over and the darkness had been banished it was a novel situation for them, a sort of mini-adventure they could tell their friends about when they got back to school after the Christmas break.

India's mother emerged from the gloom and bent down to her daughter.

'Are you alright? Want to come and sit with me and Daddy until everything is fixed?'

India gave Libby a quick glance before apparently deciding that the bosom of her family was perhaps the safest place to enjoy her little adventure, and Libby could hardly blame her for that. Her departure was quickly followed by that of Scarlet and Olivia, both also searched out by family members, leaving Libby to go and find a seat to wait out the pause in festivities.

Beyond the large windows was darkness, but there was just enough light from the candles and lanterns dotted around the room to show fat flakes still dropping like stones outside. Libby couldn't be certain, but the snow looked heavier now than it had been all day. Rufus had been forced to turn back far earlier than this, when it hadn't even been this bad – did that mean leaving at the end of the night was going to be impossible for anyone?

She supposed there were worse places to be stuck. It was warm and dry and comfortable, pleasant to look at, and she was surrounded by nice people (mostly, she thought, glancing to where Rufus had been, though in the current gloom it was difficult to make out the bar area from where she sat). Perhaps it wouldn't be so bad, despite the unwanted expense. Perhaps it would even be fun – better than an empty flat and a dull Christmas lunch with her well-meaning but bound-to-say-the-wrong-thing parents.

'Well, this is an unexpected bit of drama…'

Libby turned to find Noah at her side.

'You can say that again,' she replied. 'How long do you think it will last?'

'Who can tell? I overheard someone saying the snow had brought power lines down, but I have no idea how they know that – could be a case of Chinese whispers. I suppose we'll only find out if they were right or not if the hotel manager chooses to tell us. I know one thing; it's going to be an interesting night if it lasts.'

'There'll be nothing to do. Poor Willow – this is the last thing she needs on her wedding day.'

'It's the last thing anyone needs on any day, I suppose. As for nothing to do… we might have to get creative, that's for sure.'

'Charades by candlelight?'

'Something like that.' He held out a glass. 'I brought your drink over; I think you forgot it. It might be a bit warm now… ice has melted.'

'Oh, thanks – I had forgotten it actually. Too much excitement.'

'Too much fun dancing with your little friends, eh?'

'That too,' she said, smiling. 'Thanks for keeping hold of it – I could definitely do with it about now.'

'I think we're all about ready for one now. The longer the power's off the busier the bar will be – like you say, not much else to do.'

'Ah, so you think it's a cunning plan to get us to buy more booze? Crafty!'

He grinned. 'Isn't it?'

'The question is, will it work?'

'On me it will!' he said, laughing. 'I need no encouragement! How about you?'

'I'm sure I could manage a few more – just for something to pass the time, of course.'

'Of course,' he said, trying to look serious. 'I wouldn't imagine it would be any other reason. I mean, it's not like it's nearly Christmas or we're at a wedding reception or anything…'

Libby was distracted by Willow's voice – she didn't sound happy, and Libby could well understand why. She scanned the gloom, picking out the unmistakeable silhouette of the gown across the room.

'I'm so sorry.' She turned to Noah. 'Would you mind if I…? I have to go and talk to Willow for a minute; I think she's getting stressed.'

'I can imagine,' he said, following Libby when she started to walk, even though he hadn't been asked to.

'Are you alright?' Libby asked urgently as they located Willow.

'Yes,' Willow said, before launching into a tirade that begged very much to differ. 'I can't believe this is happening today of all days! I feel as if my wedding is cursed! First people couldn't get here, then the ones who did couldn't get home, and now this! What's next? It's bound to be something disastrous! We're going to get snowed totally in and die of hypothermia or squashed by an avalanche or something!'

Libby rubbed a soothing hand down her friend's arm. 'Where's Tomas?'

'Gone to see the manager to see what can be done.'

'Not much, I would imagine,' Noah said. 'I'm sure he's as unhappy about it as we are but I don't suppose he's got very much control over the weather or the power grid.'

'You'd think they'd have a backup generator,' Libby said.

Noah appeared to battle a frown. 'In a hospital, maybe, or a very important building. I'm not sure they'd need one here.'

'Why not?' Libby demanded. 'Wouldn't they have one for just such a situation as this?'

'I shouldn't have thought so,' Noah said. 'I shouldn't imagine they get many situations like this. We certainly don't get snow like this in England ever – probably what took the power down; system couldn't cope because it's not built for extreme weather.'

'Well that's stupid – it ought to be.' Libby glanced at Willow, who seemed more upset by Noah's words of wisdom. She had the sudden urge to tell him to stop being such a know-it-all, but she supposed he was only trying to help. They were all feeling pretty helpless in the face of things they couldn't influence in any way and nobody really knew what to do or say – conversations like this were probably happening all over Lovage Hall.

She ran her hand down Willow's arm again. 'It'll be alright,' she said uncertainly. 'I'm sure the electricity company has people working like mad on it – they'll have us back on in no time.'

'What if they can't even get to the fault to work on it?' Willow asked. 'Nobody from here has been able to get through the snow when they've tried to leave so why would the power company be any different?'

'But the guests here aren't driving big trucks, are they? The electricity people will have better vehicles.'

'What if they decide it's too dangerous to send people out in this?' Willow insisted. 'I mean, I wouldn't like to think Tomas was going out if he worked for them.'

'The difference is, they know what to expect and how to stay safe,' Noah put in. 'I expect they're trained for this sort of stuff.'

Libby wasn't sure that was altogether true but at least it was a more positive spin on things, something that would make Willow feel better and that she herself could get behind. 'Noah's right,' she said. 'They learn what to do in all sorts of emergency situations.'

'But you said yourself England never gets snow like this,' Willow sniffed. 'How could they have been trained for weather this bad?'

While Libby could understand her friend's meltdown, she also reflected that it wasn't helpful and certainly wouldn't change anything. What it would do very effectively was get her so wound up she wouldn't be able to enjoy the rest of the night, even if the power returned quickly and the snow miraculously melted away so that everyone was free to leave when they were ready.

A shadow emerged from the gloom, and after a second Libby realised with some relief that it was Tomas. He shook his head slightly at Willow, and any hopes of good news were dashed.

'There's nothing anyone can do – we really are at the mercy of the power company and the weather,' he said. 'We'll have to sit tight and make the best of it.'

'What about all the guests?' Willow asked. 'There are so many who can't get home!'

'The manager says he'll make as many rooms as he has spare available. The bad news is I don't think it will be enough for everyone who's stranded.'

'For free?' Willow asked hopefully.

'Afraid not,' Tomas said. 'It would have been the ideal solution but I suppose it's out of his hands. They're not running a charity.'

'I don't suppose there'll be any kind of discount either,' Libby said. Tomas shook his head.

'If there's one thing they're not going to do, it's give away rooms when they have a captive audience who will gladly pay.'

'But some people won't be able to afford it,' Willow said.

'I know,' Tomas said. 'I told him that. He also said he's happy for people to bunk up with someone else who has a room – as long as they comply with health and safety regs – or if they can manage they're welcome to spare blankets and pillows so they can make themselves comfortable on the chairs and sofas down in the public spaces.'

'People aren't going to like that,' Willow said.

'Maybe not, but it's all we have. They'll understand that there isn't much of an alternative. Other than try to battle through, which I'm sure nobody wants to risk, they don't have a choice but to sit it out. If the snow stops overnight and our guests choose to risk it early doors so they can be at home on Christmas Day, that's their call, but personally I wouldn't go as things are right now. At least we can put it to people and give them that choice, I suppose.'

'Perhaps I can start going around to talk to everyone to see what people would like to do,' Libby said. 'I can get an idea of who'd like a bedroom and who'd be willing to manage down here. Personally, I think it's better that we do things a bit more democratically – make certain the more needy people like the pensioners and the kids get a bed to sleep in. I don't mind putting that to people as I go round. What do you reckon?'

'I'd be happy to give my room up,' Noah said. 'If someone needed it, I could sleep on a chair, no problem.'

'But you've paid for that room already,' Tomas said.

Noah shrugged. 'Any other time I might agree but, as we've all said, these are exceptional circumstances. I'd hardly sleep easy in my lovely paid-for bed knowing some poor granny was on a chair down here, so it wouldn't have been worth paying for anyway in the end.'

'That's so kind of you.' Willow still looked troubled, but she sounded more positive now that they were forming some kind of plan.

'It's one night,' Tomas said, folding her into a protective embrace. 'One night. Surely we can all manage that?'

'Not exactly the wedding night you're supposed to get, is it?' Libby said.

Willow pulled herself from Tomas's arms and smiled ruefully. 'I suppose it's something to tell the grandkids.'

'It's definitely that. If you want me to start asking around, I'll go and grab people now before they drift off to do other things.'

Noah looked at Tomas. 'I think that's a good idea… I could help. It's going to be a less stressful process if we start sorting it earlier rather than waiting until everyone is drunk at the end of the night, or, as Libby said, have wandered off.'

'If they already have rooms, people might just go off and spend the rest of the night in them if they have nothing to do down here,' Willow said.

Tomas looked at her. 'And sit up there in the dark?'

'But there won't be anything happening down here.'

'Just because there's no disco doesn't mean we can't make it a party,' Noah said. 'All you need is good company, good food and plenty to drink, and we have all that. There's no reason the celebrations have to stop.'

Libby nodded agreement. 'If we can't all chat for a couple of hours with a few drinks and nibbles then it's time to give civilisation up as a bad job.'

'Exactly,' Noah said warmly.

'So I suppose we ought to start doing something about all this,' Tomas said.

'Not you.' Libby looked at Tomas and Willow in turn. 'This is your wedding day; you shouldn't be rushing around worrying about stuff like this. You've got me.'

'And me,' Noah said. 'Your very own dynamic duo. Leave it with us.'

'We'll get some numbers and go and see the hotel manager with them,' Libby said. 'We can go from there.'

Noah looked towards the bar. 'I'll go and see if they have a writing pad and pen over there so we can make a proper list of who wants a room and who might be willing to do without.'

'Sounds like a good idea,' Libby said. She smiled at Willow. 'Don't worry – we'll get it all sorted, and I expect when the power is back on things will look brighter again.'

Noah grinned. 'Quite literally.'

Libby gave a light laugh and Willow's hand a reassuring squeeze. 'So you're alright? Stress levels gone down a bit now?'

'A bit,' Willow said, clearly doing her best to rally, if only to look grateful for the help.

'Go on,' Libby said. 'Back to your guests. We'll do the rounds and get everyone sorted.'

Willow's smile grew a little. 'Have I ever told you how much I love you? If I hadn't already married Tomas today I might have to marry you.'

'Apparently I'm unmarriable,' Libby said glibly, 'so you'd soon regret that decision.'

She looked round to ask if Noah was ready to start, only to find that, without a word to any of them, he'd already gone to the bar to ask for their paper and pen. She wanted to ask if Willow or Tomas thought it a strange turn, but perhaps she was reading too much into nothing much at all.

A minute later he returned with what they needed.

'Your friend says he can sleep in a chair.' Noah handed a sheet of paper and a pen to Libby.

'Who?' she asked, taking them.

'The guy you were talking to earlier… Rufus, I think his name is?'

Willow and Tomas shared an awkward glance. Perhaps they were feeling guilty about the fact Rufus was there at all, but Libby had moved past that already. He was here and he was stuck. Now all she wanted to do was concentrate on getting through the night with as little interaction with him as possible, and she hoped he'd play his part in achieving that aim now she'd made her feelings clear.

'Oh,' she said briskly, moving into the range of the nearest candle. 'I'll write that down then.'

'Shall we make two lists?' Noah asked amiably, obviously unaware of any discomfort he'd caused by chatting at the bar with Rufus.

'Willow…'

They turned to see Adrienne standing behind them.

'Sorry,' she said, giving them all an apologetic half-smile. 'Could I borrow you, sweetie?' she continued to her daughter. 'It's your gran… she's having a bit of a moment and I think she wants to talk to you about what's happening…'

'Oh, we're going round to talk to everyone shortly,' Libby said.

'I think my gran might take it in better coming from me,' Willow said. 'I'll let you know what she says but I would imagine if we can get her a room that would be best.'

Libby nodded and Willow turned to her mum. 'I'll come and talk to her.'

'I'll come with you,' Tomas said.

'Right.' Noah looked at Libby as the others left them. 'Back to that list… or rather, two lists…'

'People who need a room and people who are happy to camp down here?' Libby asked. 'Sounds like a good idea. We'll get all the room requests down and then we can see what we have to play with – whether there's too much demand, in which case the less needy will have to get bumped off the list, or if we have rooms to spare so we can offer some to those with a bit of spare cash who had been planning to sleep on chairs. But we'll need to organise how to do it – no point in us both asking the same people twice. Maybe split the rooms; you take half and I take half. Or we could go round together and you note the people who don't need a room and I note the people who do, or the other way round if you'd prefer… Although' – Libby tapped the pen on her chin thoughtfully – 'that would take twice as long and we'll be here all night… Maybe we should go with the first plan of splitting the canvassing…'

Noah grinned.

'What?' Libby frowned.

'I'll bet you're a scary manager.'

'Me?'

'Yes, you. The way you did that then; so ruthless and efficient. I wouldn't be ringing any sneaky sick days in, that's for sure.'

'It's not a very attractive trait, is it?' she said ruefully.

'Actually,' he said, already walking into the crowd gathered at the edges of the dance floor, chatting earnestly amongst themselves, 'it's kind of sexy.'

Libby hardly realised her mouth had fallen open for a moment. Talk about confusing signals! One minute interested, the next playing it cool, the next practically asking her to bed.

With a tiny shake of her head she put the thought to one side. There was work to do, and it was at times like these that she really got to prove her worth.

Chapter Eight

An hour later, Libby and Noah were sitting in the quiet of the orangery comparing their lists before going to see the hotel manager to organise rooms for everyone. Dots of candlelight were reflected in the dark windows like tiny suns and it was almost impossible to see the gardens beyond, save for the vague shapes of snow-covered features on the terrace. Noah's face was bathed in a warm glow that flattered him – not that he needed flattering. If Libby had thought him handsome in the daylight, now he seemed almost godlike. She tried to banish the thought and concentrate as she watched him twiddle his pen between his forefinger and thumb.

'Most people seem very happy to have whatever is spare,' she said.

Noah looked down his list. 'I found the same. Not afraid of roughing it round here, are you?'

Libby laughed. 'Us? Don't forget you used to be from around here… although I don't suppose anyone roughs it in Hollywood.'

He grinned. 'Perish the thought! We have to keep up appearances. If I'm honest, the prospect of roughing it right now seems quite fun.'

Libby raised disbelieving eyebrows.

'Seriously,' he said. 'All-night drinks, a comfy chair, the snow out of the window and good company – I'm not sure that even counts as roughing it really.'

'When you put it like that…' Libby glanced at the windows. 'I just wish I'd brought something more with me than this bloody dress.'

'Could you borrow from someone?'

'Not from Willow – she's about two sizes smaller than me. As for anyone else… I don't feel like I know anyone else well enough to ask and, to be fair, most will only have the clothes they're standing in like me so won't have anything to spare anyway.'

'You could borrow a T-shirt and shorts from me… I mean, they'd be huge, and it might be a bit weird, but if you could move past that…'

'That's nice of you, thanks, but I don't think so.'

'Not cool enough for you, eh?'

She laughed. 'No. It's just… well, I don't know… I'd just feel kind of… I wouldn't want to mess up your stuff. And how would I wash it and get it back to you?'

'It's only old stuff. You're not planning a food fight later, are you?'

'I might be for all you know. God knows this party needs something… poor Willow. She must be freaking out by now – still no power and the snow coming down. Remind me never to get married on Christmas Eve.'

His smile was oddly humourless. She'd expected more banter in reply to her quip, but he fell strangely quiet, turning his attention back to his list.

'Are you sure you want to give up your suite?' she asked into the silence. He looked up again.

'I don't need it as much as some.'

'But I think there might be enough rooms for those who said they wanted them, so you could keep it.'

'I think some of those people said they didn't need a room to try and be helpful. I bet they'd take one if it was offered.'

'Maybe…'

'What about the kids?' he asked.

'You mean the trio of torment?'

It was Noah's turn to raise an eyebrow.

'I know, they're not that bad,' she said, laughing. 'In fact, they're quite sweet; it's just… well, they're a bit of a handful at times and I don't really know how to communicate with anyone under the age of twenty.'

'That makes two of us,' he said. 'They're like an alien species, kids.'

'Yeah…'

'So, do they need a room? Have they asked for one? I'm guessing you spoke to their parents.'

'I did. They all said they could manage downstairs if they needed to.'

'I'm sure they'd be better in a room. Maybe we should ask if they want the suite?'

'All of them?' Libby asked doubtfully.

'Well, the girls at least.'

'I suppose it would be like a sleepover for them,' Libby said. 'I bet they'd love that. But I'm sure the hotel would want them to have adult supervision and there isn't enough room in the suite for all their parents.'

'Maybe one or two of them will volunteer to supervise?'

'It wouldn't be me, that's for sure. I'd take my chances with neck ache from the chairs. I could ask them what they think. If they're having your suite then we don't really need to worry about it right now anyway; it's already booked. We'll get all these others reserved first and then we'll put it to them.'

'Good plan. God, you're scarily efficient.'

'I want to believe that's a compliment but I'm not sure.' She shot him a sideways look.

'Believe me it is. Efficiency is one thing I sorely lack. If I'm not flying by the seat of my pants then I'm not conscious.'

'I'm sure life is more fun that way.'

'It gets you into more trouble.'

'Aren't they the same thing?'

'Could be.' He grinned.

'It's good of you to help at all,' she said. 'You didn't have to.'

'You didn't have to do any of this running around either.'

'Yes, I did. Willow's my best friend, and I suspect there might be some kind of unwritten wedding etiquette that it goes with the chief bridesmaid territory to help sort out problems.'

He held her in a thoughtful gaze for a moment. 'I think you'd have done it anyway.'

'I think you're right. I have to admit, I can't resist the chance to organise things.'

'Well, if I was voting for someone here who could handle a crisis I'd be casting it for you.'

'Thanks… I think. I guess we'd better get all this sorted then before my apparent reputation for efficiency and extreme boringness goes out of the window.'

'Ah – nobody said anything about boring.'

'No, but you said efficient, and I think that's kind of the same thing.'

'Like fun and trouble are the same thing?'

'Exactly!'

As it looked very much like they were going to be stuck at Lovage Hall for a long time, and as she couldn't put the conversation off any longer, Libby decided to phone her parents before she did anything else, to tell them she might not make it to their house for Christmas lunch. And with no knowing when the power might be back on, she also didn't know when she'd next be able to charge her phone, so there was that too – the last thing she wanted was to be stuck without a way to contact them in good time if it came to that.

Dread knotted her stomach as she looked for somewhere quiet to make the call, aware they weren't going to be happy and would have no problems making their feelings known. And then there was her poor grandma, who was relying on Libby to be there and who Libby wanted very much to spend the day with. With her grandma's illness, every extra day with her was a precious gift. However, ever-practical Libby couldn't ignore the fact that if she was stuck there wasn't a lot she could do about it; she could only hope she'd be able to get a cab early enough tomorrow so she'd arrive at her parents' in time for lunch.

In a quiet spot on an ornately upholstered chair in the marble-floored reception, she dialled the landline. Her mother picked up.

'Hey, Mum,' Libby said brightly. 'How are you?'

'Libby…? Aren't you at Willow's wedding?'

'Yes.'

'Oh, then why are you phoning?'

'Hmm, well, it's just… have you seen the snow?'

'Yes. Your dad has cleared the drive three times already tonight. I told him not to bother as we aren't going anywhere but you know what he's like.'

'Yes, I do. Anyway, if it's bad where you are then it's probably way worse out here, right?'

'It usually is.'

'So, we're kind of stuck.'

There was a pause. 'At Lovage Hall?'

'Yes.'

'For how long?'

'Well, it looks like it will be for tonight at least. Which means I'm probably not going to make it to yours on time. I mean, really, I probably wouldn't have made it anyway – the snow is quite bad everywhere, I expect. You just said it's bad there too, so...'

Libby chewed on her lip. She hated chewing her lip but, somehow, conversations with her mum always resulted in chewing on lips. It was, in fact, the only time it ever happened, which made it all the more telling. Libby loved her mum and her mum, she was fairly certain, loved her, but they didn't seem to like each other very much. At least, Libby often felt her mum didn't like her and she definitely knew she was a disappointment to her.

'So you're not coming for lunch?' her mum said after a long pause in which Libby considered cutting the call and blaming a poor signal.

'I expect not. I mean, how can I?'

'What time could you get here?'

'There's no point in waiting around for me to start everything because that would make things later for you and Dad. You don't want to be eating at midnight, do you?'

'You're going to be stuck for that long?'

'Well, I don't know – that's what I'm trying to tell you. It could be late, that's all, and I don't want you to wait around for me. Might as well cook lunch and assume that I'm not going to make it. If I do then I'll just eat what's left – you and Dad always cook mountains anyway so there's bound to be enough for another lunch.'

'So you're not coming at all?' her mother said sharply, and Libby could just picture her lips pursed in a tight little O, an expression that was a depressingly familiar one.

'I might not be able to,' Libby said, and then wanted to slap herself for not having the backbone to just come out with it. 'I mean, I really want to, but it's not looking good.'

'Well, that's just perfect. Ruin our Christmas, why don't you? Your grandma is already here; she struggled over especially this morning and she's really not well as you know, what with her Parkinson's getting worse.'

'I know, Mum. But she would have come to see you anyway.'

'That's hardly the point. She's come to see all of us. Christmas is a family time – it's always been that way. Think how disappointed she'll be if you're not here; the family won't be complete, will it?'

'I have thought about that, but I can't help it,' Libby said, feeling guiltier than ever. She recalled only too well how her grandma had supported her with kind words and tea and warm hugs when she'd lost her baby and later when Rufus had left her. Her grandma was the most important person in Libby's life right now – of course she didn't want to disappoint her. 'I know, Mum. Really, I will come if I can but I'm warning you I'm quite stuck and it doesn't look good for tomorrow. Honestly, nobody's getting out. Even…'

She was about to mention Rufus's attempts to leave being thwarted, but bringing him up now would open a whole new conversation that she just didn't want to have. 'I mean the lanes are really bad up here.'

'And your dad's bought a goose.'

'A goose? Who even eats goose these days?'

'That's what I said. But he wanted to make it posh, something about cheering you up because… well, all that nonsense happening earlier this year.'

You mean me losing a baby, getting jilted and cheated on with my own cousin? Libby thought. *You mean* that *nonsense?*

'That's sweet of him,' she said. 'I honestly do feel just terrible that I won't be able to make it. Will a portion freeze, maybe? I could come over and eat it another time? As for Grandma, I'll give her a call and explain.'

'It won't be at Christmas, will it? You can't randomly eat goose at any old time.'

'I'm pretty sure you can.'

'Oh, so you're a goose expert now? And in answer to the rest of your excuse, you can explain to your grandma now because she's here… and don't think I'm going to soften the blow beforehand.'

Libby was suddenly aware of a sharp pain and realised she'd chewed her lip just a little too hard. She tried to straighten her face and took a deep breath. Was it bad that secretly she was now glad she wasn't going to be able to make it for Christmas goose? This phone call – torture. But the prospect of a Christmas Day that didn't involve her mother? Bliss, though she'd never be able to admit it out loud. But then there was a pang of guilt, because this particular, unusual Christmas might mean a break from her mum, but it would also mean missing time with her grandma, which Libby never wanted to do. Mum was right, Grandma would be disappointed. Perhaps she ought to try harder to make it home after all.

'Well, that's that,' her mother said into the silence. 'I expect we'll see you next year.'

'Oh, Mum, don't be like that. You know I'd be there if I could.'

There was a muffled voice, and what sounded like a mild debate, and then Libby's grandma was on the phone.

'Hello, Libby. What are you falling out with your mum over now? Honestly, you're always managing to be at loggerheads over something or other.'

'Oh, hey...' Libby said, that guilt squirming again. 'How are you feeling, Grandma?'

'I'm not too bad right now. What's happening at your wedding?'

'We're kind of snowed in. I'm not sure I can make it for Christmas Day. I'm sorry, Grandma. I mean, as soon as the roads start clearing I'll see if I can manage—'

'Don't you worry about it,' her grandma said firmly. 'I know you'd be here if you could. It's just a day, like any other, except we happened to put a label on it. We can have our lunch any old day and I'd like it just as much.'

'But, Grandma, it's—'

'Don't think on it for another minute,' she replied, and Libby could imagine her brown eyes disappearing into her face as she smiled broadly. 'You have a lovely time there and I'll see you after Christmas.'

'If you're sure,' Libby said.

'Of course I'm sure! Oh, hang on... your mother wants the phone.'

'OK, love you, Grandma.'

'I might have known your grandma would let you get away with it,' Libby's mum said before her grandma had managed to reply. 'Thick as thieves, you two; she always did let you get away with murder.'

'I'm not sure what I'm supposed to be getting away with, Mum, but it's definitely not murder. I've told you I'd be there if I could. Do you think I'd be doing this on purpose? Have you even looked out of the window?'

'Of course I have. People are out and about as far as I can see.'

'In the town, maybe. But we're out in the countryside, aren't we? The road conditions are always worse out here.'

'Hmm. Seems to me you could be trying a bit harder. You're telling me nobody can get in or out of that place?'

'That's exactly what I'm telling you. Nobody can leave.'

'That's ridiculous. In this day and age, people can't get about in a bit of snow?'

It was on the tip of her tongue to fire a reply back that if her mum thought it was so easy, she ought to come and pick Libby up. She quickly swallowed the jibe, because knowing her mum she'd find a way to do just that, and Libby would never hear the end of it. Not only that, but she'd be forced to eat goose with them and, right now, nothing was less appealing.

'Well, your father will be devastated.'

Which meant her mum was furious, but she was going to pin everything on Libby's unsuspecting dad. She'd tried Libby's grandma and that hadn't worked so she needed a new angle. Because that was what she did – transferred her own ire so it looked as if it was coming from someone else. That way, she came across like the reasonable one. Libby used to be fooled by the act, but those days were long gone.

'I'm sure he'll get over it,' she said evenly. 'I'll explain to him – want to put him on?'

'Oh, he's putting the shovel away.'

Sure he is, Libby thought. More like if he came to the phone he'd tell Libby he was completely fine with her missing Christmas dinner, just like her grandma had, and then her mum would look like the villain of the piece after all.

'I'm sorry, Mum…'

'Not nearly as sorry as we are.'

'It's really unavoidable.'

'I'm sure it is,' her mother said stiffly. 'So when will we see you? Boxing Day?'

'I'm working.'

'All evening too?'

'Oh, well… you know I'm usually tired by the time I close up. Maybe – I'll try.'

'Don't bother if it's that much trouble. Wouldn't want to wear you out with our company.'

'Right.'

'Libby…'

'Yes?'

'You know your father and I… we just want to know you're alright. We invited you over because you had a difficult year and we didn't want you to spend Christmas Day alone, but if our concern isn't welcome—'

'Of course it is! Mum, don't think that, please! And I'm not alone so you don't need to worry about me. There's a hotel full of guests all stuck with me, including my best friend and her new husband, so I'm going to be completely fine.'

'So we'll see you afterwards?'

'Yes, absolutely.'

'Your dad will freeze some goose for you.'

'Sounds perfect.'

'Right then. Well, I'd better say a merry Christmas now, hadn't I?'

'I can phone you in the morning.'

'I expect your dad will answer – I'll be peeling the sprouts so I'll be busy.'

'Oh, OK, well, it'll be nice to speak to him anyway.'

'As long as he's not gibleting the goose.'

Libby wrinkled her nose. 'OK. Bye then.'

'Goodbye,' her mum replied in a weirdly formal tone that suggested she'd just suffered a flashback from her days as a telecom operator.

Libby ended the call, let her head fall back onto her seat and let out a long sigh. On the scale of trying events, a telephone call to her mum usually registered a five or six. That one was definitely a nine.

An hour or so later, the great hall was much quieter. People had drifted off to sit in little cliques, some at tables by candlelight, some on sofas in the orangery watching the snow through the window, some gathered at the bar. Everywhere was the low hum of conversation, the occasional snatch of laughter and even the odd slurred/sung bar of a Christmas song. But it was all underwritten by a vague anxiety. There were worried conversations that the power wouldn't come back on at all that night, that they'd be stuck the whole of Christmas.

The braver souls found it funny.

'There goes dinner with the in-laws.'

'Oh no, I won't be able to spend all day cooking – such a shame…'

But others were getting stressed and the atmosphere of general anxiety was spreading a little too fast for Libby's liking. Everyone was trying so hard to shield Willow from it, and Libby wished she could go round and tell people to shut up because it was ruining her friend's big day. But she couldn't, of course. When she ran into someone with negative opinions, all she could do was try to reassure them, and tactfully suggest – without saying it explicitly and possibly causing offence – that they might want to try to sound a bit more cheery because their fear was causing fear to others who would otherwise have been perfectly content to wait patiently for things to return to normal.

Libby and Noah had kept their promise to Willow and organised sleeping quarters for everyone who needed them, and everyone else was prepared to fend for themselves as best they could. Libby had already eyed up a spot on a squishy-looking sofa in the orangery, her now favourite room at Lovage Hall. She didn't know where Noah was planning to bed down for the night and it seemed a little forward to ask him, because it implied that she was interested out of more than concern for her fellow guest. Not that there would be any privacy to be had for any inappropriate behaviour, even if she might have secretly hoped for it.

Adrienne, Willow's mum, had a spare set of pyjamas and she'd offered to lend them to Libby. Ordinarily it might have felt very strange and unsettling to be sitting around in them in such a public place but, faced with the alternative of trying to sleep in her bridesmaid dress, Libby had accepted the offer gratefully. The pyjamas were now folded neatly on a chair at her side as she shared a drink with Noah. She'd lost count of what round of drinks they were on now as they counted down the hours until the bar closed, and being distinctly tipsy also helped with the whole feeling-embarrassed-about-having-to-wear-her-pyjamas-in-a-roomful-of-strangers thing too.

Noah had just returned with two new bottles of wine and a bottle of lemonade so Libby could make her own spritzers after the bar had closed for the night.

'You think of everything,' she said as he sat down.

'Well, as we're in for a long night... No ice, I'm afraid, and the bottles aren't that cold as the fridges behind the bar are warming up a bit now with not being switched on.'

'We could always open the doors and stick the bottles in the snow for a bit.'

'Open those doors right now and we might just let in an avalanche.'

Libby giggled. 'You might have a point there.'

Willow came over to their table. She looked tired but happier than she had when the power had first gone off.

'Are you going to be alright?' she asked Libby, who nodded. 'You're sure? Everything you need?'

'Stop fretting – I'm fine. It's a few hours in a chair until the morning – how bad can it be? A pretty comfy chair too. Are the trio of torment sorted out?'

'Yes…' Willow smiled at Noah. 'They're thrilled to have your suite and their parents are so grateful.'

'I know,' he said. 'They keep trying to give me money for it but it's really not necessary.'

'A lot of people would take it,' Willow said.

He shrugged. 'This is a one-off situation, isn't it? Perhaps another time I'd have taken some money but it doesn't seem right today. I'm sure it's an expense they can do without and it's Christmas… I'd feel terrible taking anything from them and it wouldn't be very charitable of me, would it?'

Willow's tired smile spread. 'Well, it's very sweet of you. Tom and I are grateful…' She glanced at Libby. 'To both of you for sorting everything for us.'

'People are starting to go up to their rooms now?' Libby asked. 'It sounds quieter in the hall.'

'Not much else for them to do, is there?' Willow said, her smile fading until she just looked tired again. Libby could understand why – it had been a long day for all of them but especially for Tomas and Willow.

'You're not still fretting about everyone having a terrible time, are you?' Libby asked.

Willow shook her head. 'Actually, a few people have come over to say how nice it's been, just to chat and catch up with old friends… chilled, you know? So I suppose that's one positive from all this.'

'I think so too,' Noah said.

Willow was about to say something else when Rufus wandered into the orangery. He took one look at Willow, Libby and Noah and then left again.

'Probably looking for somewhere to sleep,' Libby said awkwardly. What she didn't add was that she wondered if he might have intended to come and talk to her – or at least try to. She would have given him the same reply as she had earlier that day: she was tired of going over old ground and she didn't want to do it again, not ever and especially not today.

'There are plenty of sofas to spare in here,' Noah said. 'He could have used one of them – nobody would have minded.'

Libby exchanged a look with Willow and then turned back to Noah with a vague shrug.

'Perhaps he wanted somewhere more private,' Willow offered.

'Good luck to him finding that,' Noah said wryly.

'Tomas and I are going to turn in,' Willow said. 'I just came to let you know and to make sure you were going to be alright.'

'That's OK,' Libby said. 'Any more news on the power situation?'

'No. I think everyone is resigned to it being off until tomorrow and I suppose once they're asleep they won't care so much.'

'This will definitely go down as one of the more interesting Christmases I've had,' Noah said.

'If we're still stuck everyone will be saying that tomorrow,' Libby agreed. 'We certainly won't forget it in a hurry.'

'No,' Willow said, 'we won't.' She leant to kiss Libby on the cheek. 'Goodnight. And thanks again for everything.'

'Goodnight,' Libby said with a smile. 'And there's no need.'

With a long sigh, Willow turned to leave. Noah and Libby were silent until she'd gone.

'Poor Willow,' Libby said quietly as she went out of the door.

'Not the wedding she'd hoped for, I suppose.'

'You could say that. Is it the wedding anyone would hope for?'

'I suppose not. She'll probably look back and laugh about it all in a few weeks...' Noah reached for one of the wine bottles. 'You're not planning to go to sleep yet?'

'No.' Libby held out an empty glass. 'What would be the point? It's hardly restful with so many guests still wandering around. I'll try in a while when others have started to settle.'

He nodded as he filled her glass, leaving enough room for her lemonade top-up.

She smiled. 'Thanks.'

As he put down the bottle, his eye caught a delicately patterned ceramic clock on the wall, and then he looked at Libby with a grin.

'It's just gone midnight. Christmas Day arrived and we never even noticed.'

'So it did,' Libby said, pouring her lemonade. She held out her glass. 'Merry Christmas then.'

He touched his glass to hers. 'Merry Christmas. Here's to the most surprising Christmas Day ever!'

Chapter Nine

Somehow, though they hadn't discussed it, Noah had ended up settling down to sleep on a neighbouring chair. Libby had slipped Adrienne's pyjamas on in the ladies' toilets, returning with a blanket wrapped around her shoulders so that she felt a little less conspicuous. When she got back, Noah had already made himself comfortable; his only concession to getting ready for sleep was kicking off his shoes, removing his tie and loosening his top shirt buttons. He had stuff in his room, but when Libby had pointed that out he'd laughed and told her he was too drunk to go and get any of it. They were both pretty sozzled by now, Libby had to acknowledge, probably drunk enough to sleep on a bed of nails if they had to.

At least, Noah would. It was gone 3 a.m. and despite being well-oiled, warm and cosy, with the weirdly reassuring presence of Noah close by, Libby still hadn't managed to fall asleep. It was a strange situation, she supposed, and the oddly pervasive sense of feeling marooned wasn't exactly helping. Nor was knowing that Rufus was in a chair somewhere nearby, maybe even awake like her, unable to nod off. It was at times like these unwelcome thoughts of what she'd had and then lost at his hand came to plague her.

They would have been married now if things had been different. It was on Rufus that they weren't and that it would never happen now, but sometimes it felt like her fault too. If she'd been more careful, if she'd taken it easy at work, if she hadn't fallen on the stairs on the way down from the stockroom that day, then maybe she wouldn't have lost their baby. And then maybe that wouldn't have started the beginning of the end, the distance between them, the inability to communicate, their failure to recognise the form of each other's grief and that it was different from their own, and that the other needed different things than they did. And maybe, much as she liked to make Rufus the villain, he wouldn't have felt the need to seek solace with another woman and maybe he wouldn't have ended up falling for her.

Were those things enough on their own to cause their eventual end? Had there always been warning signs? Would Rufus have strayed eventually anyway? Libby had asked herself these questions and others like them a million times and she'd probably ask them a million more.

Her mother had said that if a man was the type to think about it then he would have done it regardless of whether they did or didn't have problems, and that it was better for Libby to discover what sort of man he was sooner rather than later. She'd told her she'd had a lucky escape and that while losing her baby was tragic, perhaps it had never been her fate to end up as a single parent.

It was insensitive views like that which made it difficult for Libby to spend time with her parents, and, though she loved them dearly, why part of her was secretly glad she was unlikely to make it to their house for Christmas lunch this year. They'd have gone over old, painful ground, and they'd have said the wrong things, their advice completely off and failing dismally to read the room. Far from a happy Christmas, the day would have been like torture wrapped up in kindness and Libby would have left in the evening feeling wretched.

One of the other questions she often asked herself was whether she still felt anything for Rufus. Maybe, in a strange and unrecognisable way, she still loved him. Sometimes she thought yes and sometimes no, but she was always consistent in her one main regret – she was sorry things had come to this. Once she'd thought he would be her future; now he was a shadow from her past to be avoided at all costs.

A sudden urge to see if he was OK seized her. The rooms where people had made themselves comfortable for the night were still well lit with rows of candles and lanterns. Wrapping her blanket around her, Libby got up and padded out of the orangery. She walked through the great hall but didn't see Rufus in there, though she smiled and greeted a few guests who were still awake. She didn't even know why she wanted to see Rufus, or what she'd say to him if she did find him still up. She only knew that something, perhaps a remnant of the love she'd once felt for him, was driving her.

Her search took her through the huge entrance hall and into a formal drawing room. A few of Tomas's single friends were on sofas in here and, on an armchair, his head to one side as he slept, was Rufus. Libby stopped and stared. What now? Did she wake him? Did she take this opportunity, while everyone else was asleep, to have the talk he'd pushed so hard for? Would that be closure, or would it open painful wounds again, wounds that didn't need to be opened? She could, and perhaps it would be sensible to address their issues head on. It might clear the air between them so that they could get through the rest of this wedding reception on more comfortable terms.

But, in the end, Libby couldn't do it. She was afraid of what he might say, and what she might say, and what that might start. At least now, they both knew where they stood, even if there was animosity. She couldn't be tempted to give him that second chance and she was afraid she might be if she let him speak. Instead, she watched him sleep for a moment, feeling slightly like a stalky ghost in her blanket, hovering over him. The sight of him made every fibre of her miserable; a sad end to what was supposed to have been her happy ever after.

Someone on another sofa stirred, and Libby took that as her cue to leave. As quickly and quietly as she could, she made her way back to her own sofa in the orangery and settled down.

She hadn't even realised she was crying until she noticed her pyjama top was wet. As she hastily dried her eyes, she felt someone's gaze on her and looked to see that Noah was awake.

She forced a smile. 'I thought you'd gone to the land of nod.'

'I had… something woke me.'

'You must have heard Santa's bells.'

'That must have been it,' he said with a sleepy grin. 'Hope he's left me something good.'

'If he hasn't then there's always the leftover wine.'

He stretched before wriggling to get comfortable again. 'God no! I'm done for tonight – and it's not often I admit defeat so we must really have gone some.'

'It's a shame to waste it.'

'You have it.'

'I can't drink any more either – I'm a bit past it now.'

'Definitely. Me too.'

They were silent for a moment. Some of the candles had burnt down and were almost finished, sending dark smoke into the air. Libby could smell that peculiar odour of spent wax. There were still plenty in flame around the room though, throwing a warm glow over Noah's dishevelled hair and sleepy features. He'd looked good earlier that day, but in this light, all relaxed and casual and with a good measure of wine inside her, it took some willpower for Libby not to reach over and kiss him. But was this just a reaction to her sadness over Rufus? Was this a rebound attraction? Noah gave her a languid sideways glance and her heart lost a beat. If this was a rebound, she was going to have a fight on her hands resisting it.

'Do you think we'll get home tomorrow?' she asked, more to take her mind off his lips than because she didn't know what the answer to her question would be.

'I hope so at some point. My mum will never forgive me for missing Christmas dinner, especially when I'm usually not even in the country for family get-togethers.'

'Same. I mean, obviously I'm in the country but family get-togethers haven't been all that high on my list of priorities anyway. If you met some of my family you'd try to get out of them too.'

'Will there be a lot of them waiting to greet you for Christmas lunch?'

'No, it'll just be Mum, Dad, Grandma and me. I can probably just about handle them. I did phone my mum to warn her I probably wouldn't make it and, to be honest, she was so pissed off that even if I did, I hardly think I'm on her list of favourite people right now. She'd probably burn my dinner on purpose to teach a lesson.'

'Well, not sure if it makes you feel better or worse but you might not have to. If the snow keeps coming down like this we'll definitely be stuck.'

'If the snow keeps coming down like this I feel like we might be stuck here forever, not just Christmas!'

'In my present company I'm not sure that's such a bad thing,' he said.

At that moment she was thankful for the candlelight. At least nobody could see her blush. 'You'd soon get bored of me.'

'I'm not bored yet.'

'That's because we've been drinking all day. Trust me, without the beer goggles you'd see things differently.'

'So, are the beer goggles the only reason you've spent so much time with me today?'

'No, I'm just desperate for attention.'

His grin spread. 'I knew it. There was no way a gorgeous woman like you would be here with me for any other reason.'

Libby blushed again, annoyed at herself that she couldn't help it.

'Shut up!' she said, trying to sound stern. 'And go to sleep!'

'*You're* not asleep.'

'That's because I'm talking to you. You go to sleep and then I'll be able to go to sleep.'

'I can't now I've woken – I've got my second wind.'

'Well…' Libby shrugged. 'Santa won't leave you a present, will he?'

'He wouldn't anyway – I've been on his naughty list for years and it's gone too far for him to take me off it now.'

'Me too,' she said. 'But you never know – we've been pretty good today.'

'True,' he said. 'Is one day enough? It feels like a bit of an afterthought.'

'If Santa doesn't leave you a gift then I'll give you one myself for helping me today. I don't know what I would have done without you but it would have taken me twice as long to get all those rooms sorted for a start.'

'You already have.'

'Have what?'

'Given me a gift. Your company today.'

Libby bit back a grin. 'You had plenty of company today – you didn't need mine.'

'True again, but I liked yours.'

'You didn't like anyone else's? I'd keep that to myself.'

'Alright, I did enjoy a few other conversations, but none of those people were as good to look at as you.'

'Now I definitely know you have your beer goggles on.'

'Wine goggles,' he said with a lazy smile. 'And I admit I might be the worse for wear now, but I thought you were gorgeous before I'd started drinking; I just wasn't drunk enough to pluck up the courage to tell you so.'

There was a cough from the darkness beyond the glow of the candles, and then a grunt that seemed to suggest someone stirring. But all stayed silent, save for Noah and Libby's low conversation. It would almost have been a blessing if someone had woken up because it would have saved her the need to find a reply. What was she supposed to say to that? Was it a come-on? He'd been so hot and cold all day she didn't know what to think.

'I…' she began, but the grunter let out a huge snort which then led into the low rumble of steady snoring.

'Well, neither of us will be going to sleep now,' she said.

Noah got up, padded across the room and prodded the offender, who mumbled a complaint, changed position and then drifted back to thankfully silent sleep.

'Impressively done,' Libby said as Noah returned to his chair. 'Where were you on all those childhood caravan holidays when my dad kept me awake night after night doing his impression of a tractor?'

'It's good to know someone appreciates my talents.'

Libby smiled, though she was troubled by the vague thought that it was an odd thing to say. Surely someone as successful as him was appreciated for his talents all the time. It was a glib saying, of course, but there was something else hidden in his words – she felt certain of it. She thought for a moment about asking him if it meant more than it seemed to, but by the time she'd made her mind up about it he'd already closed his eyes again. She watched him for a moment: perplexed, insane with curiosity and still itching to kiss him before closing her own eyes and snuggling under her covers.

A high-pitched squeal woke Libby. For a moment she was confused, until her faculties returned and she remembered that there was a perfectly reasonable explanation for her being on a sofa in the orangery of a stately home wearing someone else's pyjamas. She was also cold, which was the second thing that occurred to her. That was quickly followed by the third – the almighty headache.

'I hope someone has an aspirin.'

She looked to see Noah was awake too and he'd taken the words right from her mouth.

'I hope they've got a good supply,' she replied with a yawn. 'Otherwise I might have to fight you for them.'

'I wouldn't dare fight you; you'd win for sure.' He stretched and rubbed a hand through his hair as he turned his gaze to the window. Beyond it was white sky and whiter land. The candles had all burnt down during the night, leaving the room washed in the cool greyness of a cloudy winter's morning. 'Still coming down but it looks lighter – don't you think?'

'It's hard to tell but I think so. I wonder if the power's back on?'

'I wonder what the squealing was that woke me.'

They got their answer when there was another one. At least it sounded very much like exuberance and not distress, an assumption that was proved right when Scarlet raced into the orangery sending out another one and grinning all over her face.

'It's Christmas Day! It's Christmas Day!'

'I know.' Libby smiled. 'Happy Christmas.'

'We're opening presents just as soon as we get home!' Scarlet continued breathlessly. 'Mum says Santa had to leave them at our house but she knows he's been because she texted him to check. I can't wait! I think I'll explode!'

'I hope not,' Noah said. 'I don't fancy cleaning up the mess if you do.'

Scarlet giggled. Her hair was loose and she had her bridesmaid dress on again, though some of the buttons were undone at the back and it was definitely looking worse for wear today. The look was completed by her bare feet – she had the vague air of a Dickensian urchin who'd once been quite rich but had fallen on hard times and had only her fine but now ragged dress left to remind her.

'I want to go outside!' she said.

Libby shook her head. 'You'll freeze to death in that dress.'

Scarlet pouted. 'That's what Mum said.'

'You could wear my jacket,' Noah said.

'I think you might need to find some shoes too,' Libby added, giving Scarlet's feet a meaningful nod.

Scarlet chose to ignore the shoe bit; she simply beamed at Noah. 'Really?'

'Why not? I'm not using it right now so you might as well.'

Scarlet bounced up and down and then turned to race out of the room. 'I'm going to ask my mum!' she yelled as she went.

Libby turned to Noah. 'You know her mum will say no?'

'Well, I offered – I can't do more than that.'

'And if she says yes, the other two-thirds of the trio of torment will get wind and they'll want to go out in the snow as well. How many jackets do you have with you?'

He grinned. 'I'm sure I could figure something out for the other two.'

'You're just a big softy, aren't you, Mr Hollywood-Big-Shot?'

'Yeah, but don't tell anyone,' he said, stretching. 'God, I feel stiff as a board. I wonder if they've got coffee on anywhere.'

'You'd think so. I could go for some breakfast too... and those aspirins while I'm at it.'

'You're quite demanding, aren't you?'

'It's been said before.' Libby stretched lazily, mirroring him. 'I'm going to get dressed and then see if there's food anywhere.'

'Why bother? Wouldn't you be more comfortable as you are for breakfast?'

'I'd feel weird, walking round in pyjamas in public.'

'No one will care. I would if I had mine on.'

'You can put these on if you like – I'm sure Adrienne won't mind.'

He grinned. 'They're not really my colour.'

'Oh, I don't know... I think more men should embrace rose pink.'

'I've got no issue with rose pink on a Hawaiian shirt, but that's about it.'

'Oh, so you wear a lot of Hawaiian shirts then?'

'I've been known to sport one... I bet you don't sell those in your fancy suit shop, do you? I bet you'd be horrified if someone walked in wearing one.'

Libby laughed. 'We're not that snobby! There's a time and a place for Hawaiian shirts and it's probably California, so if you wear them at home then good for you. Although…'

'What?'

'I didn't really have you down as the palm print type.'

He waggled his eyebrows, making her burst into laughter. 'You'd be surprised.'

As the laughter died down she wrapped her blanket around her shoulders. She was stiff too, as well as cold, and it took a moment to get everything moving. 'I'm going to get dressed. I won't be long; you go and hunt for sustenance and I'll come and find you when I'm done.'

Libby could smell coffee coming from somewhere as she walked down a lavish hallway papered in a William Morris print. It smelt good – rich and bitter and just the thing to warm her up and banish her hangover – but it would have to wait. First was a trip to the ladies' to get washed and changed.

'Good morning…'

She spun around to see Rufus following her down the corridor. His suit was crumpled but he looked bright enough – refreshed even. He certainly appeared a lot more put together than she did right now, but then, he'd always woken looking good.

'Oh… hi.'

His greeting had caught her off guard. There was nothing in it but civility, but still…

'You slept OK?' he asked.

'Yes,' she lied, though she didn't really know why she was bothering – the evidence of her terrible sleep was right in front of his face. 'You?'

'I've had better nights. It's been a weird one, hasn't it?'

'I suppose it has.'

'Will you try to get home before lunchtime?'

'Will you?'

'Depends on what the traffic reports say. I might wander out and take a look at the car – see if I can get it to move...'

'Hmm, that's probably a good idea.'

He sank his hands deep into his pockets and took a long breath, and Libby recognised only too well that he was about to launch into something a lot more serious than whether he'd be able to move his car before lunch or not.

'Listen, Lib... I—'

'Don't do this, Rufus,' she cut in. 'Not now.'

'Then when? We're going to have to talk sooner or later.'

'Why?'

'Because we're both stuck here and we can't spend the time until we can leave ignoring each other.'

'Yes we can. Watch me ignore you – I can do it admirably.'

His smile was so sad she almost reached for him. Instead, he reached for her. 'Libby... please...'

She batted his hand away. 'I said don't and I meant it. I'll be civil in passing but I have nothing to say that hasn't already been said, so what's the point in dragging it all up again?'

'All that was said isn't all that needs saying.'

'Well maybe I don't think any of what's left needs saying. It's old news, Rufus – history, dead and gone. Why can't you just leave it? You were happy enough to let it lie when Kylie was in your bed... I suppose that's it, isn't it? Nice to know I meant so much to you that you didn't bother trying to say all these important things to me until she'd gone.'

'You wouldn't have listened anyway.'

'So what makes you think I want to listen now?'

'Did you spend the night with that guy?'

Libby stared at him. 'In a way we all did,' she said coldly, 'inasmuch as I was sleeping in a chair in close proximity to his, yes, but even if I was in his room it would be nothing to do with you anyway.'

'He had a suite.'

'Yes, he did.'

'I thought…'

'That he'd be ruled by his libido like you are? If you'd bothered to look you'd have seen us both sleeping in the orangery. He gave his suite to the little girls to sleep in because he's an actual nice guy – something I'm starting to discover is a real rarity in the world.'

'Oh, right… I thought…'

'I know you did – that's your problem, you always think the wrong thing. Maybe you shouldn't be so quick to judge others by your standards, eh?'

'I just wanted—'

'I've got to get changed, so if you'll excuse me…'

Before he could say anything else she hurried down the corridor towards the toilets. But she was shaking. How dare Rufus comment on her life? How dare he care now, after everything he'd done? Perhaps he should have cared more when he was carrying on with Kylie behind her back, and then maybe they wouldn't be in this mess. How dare he tell her who to talk to or who was good for her? Whatever place his concern was coming from he had no right to air it and, even if he did, he was wrong. What gave him the right to make snap judgements about people he barely knew?

And why did she still care what he thought of her? Because now, as she recalled their brief exchange and his comments about Noah, she realised she did.

When she got to the loos India and Olivia were in there with their mums.

'Oh, morning…' Libby said stiffly, doing her best to shake off the thunderous mood her run-in with Rufus had left her in. 'Merry Christmas.'

'Are you alright?' Olivia's mum asked, peering at her.

'Me…?' Libby smoothed her features. 'Oh, yes, of course… hangover, that's all. Nothing some coffee won't sort out. How's your morning been so far? You all slept OK?'

'We won't be able to open our presents for ages!' India put in.

'You might have to wait but it can't be helped,' her mum said. 'We talked about this already and I thought you'd got it.'

'I know…' India let out a huge sigh. 'We're stuck; it's not safe to leave…'

Olivia patted her on the shoulder. 'Scarlet's mum texted Santa and he's left their presents at her house for when she gets home. I expect he's done that with yours too. Scarlet says the hotel might give us presents too!'

Libby couldn't imagine what the hotel could possibly give as presents other than the free toiletries in the rooms, but the idea seemed to cheer both girls, so she simply smiled. 'They might; that would be nice, wouldn't it? It'd be extra stuff you weren't expecting so it would be a nice Christmas surprise.'

'Exactly,' India's mum said. 'The whole of today is an extra Christmas surprise. We can think of it as a Christmas Day party here and then we can do our own Christmas as well when we get home. Two Christmases!'

'Has anyone said they might try to get home this morning?' Libby asked.

Olivia's mum tied her daughter's hair with a band. She glanced up at Libby as she straightened it out. 'Mike – my husband – said he was going to take a walk out to check the lanes after breakfast but I'm not all that hopeful they'll be any clearer than last night. If by some miracle they are or the snow stops for long enough we might try to make a run for it but, actually, I'm quite enjoying being here. I know we've got no electricity, but we also don't have the pressure of racing around all day trying to make everything perfect. Personally, I always find this time of year exhausting – but here we're forced to stop and enjoy the moment with no opportunity or obligation to do anything.'

'Yep,' India's mum agreed, 'there is that. We couldn't really do anything here today even if we wanted to apart from have drinks and sit around and I'm all for that for a change.' She looked at Libby. 'How about you? Thinking of trying to get home?'

'I'm a bit more stuck because I don't have my own transport. I might if someone else is driving out and I can get a lift with them but I wouldn't dream of asking a taxi or anyone else to try and get through to pick me up – it's far too risky.'

'We could let you know if we decide to make a bid for freedom and you could come with us,' Olivia's mum offered.

'That's really kind of you,' Libby said. 'If I could that would be great.'

But even as she said it, she wondered what the hurry was. Perhaps it wouldn't be so bad to stick around at Lovage Hall for a while. She'd squared it with her grandma and at least here she wouldn't be on the receiving end of her mother's constant withering looks. Her mum would criticise everything Libby did in the kitchen and redo it when she wasn't looking, they'd eat and make small talk (or worse, start dissecting every mistake she felt Libby had made in her entire adult life), pretend to be jolly and then her mum and dad and even grandma would fall asleep in front of the Christmas Day film – usually something Libby had seen before.

Here... she could make a day of it with new people, people she found interesting (if only the less interesting ones would stay out of her way). Noah might stay for a while – he'd said he had nowhere to dash off to apart from to his parents, who completely understood that he was stuck. He didn't exactly seem in a hurry to get off either. Willow and Tomas had always intended to spend their Christmas here as part of their wedding celebrations and Gene and Adrienne were staying too.

'Have you got anything else to wear but your bridesmaid dress?' India's mum asked Libby, who shook her head.

'They do say you should be careful what you wish for,' she said ruefully. 'When I was a little kid, I'd have dreamt of spending my every waking hour in a huge silk dress – now, on day two, I'm sick of the sight of it.'

'Maybe you could borrow from someone? I don't have any spare either and quite frankly I'm not that happy about how grotty I feel in yesterday's clothes, despite being glad of the break from routine, but at least my clothes are a little more functional than yours. It must be a nightmare walking around in that all day and you must be cold.'

'Actually, I'm not particularly cold as long as I stay inside, but it is a pain. I can't think who might have something suitable to lend me to be honest. I guess I'll manage for now. I do wish I'd brought a toothbrush though – my mouth tastes pretty disgusting right now.'

'Oh! I have these!'

Olivia's mum rifled in her handbag for a moment before pulling out a small plastic tube. She popped out a tablet and handed it to Libby.

'Tooth-cleaning tablets!' Libby smiled. 'That's lucky!'

'I've always got those in my bag – you never know when you're going to want to kill some garlic. It's lucky at times like these that I'm so paranoid about bad breath!'

'Lucky for me,' Libby agreed. 'I don't suppose you also have aspirins, a slice of toast and some clean knickers in there too?'

Olivia's mum grinned. 'Afraid not.'

'I have aspirin,' India's mum said.

'You do? Brilliant!' Libby smiled at both women. 'You two are lifesavers!'

'Always equipped,' India's mum said.

Olivia's mum nodded. 'It's a mum thing. One day you'll be the same.'

Libby's smile faded. People said things like that all the time, never thinking anything of it, never intending to cause pain. Of course they couldn't know what she'd been through that year and it wasn't something she felt like sharing widely. She pushed the smile back across her face as she accepted a blister pack and popped out a couple of aspirins.

'Thank you,' she said. 'This will definitely help me feel a bit better about all the other stuff.'

'I think there's coffee on in the great hall at least,' India's mum said.

'I wasn't sure there'd be anything at all with the power being off,' Libby replied. 'I thought we might be drinking warm lemonade and fighting over last night's leftover party food.'

'I think we still have a gas supply,' India's mum said. 'And they might have gas ovens, which means if we're very lucky we'll also get a lovely cooked breakfast. I think the fridges and freezers stay cold for a good few hours if you don't open them, so maybe the food won't have spoilt.'

'Well, we've definitely been good, and we deserve a Christmas morning treat,' Libby said.

'Oooh, I've been good!' India squeaked.

'And me!' Olivia agreed, suddenly more animated than Libby had seen her that morning.

'Well,' Libby said, 'in that case we'd better go and see if we can get our treat!'

Toast was off the menu – electric toasters – but the kitchen was instead able to offer fried bread, fluffy French toast or pancakes as an alternative; not bad alternatives as far as Libby could tell. They had made real coffee on the stoves of the vast kitchens and they'd also cooked up the bacon and eggs that had survived the fridges being off by being stored in containers out in the snow.

Libby was enjoying her choice of French toast as she sat with Adrienne and Gene, wondering vaguely if the hotel had bought turkey in for the Christmas guests they'd anticipated before these very exceptional, unforeseen circumstances, and whether those birds had survived the lack of power too. It would be a shame if they hadn't, and it raised the question that if everyone was still stuck here at lunchtime, what would they all eat?

Despite these minor niggles, she was impressed with the dedication of Lovage Hall's staff, who were stranded too, the majority of them not scheduled to work today and yet all busy on duty trying to keep the guests stranded alongside them comfortable. When all this was over they deserved a hefty bonus in their pay packets, and Libby hoped they'd get some kind of recognition for their efforts. If it had been her staff she'd have been fighting their corner, that was for sure.

'This breakfast is amazing, all things considered,' Gene said, echoing her thoughts. 'I don't know how they've managed to rustle it all up but they deserve a round of applause.'

'Yes,' Adrienne agreed, 'considering we have no power and there were bigger numbers here than they were meant to have it's a minor miracle. It's absolutely lovely too.'

'The French toast might be the best I've ever had,' Libby said. 'Although, if I eat much more I'm going to have to undo the zip on my dress and that will not be a good thing.'

'I wish I could offer you something spare to put on,' Adrienne began.

Libby put a hand up to stop her. 'It's fine, really. Most people only have the clothes they came in yesterday and anyone with spares isn't the same size as me.'

'I told you last night you could borrow a shirt from me to put over your dress if you get chilly…'

They looked up to see Noah at their table with a plate of bacon and egg. 'Mind if I join you?'

Mildly surprised by the request, Libby glanced at Gene and Adrienne, who seemed perfectly content to allow it, before nodding.

Surprised, because she'd expected him to sit with his old university buddies this morning for more catching up, but he'd clearly come looking for her – evidenced by the fact that the buddies in question were in clear view a few tables away and laughing loudly enough for anyone to notice their presence. Not that she minded one bit; the idea was a welcome one, though she tried not to let it mean anything. Trying to second-guess his intentions – she was beginning to see it wasn't that simple.

'Of course,' Gene said. 'Can't have people sitting on their own like sad sacks at breakfast, can we?'

At that precise moment, like some supreme cosmic irony, Libby's eye caught Rufus walking into the dining room with a breakfast plate of his own. He stopped for a moment, scanned the crowd, his gaze connecting with Libby's for the briefest second before settling on Noah, who was currently taking his seat at her table. Then he finally headed to an empty table by the draughty windows. With Gene's words still in her ears, Libby squirmed at the sight. Nobody ought to be sitting alone on Christmas Day, not even Rufus. Though she baulked at the idea and how it might send out the wrong message, she pondered for a moment suggesting they ask him to join them at their table. She could stand his company for an hour, surely? For the sake of a little Christmas kindness – for the sake of what they'd once had?

But then she noticed India's mum go over to him. They spoke for a few seconds, after which he took his meal to join her family at their table. It was hard not to heave a silent sigh of relief. Libby had been about to ask him over herself, but who knew what sort of mischief him joining her for breakfast might have caused. Lucky for her the crisis was averted, although something still troubled her about it all.

Today wasn't just about the kindness of strangers but about being in the thoughts of friends. She and Rufus were no longer together, and she could never forgive him for what he'd done, but he did seem truly sorry and like he was trying to build some kind of bridge. He'd meant a great deal to her once, hadn't he? They'd been through a lot together before it had all turned to shit. Perhaps today was a good day to if not forgive then at least to try and put the bad parts of that past behind them and acknowledge and respect the bits of it that had been good?

'Ladies and gentlemen!'

The bustle of the hall was silenced as everyone turned to see the manager, looking slightly dishevelled and very tired, addressing them. Libby assumed he would have expected to work today but probably not taking care of quite so many people in such trying circumstances. It was no wonder the poor man looked frazzled.

'I just wanted to take a moment to update everyone. The weather reports say that the snow should stop in the next hour or so and operations to make the roads passable again will commence shortly afterwards.'

'What about the electricity?' someone asked.

'Yes, I'm in regular contact with the energy company and they assure me they're working on it but, as you can imagine, the weather is making things a lot slower than they'd usually be. I'll keep everyone updated and we'll do our best to keep everyone comfortable regardless. You are welcome, of course, to stay with us for as long as you like today – we want all our guests to stay safe and so not only are you welcome, but I would advise at this time that it's probably better to stay with us until we have confirmation that the roads are clear and a route through is safe and possible.'

'What about Christmas lunch?' someone else asked.

'We will do our best to provide what we can. We find ourselves in unusual and unexpected circumstances, but we have good supplies in our larders and our fridges and freezers have held up well. We have the snow, of course, a natural freezer at a pinch. You might not get a traditional Christmas roast as you know it but there will be plenty for everyone and our talented kitchen team will make sure it is delicious. Just like you, they find themselves in unprecedented circumstances and working under difficult conditions, and I hope you'll all join me in thanking our hard-working and dedicated staff who have risen brilliantly to the challenge.'

'They're all missing their Christmas Day too,' someone said, and a chorus of agreement rippled through the tables, followed by a solo handclap which then grew until the entire room was giving awkward-looking staff members a round of applause.

The manager smiled and as the applause died down, he spoke again. 'Thank you for your appreciation and your understanding at this time. I'll leave you to your breakfasts. If anyone needs me they can ask at reception, who will contact me on your behalf. Of course, I will keep everyone updated on any developments. And merry Christmas to you all!'

'Merry Christmas!' everyone chorused back, and despite being stranded, many in the clothes they'd worn for a day and night and without the gift of tooth-cleaning tablets, most of them looked remarkably cheerful. There was a strange kind of camaraderie that only a situation like this brought out in people, and that, coupled with the spirit of goodwill that came with Christmas, gave the room full of wedding guests an almost visible warm glow.

The manager left and everyone went back to their meal.

'I don't envy his job today.' Noah cut into his bacon then put a forkful into his mouth and chewed with satisfaction. 'God, this is good. It's ages since I had decent bacon – the stuff in the US is not like this at all.'

'Oh yes,' Gene agreed, 'this is good stuff. Don't they have that crispy nonsense in America? Give me a thick slice of organically raised back any day. I'll bet you miss the food here, don't you?'

'I don't miss much from home and food out there is pretty good but I definitely miss some of our food. It's the simple things really, like a decent chip butty.'

'Can't you buy some English food there?' Adrienne asked. 'I mean, there are places here where you can buy American food.'

'Some of it I probably could,' Noah said. 'Things like chocolate. It's funny though – I don't really think about doing that. It's one of those situations where you don't realise you're missing it until you have some again. Although, it might be a good thing I don't get British chocolate sent over; stops me eating too much of it.'

'I'll bet it's all wheatgrass smoothies and nuts in California, isn't it?' Libby said. 'To keep all the beautiful people looking beautiful?'

'California?' Adrienne turned to Noah. 'Is that where you live now? How lovely!'

'It is gorgeous,' Noah said. 'I haven't seen as much as I'd like of it, but one day I'll get round to a tour. I'd love to travel from the top of the state to the bottom, see everything it has to offer.'

'That sounds like an amazing trip,' Libby said. 'I'd love to do something like that.'

'You should.'

'I'd have to stow away with you.'

'I'd love that,' he began with a grin, but the moment he did he looked suddenly mortified and turned to his plate. 'I mean... you should visit California one day; it's such an amazing place and... you know... if you did, we could absolutely meet up for... you know...'

Libby held back a frown. 'Maybe one day,' she said, wondering what on earth he actually wanted her to say. Every conversation with Noah seemed to turn on a sixpence: one minute he was all flirting and open enthusiasm, the next he was pushing her away, barely able to look her in the eye. She was beginning to feel like a piece of cheese being lusted after by someone who was lactose intolerant – they wanted it but knew they shouldn't. Which didn't make any sense, unless...

There was something he wasn't telling her – or anyone else for that matter. He was at the wedding alone but maybe there was a girlfriend back home? If that were the case then no wonder he was being weird, but, even worse than that, if there was a girl tucked away then he had no right being flirty with anyone at all. Libby had had her fill of duplicitous men and had no desire to tangle with another one for as long as she lived.

It wasn't a question she felt she could ask outright; for one it would imply she was convinced of his interest in her, and if he wasn't actually interested then that was potentially horribly embarrassing. She'd find Tomas later, she quickly decided, and somehow shoehorn the question into a conversation and get the answer in a much more subtle way. Embarrassment averted and nobody would have to get hurt... apart from Libby's pride, of course, because if Noah was hiding something like that from her, how stupid did it make her to show the slightest interest in him? Played by yet another man leading her a merry dance – she might well consider binning her dance card for good.

'I've never been to America,' Gene said, 'but I've always wanted to go.'

'Well, you're more than welcome to look me up if you ever make it to California,' Noah said.

'I'd love to see New York,' Adrienne said in a dreamy voice. 'And Niagara Falls, the Great Lakes, New England in the fall... Boston... Nantucket...'

'I've never made it that far east myself,' Noah said. 'I plan to some day when I can make the time.'

'I suppose it's a big country,' Gene said. 'I should imagine it's very difficult for anyone to see all of it, even people who live there.'

'Yes, exactly,' Noah agreed. 'We don't realise how vast the distances are. Here in the UK we think a four-hour drive is a long one; over there it's a trip to the shops. They drive for hours and hours and think nothing of it.'

'The roads are built for it,' Gene said. 'At least that's how it seems when you see them on the television.'

'They're certainly more suited to driving than ours,' Noah said. 'I think being stuck here today is proof of that.'

'Very true,' Gene said ruefully. 'What are your plans for today?'

'I don't really know. I suppose we'll all just take things as they come.'

Gene turned to Libby. 'What about you?'

'The same. It's hard to plan anything when you don't know how long you're going to be stranded somewhere.'

'The hotel is going to try and provide some kind of Christmas lunch at least – catering for a lot more than they'd bargained for, of course – but other than that we're really just sitting around, aren't we? You're both more than welcome to sit around with us if you like.'

'Thanks,' Libby said. 'I feel sorry for some today who won't be happy sitting around waiting to escape. Some will really be missing their Christmases with loved ones, won't they? Missing plans with people at home they really want to be with. That's such a shame.'

'It is,' Adrienne said. 'But it can't be helped.'

'It would be nice to do something to include everyone, pull them together somehow,' Libby said. 'So the place isn't filled with sad, silent bunches of people pining for home.'

'You mean make an occasion of it?' Noah asked.

'Why not? If people don't have a choice about being here at least we could make it memorable in a positive way.'

'What do you have in mind?' Gene asked.

'I don't really know,' Libby said. 'I was just thinking it would be nice if we could do something to draw everyone together.'

'Won't they come together at Christmas lunch?' Adrienne asked.

'Well, yes, but that's only an hour or two. What about the rest of the day?'

'We need some kind of event,' Noah said. 'Like carols or something.'

'I like the sound of that,' Libby said. 'It's the sort of thing that will turn the day into one that people might look back on and treasure rather than feel that was the Christmas Day they wasted stuck in the middle of nowhere in the snow.' She turned to Gene and Adrienne. 'What do you think?'

'I think our Willow was very lucky to make friends with you all those years ago,' Adrienne said fondly. 'It's a lovely idea and just the sort of thing you'd come up with.'

'Actually, I think it was Noah's idea,' Libby said with just the merest hint of a blush colouring her cheeks.

'It was a joint effort,' Noah replied gallantly. 'We could come up with other activities too perhaps. I don't know how long carol singing would last but it's not going to be the whole day. Maybe we could give people more than just that to look forward to and organising it all would be something to occupy us.'

'You'd want to do all that work?' Libby asked doubtfully.

'Of course I would!' Noah smiled. 'Beats sitting around all day, bored out of my tree, getting blind drunk just for something to do.'

'Alright…' Libby tried to keep her excitement in check. If there was one thing she loved it was organising, and it was like Noah could read it in her. The fact that he was so eager to help… well, she couldn't deny that he probably was just trying to stave off a day of boredom, but surely there were other ways to do that. Was this an excuse to spend time with her? Like, real, quality time where they could get to know each other?

That little voice of reason reminded her that even if it was, it wasn't necessarily a good thing and she packed away the building sense of hope and anticipation. For now, she needed to take all this at face value – he was just trying to make the best of a less-than-ideal situation, as they all were.

'What kind of things do you think we ought to do?' she asked him.

'I definitely think some kind of singalong is a great idea,' Gene said. 'What would we do for backing music? There's no electricity so the hotel wouldn't be able to give us CDs or anything.'

'There's a piano in one of the rooms,' Noah said. 'I've seen it.'

'You play piano then?' Gene asked.

'Not brilliantly, but if we could get hold of some sheet music I could probably bang out a couple of Christmas tunes well enough for everyone to sing along.'

'I'll bet there's sheet music online if we can get a decent signal and someone has enough charge on their phone to find it,' Libby said.

'For sure,' Noah agreed. 'You can easily get free music if you know where to look.'

Libby beamed at him. 'Brilliant! So what time do you think we ought to plan the singing for?'

'Maybe after lunch? People can take it easy this morning, take time to sleep in if they want to…'

'I think most people are up already,' Libby said. 'It's not really a place to sleep in, especially if you've spent the night in a chair downstairs like we did. I wonder if we ought to do it this morning. Or if not the singing then something else – something family-friendly like games for the kids or something?'

'I suppose it would be good for the kids to have something to take their minds off the fact that they don't have presents to open this morning,' Gene said. Adrienne nodded her agreement.

'You're right,' Libby said, 'but will the adults really appreciate us turning Lovage Hall into Butlin's? It's one thing organising a few carols but another having games.'

'Nobody's going to be forced to join in,' Noah said. 'We could use a small space – the orangery or piano bar. That way if people want to stay out of the way of it, they can.'

'I suppose India, Scarlet and Olivia would love something to keep them occupied,' Libby said thoughtfully.

'We don't have many kids staying over but I'm sure they would all love it,' Noah said.

Libby smiled at him. 'You really are enjoying this, aren't you?'

'Well, it's Christmas and it's a big deal for kids…' He shrugged. 'I just thought it would be good to do something for them.'

'It *is* a big deal for kids,' she agreed. 'My mum says I used to get so excited about it I'd make myself sick.'

'All the more reason to make it a good one then,' Noah said.

'So how are we going to do this?'

Noah's words had given Libby a warm feeling that she tried to ignore. She couldn't allow herself to place too much value on them; after all, he seemed like a sweet guy and that was probably all there was to it.

'I say we figure out what exactly it is we want to do,' Gene said. 'We've thrown around quite a lot of suggestions but what do you think most people would be happy to participate in?'

'Nothing too demanding,' Libby said. 'At least that's my view. I think the main thing people want from today is to have a rest and spend a bit of quality time with people they like.'

'Or with people who drive them a bit mad but whom they love anyway?' Gene said, while Adrienne threw him a sideways glance that said she was less than impressed with his quip. 'Only joking, my love,' he added with an impish grin.

'*Anyway…*' Libby cut in, heading off any further segues. 'We want to keep it low-key, that's what I think. If it's too much effort people won't bother. We just want ways for everyone to come together where they won't feel pressured – there's nothing worse than forced jollity.'

'I'm in total agreement,' Noah said. 'Believe me, I've been to plenty of parties over the last few years that I didn't want to be at and forced to pretend I'm having a great time participating in some "event" when I'm not; there's nothing worse.'

'For your job, I suppose?' Libby asked. He gave a vague shrug.

'That, and other things…'

Other things? Talk about cryptic. Something told Libby she wasn't going to get any more than that and his next utterance proved her right.

'I'd say songs around the piano are a definite winner. But that could just be because I'm always happy to have an excuse to bash at a piano and it doesn't happen as often as I'd like these days.'

'Bingo!' Adrienne said. Libby gave a slight frown. Was she referring to the game, or was she just excited for Noah's piano opportunities?

'Sorry?'

'Everyone loves bingo!' Adrienne said. 'What about some kind of Christmas-themed bingo?'

Gene looked as doubtful as Libby. 'What would people win?'

'It doesn't matter. It's not the winning that matters today; it's the playing. It could just be a drink from the bar or something.'

'Drunk Christmas bingo?' Libby grinned. 'I could be into that! So... songs and bingo. What else?'

'What about something more traditional, like a big game of charades or something?' Gene suggested.

Noah nodded slowly. 'Could work. Easy to do – no equipment or prizes necessary and most people find it fun.'

'It's not everyone's cup of tea,' Adrienne said.

'You mean it's not yours,' Gene replied wryly.

'No, not since Christmas 1989,' Adrienne said meaningfully.

'Why?' Libby asked. 'What happened?'

'My uncle Mick lost it playing a very competitive game of charades and punched my uncle Donnie in the face. What a Christmas that was...'

Gene chuckled, which was handy because Libby didn't have a clue how to react to Adrienne's revelation. She exchanged a brief, perplexed glance with Noah before continuing.

'Like Noah said, I suppose people can join in or not, whatever they want. It might be that some people don't want to do any of the things we've come up with, which is fine, of course, but…'

'We want to, don't we?' Noah looked at Gene and Adrienne, who both nodded.

'Of course we do,' Adrienne said, though Libby got the sudden impression she might only be saying that because they thought organising these activities was something that meant a lot to her. She didn't know whether to be flattered or unsettled by the notion.

'So, would you like me to draw something up?' she asked. 'Maybe see if the manager can post some notices around the place? Should we have some kind of sign-up sheet posted too?'

'All sounds a bit formal,' Noah said. 'Wouldn't it be more appealing if it was all a bit loosey-goosey and people could drop in if they fancied it or not if they didn't? A sign-up sheet sounds a bit like a commitment; people might feel they're being held to a promise and it might be a bit off-putting.'

'As would them feeling as if once they've signed up they're obliged not to change their minds or plans later on,' Gene agreed. 'It might put people off signing up if they think it's a binding thing.'

'Surely nobody will see it like that,' Libby said doubtfully.

'They're not drawing up a will,' Adrienne added, taking Libby's side. 'I don't see why sticking your name on a list is a problem – we're hardly going to hunt them down if they don't turn up.'

'Of course not,' Gene said patiently, 'but you must see what I mean.'

'OK.' Libby took an executive decision. 'No sign-ups. Posters are agreeable to everyone? We need to let people know when and where things will be happening.'

'Yes,' Gene said. 'I think that's enough.'

'Well, I can deal with that easily,' Libby said.

'Now, I'm beginning to learn that you're Miss Efficient and that you could probably organise all this with your eyes closed, but you know what might be a better idea?'

Libby tried to look as receptive and open as possible while still wondering what on earth Noah was going to suggest that was better.

'You could ask the little bridesmaids to do the posters,' he continued. 'I bet they'd love it. It would give them something to be occupied with and make them feel involved.'

'The trio of torment?' she asked, and Gene burst out laughing.

'I'm glad you came up with that nickname because I'd never dare!'

Libby gave him a sheepish smile before turning back to Noah. Actually, when she thought about it, Noah's idea was a very good one and much better than her designing the posters.

'I think Noah's right,' Gene said. 'I wonder if there are coloured pens anywhere? The hotel staff might be able to help out with that?'

'I'll ask,' Noah said, getting up and striding out towards the reception area.

'You know, he's lovely,' Adrienne said as they watched him go. 'One of Tomas's old friends, you say?'

'I think so,' Libby replied. 'I don't really know much about him apart from that he knows Tomas from way back.'

'Hmm.' Adrienne was silent for a moment, but then broke into a mischievous smile. At least it looked full of mischief to Libby. 'I think I'll have to do some investigating of my own.'

Gene looked at her. 'What for?'

His wife tapped the side of her nose, but the look she gave Libby was enough to make Libby suspect some kind of matchmaking was afoot and that it probably involved her. She hoped not. Things were complicated enough with Rufus still stranded there and Noah blowing hot and cold; she certainly didn't need anyone else adding to it.

Chapter Ten

For obvious reasons there hadn't been much gift-opening that morning. Most people had spent the hours between breakfast and the first activity of the day as they'd spent the previous evening — sitting in groups with friends and family and talking about the quite remarkable weather.

The trio of torment were only too happy to design posters and were diligent in their efforts. Libby sat with them for a while to guide them with the details they needed to include, and she even tried to get involved in the artwork but quickly realised that they didn't need her, didn't really want to delegate any of it to her, and were doing a better job than she could anyway. Most importantly, she'd never seen the three of them so content and focused. They lay on their fronts on the floor of the piano room, tongues at the corners of their mouths or foreheads lined with concentration as they drew bright, Christmas-themed designs around clunky lettering. In the end, Libby had to concede that Noah's idea to involve them was a masterstroke, if only because the sight of those childish scribbles couldn't fail to entice the most ardently antisocial soul to come along and join in the fun, and that was what they were hoping for. There was no point in organising these things if nobody cared to make the effort. Even so, she was filled with doubt.

Would anybody bother to come to their little singalong? There were no guarantees their events wouldn't all fall flat, even the carols, which seemed the safest bet, and if nobody came she'd feel a bit silly for trying to organise them. Noah, at least, seemed confident that people would gather at the drawing room's grand piano at the allotted time and that they'd all have fun. She suspected that would be true for Noah himself if for nobody else, because he seemed very excited at the prospect of playing the grand piano and to have an audience too.

Her suspicions were definitely strengthened by the fact he'd spent a good hour of his morning practising the list of songs they'd picked out. Every so often she'd pass the open door to the grand old drawing room and take a moment to listen. Sometimes he'd be so engrossed he wouldn't notice her there, but at others he'd catch her eye and give her a dazzling smile. He was pretty good – better than he'd had her believe – and he looked about as content and at ease on a piano stool as she'd ever seen a man look anywhere.

She couldn't deny that he looked kind of sexy too. It was kind of the same as the suit... a handsome man in a good suit was a sure aphrodisiac for Libby, but a man who could play a cool instrument was almost as hot. Noah, at this precise moment, was rocking both looks with some panache. But she reminded herself that she had reasons to suspect she'd be wise to keep her distance – at least in that way – and that she didn't know if she could trust him, even though she wanted to.

Rufus had crossed her mind a few times while all this was going on, but she hadn't seen him since breakfast. Willow thought he'd gone to someone's room to get cleaned up but she wasn't sure. She offered to find out, but Libby didn't want to put her out so left it at that.

They'd scheduled their carols for just before lunch. An hour was about the length of anyone's attention span for that sort of thing, they'd agreed, and so by eleven the room was – to Libby's mild surprise but also pleasure – starting to fill up with singers.

They gathered in the shadow of bay windows that ran the full height of the wall dressed in sumptuous cream damask curtains, and the snow lay piled on the terrace beyond. The walls of the drawing room were a deep, warm red and a gleaming, dramatic chandelier hung above the walnut grand piano that sat on an antique oriental rug at the centre of the space. More than once, as Noah had sat with great delight tinkling lovingly on the keys, she'd thought about lying across it seductively like they did in old movies, just to see if it would tempt him to kiss her. But, of course, she'd done nothing of the sort. She'd dashed around making sure everything was ready, chattering like a machine gun about all the things she wished she had the resources to do.

'You never stop rushing around, do you?' Noah had said at one point, looking up with a languid smile, his fingers still stroking the keys even though he'd paused his playing. Libby had wondered more than once whether he might actually cry when the time came to leave it, because he seemed to be getting very attached to Lovage Hall's grand piano.

'I want everything to be perfect,' she replied, a little flustered.

'A people-pleaser,' he said sagely. 'Don't you ever just want to please yourself?'

'Of course. Doing this is making me happy.'

'You've been fretting all morning. Come and take a break.' He patted the seat next to him. 'Want to learn a bit? I could teach you a few notes.'

God, she wanted nothing more than to sit close to him and feel the heat of his body pressed against her as he guided her hands across the smooth keys of the piano, but she shook her head.

'Water!' she yelped. 'We need jugs and glasses of water – people will get parched!'

And with that, cursing herself for not being cooler, she'd dashed off to find someone who could provide the quite unnecessary pitchers.

As there was no electricity they couldn't use the printers, so Libby and the other bridesmaids had made handwritten copies of the lyrics to the songs they planned to sing, but only enough for families to share a copy between them. Some of them were clearer than others too, but she trusted that the majority of people knew most of the lyrics to the very famous songs and would be able to work out what they couldn't quite read – at least enough to make a fist of singing along. They'd kept things light and cheery with all the usual suspects: 'I Saw Mommy Kissing Santa Claus', 'Jingle Bells', 'White Christmas', and so on. They were busy distributing the song sheets as the last participants arrived piano-side, ready to start.

Noah beamed at Libby. 'This is a great turnout!'

She let her gaze wander the crowd and allowed herself a wide smile too. The room was full of eager chat and anticipation, the woes of being stranded and still without power temporarily forgotten and the spirit of Christmas very much in evidence in the bright faces that smiled back at Libby whenever she caught an eye. It was wonderful to see so many more people than Libby had imagined would turn up.

Noah swept a hand down the keys of the piano in a tinkling crescendo and the chattering stopped.

'Right, you lovely people!' he announced, his grin now so manic it almost had a life of its own. 'Let's do this!'

It all promised to be rough and ready from the start, but there was something quite joyous about the musical chaos that ensued.

People were out of time, off-key, sang the wrong words and choruses where verses should be, and hardly anybody ever knew what song was coming next until Noah had started to play it because he'd stopped using the set list Libby had written for him almost as soon as the concert had started. Ordinarily that sort of transgression would have fried Libby's order-craving brain, but today, with him, somehow she didn't mind. If she couldn't allow a little crazy on such a crazy day as this, then when could she? The main thing, when she ignored all this other stuff, was that people were having fun and that had been the point, after all.

It seemed nobody (even the trio of torment, who were dancing around like loons) was having more fun than Noah, who'd said he'd been deprived of a piano in California – and it was now evident that he'd been deprived for far too long. Even though she was way out of her comfort zone because public performance was definitely not her thing, Libby was having almost as much fun too, until she noticed Rufus sneak in and stand near the door to watch, which instantly popped her fun balloon like a devilishly sharp pin. Despite this, she tried valiantly not to let him bother her, and even more importantly tried not to let the fact she'd noticed show, but it was hard not to get wound up.

He probably didn't know what to do with himself, she thought, trying to be charitable. He probably only wanted to see what was going on and to be a part of the Christmas celebrations; he was stranded on Christmas Day, after all, just like everyone else. But he didn't look much like someone who wanted to be a part of happy celebrations. He stood and watched in brooding silence, until other people started to notice him. He was slightly killing the mood, and if Libby had been strong enough to pick up the piano she might have been tempted to hurl it at him.

When she could ignore his presence no longer she resolved to go and give him what for, but then she saw Tomas heading over to have a word. She couldn't tell what they were saying, but a moment later Rufus skulked off and Tomas rejoined the singing. She'd have to grab Willow's husband when she could to ask what had happened. Then again, that might imply that she cared, so maybe not. It wouldn't do to give Rufus any extra ammunition when he already had quite enough. Instead, she turned her thoughts back to the singing, though her mood was just that little bit darker than it had been.

As Noah played the opening bars to 'Santa Claus Is Comin' to Town', Libby rifled through her song sheets to get the right one. Almost everyone did the same, but some decided to give it up and wing it and started singing pretty much any lyric they fancied. It would have been funny had Libby's mood not been ruined quite so dramatically. Though she didn't want to, she might have to talk to Rufus to sort this situation before it got out of hand. It looked as if he was determined to stay after all, so it was either that or do a much better job of pretending he wasn't there.

As the song built and everyone figured out it was the last, the singing got louder and more raucous, and people started to clap along and stamp their feet, and it was hard, even for Libby, to stay mad when she was surrounded by such joy. She put her song sheet down and clapped too and did her best to get the lyrics right, even though it didn't seem to matter to anyone anymore.

After a couple of minutes of this madness, Noah finished the song with a flourish.

'That's it, folks!' he shouted. 'Thank you so much for coming!'

Libby half expected him to leap up onto the piano to take a bow, but instead he grinned as everyone cheered, and his expression was so adorably, ridiculously happy that she didn't think he'd looked so hot since the first moment she'd clapped eyes on him. She did her best to dismiss the thought and started to gather in some of the discarded song sheets but was interrupted by people calling for an encore.

Noah laughed off the demands, though he was clearly itching to oblige. 'We've got stuff to do!' he said.

But they kept shouting for him to play again, until, in the end, he relented. Of course he was going to do an encore.

'Which song?' he asked. There were many yelled answers, even suggestions of non-Christmas classics like 'Hey Jude', but Noah didn't have the music for those and told them his own repertoire was a little rusty. So they decided on 'Rudolph the Red-Nosed Reindeer', and as the song kicked in again people were practically shouting the lyrics and laughing hysterically as they did. By the time the song had come to an end it was audible chaos.

'And that, folks, is definitely that!' Noah said, grinning. Libby suspected that if he could have sat there and played for them all day he would, but even he knew that good things had to come to an end and that some people would need time to find significant others and get ready for lunch.

Libby thanked the people nearest to her as they handed back their song sheets.

'It's been lovely,' one lady who might have been Tomas's great-aunt said.

'It has,' Libby said. 'Thanks for coming.'

'Oh, no, thank you for organising it!' The woman had to be eighty, if not older, but as she left she turned to throw a last wink at Noah and mimed a telephone. 'Call me, hot stuff!' she said, before leaving in fits of laughter.

Noah stared after her, and then at Libby, before they both began to laugh too.

'Wow!' Libby said. 'We'll have to watch out for that one!'

'She must have had a good time,' he said.

'Everyone did…' She threw him a sly smile. 'I think you had more fun than anyone.'

'Maybe,' he replied with a sheepish grin.

The last guests were filing out, and Libby decided to make a quick tour of the room to make certain it was clean and tidy and would be left just the way they'd found it.

'It's ages since I played a decent piano,' Noah continued, 'and that one is amazing!'

'I think you rather enjoyed the audience too,' Libby said.

'Maybe a little bit. I mean, who wouldn't, right?'

'Not me, that's who wouldn't. Performing is possibly my worst nightmare, but I can see why you like it – you're really good too. Have you ever played professionally?'

'Oh, no… just local concerts with the school orchestra, that sort of thing. I used to enjoy it but, you know, unless you're a virtuoso there's not much money in it as a career.'

'I get it. You still ended up with a pretty cool career though.'

He grinned. 'I did, didn't I? I'm not complaining at all; today just made me realise how much I miss playing. I wish I had more room in my apartment for my own piano… I've got a little keyboard thing but it's just not the same.'

Libby peered under a row of chairs to check for discarded paper. 'Maybe Santa will get you one if you're extra good.'

'I don't think we have the same Santa, because mine definitely can't afford gifts like that, no matter how good I am.'

'No, come to think of it, mine can't either.'

He sat back on the piano stool and watched for a moment as she carried on her inspection. After a silent moment, she realised it and glanced up, and the way he was looking at her was enough to melt her. She blushed and put her head down again, pretending to check the carpet as her face burnt. But when she finally regained her faculties and looked up again, he didn't seem to realise he'd any effect on her at all.

'So we have half an hour or so to kill before lunch. What are you planning to do?'

'Not much. Maybe finish up here and then...'

'Because I was thinking maybe we could... I don't know... get a drink?'

'I'm not sure my liver will thank me for more drinking,' she said with a self-conscious laugh.

'It doesn't have to be an alcoholic one.'

She smiled. Noah had other friends staying at Lovage Hall, but he was asking to spend even more time with her. She couldn't help but be flattered; he had plenty of choice, and his choice was her.

During the years they were together, Rufus would tell Libby that she was difficult to spend time with, critical, demanding, too serious, and so many other negative things she'd lost track of them. But the way she saw it, she just wanted things to be right and if that was who she was, then why pretend to be anything else? Rufus was her partner, he'd promised his life to her, so surely that meant acceptance of everything she was, the good and the bad? Those were her logical thoughts on it, but since their split she'd begun to question that logic. The way their engagement had ended had stripped her confidence and her belief that she shouldn't have to change to be accepted. But here was Noah, who seemed to like her even though he'd seen that madly ordered side to her first-hand and didn't appear to have been put off one bit. But it wasn't so easy to shake doubts that had festered for years, and they still persisted now; Noah might seem interested and accepting, but it was probably too good to be true.

A drink couldn't hurt though, could it? It wasn't like she was planning to sleep with him or anything.

She was about to take him up on his offer when there was a trio of footsteps accompanied by breathless giggles, as India, Scarlet and Olivia raced across the piano room.

'Libby, will you come out and play snowball fights with us?' Scarlet cried. 'Mum doesn't want to but you like the snow, don't you? You said yesterday…'

'Yes, please come!' the other two chorused.

'Well, I…' Libby looked hopelessly at Noah for some kind of intervention that would help to excuse her. She'd humoured them the night before by going outside to stand in the snow for a short while but it was hardly the same as a full-on snowball fight. Facing a barrage of sopping-wet, freezing-cold missiles was hardly her idea of fun. But Noah simply grinned and offered nothing and she didn't know whether to be amused by the fact he clearly knew she was silently begging for help or to start planning her revenge.

'We're hardly dressed for it,' she said lamely, feeling slightly guilty the moment their expectant faces fell. 'Aren't your parents worried about you getting cold?'

'My mum says if I want to catch my death that's my stupid lookout,' India said. She didn't sound very concerned about her mother's warning at all and Libby wondered if she ought to be, because it sounded very much to her like India's mum was really saying: I don't want you to go out but I'm crumbling under the pressure of your nagging and I've gone past caring.

'My mum just told me not to be out long because lunch would be ready soon,' Scarlet said.

Olivia put her hand up as if in class and Libby smiled at her. Of the three, she was definitely the quietest, shyest one, but Libby suspected those outward qualities hid a bit of a naughty streak. 'My mum was talking to my dad about oil in the car so I couldn't ask. I don't think they'd mind if I went outside. Yesterday Mum told Dad I wouldn't get into trouble no matter where I went at Lovage Hall.'

Given that intruders from outside were quite unlikely in the current weather conditions, Libby could hardly disagree with that. She hated to disappoint her little friends but, despite their assurances, she wasn't convinced their parents actually would be happy at the idea of her taking them outside in the snow. And even if they were, it didn't seem sensible anyway.

'What if I came out with you?' Noah said.

'But your suit will be ruined!' Libby said.

'I can imagine how that might be stressful to you,' he said, laughing. 'In your line of work.'

Libby folded her arms and gave him a scolding look, and he laughed even harder.

'And your shoes,' she continued. 'They're hardly waterproof.'

He shrugged. 'They're only shoes. Can't say I like them all that much anyway. Today feels like a good day to throw caution to the wind and live a little, even if that means a few water marks on some Italian leather.'

'Will you?' Olivia asked him. 'That would be *so* fun!' She looked up at him with that particular awe that little girls reserve for only the very coolest men in their lives. It was obvious Noah was making an impression on more people at this wedding than just Libby.

'Are you sure you don't fancy it?' Noah turned to Libby. 'You can wear my jacket if you like, and the fires will be lit in the great hall so we'd dry out pretty quick afterwards.' He waggled his eyebrows. 'Come on... you want live a little, right? Take a walk on the wild side?'

'It's hardly trekking through the Himalayas,' Libby said with a grin. She looked at the window again – she would bet a hefty portion of next month's salary that it was bloody freezing out there. But then she turned back to three hopeful little faces and one a bit bigger but equally as expectant. How could she say no without being a major stick-in-the-mud? Stick-in-the-mud was usually her default setting, of course, but maybe Noah was right – maybe today was a good day to throw caution to the wind... or at least snowballs at little girls. And they wouldn't have to be outside for long because they'd need to come back in and get dry for dinner, so it would be maybe fifteen minutes tops. She could do fifteen minutes, couldn't she?

'OK,' she said finally.

'Yay!' the trio shouted in unison.

'Teams?' Noah asked.

'It's a bit of an uneven split,' Libby said.

'The girls versus us?' he asked. He grinned at the little bridesmaids. 'That way we can annihilate you.'

'No way!' Scarlet giggled. 'We'd win!'

'Maybe I take two of the girls and you take one?' Libby suggested, and a bit of her already wondered if she was putting way too much thought into making this fair. But old habits died hard and she quickly dismissed the idea.

Olivia's hand shot up again. 'I want to go with Noah!'

'No, me!' India shouted.

'That's not fair!' Scarlet pouted. 'I want to go with Noah.'

'Way to make me feel popular,' Libby said, though she was smiling. It was hard to deny he had a palpable charisma that was almost impossible to ignore and she could well understand why all the girls wanted to team up with him. Hell, she wanted to team up with him and she was old enough and wise enough to know better.

'Sorry...' Scarlet looked mortified, and Libby laughed lightly.

'Don't worry, I get it. He does look like he'd be quite good at snowball fighting and me... not so much. Why don't we go with the original plan? You three against us two?'

'You and me?' Noah grinned at her. 'I see, so you're handing the advantage to the girls; noble of you.'

Libby put her hands on her hips. 'Oh, which of us is the disadvantage then?'

'Well, it's obviously not you,' he said, chuckling. 'If your snowball throwing is anything like as efficient as everything else you do then it will be almost impossible to beat you.'

'I'm pretty sure that's not true but I'll take it.' She turned to the girls. 'OK with you? The teams, I mean?'

'Maybe we can swap round after a while?' Scarlet said with a sly, longing glance at Noah. The grown-ups weren't getting away with things that easily and it looked as if Scarlet, at least, was determined to get her man. Well, her marksman anyway.

'We might not be out long enough to swap round,' Libby said. 'We've got to be back in for lunch, don't forget, and they're serving very soon. It's freezing too – three snowballs and I'll probably turn into an icicle myself.'

'We'll work something out,' Noah said cheerily.

Scarlet nodded. It was then that Libby noticed the girls were each clasping a garment. As Scarlet unfolded hers it was revealed to be a huge sweater. Borrowed, clearly, way too big and manly to belong to any of them, and so Libby guessed they or their parents had been on the hunt and improvised some cold-weather gear. She didn't imagine they'd be warm, even with their pilfered clothing, but she supposed they wouldn't care. At that age, she supposed she wouldn't have either.

'You want that loan?' Noah asked as he held his jacket out to Libby.

'What about you?'

'Don't worry; I can run up to my suite and get something else. I must have something suitable in my spare clothes.'

'Thanks then.'

She took the jacket, unable to prevent the instant inhalation of the scent that clung to it that smelt just like him. It did strange and wonderful things to her, and she only hoped nobody would notice.

Chapter Eleven

Ten minutes later they were out in the Italian gardens of Lovage Hall. The staff had thankfully been busy clearing some of the paths now that the snow had stopped, because ankle-deep in snow wearing open-toed sandals was not Libby's idea of fun. That wasn't to say her feet weren't cold as it was, but at least she wasn't in immediate danger of frostbite. Maybe in an hour that threat might become a reality, but she wasn't planning on being out there that long. Noah had offered spare socks to go with his jacket, but Libby had decided her pride just wouldn't survive men's socks inside her fancy sandals, certainly not to be seen by other human eyes – she wasn't vain, but she had standards.

That wasn't the only betrayal Libby's sandals were subjecting her to. Skidding and slipping on the paths hardly helped her aim in the snowball fight either, and she and Noah were currently being trounced by the opposing team. She'd have liked to pretend it was because she and Noah were allowing the girls to get the upper hand, but the sad fact was that the two adults really were that useless.

'I can't remember the last time I did this,' Noah said as he ducked a handful of snow that had been launched by Scarlet.

'I can't remember the last time I was this humiliated,' Libby cried, but she was laughing at the same time. She scooped a missile from a nearby grass verge and hurled it, with terrible aim, at Olivia. It fell sadly short and landed with a pathetic plop onto the snow-covered sundial. Noah raised his eyebrows.

'I hate to say it, but you weren't kidding when you said you'd be no good at this – you're even worse than you promised to be. I should have taken the kids up on their offer.'

'Oi!' Libby squeaked and sent her next one in his direction. It hit him squarely in the mouth, and the look of shock on his face was enough to send her into spasms of giggling.

'Now she decides to get good,' he said wryly as he wiped his face. 'Aren't you supposed to be reserving accuracy like that for the enemy?'

Just then another snowball hit the side of his head and they both turned to see India grinning at them.

'Gotcha!' she shouted.

'You little…' Noah bent to get more snow, but as he did he was pelted from all directions, including Libby's. Then he straightened up and mock glared at Libby. 'Did you just throw with them? You're supposed to be on my side!'

'I was until you said I was rubbish. I'm just proving to you I can hit the target when I really want to. Also, sorry but I've just defected.' She skipped to the other side of the path, which represented where the battle lines had been drawn up, to join Olivia, Scarlet and India. 'I'm on their side now.' She winked at the girls. 'Solidarity for us, right, sisters?'

'Yeah!' the three little ones shouted.

'Oh God!' Noah yelped. 'I'm doomed!'

A moment later the air was filled with squeals of joy and peals of laughter and flying snow. For a frantic couple of minutes Libby could barely tell who was pelting who. The battle line was breached and everyone was wherever they fancied, hitting anyone they fancied with snow. One thing she did know was that she could hardly catch her breath for laughing. She couldn't remember the last time she'd felt this free, laughed this hard and with such abandon. And then she reached for an inviting pile of glistening snow at the same time as Noah and their hands touched. Her fingers were numb from the cold but that did nothing to dampen the jolt that passed between them. Her laughter died in her throat and, as she lost herself in his eyes, she realised his laughter had stopped too.

A snowball to the back of his head broke the tension, but not before the most delicious scenario had run through Libby's head, one in which she pushed him to the ground and kissed the life back into her frozen lips.

He spun to try and locate the source of the attack, but all three little girls were laughing.

'Bet you don't know who threw that!' Scarlet shouted gleefully, giving away that it had probably been her.

'You little minxes!' he said, laughing, before throwing armfuls of snow in all directions like a mad human snowplough – they rained down on everyone and soaked them even more than they already were. 'If I can't find the culprit I'll just have to punish you all!'

Still laughing, the three girls scattered in all directions with raucous squeals and he made a dash towards them. But he'd only gone a few feet when he slipped on the icy path and flew comically into the air before landing on his back.

'Oh shit!' Libby cried as she slip-slid her way over. 'Noah! Are you alright?'

'I'm fine,' he gasped. He seemed winded but otherwise unharmed and didn't look too distressed, all things considered. 'I mean, I feel like an idiot, of course, but that's not exactly a new sensation for me so I guess I'll survive.'

Libby offered a hand to help him up but he refused it.

'Better if I get myself up,' he said. 'I'm more likely to pull you down as well otherwise.'

Libby half thought that she might not mind so much ending up on the ground in his arms, but she kept it to herself. 'Are you saying I'm a weakling?'

'I'm saying I'm that much of a klutz.'

India, Scarlet and Olivia were standing over him now too, and as Noah got to his feet and smiled down at Libby, she tore herself away, once more, from his clear, winter-blue eyes to see Scarlet and India whispering and giggling behind their hands and got the distinct feeling that she might be the subject of their joke. Or maybe her and Noah both. Much as she'd like to believe otherwise, it was hard to deny the obvious attraction and harder, it seemed, to hide it, even from three supposedly clueless children.

Part of her, against her better judgement, didn't want to deny it, but she also knew it was probably a good idea to hide it while Rufus was still skulking around.

She held in a sigh. Would life always be like this now? Would she always have to pussyfoot around whenever Rufus was nearby? And why did she care so much about sparing his feelings? It wasn't like he deserved that kind of consideration and he'd certainly never showed the same to her.

She was spared further deliberation by a cheer going up inside Lovage Hall and shot Noah a silent question.

'I wonder if something has changed with the travel situation,' he said, and Libby could have sworn he looked disappointed at the possibility.

'I suppose we ought to go and find out,' she replied and, despite what common sense told her, the idea was suddenly a disappointing one to her too. It wasn't every day you were handed the perfect excuse to forget about obligation and responsibilities and allow yourself to live purely in the moment – even if it was only for a short time. Being stranded here at Lovage Hall had given her just that. After all, what else was there to do here? And she was just starting to relax and enjoy it way more than she'd have thought possible.

'I suppose so,' he said. 'I expect you're getting cold too, so it's probably for the best.'

Scarlet, India and Olivia voiced their disappointment far more vocally than Libby's silent grudging acceptance, but they trudged in behind the adults just the same, which led Libby to suspect they were all colder than they'd admit to as well, and secretly glad of the opportunity to get warm and dry again.

The reason for the cheering became obvious very quickly. As soon as they walked in from the gardens they were greeted by soft music piped in through the sound system that provided the background ambiance for the orangery bar. Christmas tree lights twinkled and spotlights illuminated the bar area.

'Looks like we have electricity at last,' Noah said. 'About time too – I can get a shower at last.'

'A shower…' Libby said longingly, 'sounds so good about now. I wonder if there's any news on getting out of here – I'm dying for a shower myself, but as I have no room booked it will have to wait until I'm home.'

'Shower in my room,' Noah said. 'You only have to ask for my key anytime. While I still have access to my suite you can use it as much as you like.'

'Oh, but I didn't like to…'

'Don't be silly!' He smiled. 'What's a hotel bathroom between friends?'

'Well… as you put it like that…'

Yet again, she was forced to wrench her gaze from his, and when she finally managed it, she noticed that their three snowball-fighting compatriots had already wandered off.

'Dropped like a hot brick,' Noah said, grinning as he spotted they'd gone too.

'Like a very cold brick in my case,' Libby said.

He shrugged. 'Girls… I've been there too many times before to get upset – they're learning fast, those three. Before long they'll be abandoning boys and breaking hearts all over the place.'

'We're not all like that,' Libby replied, the vaguest sense of annoyance creeping in to steal her good mood. Was that a dig at women in general? If he knew half of what she'd endured at the hands of a man he wouldn't be so quick to judge.

Then a thought occurred to her. Where was Rufus? She hadn't seen him since the start of the carols earlier that morning. She ought to have been relieved but instead the fact bothered her; she simply didn't trust that he could sit quietly minding his own business somewhere but she couldn't imagine what he might be doing instead, and that was what troubled her.

'At least this means ice in the drinks and music at lunch,' Noah said, breaking into her thoughts.

'I suppose it does. I might go and find the manager to see if there's any news on travel.'

'Wouldn't we find traffic updates online?'

'I don't have much battery left on my phone. I'll go and ask him – give me an excuse to check in to see if the poor guy is coping too.'

He smiled. 'Sounds like something you'd do. I'll come with you then,' he said.

She threw him a sideways look. She liked that he wanted to continue spending time with her but surely there were other people staying at the hotel that he wanted to spend time with? But it didn't seem that way, because so far today he'd pretty much stuck to her side like they were magnetised.

'Just so I can get the low-down and help you feed back to everyone,' he added, seeming to read her thoughts. 'I figured that was why you wanted the update?'

'Yeah,' she said. 'You know me – Miss Organised.'

'Don't say it like it's a bad thing. We all need a you in our lives – God knows I could do with someone to organise me a bit better at times.'

Well, that made his interest in her sound rather less sexy. He valued her organisational skills? *Wow, be still my beating heart!* She'd have taken beautiful blue eyes or charming laugh, but her ability to put together a schedule? She pushed a smile across her face to humour him.

'You'd hate me. I'd drive you mad like I used to… oh, never mind.'

Rufus used to poke fun at her rigid routines all the time, but she didn't want to think about that right now and she certainly didn't feel like sharing it.

'Libby!'

They turned as one to see Willow coming towards them.

'I've been looking for you everywhere!' she continued, sparing a quick, curious glance at Noah before turning back to her friend. Libby recognised the look and she could imagine the cogs whirring as Willow tried to work out what was going on between her and Noah, how far they'd got and how she felt about it.

'I've been outside in the snow,' she said with a self-conscious laugh. 'You couldn't tell from the state of me?'

Willow blinked. 'Like that? In your dress and shoes?'

'Yes.'

'What...? What were you thinking?'

'Oh, I don't know...' Libby shot a mischievous glance at Noah now before turning back to Willow. 'It just feels like a good day to throw caution to the wind.'

At this Noah grinned broadly. 'Doesn't it just.'

Willow said no more about it but seemed to be struggling to hold back a disapproving frown. 'OK... can I have a word now I've found you?'

Libby gave Noah an apologetic look before following Willow to a corner a few feet away.

'Rufus has been looking for you,' she began, lowering her voice. 'I thought I ought to give you fair warning because he's got that weird look on his face where he might get a bit... unpredictable.'

'Hmm,' Libby snorted. 'Let him look.'

But despite her careless tone she was suddenly gripped by anxiety. She knew that weird, unpredictable mood well enough, but why he'd be prey to it now was beyond her. Hadn't she made her feelings clear already? Why couldn't he drop it?

'I just thought...' Willow sent a wary glance towards Noah. 'Are you two...?'

'Noah and me?' Libby asked. 'Of course not!'

'Right...' Willow looked relieved. 'Only he's—'

She was cut short by Tomas hailing them.

'This is where everyone is hiding!' he shouted across the orangery. 'I was beginning to think I'd been abandoned!'

Noah stuck his hands in his pockets and sauntered over to where Tomas had now joined Libby and Willow. As Willow didn't argue,

Libby took their conversation to be over – at least for now – though she had to wonder what her best friend had been about to tell her.

'I've been in a brutal snowball fight with a gang of girls,' Noah said. 'Most of them were school age, of course…'

'Oh, the bridesmaids,' Tomas said, laughing. 'God, I bet they pasted you.'

'They did a bit – hence why we're both soaked and they're not.'

Tomas clapped him on the back. 'Well, we have the power back on now, which means I'm thinking we should have the disco we never got to have last night…' He grinned at his wife. 'Right, Will?'

'And I told you everyone will probably want their lunch and then they'll want to see if they can get home,' Willow said.

'We'll see…' Tomas was slurring his words a little and Libby was quite certain he'd carried his celebratory drinking from last night through to today. He was probably allowed, in the circumstances. If you couldn't get plastered at your wedding reception at a hotel that was snowed in and without power, then when could you?

'I've got nowhere to rush off to,' Noah said. 'If you have a disco later I'll stay for it.' He turned to Libby. 'Will you stay a while?'

'I don't think I have a choice at the moment,' Libby said, which was partly true, though she suspected if she really tried very hard she might be able to get home sooner rather than later. She wasn't going to say that though, because she hadn't really made up her mind how she felt about staying longer if it meant more time with Noah.

'Come on, my darling wife…' Tomas draped an arm around Willow's shoulder. 'Let's go and see who else we can persuade to stay.'

'But…'

They left, Willow grumbling at Tomas but clearly trying to be diplomatic in order to avoid a full argument, even though it was equally clear she wasn't entirely on board with his plans.

'That might put paid to our afternoon charades,' Libby said. 'If the disco is setting up we won't be able to use the room.'

'I'm sure we can work something out,' Noah said cheerfully. 'Where there's a will…'

'People will probably be thinking of going home too,' Libby said. 'I mean, the roads must be a bit more passable now anyway.'

'Well, if they weren't really up for our Christmas activities then we won't miss the miserable gits if they do decide to abandon us and go home. Doesn't mean we can't still make the most of the rest of the day.'

'I think we should go and see what's actually happening,' she said. 'Come on, let's find the hotel manager like we planned to and see if we can get the low-down. Knowing tipsy Tomas, he's the only person realistically expecting a disco for no other reason than he fancies a drunken boogie.'

'If I still know Tomas like I used to then that's probably true,' Noah said, laughing. 'Right then – low-down first, hoedown later!'

If the flurry of activity in the corridors and main rooms was anything to go by, it seemed news had already reached almost everyone that not only had the power returned, but there was movement on the frozen lanes out of Lovage Hall too. It was confirmed when Libby stopped a guest carrying a bulging overnight bag to ask.

'I guess it's saved us having to track down the manager,' Noah said, though he looked far from pleased about the turn of events – certainly less happy than he ought to given they'd been stranded for the last twenty-four hours or so.

'You really wanted the activities to go ahead, huh?' Libby asked.

He shrugged. 'You have to admit, being stuck was kind of fun in a way. I just thought maybe we could have squeezed a little longer out of it. And I liked having everyone around; you know, all the noise and bustle… It was a welcome distraction.'

'Yeah, I get it. I felt like it was too – certainly beats sitting in an empty flat alone on Christmas Day. But you can't blame people for wanting to go home.'

She'd mentioned her own home situation but she didn't ask about the one he'd alluded to. He'd wanted a distraction, he'd said, but he didn't say from what and it didn't escape her attention that he'd said it at all. It was a strange thing to say and certainly not the sort of thing you told someone you'd just met unless it was really playing on your mind. But she supposed that if he wanted to elaborate or share more of what was troubling him he would, and perhaps now wasn't the time to press the issue.

'Some people will stay, I expect,' she added. 'For a bit longer anyway. We could do stuff with them. Like Willow and Tomas had booked to stay over Christmas regardless of the weather keeping them here. Gene and Adrienne too. And there are bound to be others who don't want the fun to end.'

'I know, I thought… well, I thought you'd want to go home too, now that the roads are open. You kept saying how you were ill-equipped to be here and there's your family waiting for you.'

'Well, that's true, I probably did moan a bit at first. But like you I'm in no real rush, and I guess I can keep this shabby old dress on a few hours longer. I've already pissed off my parents with my no-show for Christmas dinner—'

'But that wasn't your fault!'

'Try telling them that. After the phone call I had with my mum I have no real desire to go there even though I can now. My grandma understands. When I spoke to her, I think she was more worried about the idea of me trying to get home in the snow than anything else. So she won't have any issues with me staying and we've already agreed that we'll do Christmas lunch take two on another day. I might as well have lunch here like we'd planned before the roads cleared.'

She grabbed a handful of tulle from the bottom of her dress and shook it.

'I bet you're freezing. I never thought to ask.'

She let the skirt drop. 'It's a bit wet at the bottom but your jacket kept me pretty warm. And now that we're inside my feet are thawing out a bit; I'll have to check to be sure, but I think I still have all my toes.'

He relaxed into a smile. 'The jacket suits you – it's a look.'

'Actually, I wear something very similar to this for work – it fits me a bit better, of course – so I can't see me adopting this look in my spare time, but thanks for the compliment. It's a very nice jacket too, good quality. I suppose it came from some swanky Hollywood tailor?'

'Nah, I think I picked it up from a thrift store or something when I first moved out there. I don't earn quite as much money as you think.'

'Well, it's a real find if you got it second-hand.'

'You know, the offer's still open if you want to use my suite to get dried off or have a quick shower before lunch or… you know… whatever you need. I can wait down here.'

'I don't think there's time before lunch.'

'If you're quick and you go now I reckon you could manage it. If you're as organised in your personal grooming as you are with everything else I reckon you could manage it with time to spare.'

Libby gave a light laugh. 'I suppose a shower would be quite nice. I'm not sure how I'd get my dress dry but at least I'd be clean.'

'Borrow some of my clothes.'

'They'd never fit me. And it would be... well, a bit weird. We hardly know each other.'

'I didn't know the guy who donated my suit to the thrift store but I'm still wearing it. Besides, I think we know each other pretty well by now. Nothing like a set of extreme circumstances to escalate a friendship. For what it's worth, I think you'd rock the oversized borrowed-from-the-boyfriend look... I mean,' he added hastily, 'of course, with us, you know, it's more like *borrowed from a boy who's a friend... not a boyfriend...*'

'Yes, I get what you mean,' Libby said, smiling. He was suddenly all kinds of flustered, something she hadn't seen in him before, and it was actually kind of adorable. Kind of sexy...

She shook the thought.

'Will you have enough for yourself if I borrow some?' she asked. 'I'd hate to deprive you of dry clothes.'

'Oh, don't worry about that. I can keep this on for a little longer – it really isn't that bad.'

'Your suit?' She raised an eyebrow and gave him a meaningful once-over. 'Not that bad? It looks pretty soggy to me.'

'Yeah, maybe a little, but this fabric dries quickly. But then... you can probably tell that by the feel of it, being a bit of an expert and all that.'

Libby took a lapel between her fingers and gave it a gentle rub. 'I'm not exactly an expert but yeah, you're right, it probably dries quickly. If you're sure, I can't deny I'd love to put something a bit cosier on.'

'Honestly, help yourself. Take my key and do what you need to do. I'll get the drinks in down here while I'm waiting.'

'You're so kind… what did I do to deserve you?'

Libby took the offered key card from him. The room number was printed on a slip of paper attached to it; she figured he'd probably left it on there so all the other people who'd borrowed his facilities (and she knew of a few, including the trio of torment who'd slept there, of course) would know where to go. He really had been more than generous over the last twenty-four hours, and she had to wonder how many others would be that charitable.

Leaving Noah to make his way to the bar, Libby walked to the lift. Despite saying she wanted to stay, she had to admit she was starting to feel weary now. A night struggling to sleep properly and a morning dashing about – including a mad snowball fight – had left her about ready for a nap, and the idea of having five minutes on Noah's bed was very tempting indeed. It probably wasn't cricket, especially considering he was getting drinks in and – knowing what she did already of him – would probably wait for her to return before he even considered going for lunch, even if that meant missing one or two courses. So a sleep was out of the question, but maybe a shower and a change of clothes would be enough to perk her up. It would have to be, regardless.

Just as the lift doors closed to take her up to the floor to Noah's suite, Libby noticed Rufus striding across the foyer towards her. The

doors shut before he made it and, as the car jolted into action, she
held her breath, certain he would call it back down so he could get
in with her. As far as she knew, he had no reason to go to the next
floor where the bedrooms were as he'd never hired one, so he must
have had another motive for being so hell-bent on getting to the lift,
and the only one she could think of was to give her another grilling
on what she was or wasn't currently doing and why she ought to give
him another chance.

But the lift carried on going, and as the doors opened at Noah's
floor she heaved a sigh of relief, only for it to be cut short by the sight
of Rufus coming from the stairwell, where he must have fairly bolted
to get there at the same time as her. As she stepped out and the doors
closed, he strode towards her.

'Shit,' she muttered, turning towards Noah's suite and picking
up the pace.

'I know you've seen me,' he called. 'Libby, stop, I just want to—'

'Not now!' she shouted without stopping to look back. 'I'm kind
of busy; I need to get changed before lunch.'

'Two seconds – please.'

'You won't get much said in two seconds. Talk to me later – after
we've eaten.'

'You'll go missing again.'

'I won't.'

'I don't believe you.'

'Rufus, this is ridiculous…'

She stopped at a door, checked the number attached to the key
card and lifted it to swipe.

'Libby, isn't that…?'

'Don't you have a girl to chat up somewhere?'

'Isn't that *his* room?'

This time she turned to face him, the card at the door but not yet activated.

'What's *wrong* with you?' she asked incredulously.

'Wrong with me? What's wrong with you?'

'I'm not the one obsessing about a man I barely know – and who doesn't deserve your borderline stalking – just because I'm not big enough to accept that I screwed things up with the woman who would have married me. So what if this is Noah's room, Rufus? It's none of your business if it is, and, quite frankly, your behaviour at the moment is so many levels of wrong. You shouldn't know this is his room unless you've been doing some seriously inappropriate digging. And don't tell me you just happened to see him go in one time because I know you've had absolutely no reason to come up here other than to spy on him.'

Rufus shrugged, and if anything, looked slightly vindicated. 'Actually, I have. He let me use his sink for a wash after breakfast.'

She let out a sigh. Of course Noah would have offered to help Rufus out. Big-hearted, guileless, trusting Noah. The more she saw of him, the more she saw a man who was open and generous – he would have done the same for anyone. He wasn't to know there was a real past between her and Rufus; he no doubt just thought he was doing Libby's *old friend* a favour. And even if he had, he'd probably have helped Rufus out anyway. It would also explain where Rufus had got to when Libby hadn't seen him for a while – Willow did say she thought he'd gone to use someone's room. Of course it would be bloody Noah's.

She had to wonder how much Rufus might have told him about their past when they'd had their brief chat at the bar the night before. What if Noah actually did know the truth but hadn't mentioned it to Libby out of respect for her privacy? Was he waiting for her to say something? Maybe he didn't think he needed to know, because maybe he wasn't as into her as she thought.

Whether or not Rufus had told Noah the truth about their past, she wasn't about to give her ex the satisfaction of knowing she cared, so she didn't ask.

'Yes,' she said coldly. 'He's nice like that, and that's what I'm doing now, grabbing a quick shower, so if you don't mind…'

'Lib, just one more minute—'

'For God's sake! Don't you have a home to go to? The roads are open now so you can bugger off and leave me alone!'

'I know they are, I just—'

Libby flicked the card at the reader and the door clicked to unlock.

'Bye, Rufus,' she said shortly, stepping in and allowing the door to slam shut behind her.

A second later he knocked.

'Come on, Lib! I just want to talk! Is that really too much to ask?'

'That's just the problem!' she shouted back through the door. 'It's always about what you want – it always has been. You did all the talking and I was supposed to do the listening. It never occurred to you that I was hurting, that I was struggling, and instead of being patient you looked elsewhere for the attention you constantly crave. Well, Rufus, you reap what you sow and I don't do reruns so, if you don't mind, I'm going to get my shower and you can bog off!'

'But, Libby!'

She marched to the dressing table and picked up the TV remote, switching on the set and cranking up the volume as high as it would go. There was a Christmas cartoon on, something she'd seen years before as a kid. It didn't matter what was showing, only that the noise drowned out Rufus's voice, but she couldn't help staring at the screen for a moment as a flood of childhood memories carried her away.

Suddenly, she was transported, sitting on her grandpa's lap with a bag of sweets from a gift she'd opened earlier that morning, snuggled against his broad, comforting chest as she watched the lonely little reindeer's adventure unfold until he became Santa's most important helper. Grandpa had been dead for ten years, but his scent came back to her now, as clear as if he was in the room. Little Libby would have been transfixed, munching solemnly with wide eyes, learning the lesson, without even realising, that the most insignificant person matters. It was a lesson easy to learn in childhood but much harder to cling on to as the rough winds of adulthood did their best to shake every bit of confidence loose.

She sniffed back a tear as she sat on the bed, mesmerised as the story continued to unfold.

But then another hammering at the door pulled her from the memories and reminded her she had things to do. Rallying, she went to the bathroom and switched on the shower. Luckily the hotel had free toiletries in every room, otherwise she'd have been forced to used Noah's uber-manly stuff.

Letting her sodden dress drop to the floor, the music of the old cartoon still playing in the other room in her ears, she stepped into the warm jets of the shower and felt instantly better.

Chapter Twelve

Noah's clothes were hanging in the wardrobe. Just a pair of jeans and a couple of sweatshirts – all too big for her, of course, but with the jeans pulled in with a belt and rolled up at the legs, and the sweatshirt arms folded, Libby felt as if she was wearing her cosiest, comfiest loungewear. It was a bonus that they smelt like Noah too (though she tried not to think of it because it was *very* distracting), in that peculiar way that all clothes, even freshly washed, seemed to smell like their owner. And the owner of these particular clothes smelt very good indeed.

She held a sleeve up to her nose and breathed deeply, allowing a little thrill to run down her spine. Try as she might, she couldn't deny the ever-growing attraction and certainly couldn't fight it. It would be wise to try, she kept reminding herself, because there was a lot she didn't know about him and a lot she couldn't trust. Of course, he was lovely and kind and fun to be around and she wanted to trust him, and maybe she could, but she couldn't quite believe it. When she really thought about it though, perhaps the problem stemmed from Rufus rather than Noah himself. Her ex had done enough damage to make her feel she'd never trust a man again, even the most open and transparent of them – which Noah, generous and charming as he was, was not.

She hung the hairdryer back on the peg provided at the dresser and shook out her clean hair, then gave herself a once-over in the mirror.

She looked like a jumble sale reject but there was no finer feeling than that of being freshly showered after a long night. She'd left her wet gown on the bathroom floor, uncertain what else to do with it, and was just about to bundle it up to take downstairs with her when there was a knock at the door.

She let out a long, impatient sigh. Didn't that man ever give up? How long had Rufus been out there? She'd been in the shower for at least ten minutes, so it had to be as long as that. What had he done – sat on the floor of the corridor like a homeless puppy? Well, if he thought she was going to feel guilty, or that it might soften her stance on letting him speak, he was in for a shock.

'Libby? I just thought I'd pop up to see how you were getting on… and to confess I drank your gin because you didn't come down and the ice was melting… Sorry about that. How's it going? Found everything you need?'

Libby rushed to the door and yanked it open to find Noah grinning at the other side.

'I'm so sorry – I didn't realise I'd been so long!'

'Don't apologise,' he said amiably, glancing down at her change of clothes. 'They look good on you – better than they do on me.'

'I doubt that, but thank you. I do feel a little bit like a toddler playing dress-up in her dad's clothes though.'

He raised his eyebrows. 'Are you saying my taste in clothes is dad-like?'

'Oh.' Libby laughed. 'That came out very wrong, didn't it? I just meant because everything is rolled up and folded back to fit.'

'I think it works. In LA you'd be starting a new trend if you stepped out in it – they love a trailblazer out there.'

'Really? Well it's the first time I've been called a trailblazer.'

Noah smiled. 'So… I think lunch is almost ready. Lots of guests have decided to leave, I'm afraid, so we're a bit thinner on the ground than we were…'

'It's disappointing but it can't be helped.' She rallied a bit of cheer for him, because it seemed to her that even though she'd said she was disappointed, he was feeling that particular emotion a lot more. 'At least the most fun people are still here, eh? And more lunch for us.'

'Can't argue with more food. So if you're ready, shall we go down?'

She was ready, but there was sudden hesitation. Clearly Rufus hadn't been hanging around outside the suite when Noah had come up to fetch her, but she wanted to know if he'd left the hotel like so many others had. She got the feeling the answer to that question would be a frustrating negative because Rufus had never made her life easy – not while they were together and certainly not since they'd parted. She almost didn't dare step into the corridor in case he was lurking out there, but without telling Noah any of this she'd have to, and she wasn't going to tell him because it probably sounded a bit nuts.

Taking her hesitation to mean she wasn't ready, Noah frowned slightly. 'I could give you a few more minutes? I could wait downstairs if you're not finished.'

Libby shook herself. 'No, no… I'm good to go. I was just wondering what to do with my damp dress.'

'You could hang it in here; collect it before you leave later?'

She nodded. 'That's a good idea if you don't mind me doing that. It makes sense; I'll have to change back into it later anyway so you can have your clothes back, so if it's alright me using your suite again to do that…'

'Of course! Although, there's really no rush for the clothes if you wanted to wear them home.'

'But I won't see you again after today... how will I get them back to you?'

He shrugged. 'I guess...' There was a pause, and then another shrug. 'It doesn't matter. Let's figure it out later. Lunch first; I'm starving and I can't problem-solve on an empty stomach.'

'Actually, I'm ravenous now too.' Libby hung her dress over the towel rail in the bathroom before joining him in the main room. 'It'll have to do in there for now, and if it doesn't dry before home time I'll just have to suffer for the drive back. So I'm ready when you are.'

She followed him out into the corridor, the suite door swinging closed behind her with a heavy clunk. Glancing up and down and seeing no Rufus, she felt immediately easier.

'Oh, your key,' she said, handing it back to him. 'Thank you again for all this.'

'No problem.'

The jeans she was wearing bagged around her thighs, and the heavy rustle of the fabric echoed around the silent corridor as they walked side by side. Noah had said she looked good, but he was definitely being kind to make her feel better because good wasn't the word she'd use. Odd was more like it – her huge clothes finished off with dainty (and expensive) sandals and still-damp, untouched-by-product hair made her feel like a homeless lady who'd lucked out with a clothing find in a posh dumpster.

Noah walked close, perhaps closer than was appropriate for two relative strangers to be, but she didn't mind. In fact, she itched to be closer still, and when he looked down and gave her a vague smile at the lifts it was all she could do not to grab him for a kiss. She'd always prided herself on her logic and self-control and the fact she didn't do erratic emotions, but this never-ending wedding reception was unravelling that. Whether it was simply having Noah around, she didn't know, but strange things were happening to her. She was doing things she'd never normally do, like singing in public, snowball fighting in a silk dress, showering in a stranger's room. It was almost as if being here in Lovage Hall was like some kind of bubble of alternate universe where the normal rules didn't apply and Libby could do whatever she wanted without consequence. But, of course, that wasn't real, despite feeling like it, and actions did have consequences, and no matter how this strange two days made her want to throw common sense out of the window and take a chance on this incredibly attractive, magnetic, charming and funny man, she had to remember that.

She made those last warning thoughts her mantra as they stepped into the lift together, where they were gifted total privacy and a few torturous moments during which she couldn't get the idea of them kissing in there out of her head. Lucky for her, Noah broke the spell by wondering aloud at the possibility of pigs in blankets at lunch, which made her laugh self-consciously. She really needed to get control because clearly, if he was pontificating about tiny sausages, he wasn't thinking about kissing at all.

As the lift hit the ground floor and the doors opened, they were greeted by the smell of roasted vegetables and meat wafting in from the grand hall and Libby's stomach started to gurgle. It was quite nice to be taunted by a different kind of craving, one she definitely could satisfy without consequence. She'd eaten plenty at breakfast and ordinarily wouldn't be hungry again for most of the day, but being so busy all morning and running about in the snow like a big child, she'd worked up an appetite.

'God that smells good!' Noah stuck his nose in the air and breathed in. 'I hate to say it, but I think this is going to be so much better than what I would have had at my parents'. And if you ever meet my mum, please don't tell her I said that!'

Libby shot a sideways glance his way and he laughed.

'Even my mum knows she's not the best cook. Dad sometimes takes on Christmas lunch, but let's just say he's no Jamie Oliver either.'

'Well, as I'm very unlikely to meet your mum or your dad I think your secret is probably safe.'

'You're a pal.' He grinned down at her and they began to make their way to the dining area.

'My dad's a pretty good cook actually,' Libby said, more to distract herself from the fact she was thinking about kissing again than because she wanted to discuss her father's culinary merits. 'Mum, not so much. If I hit a lucky year, Dad will be cooking; any other time I just grin and bear it. Although, saying that… we were supposed to have goose today. Dad's bright idea apparently.'

'Goose? Pushing the boat out, eh? Who's your dad, Charles Dickens?'

'Very funny.'

'So you're not going to be missing the food today?'

'I'm really not sure about the goose. I might be missing Dad's epic roast potatoes but I have to admit to being quite happy about also missing the lecturing that usually comes with them. I can't remember the last time we sat down for a meal together and my mum didn't use it as an opportunity to tell me everything she thinks I'm getting wrong in my life. She means well, of course, but…'

'Oh, I get that too,' Noah said, and for some reason his tone had suddenly taken on a darker hue. 'My mum's never met a piece of unwelcome life advice she didn't want to offer up to me.'

'Parents, eh?' she said cheerily, trying to lighten the mood again. 'I wonder if that ever changes, or maybe they're still lecturing you when you're old and grey?'

'Mine will be – it's her favourite hobby so there's no way she'd give it up.'

She glanced up at him again. 'Are you sure we don't have the same mum? I don't know about any secret adopted brother but you're painting a startling picture of the same woman here.'

'God, I hope not!' he said, and Libby was glad to hear humour in his voice again. 'Because if there was any possibility of that, the things I'm thinking about would be very wrong... Hey, Tomas!'

Libby looked across the foyer to see Willow's new husband staggering towards them.

'Hey, you two!' he boomed. 'Merry Christmas!'

'Merry is certainly the word for your Christmas so far,' Libby said, laughing. 'Have you actually stopped drinking since yesterday?'

'Of course!' Tomas winked. 'When I was asleep last night. So that's... maybe about three hours...'

'Such restraint,' Libby said wryly.

'I know,' he replied with a grin. 'Dinner's ready!'

'Good, at least some food ought to sober you up.'

'Aw, come on... it's Christmas! And my wedding! I'm allowed to be drunk before lunch today!'

Noah shrugged at Libby. 'We can't really argue with that. While we're on the subject of drinking, want something from the bar to take to lunch, seeing as I drank yours earlier?'

'That's OK,' she said. 'I'm sure there will be wine at the table.'

'Fair enough.'

'I'll have one if you're offering,' Tomas said.

Noah grinned at him. 'Later for you, my friend. First of all, concentrate on getting to the dining table, then we'll talk more drinks.'

Noah got sidetracked by the same old uni buddies who had taken him from Libby the night before and ended up on their table for lunch, while Willow, Tomas, Gene and Adrienne demanded that Libby come sit with them. Much as she wanted to argue otherwise – she was disappointed to be separated from Noah, having been looking forward to having lunch in his company – she supposed she'd just have to deal with it. At least it would shut Rufus up for a while – he was, annoyingly, still at the hotel, as clingy and persistent as a bogey hanging from a toddler's nose. What was his game? He really had no reason at all to be there now, although it was almost worth the annoyance just to see the look on his face when he clocked her wearing Noah's clothes.

Willow's reaction to that, however, wasn't nearly as satisfying.

'What the hell have you got on?' she asked as Libby sat down.

'Clothes,' Libby said. 'And thanks for making me feel super confident about my appearance.'

Willow's face fell. 'Oh no, I'm sorry, I didn't mean... It's just that you're always so smartly turned out – you never wear anything that doesn't fit perfectly.'

'Well, that's partly an occupational hazard. Just because I have to be smart for most of the time doesn't mean I can't do fast and loose when I want to.'

'You got the loose bit right,' Willow said, trying not to grin.

'And again, thanks for the confidence boost,' Libby said, rolling her eyes.

'Sorry,' Willow said, straightening her face again. 'I told you to borrow something of mine.'

'Your stuff doesn't fit me.'

'And that does? I'm sure I would have been able to find something that would have been closer to your size.'

'Well, I wasn't planning to change at all, but the opportunity was just there and I seized it. I'm allowed to be less than perfectly turned out every now and again, aren't I?'

'Hey, on a day like today you're allowed to do anything you want.' Tomas leant in with a beery grin. 'I think it looks cute.'

'*Thank you, Tomas*,' Libby said very deliberately. 'Thank you for giving me such a lovely compliment.'

'Where did you get it from?' Willow asked.

'Um… Noah lent it to me.'

Willow paused. 'Noah?' she asked finally. 'Oh, right…'

Libby waited, sensing there was more to come on that subject. She was ready with the reply that she was a grown woman who knew perfectly well what she was doing, and that actually it was nothing anyway and why couldn't she borrow clothes from a well-meaning friend, and she was most definitely not falling for a guy she'd just met and knew nothing about, and especially not right under her very needy ex's nose. But she never got to say any of that because a cheer went up as the food started to arrive at the tables and the newly restored power allowed for the sound system to start playing Christmas songs. Whatever lecture Willow had in store – and Libby's affronted reply – would have to wait.

'Oh man, I can't wait for the turkey!' Tomas sighed.

'You've got starters first,' Willow said. 'You'll have to hang on for your favourite bit.'

'Aww…'

'Idiot,' Willow said, but she was half laughing.

'Correct, darling wife,' Tomas said cheerfully, 'an idiot who is so grateful you were charitable enough to marry me so you can make sure me being an idiot doesn't end in tears.'

Willow rolled her eyes and Libby smiled at them.

'I'm very hungry myself,' Libby said, 'and I am looking forward to turkey cooked how it's meant to be.'

Willow laughed. 'I won't tell your mum you said that.'

Libby grinned. 'You wouldn't dare.'

'That's true,' Willow readily agreed. 'She'd have no issue with shooting the messenger.'

Libby went for the melon to start with. The hotel had smoked salmon pâté on the menu, but everyone was avoiding it because, even though they'd been assured the fridges were top-notch, very efficient, and had stayed relatively cold for the duration of their power cut, it didn't seem a very good idea to risk fish.

Despite this, nobody avoided the turkey, even though it had been stored in the same fridges. No matter what else was on offer, for Libby and for everyone else, it seemed, Christmas lunch was all about the turkey, a fact she and Tomas agreed quite vocally on. And surely the hotel wouldn't serve it if there was any danger of it being unsafe? So she put her worries behind her and decided to go for it.

While the plates came round, she chanced a glance at Noah, who was seated a few tables away with his old friends. He was laughing at something one of them had said, and, try as she might to fight it, there was a tingle of anticipation that had nothing to do with the imminent arrival of her food. She'd be having a word with the universe too, for forcing him to sit elsewhere and depriving her of the pleasure of his company for the next hour or more.

She realised she'd been staring for some time only when Willow tapped her on the arm to say something, and, as she turned back to her friend, Rufus caught her eye. He looked quickly away, and it was obvious that while she'd been watching Noah, he'd been watching her.

Why couldn't that man just bugger off? What she wouldn't give for a voodoo doll and a pack of pins right now. Still, she didn't have to let him ruin her day. Perhaps the only power he really had over her was what she let him have. Perhaps if she didn't allow herself to care what he was doing it would be enough to disarm the threat. She could choose to ignore him and surely that would do. If he was trying to win her over, all he was doing was driving her away. Yesterday, she'd felt she might crumble if he got a moment alone to talk her round, but today she felt much more stoic about it. It was strange how a bit of stalking could do that to you.

'How long do you think you'll stay?' Willow asked.

'Here?' Libby replied, tearing her gaze from Rufus. 'I don't know. I guess it depends on what's happening here and whether the hotel asks us to leave; we've probably already outstayed our welcome.'

'The manager did say people could spend as long here as they wanted. I mean, with a captive audience they're probably making more money at the bar than they would on a normal Christmas Day for a start. I don't see why they'd be keen to get rid of us.'

'Maybe, but that was before the roads reopened and the snow stopped. I certainly couldn't stay another night.'

'But you could stay for the disco?'

'You mean the replacement that Tomas is determined we're going to have? Will anyone be here for that? Will it be worth the hotel putting it on?'

'I've asked them and they said yes. I think Tomas might have a point and we should have it regardless of who is still here. It's not every day you get the opportunity of a great big hall to jump about in and a decent sound system. I mean, I didn't get a proper party yesterday and it is my wedding after all, and doesn't a bride get what she wants?'

'I can't argue with that, but it might be a bit of a tumbleweed moment if everyone's gone.'

'As long as the most important people stay I won't care.'

'Like who?'

Willow laughed. 'You, silly! You're the only person I need here... apart from Tomas, of course. We have a duty to relive our wild youth on the dance floor one last time before I turn into an old married woman.'

'I think you're mixing me up with your more exciting friends,' Libby said. 'I'm pretty sure I was never wild – on the dance floor or otherwise.'

'Oh, I wouldn't say that. We definitely had our moments. Say you'll stay. For a while at least.'

Gene leant over. 'Sorry to butt in, but we'll make sure you get home safe if you do stay,' he said.

'Thanks, Gene,' Libby replied. 'That's kind of you.'

'Well, we'd never let our favourite honorary daughter get into trouble, would we?'

'Honorary daughter?' Libby asked, flushing with pride.

'Absolutely!' Gene smiled. 'Have we never told you that before?'

'No, but I like it.'

'OK, so now you know. And as my actual daughter has now flown the nest, feel free to move in and take the job on full-time.'

Libby laughed. 'Oh, right, thanks. And what would my duties be?'

'Well, using the current job description as a guide, you'll mainly be there to argue with me and spend all my money.'

'Hey!' Willow squeaked, and Gene chuckled.

'You know I'm only joking.'

'Do I?' Willow scolded.

'Your dad's had too much to drink already,' Adrienne cut in. 'Ignore anything and everything he says.'

'Turkey, madam?'

Libby looked up to see the servers had reached their table. There was a hostess trolley laden with platters and tureens containing meat; roast, boiled and mashed potatoes; vegetables; stuffing; tiny sausages – which Libby reflected would make Noah very happy – and just about every other accoutrement you could associate with a decent Christmas lunch. She was impressed with the spread considering the obstacles the hotel had faced producing it. She was impressed with the fact there was anything on offer at all.

'It all looks lovely,' she said. 'Yes please.'

'And the sides, madam? What would you like?'

'Oh everything! No need to go through the list with me!'

The waitress smiled as she started to deposit a portion of everything onto Libby's plate. Then she moved on to serve Willow, leaving Libby to tuck in. It was every bit as good as it looked – the meat moist, the vegetables herby and cooked to a perfect al dente, the roast potatoes crisp and golden on the outside and fluffy in the middle. It would have been good anyway, but the fact she'd worked up quite an appetite made it ten times more delicious. In fact, Libby couldn't remember the last time she'd eaten a Christmas lunch this tasty.

Because there were a lot of guests to get round (Libby had heard someone saying they were a little short-staffed too), and waiting for service to be finished would mean the first plated meals going cold, everyone started to eat as soon as they got theirs, so although the waiters were still doing the rounds, the hall was now filled with the clanking of cutlery on china and satisfied exclamations about the food.

One by one as they got their meals, everyone on Libby's table stopped talking and got stuck in. She took the opportunity to glance across to where Noah was still talking to his friends, only this time she took care not to let her gaze pan around as far as Rufus. Despite this, she was somehow certain that he was looking at her anyway. What was he hoping to achieve? Surely he'd realised by this point he really wasn't wanted. Couldn't he see that the best thing to do now was go home? The roads were clear – what was he waiting for?

As these thoughts ran through her head, she became aware of someone approaching their table.

She looked up and Santiago smiled at her, a sort of secret, more-than-professional smile that told Libby he hadn't forgotten their flirting the day before.

The funny thing was, now that she looked properly, though he was still very obviously handsome, his finely balanced, close-to-perfect features weren't having quite the same effect on her as they had then. She could still appreciate his beauty, but for some reason she wasn't moved by it now.

'Wine for you?' he asked.

She held up her glass. 'Thank you.'

Willow leant in as soon as he was out of earshot. 'He totally fancies you, Lib! Whatever perfume you're wearing today is seriously working hard for you. Is there a guy in this room who doesn't fancy you?'

Libby blushed and waved away the compliment. 'Santiago?'

'Santiago! Jeez, you even know him by name! You're a dark horse!'

'There was a bit of flirting going on yesterday... harmless fun, that's all.'

'Please tell me you're going to get his number – he's an absolute god!'

Libby sipped at her wine. It was crisp and sort of peachy but very good. 'Maybe. Aren't the good-looking ones always trouble though?'

Willow laughed. 'With a man that fit I think the trouble might be worth the reward. He's gorgeous and clearly into you – I'd say go for it and see what happens.'

'Hmm...' Libby said vaguely.

Without realising it, her gaze travelled the room until it found Noah again. He was engrossed in an animated conversation, laughing loudly, hands flapping. His lunch was in front of him but, despite saying he was hungry earlier, he'd stopped eating – presumably to get a very important point across using the full, unencumbered movement of his arms. He looked as if he might be a little tipsy too. The wine had been flowing freely during the meal and Libby was feeling the effects of it herself, and she'd been pacing her intake. Noah probably hadn't been pacing himself quite so cautiously, as evidenced by him drinking the gin he'd ordered for her earlier while she'd been using his shower. She didn't blame him really – he had no plans to be anywhere in a hurry, after all. None of them had, she supposed.

'Lib...'

She turned to see Willow studying her. 'There's something you need to know about—'

'Yes,' Libby cut in, unreasonable irritation coming from nowhere and impossible to keep from her voice, even though later she'd regret it. 'I know I can't trust him. There are things about his life back home he doesn't mention that he's probably hiding... I already worked that out for myself.'

'But, Libby—'

'You don't need to worry; I won't get involved. I'm not stupid enough to do that again. But out of interest, what makes you think our hot waiter is a safer bet? You're all over that one. We don't know him from Adam either; what makes you think he's any better than Noah for me?'

Willow frowned. 'I never said the waiter was a safe bet; I just said he was good-looking. How should I know? But Noah...' She paused. 'I do know he's—'

Her words were stolen by a loud crash. Everyone turned to find the source of the noise, and then there was a collective gasp. One of the waitresses had passed out, falling to the floor and taking a stack of plates with her. She was out cold, surrounded by food and broken china.

'Oh my God!' Willow clapped a hand to her mouth. A second later she and Libby had leapt from their seats, quickly followed by a dozen or so others. They all swarmed to aid the girl.

'Does anyone know who the first-aider is?' Willow asked frantically.

Libby bent over the waitress. 'I know a bit,' she said. 'I'm rusty – it's been a while since I used it but I could try.'

'The manager is the first-aid marshal,' Santiago said urgently. 'I will get him.'

He pushed through the crowd and sprinted away, and then a new voice shouted up.

'I'm fully trained!'

Libby looked up as he made his way through the guests gathered in a loose circle around her and the unconscious waitress. Of course he knew first aid – was there anything this man couldn't do? She was thankful, of course, for having been saved from displaying her own muddled efforts, and also for the fact that he suddenly looked a lot more sober than he had a few minutes ago.

'Thanks, Noah,' Willow said with a tight smile of relief. She began to move some of the broken crockery and food so he would have room to work and they could make the girl more comfortable and definitely safer. The good news was she was beginning to stir already too, which Libby thought had to be a positive. Maybe it would turn out to be a passing fit that wouldn't require much intervention – at least she very much hoped so because there had been quite enough drama during this everlasting wedding reception already.

'Come on, folks… let's move back and give them some space,' Gene said. Some people had already drifted back to their tables, looking on with concern but obviously glad to hand over responsibility, but some stubbornly remained, determined to do their bit, including, Libby couldn't help but note with some annoyance, Rufus. He had a genuine motive, she kept telling herself – he only wanted to help in a crisis, but as well as that she was beginning to wonder how quickly someone could get a court injunction, because right now he was like a third arm.

'Is there anything I can do?' he asked.

'I think we've got it covered, thanks,' Noah said. The exchange was good-natured enough on his part, even if it wasn't quite so guileless on Rufus's.

The girl on the ground began to open her eyes and tried to sit up.

'Steady,' Noah said gently, catching her.

'Oh... how embarrassing,' she said weakly.

'Nobody is thinking that,' Libby said. 'Everyone gets ill – it's not your fault.'

'What matters is you're OK,' Noah said.

The girl gave her head the tiniest shake. 'I used to have fainting fits when I was young but it hasn't happened for years.'

'It's alright,' Noah said.

It was then she seemed to notice the mess around her. 'Oh God... I didn't have time to put anything down and by the time I realised I was going to hit the deck—'

'It's only stuff,' Noah said. 'Nobody cares about a few old plates, only that you're OK. Did you hurt yourself?'

'I don't think...'

This time she pushed herself from Noah's support to sit by herself. Libby put a hand to her back to help ease her up.

'I don't think so,' the girl said. 'Maybe a few bruises, but I don't think there's anything else.'

'You should check for concussion,' Rufus said to Noah.

'I didn't hit my head,' the waitress said.

'Still,' Rufus insisted. 'I didn't see you go down and you couldn't really know if you hit your head or not.'

'It doesn't feel as if I did. Not hard anyway.'

'But I think—'

'She says she didn't hit her head!' Libby repeated, trying not to make her warning glance at Rufus obvious to anyone else. She turned back to the girl. 'You should sit quietly for a while... away from everyone. Have a glass of water, catch your breath. And then you should go home. The roads are open again so you should be able to get through.'

'But I haven't finished my shift.'

'You shouldn't be working if you're not well,' Libby said sternly. She turned to Noah. 'Give me a hand…'

He might have had his own thoughts on it, but he kept them to himself and seemed perfectly content to help Libby getting the waitress to stand. Between them, taking an arm at either side, they supported her as they walked her out of the dining room.

'Is there somewhere nearby that's suitable?' Libby asked as she glanced behind for a second to see Rufus looking faintly annoyed. At what she didn't know and didn't care, but presumably it had something to do with her departure and his exclusion from the proceedings. He always did want to be the most important person in the room – it was just another of his less attractive traits – so he'd have hated being surplus to requirements in this case.

'There's a staff area next to the manager's office where we keep our stuff,' the waitress said. 'But it's alright – you needn't come with me.'

'We'd rather,' Noah said. 'I'm sure Libby would agree – we'd rather see for ourselves that you're alright.'

The hotel manager met them in the corridor.

'What happened?' he asked urgently.

Libby had to feel sorry for him at that moment – if she felt as if she looked a little worse for wear after being stuck there all night, he looked positively frazzled. She could see why – he must have been under a lot of pressure in one way or another since yesterday and this was probably the last thing he needed on top of making certain his guests were all looked after.

'She fainted,' Libby said.

'I'm sorry,' the waitress put in. 'I'm alright now but…'

The manager's frown became a look of worry. 'Are you hurt?'

'No,' the waitress replied. 'I'm fine but I made a bit of a mess in the dining room.'

'Oh... Right... then I'd better get someone to sort that...'

'We'll take care of...' Noah gave the girl an apologetic look. 'I'm so sorry, I didn't ask your name.'

'Josie,' the girl said.

'Pleased to make your acquaintance, Josie. I'm Noah and this is my new best friend, Libby.'

Josie gave them a weak smile and then Noah turned back to the manager.

'We can look after Josie for a while if you want to get things under control in the dining room.'

'Oh, I couldn't—' Josie began, but Libby cut in.

'It's fine,' she said. 'We want to help.' She looked at the manager. 'You've got your hands full and, speaking as a manager myself, I know how stressful these situations can be. Your instinct is to make sure your staff member is OK, but you'll be worrying about complaints from your guests. Leave Josie with us; it's not a problem at all.'

The manager paused, but then after a moment's consideration he nodded. 'Thank you. I'll try to be as quick as I can.'

They watched for a second as he strode off and then they returned to their own task.

'Thank you,' Josie said. 'This is so kind of you both. The room's just here...' They stopped at an inconspicuous-looking door. 'There's a code; I'd better just punch it in.'

Libby turned away as Josie keyed in the number – mostly because she didn't want Josie to worry she'd given away access to their personal staffroom. She was gratified to see Noah had the sense to do the same. Then they followed her in.

By now Josie was recovering well and she didn't need their help walking, but Libby still didn't trust the situation enough to leave her alone, and she suspected Noah felt the same. The room was cramped and dingy, more like a store cupboard really, with a tiny barred window, room enough for a few threadbare chairs, a sink and a shelf full of mugs and a row of lockers. It was a far cry from the grandeur of the rest of Lovage Hall. Libby vaguely wondered what purpose this room had served during Lovage Hall's heyday. A scullery, perhaps? Some kind of walk-in larder or meat safe?

Libby rinsed a mug from the shelf and filled it with cold water before handing it to Josie, who took it with a grateful smile and settled on a chair.

'Thank you,' she said. 'I feel just awful having you both look after me like this.'

'You've been looking after us for two days straight,' Noah said.

Josie took a sip of her water. 'Yes, but I get paid for it.'

'I think it's been above and beyond your pay grade though,' Libby said. 'All of the staff here have been amazing. I'll bet you should have been at home today, not here skivvying for us.'

'Well, I should have been having dinner with my boyfriend and his little boy… he has an eight-year-old from a previous relationship… But when the weather turned, I thought, I'm stuck anyway so I might as well work. We all did and there was plenty to do – kept us from thinking too much about what we were missing at home.'

'I bet your boyfriend wasn't too happy,' Noah said.

Josie shook her head ruefully. 'He wasn't. But he understood there was nothing else we could do. We'll just have to have our Christmas Day tomorrow instead.'

Noah smiled. 'Good for you. Glad to see you haven't given up on your plans.'

'I guess we'll all be doing that with the people we were meant to see today,' Libby said.

'Some of us,' Noah said.

Libby glanced at him, sensing there was more to that statement – something he didn't want to say.

'Did you have plans then?' Josie asked.

'Dinner with my parents,' Libby said.

'Same here,' Noah said.

'Oh, that's good,' Josie said. 'I mean, not good, of course, but at least you're not ditching spouses or children or anything. So I suppose that's better, isn't it?'

'No, nothing like that,' Noah said.

'Me neither,' Libby said, smiling. 'In fact, I've quite enjoyed being stuck here in a strange sort of way.'

'To be honest, so have I,' Noah said warmly, and for the briefest moment, as Libby looked up to meet his gaze, she found herself trapped in it.

She reminded herself she'd promised Willow she wouldn't do anything silly for a reason she had yet to discover, but one her friend clearly thought she needed to know and would have divulged had they not been interrupted. She half wondered whether she ought to ask Noah himself. But would he admit to anything, or even see whatever it was as something worth worrying about? Plus, Libby would have to find a moment to do that and a diplomatic way to ask without causing offence. It all seemed like a bit of a minefield really and, as they'd be going their separate ways later that evening, was it even worth the bother?

Pushing the matter from her thoughts, she focused her concentration where it was needed once more – on Josie.

'How are you feeling now? Better?'

'Much,' Josie said. 'The thing about these silly fainting fits was that I never felt ill for long; I used to just keel over all of a sudden and then I'd recover really quickly. It used to be linked to my hormones – so the doctors told me – and I haven't had anything like it since I was about eighteen or nineteen, so that's like… about seven years ago at least.'

'It is weird you've had one after all these years then,' Libby said thoughtfully. 'Hormones, you say?'

'Yes, I—'

Josie stopped dead and stared at Libby. 'Oh…' she said quietly.

'What's wrong?'

'Well, my boyfriend and I, we… well, he has his little boy with his ex, but we wanted our own and we'd just decided to try. But surely we wouldn't…? Not that quickly? I mean, we literally just made our minds up a couple of weeks ago and with me doing shifts there hasn't been a lot of time for… well, for us to be together.'

Libby broke into a slow smile. 'You might be pregnant? If that's the case then that's wonderful! Even more reason to take the best care of yourself though.'

She wanted to add how she ought to know that better than anyone and how she wished someone had persuaded her to take it easier, and how she might have been married and a mother herself about now, but that wouldn't be fair to Josie. This was her life, her moment of joy, after all, and so Libby kept it to herself.

'So nobody knows?' Noah asked.

'Even I don't know for sure!' Josie gave a shaky laugh. 'So how could I tell anyone else?'

'Maybe your first stop when the shops open again should be to buy a test,' Libby said. 'Then you may well have the answer to today's mystery fainting episode and you'll be able to make plans for your pregnancy.'

'*Possible* pregnancy,' Josie corrected. 'I still can't quite believe we'd have managed it that fast.'

Libby smiled. 'Yes, of course. But it will be a pretty cool Christmas present if it's true, eh?'

'God, yes!' Josie said, though she looked a little shell-shocked by the idea. Or perhaps she was still recovering from her recent swoon – it was hard to tell.

There was a knock at the door and then it opened to reveal Santiago. He took a moment, glancing between Libby and Noah, and then looked at Josie.

'What happened?' he asked her.

'Oh, it was nothing really,' she said.

'Nothing?' he asked incredulously.

'I'm fine, really, Ti. Five minutes' sit-down and I'll be good to go—'

'Um, I hope that sentence was going to end with the word home,' Noah chided like an old mother hen. 'You told us you'd go home, remember? And' – he raised his eyebrows and gave her a meaningful look – 'after what you've also just told us you should be going home to rest, even if I have to carry you there myself.'

'But really, I'm fine.'

'Noah's right,' Libby said.

'I think so too,' Santiago said. 'You look pale, Josie.'

Josie gave a vague frown, but then let out a weary sigh. 'Right. I suppose I can talk to Manny to make sure that's OK and then call a cab.'

'I'll tell Manny,' Santiago said. 'He already told me he was expecting you to go home so it will be fine. Phone your taxi – you may have a little wait anyway.'

'Manny's the manager?' Noah asked, and Santiago nodded. 'In that case I'll have a word to be certain there are no issues; he can hardly argue the toss with a paying guest, can he?'

'Oh, please don't do that,' Josie said. 'I can talk to him and I'm sure it will be alright anyway.'

Santiago sat next to his colleague and looked up at Libby and Noah. 'I can stay with her now. Please return to your meal or it will be over.'

'OK,' Libby said. 'If you're sure…'

'I am,' Josie replied. 'Thank you so much.'

'We'll be phoning the hotel,' Noah said. 'We want to know the news when you do.'

Josie gave a little laugh. 'OK. You can do that but there may be nothing to tell.'

Noah smiled. 'I hope there is.'

'Me too,' Libby agreed. 'Take care of yourself and go home as soon as you can.'

'I will,' Josie said.

Noah opened the door and allowed Libby to go through first before following her out into the corridor.

'Well, that was a fun little distraction,' he said wryly.

'I hope she's going to be alright,' Libby said.

'She seems to have her head screwed on so I'm sure she will be.' He cast a glance in the direction of the dining room. 'Do you think we've missed pudding?'

Libby laughed. 'Just like a man to worry about pudding. Possibly, though I'm actually already so full that if we have missed pudding it's probably done me a favour.'

'But you can't have Christmas lunch without pudding.'

'Who says?'

'Everyone!'

'Right… I'm sure we could track some down if you get desperate. Personally, I'm not bothered either way, and it's better not to be too full by the time the disco starts anyway.'

'You're staying then?'

'I might as well. Like you, I've only got boredom waiting for me at home, so why look this particular gift horse in the mouth, eh? I'll warn you now though, I don't dance.'

'The evidence of last night tells me otherwise.'

'Last night I was very drunk.'

'Oh. Well, in that case I have my task for this afternoon – get you as drunk as yesterday and get you on that dance floor.'

Libby grinned. 'You can try, but I'm telling you, last night was definitely a one-off.'

'Yeah?' he said with a chuckle. 'Challenge accepted!'

Chapter Thirteen

There was no need to track down pudding; luckily, the last of it was still being served up. On the floor where Josie had fallen, all traces of the chaos had disappeared. Noah took his place back at the table with his other friends and, with a faint stab of regret, Libby took hers with Gene, Tomas and Adrienne. Willow had disappeared, and Tomas didn't seem to know where to, but it was unnerving for Libby to see that Rufus had also left the room. Were they together? If they were, what were they talking about? Libby had a horrible feeling it might be about her and hoped desperately that wasn't the case, and that Rufus wasn't pressuring Willow to act as a go-between for him in his quest to get Libby back.

Good as the Christmas pudding was, Libby couldn't enjoy it. The longer Willow and Rufus were both missing, the greater her concern. It could be totally unconnected, of course, but that would be too easy. She leant over to Tomas.

'Do you know if Rufus went home?'

'I don't know where he is,' Tomas said. 'He went out of the dining room just after you did with the waitress.' He picked up a glass of sherry that had replaced the wine to finish their meal. 'I wouldn't stress it.'

'It's difficult not to.'

'If you ask me, I think he's got the message.'

'Do you?' Libby asked, finding it hard to mask the tone of utter disbelief.

'Well he didn't follow you out earlier, did he?'

'When we took Josie out? That was probably because it was a totally inappropriate moment.'

'Exactly!' Tomas said with a triumphant but slightly soggy grin. He lifted the sherry glass to his lips and knocked the rest of it back with a grimace. 'God, who actually likes this stuff?'

'Somebody must.'

'Old people, that's who, and that's because they were brought up on suet and liver so they don't know any better.'

Libby forced a smile and Tomas gave her hand a clumsy pat. 'You wait and see – tonight is going to be a corker and you won't care whether your lame ex is here or not. You know, I always knew there was something dodgy about him, but I was nice to him because, hey, he was your boyfriend and you're Willow's best friend, right? I don't have to be nice to him now and if he causes any trouble here I'll be ready. But don't worry about that – I bet he'll go before the disco starts anyway. I mean, who's he going to dance with?'

Rufus didn't have to be dancing to be there, but it was easier not to put Tomas right – not that he was in any state to comprehend her point anyway.

'Are we still doing charades this afternoon?' Tomas asked.

'I don't know. It depends what Noah thinks as it was partly his idea. I think maybe there aren't enough guests here now and some will leave this afternoon now that we can and lunch is done, so there might be even fewer.'

'Doesn't mean we can't still have a game,' Tomas said. He let out a little belch. 'I'd be up for it.'

'Maybe we'll just do something low-key then,' Libby said. 'I'll see what Noah says.'

'He's a good lad, isn't he?' Tomas said.

'He seems it.'

'You like him.'

'He's nice. He's also going home to California in a day or so.'

'Yeah… shame that.'

Libby seized her chance. 'Tomas, what's his situation in America?'

'What do you mean?'

'I mean, does he have—'

It was then that her eye caught the figure of Josie walking across the dining room. Libby leapt from her chair and raced over.

'I thought you were going home!' she said.

Josie turned to her. 'Oh, Libby… I am, I just… well I thought I might finish my shift first.'

'What! You told us you'd call a cab!' She glanced across the room to see that Noah had noticed Josie too and was wearing a deep frown, but one of his friends was talking to him and it looked as if he wasn't able to get away to come over. Libby wondered if perhaps that was a good thing – she wanted Josie to stop working but she didn't want it to seem as if she was being ganged up on.

'I did,' Josie said, blushing slightly. 'There was an hour wait and… well, I'm not much more than that from the end of my shift.'

'Does Manny know?'

'Um… well, I haven't exactly had time to talk to him about it.'

'Oh, Josie…' Libby frowned. 'Please, I'm so worried about you. I…'

What could she say? Again, she was desperate to share her own story, but it would seem like doom-mongering and she didn't want to scare Josie. Pregnancy was supposed to be a joyous time, or at least not one when you lived in fear of every little activity. But if anyone knew how quickly things could turn bad, it was Libby.

'I promise I'll only do little jobs,' Josie said. 'I'll just be on the bar or something; I won't do anything heavy. It's just for an hour while the cab is on its way, and I honestly feel completely fine now.'

'I don't believe you, but…' Libby shrugged. What could she do? This was Josie's life, and she didn't have to take orders from anyone regarding her self-care – especially someone who was just about a stranger. 'You're taking it easy then? If I see you so much as lift a pint glass I'm going to get Noah on you!'

Josie smiled. 'I wouldn't mind that. He's nice, isn't he? Are you two…?'

'Just met him,' Libby said.

'Weddings are a good place to find a fella; I should know, I met my boyfriend at a wedding,' Josie said. 'I think Noah likes you, and if I was you, I'd get in there. It's lovely of you to be so concerned for me; and as you're so bothered, I promise I won't work too hard.'

'OK.' Libby nodded. 'I'll let you get on then.'

She threw a look at Noah to try and reassure him that everything was sorted, and his expression relaxed, which she took to mean he understood. As she returned to her table, Josie's voice halted her and she turned back.

'Thank you,' she said. 'And… I really hope you come back to the hotel one day and I'm on shift when you do.'

Libby smiled. 'Me too.'

She was still smiling when she got back to her table, but it didn't take long for her to realise that Tomas was no longer there. Couldn't that man stay in one place for a minute?

'Do you know where Tomas is?' she asked Adrienne as she sat down.

'No idea. He mumbled something I couldn't understand and then staggered off. I think he might be a bit worse for wear – God only knows what state he'll be in later.'

'Hmm,' Libby said as she reached for the sherry he'd abandoned. Her questions about Noah would have to wait – again – and even if she did catch Tomas and get a moment to ask, would she get any sense out of him anyway?

She'd barely had time to pick up her drink when she saw Willow and Tomas come back in.

'I wondered where you'd got to,' Libby said. But the smile on her lips died as she saw Willow's sombre expression. Tomas looked more serious and sober too. 'What's happened?'

'I think you really need to go and talk to Rufus,' she said. 'He's in that drawing room off the foyer.'

Libby sighed. 'I thought we'd got it all sorted.'

'Yeah,' Willow said, 'you'll think very differently when you see him.'

Libby looked between the two of them.

'Crying like a baby,' Tomas said.

Libby stared at him. 'Seriously?'

Willow nodded. 'We've done what we can but it's no good – he needs you.'

'Jesus!' Libby breathed, but she leapt from her chair and rushed out anyway.

She found Rufus in the room where he'd slept the night before. He was hunched up in a chair gazing out of the window, not crying but certainly looking as if he had been.

'You can't keep doing this,' she said. 'I'm not going to change my mind.'

'I know,' he said quietly.

'So what's this about?'

He turned to her. 'I can't be miserable if I feel like it?'

'Miserable isn't exactly the way you were just described by Willow and Tomas. Crying like a baby is what Tomas said.'

'I wasn't.'

'OK... so you don't need me then? Only Willow said I ought to—'

'It's my mum.'

'Valerie?' Libby's forehead creased into a deep frown and she took a seat on the sofa next to him. What on earth had his mother got to do with anything happening here right now?

'She's ill. I know you're fond of her, so I thought you ought to know.'

'Oh... what's wrong with her?'

'She's got six months to live.'

Libby stared at him. 'What the hell! And you didn't think to say anything before now? You've been here for two days and you're telling me now? How long have you known?'

'A few weeks. I didn't think... you never gave me a chance to tell you.'

'I gave you plenty of chances! It's the sort of thing you lead with, not just drop into a conversation when everything else has failed to get my attention!'

'I'm sorry,' he said quietly.

'No...' Libby took a breath. 'God, no, *I'm* sorry. I have no right to shout at you about it... and I was totally out of order. It's just a shock, that's all...' She reached for his hand. 'It must be hell. If you'd said something earlier maybe I could have offered some support...

at least I might not have been so vile to you. And you're right; I love your mum. I'm gutted. What's wrong with her?'

'Cancer.'

She waited for him to elaborate, but he didn't. So she nodded and figured he would when he was ready. 'Where is she now? Is she still able to live at home? Can I go and see her?'

'The family's taking it pretty hard – probably best not to at the moment. Maybe in a couple of weeks.'

Libby offered him an encouraging smile. 'Whatever's happened between us, know that I'm here for you now. If you want to talk, if you need anything at all.'

'That means a lot to me. You know, I really am sorry about everything. I know it doesn't excuse anything, but I didn't feel like I could talk to you at the time. There was this wall around you and I couldn't get in. I was made to feel like your pain at losing... well, it was private and yours alone and more important than mine. I felt like what I was going through was less and I felt silly asking you to help me with it, like I had no right because you had so much of your own. I never meant to fall for Kylie; I just wanted some company with no strings, but it was just that...'

Had she really been so blind to Rufus's pain when they'd lost their baby? Had she really kept him out, ignored him, driven him into Kylie's arms? Was everything really her fault?

'For what it's worth,' she began slowly, 'I think you're right when you say I should carry some blame too. I put my own grieving before yours and I shouldn't have done that. I didn't realise... It was partly my fault, what happened with Kylie. I know that now.'

'I never stopped thinking about you.'

'Don't...' Libby shook her head. 'Please, Rufus.'

'Don't tell me you haven't been the same.'

'Of course I have. I've thought about nothing else for months. Mostly I thought about what you were doing with Kylie and how lonely I was.'

'I was wrong to leave you for her.'

'Tell me honestly, did you really do the leaving with Kylie or was it her?'

'I know I said it was me, but it was her. Only because she knew that I wasn't over you and she said she didn't want to be second best. I only said it was me because… well, I suppose I felt stupid that I'd given you up for her and then she dumped me anyway.'

Libby still didn't know if she could believe him or not, but she let his statement sink in for a moment. If it was true, where did that leave them?

Without warning, he leant in and kissed her, and she was so shocked that she didn't stop him.

'There's the proof,' he said as he pulled away. 'You do still love me. We're meant to be together.'

Libby shook her head, though the kiss had done nothing for that resolve she could feel turning to quicksand under her feet. If things were as bad for him as he said, if his mum really was that ill, he was going to need support. He'd have his family, of course, but could Libby really leave him in his hour of need? Could she walk away from this? She'd already indirectly done it once when they'd lost their baby and she'd failed to offer the support he'd clearly needed. But if she gave this to him now, who was going to be there for her if it all turned to shit again?

'You have to understand… I want to help you and I want to offer you support, but things have gone too far between us and I don't love you now,' she said.

'I don't believe you.'

'Even if I did, this can't happen. I've come so far and it's been so hard… I can't get hurt again.'

'I wouldn't hurt you again.'

'Those are just words; easy to say. How can I trust them? How can I trust you?'

He leant in close, his forehead resting against hers, just as it used to. 'Give me one more chance and I'll show you.'

'I can't.'

'You can. It's easy.'

It took all she had to stand up. 'I'll think about it – that's all I can say.'

He smiled up at her, looking rather too much like he'd already won. 'That's all I can ask for.'

'In the meantime, please go home. You're making things super awkward here and, honestly, you ought to be with your mum today of all days.'

'I know that. But I was stuck, remember?'

'Well I don't think you're stuck now. You should have told me about Valerie. I would have gone to see her. She must think I'm such a heartless bitch.'

'She doesn't. She knows things were off between us. Don't come yet though… give me a chance to tell her you'll be visiting first.'

'I can phone her.'

'It's alright – I'm heading there now; I'll tell her.'

'OK. Will you be alright?'

He nodded. 'I will now we've talked.'

'I'll get back to the party then. I'll call you in the next couple of days.'

'Are you staying till the end of the night then? I could… well, if you needed a lift home I could… I have my car…'

'I don't think that's a good idea.'

'There wouldn't have to be anything in it, Lib… it's just a lift home.'

'No, Rufus,' she said, more gently now. 'You say there wouldn't be anything in it but inevitably there will be.'

'I swear, I just want to know you're getting home safely.'

'Well, that's good of you but I'm going to be fine. I'll most likely get a taxi with Willow's parents, so…'

'Willow's parents… right. That's good.'

'So I'll speak to you soon, right?'

'Right.'

'Thank you,' he said, and Libby left him with a vague half-smile and more questions than answers.

As she made her way back to the other diners, she didn't quite know what to think or how to feel. Rufus had thrown her a complete curveball. He was getting very good at that, it seemed.

Chapter Fourteen

'It's a film!' Scarlet cried triumphantly. Then said no more, but gazed around the room as if waiting for her round of applause.

'Yes,' Libby said patiently. 'But that's only the first bit – you need to figure out what film it is.'

'Oh…'

Scarlet turned her attention back to Noah and frowned, as if giving his next movement the deepest concentration.

Noah, Libby, Adrienne and Gene had decided charades should go ahead, but there weren't many people in attendance in the end and they'd had to move it into the orangery. Currently sitting around watching Noah perform were Willow's parents, the trio of torment, the old great-aunt who'd wanted Noah's number earlier, the bartender (ostensibly working but leaning on the bar and watching the proceedings with interest) and Libby herself. Willow and Tomas were absent as they were having a conversation with the manager about the evening's festivities.

Libby still didn't know what to think about Rufus. Their conversation kept going round and round in her head, even though she was doing her best not to dwell on it. Something about it didn't add up, and the fact she'd let him kiss her wasn't helping. One thing was oddly comforting though: the kiss, while it had rekindled some old feelings, hadn't had quite the explosive effect on her she'd feared it might. As she hadn't seen him since, she had to assume he'd stayed true to his word and gone home. Given his news about his mum, Libby was frankly shocked that he hadn't tried much harder to get home before now, but she reflected that he'd been stuck like everyone else, and perhaps she was being unfair.

As for their game of charades, she supposed they hadn't expected much of a turnout but that was OK. Now it was just about killing an hour before the party started later on rather than entertaining the masses anyway, and she had to admit that her mind wasn't entirely on it, though she was doing her best to get into the spirit of things.

Noah held up four fingers.

'Four words!' Libby called.

Noah nodded and then indicated he was about to perform the first of those words to them before holding a hand to his eyes and pretending to search for something.

'Looking,' Libby said.

'Searching,' the old aunt offered.

'Lost!' Gene shouted.

Noah shook his head to all those and then added a very deliberate shrug to the mime. So now he was looking for something he couldn't find?

'*Dude, Where's My Car!*' Libby cried, and Noah burst out laughing.

'What the hell! How did you get that from what I just did?'

'So I'm right?' Libby asked excitedly.

'No, of course not!'

'You're not supposed to talk then,' Libby said with a vague pout that made him laugh all the more.

'You don't like being wrong, do you?' he asked.

'Oh, she doesn't!' Gene put in with a grin.

'Hey!' Libby turned to him. 'Who rattled your cage?' She flicked her gaze to Noah. 'And you're not supposed to talk!'

Noah grinned broadly and then mimed zipping up his mouth. He held up his fingers to indicate he was going to attempt the fourth word in his title and then turned around and started to waft at his bum.

All three of the trio of torment erupted into giggles.

'Smelly!' Olivia said.

'Poo!' Scarlet offered.

'Stinky bum!' India cried.

Noah shook his head and tried again, this time grimacing as if he was forcing something out, and then wafting one hand across his backside again while using the other to peg his nose.

'Farty bottom!' Olivia shouted, almost unable to breathe she was laughing so hard now.

'Trump man!' Scarlet called.

'Batty bomb!' Tomas's old aunt shouted and started to laugh more hysterically than the children.

Libby turned to stare at her.

'None of those things are four-word answers and are certainly no films I've heard of,' Adrienne said, appearing to miss the joke entirely and looking quite perplexed. 'Do the first word again, Noah,' she said.

Once again, he began to mime something that looked like an unsuccessful search, and Adrienne frowned. But then her expression cleared and she gave a hopeful smile.

'Is it *Gone with the Wind*?' she asked.

'Yes!' Noah gave her a little round of applause. 'At least there's someone who doesn't have their mind in the gutter in this room!'

Libby blinked. 'So you wafting your backside was supposed to be wind? And you're surprised everyone was thinking about farting?'

'Well how else was I going to do wind?' he asked practically as he returned to his chair and gave Adrienne the floor to take her turn.

'*Do wind*!' Scarlet guffawed, and the other girls erupted into laughter again too.

'I told you to ease up on the sprouts at lunch,' Gene said, making the girls laugh so hard now that Libby was seriously concerned she'd be called on for some kind of first aid after all.

Adrienne held up two fingers, but then indicated that it was a compound word and mimed that it was a film. The giggles quietened as everyone gave her their full attention. She appeared to open an imaginary coat out wide, before jiggling around on the spot.

'Oh!' Tomas's old aunt cried. '*Flashdance*!'

Adrienne stared at her. 'So fast!'

'I'm good at this,' the aunt said.

'You are,' Adrienne agreed.

The aunt got up and swapped places with Adrienne at the front of the room. She indicated a film of two words and then told them that the first part of the first word was the number nine. So far so simple, but things quickly went downhill after that, as nobody had a clue about the next bits. Exasperated, the aunt gave up on literal clues and started to groan and gyrate in a most disturbing way.

'What's she doing?' Scarlet whispered to India, who shrugged, while Olivia had taken to staring out of the window.

Was the first aid required again, Libby wondered, as the aunt started to breathe heavily, while Gene looked deeply uncomfortable and Noah simply stared in a state of vague shock.

'I give up,' he said after a few more excruciating moments.

'Me too,' Gene said. Adrienne nodded.

'I'm afraid you're going to have to tell us,' Libby said.

The old aunt sighed. 'Honestly…' she said. '*Nine and a Half Weeks*!'

Libby blinked while Noah grinned; Gene and Adrienne didn't know quite where to look.

'I don't know any of these films,' Scarlet complained, while the other two girls murmured agreement with her.

'That means I get another turn, right?' the old aunt asked.

Libby nodded and tried to look agreeable, but she was beginning to wonder if this game had been such a great idea after all. With clues like that, they were never going to guess any of her titles… What had started out as an hour to kill might turn out to be a very long afternoon. She glanced at Noah and wondered if he was thinking the same thing, and he mouthed something she couldn't quite make out. But if he was on her wavelength like she thought he was, then it was probably: help!

Libby's dress had dried out, and although she was quite enjoying the ease and comfort of Noah's clothes, dancing in them was quite another matter. She'd told Noah she had no intentions of dancing, but even she knew better than to think his plan to get her tipsy and then persuade her to step onto the floor wouldn't work. With some foresight of this happening, she was on her way up to his suite to change back into her gown so she'd be cooler, better equipped to move, and have the added bonus of being able to go straight home when the time came without having to worry about getting his clothes back to him.

The lift pinged and Libby stepped in, an endless replay of her most recent conversation with Rufus in her head. And then she was at Noah's floor and the doors opened again, and, as she trudged to his suite, she suddenly didn't feel much like being here anymore, and certainly not dancing.

Had she really treated Rufus that badly? Misunderstood him and locked him out to the point where she'd made him seek comfort in the arms of her cousin? Not only that, but his mum had been ill for weeks and, even knowing how fond Libby was of her, he still hadn't felt able to tell her about it. None of it quite made sense, but it certainly did make her feel like a miserable failure.

Poised with the key card at the door of Noah's suite, her shoulders sagged in weary defeat. Maybe it would be better if she got changed, called a cab and went home. What point was there in staying now?

A sudden resolution struck her, so simple she wondered why it hadn't occurred to her before. She couldn't speak to Valerie because Rufus had asked her not to, but she didn't have to be a pointless failure. If Rufus's mum had been ill for a few weeks, maybe Kylie could tell Libby something more about it and then maybe Libby would know what to do. Surely Kylie knew. In fact, now that she thought about it, Libby couldn't quite believe that her cousin would have left Rufus to deal with such an awful situation, which was just another perplexing fact to add to the pile she already had. Kylie was such a kind soul she'd never do that, even if it meant putting his happiness above hers, even if she was desperate to end the relationship. Kylie would have seen it through – she would have stayed with him until Valerie had passed and he'd mourned her.

Libby found the number in her contacts and her finger hovered over the call button. It was Christmas Day, and Libby hadn't spoken to Kylie for months. What on earth was she going to say? It certainly wasn't a conversation to lighten anyone's mood.

She locked her phone again. No, she couldn't do this to Kylie, not today. It would have to wait for a more appropriate day.

'Libby!'

She turned to see Olivia racing down the corridor towards her. She must have come up the stairs.

'Libby! Are you going to Noah's room?'

As she was about to reply, Libby noticed Olivia's mum further back, following her daughter at a much more sedate pace.

'Sorry, Libby,' she said, 'Olivia's just realised she's lost her necklace and we wondered whether she dropped it in Noah's suite earlier when she got washed. Noah said you had the key and were coming up here – do you mind if we have a quick look?'

'Well, I was getting changed, but I suppose as we're all girls together it won't hurt.'

'You're putting your dress back on?' Olivia asked.

'Yes. I need to give Noah his clothes back before I go.'

Olivia's face fell. 'You're going?'

Libby swiped the key card and opened the door to Noah's suite, gesturing for Olivia and her mum to go in before following. 'Yes, as soon as I've got changed.'

'But the disco!' Olivia squeaked.

'I know… sorry about that. But I'm really not much of a dancer anyway so you won't miss me.'

'I will!' Olivia cried.

'She will, you know,' her mum said. 'You've made quite an impression on all the girls and especially our little Lolly.'

'Have I?' Libby asked, taken slightly aback. 'Oh… well thank you.'

'Please stay!' Olivia said fervently. 'We all want to dance with you and Noah!'

'Oh, I bet you want Noah a bit more,' Libby said with a smile. 'He's a much better dancer and I'm sure he'd be up for a boogie.'

'I think Noah would rather like to boogie with you too,' Olivia's mum said with a wry smile at Libby.

'Hmm,' Libby said. 'That's not going to happen, not after what my ex has just told me.'

Olivia's mum stared at her. The admission had come from nowhere and it was strange company to bring it up in. A near-stranger certainly wasn't her first choice of confidante, but it felt good to say something to someone, and it might be that someone with no connection to either party would end up being an inspired choice. Libby sat heavily on the edge of the bed.

'Lolly…' Olivia's mum said, 'go and check round the bathroom for your necklace – if it's anywhere it's probably in there. Look properly – underneath the cabinets and behind the towel rail.'

The little girl did as she was asked without argument, skipping off to the bathroom while her mum turned to Libby.

'A man sat with us at lunch – that was him, wasn't it? I wondered why he wasn't at the wedding with anyone, and then he kept looking over at you… a little bit obsessively, if you don't mind me saying.'

'Yes,' Libby said ruefully. 'And I don't think it's an unreasonable thing to say at all. We were meant to be here as a couple but then… well, I expect you can guess. We're not a couple any longer but he decided to come anyway. I think he had some idea about using the situation as a way for us to get back together.'

'And you don't want that at all?'

'No.'

'And I think maybe you're interested in someone else and he doesn't like it?'

Libby looked up sharply. 'Did he say that?'

'No, don't worry,' Olivia's mum said. 'It's just obvious to anyone you and Noah have the most ridiculous chemistry.'

'Is it?' Libby held back a frown. She'd tried so hard to keep her attraction to Noah in check and thought she'd done a good job of it too. It only went to show how wrong you could be about these things, and that some attractions were just too big to hide.

'Yes!' Olivia's mum said with a little laugh. 'I don't blame you either – he's gorgeous.'

'Do you know him much?'

'Not really – all I know is that he's an old friend of Tomas from way back.'

'I don't know much about him either,' Libby said. 'It's strange, he's been so open about such a lot and yet nothing all at the same time, and I have to admit that worries me. I like him but I don't feel I can't trust him.'

Olivia's mum shrugged. 'Can't you just ask him?'

'But if I ask him he'll know I like him.'

'So?'

Libby grimaced. She was aware that right now she sounded a little bit like a fourteen-year-old suffering with her first crush, one step away from passing notes around in class, but she didn't know how else to say it.

'What if he doesn't feel the same way?'

'Trust me, he does.'

'It's not that simple now. My ex has just told me his mum has six months to live. I mean, what am I supposed to do with that? He just looks up and tells me, today of all days. He's known for weeks and he chooses today to say something?'

'Hmm. I must admit, that's not the best timing. Was there something that forced his hand?'

'I guess the fact that I was refusing to talk to him… perhaps that was stopping him from saying something before. But how was I meant to talk to him? He had an affair with my bloody cousin!'

'Ouch!' Olivia's mum said with a sympathetic grimace.

'I know, right? So now he's shocked that they've split up and I don't want to discuss us getting back together.'

'Maybe that's why he brought up his mum's illness.'

Libby's eyes widened. 'You don't think she's ill?'

'I don't know about that, but he might have decided at first he wasn't going to involve you because you were no longer together, but then perhaps, when he was getting desperate, he's seen it as a way to get your attention. And it seems as if it has.'

'I suppose so.'

Libby was thoughtful for a moment. Perhaps, despite what the fallout might be, she really did need to make that call to Kylie. Or at least send a text – though was it really the sort of thing you texted someone about?

The door to the bathroom was flung open and Olivia raced in. 'It's not in there!' she announced in an exasperated voice. But then her gaze suddenly went to Libby's feet and she dived under the bed. 'Found it!'

Her mum gave an amused look. 'Well, that was easier than expected. Now that's sorted we'll leave you to get changed, Libby.'

'Are you absolutely, definitely going home after that?' Olivia asked.

Libby reached for the buckles on her sandals to undo them. 'Um…'

'Please stay for just one dance!' Olivia cried. 'Please!'

Libby sighed. 'One dance. OK, I suppose one dance can't hurt anyone.'

'Yay!' Olivia grabbed her mum's hand. 'See you later, Libby!'

The room was silent as they left and the door closed behind them. Libby picked up her phone again and stared at the list of contacts. There was Kylie's name and smiling photo. In a stark and sudden bolt, she realised she'd missed her cousin, almost as much as she'd missed Rufus, though she'd been so busy blaming them both for her woes that she hadn't really noticed it until now.

Before she'd given it another thought, she dialled the number. She half expected Kylie not to pick up, but after three rings her cousin answered. Quite as Libby had imagined, she sounded shocked.

'Libby… is everything OK?'

'Um… yes. I'm sorry to call you on Christmas Day—'

'God, no, it's fine! Mum and Dad are asleep in front of the telly anyway… It's good to hear from you.'

Libby couldn't help a smile as the tension flooded from her. Why had she been so scared of making this call? Kylie's tone was as warm and affectionate as always.

'I thought…' she continued. 'Well, you know… I thought maybe I wouldn't hear from you again.'

'For a while I thought that too,' Libby admitted. 'But we've had time to move past that, I think, and if you're happy to then so am I.'

'God, yes! I want that more than anything! I think I must have wanted my head examining!'

Libby half thought perhaps hers needed examining too. What was she thinking? What was this call going to achieve? Was it going to make her feel more sorry for Rufus, drive her back into his arms? There was a distinct possibility, but she had to know.

'It's actually him I'm phoning about.'

'Oh…'

'Don't worry... I'm not ready to kick off. I just... well, he's just told me about his mum.'

Kylie sounded confused. 'He's there with you?'

'Yes and no. It's a long story.'

'What's he said about his mum?'

'That she's really ill.'

'Valerie's ill? What's wrong with her?'

Libby paused. 'You don't know? That she has six months to live?'

'Jesus!' Kylie cried. 'When did this happen? I saw her last week when I went round to pick up some things I'd left there and she seemed fine – she never said a word about anything like that!'

'So she's not bedbound, hiding away from the family, beside herself, or in any way unavailable to have a conversation with?'

'No,' Kylie said. 'Not as far as I can tell. What's going on?'

'That's just what I'd like to know,' Libby replied.

She didn't want it to be true, because it was low, even for Rufus, but... had the whole story been a lie to get her sympathy? If it was, it had certainly worked. She'd been a hair's breadth away from taking him back.

'She's definitely OK?' Libby asked.

'I mean, I can ask her, but last time I saw her she was.'

'And that was a week ago?'

'Yes. Do you want me to phone her?'

'I don't know. It's kind of a weird conversation to have, especially if it's not true.'

'You think Rufus has made it up?'

'I don't know. What do you think?'

'I don't know... It sounds like a strange thing to do.'

'Or maybe a desperate thing to do. The sort of lie a kid makes up when he can't see another way to get what he wants?'

'I don't know what to say.'

'Me neither,' Libby replied. 'But I do know there's a certain someone I need to talk to if I'm going to get to the bottom of this.'

'Does that mean he's been trying to get you back?' Kylie asked, and her tone sounded so hurt Libby couldn't help but feel for her.

'Sort of,' she said, not wanting to admit the full extent of his efforts, knowing it would hurt Kylie even more.

'I don't think he ever really wanted me,' she said quietly.

'I don't think he was ever good for either of us,' Libby said. 'For what it's worth, there's no chance we're getting back together.'

'Would you want him, if it hadn't been me he'd gone off with? If it had been someone you didn't know?'

'I can't answer that, because it was. But I don't blame you for it.'

There was a brief silence, and Libby wondered what Kylie was thinking. She had the strangest impression that Kylie still had feelings for Rufus and would probably take him back if he decided to pursue her instead of Libby. She wanted to ask, but perhaps now wasn't the time and, besides, she had more pressing concerns. She needed to know the truth of her last conversation with Rufus – though she was beginning to form her own theories about it. She didn't want to have a conversation like that with Valerie, so that left another chat with Rufus himself.

It wouldn't be today, of course, because the one sensible thing Rufus had managed to do was finally go home, out of the way where he couldn't cause any more trouble. But as soon as she was home herself, there was a very urgent phone call to make and Libby really wasn't looking forward to it.

*

She found Noah at the bar in the orangery, their now favourite room it seemed, because whenever one of them went missing, the other would automatically head there to wait for them. It was as if, in some strange and unspoken way, they had become an unofficial item – one was rarely seen without the other and it was obviously more noticeable than Libby had supposed, as evidenced by Olivia's mum, who had seen it even with her hands full and pulled in all directions. And if she had, then everyone must have.

At first Libby had been baffled about Rufus and his story about his mum, and then furious at the thought he might have made it up, and then just plain sad that if he had, he'd felt the need to go to such lengths to get her attention. In the end, as she turned it over in her mind, the theory that it was a lie made more and more sense – from his request for her not to contact Valerie to the fact he'd only just decided to tell Libby about it at the very moment when he thought he'd completely lost her.

It should have bothered Libby, and ordinarily it would have put her in such a bad mood that she wouldn't want to socialise, but strangely, this time, it didn't. Her chat with Olivia's mum and the recent conversation with Kylie had had the opposite effect. It was like being let out of a prison, a weight lifted from her. If Rufus had thought to trap her, he'd done the opposite of that too. She now no longer cared what he thought or what he needed from her, and that sense of freedom had left her feeling uncharacteristically reckless and rebellious. It was nothing to do with Rufus or anyone else what she got up to with Noah. They were two consenting adults out for a good time, who happened to enjoy each other's company, and it was nobody's business but theirs. And so what if Noah had secrets – didn't everyone? At least they weren't whopping mean lies about his mother. And it wasn't like Libby was planning to marry him or anything.

'Hey,' Noah said, 'you're looking a bit more familiar now.'

'I'm feeling a bit more familiar.' She handed over the key card and he stashed it in his pocket. 'I'll tell you one thing, if I don't lose this frock soon it'll need surgical removal.'

'I did say you could keep my clothes for a bit longer. Tomas could have got them back to me at some point before I headed back to the States.'

'Imagine claiming somewhere so glamorous as home. It must seem very dull around here to you.'

'God no! It feels very much like home as soon as I set foot outside the airport, and that's every single time I visit. California's amazing, of course it is, but there are loads of things about Blighty that I miss.'

'It can't be the weather – I know that much.'

'Well, it is true that the weather in LA is a bit more reliable for al fresco dining, but you sort of take that and everything else about the lifestyle for granted after a while, especially when you're so busy working you barely have time to enjoy it.'

'I can only imagine… sitting on a sun-drenched hillside restaurant overlooking the sea surrounded by cool and beautiful people… I don't think I'd ever get used to it.'

'You know,' he began slowly, 'when I said this morning that you ought to come and visit, I meant it.'

'I know,' Libby said airily, trying not to attach any significance to the fact he'd brought up visiting again. 'And maybe I will… if I ever get the time.'

'I'm sure that shop you run wouldn't close down if they had to go a couple of weeks without you, right?'

'I guess not,' she said, smiling, and left it at that, because it was easier than going into the whole litany of other more complicated reasons why it wasn't as simple as jumping on a plane and then stepping off at the other end a few hours later.

He pushed a glass across the bar top towards her. 'I got you one in and I even managed not to drink it this time. I think I got it right, didn't I?'

She took a sip. 'Yep; you're a fast learner.'

The first strains of pop music came from the direction of the great hall.

'Sounds like the party's started,' Noah said. 'So am I getting that dance or not? I mean, I just need to know so I can save space in my schedule because I have a feeling I might be getting hassled by the trio of torment.'

'Ah, well, I'm afraid I'm already promised to one of their number – little Olivia.'

'Ugh, that darned trio tormenting me at every turn.'

Libby laughed. 'I kind of feel bad that you've started to call them that too, you know. Maybe we ought to stop; they're really quite sweet and not tormenting at all.'

'Well, maybe, but we need some way to identify them as a cohort.'

'Hmm, how about the trio of cuteness?'

He shook his head. 'It just doesn't have the same ring and it's not nearly as amusing. I'm afraid they'll always be the trio of torment to me from this day forth. I'll still be calling them that when they're middle-aged with kids of their own. So you're promised to dance with the little horrors – does that mean you plan to stay for a while? And didn't you say you'd have to be drunk to dance?'

'I did,' she said, smiling. 'So I suppose I'd better get this one down and refill fast.'

He gave her a cheeky grin and then turned to the bar to get the attention of the girl tending to it. 'I'll get them lined up and ready!'

*

Three gins later they were in the great hall, though Noah was the one out on the dance floor while Libby watched him twirl a delighted Olivia around. As soon as the opportunity to dance with Noah appeared, Libby had been ditched – though she couldn't say she really minded that much. She was currently sitting at a table, well oiled but not quite far enough gone to let go. Still, she was tapping her feet and drumming her fingers, occasionally doing a little shimmy in her seat, and secretly itching to get up, despite what she'd told Noah earlier about not dancing.

Scarlet was a few feet away dancing with her mum, though she kept throwing envious glances at Noah and Olivia. India was nowhere to be seen, and Libby struggled to remember seeing her or her family around for a good hour or more. Perhaps they'd decided to leave the hotel and go home after all – it was hard to keep track of the comings and goings.

While she was scanning the room she caught Tomas's eye. With a soppy grin, he beckoned her onto the dance floor to join him. He was clearly legless and very sweaty.

She shook her head.

'Why not?' he yelled above the music.

This time she shook her gin glass. 'Not enough of these yet!' she mouthed back.

'Aww… come on…' Tomas started to shimmy over. 'Don't be a stick-in-the-mud!'

'I *am not* a stick-in-the-mud!'

'Prove it!' Tomas shouted, lunging for her hand and getting hold before she had time to react. A second later he was trying to pull her from her chair.

'Dancing with you is your wife's job!' Libby said, laughing.

'Yeah, well she's dancing with her uncle or something, said I kept treading on her. I mean, as if!'

Libby winced as the tip of his shoe caught her toe and decided that Willow probably had a very good point.

There had been a Stevie Wonder classic playing – Libby knew the song but didn't know the title – but then it faded into the opening bars of 'Come On Eileen', a song that had featured at every wedding disco Libby had ever been to. Tomas roared with appreciation and now grabbed her by both hands, yanked her up and began to fling her round in a sort of drunken barn dance. All she could do was allow him to lead (in a fashion) and do her best not to get a dislocated shoulder, but she couldn't help but giggle just the same. A few moments in and she was actually quite enjoying herself too – perhaps she'd had more to drink than she'd realised.

'Tomas, calm down!' she cried, laughing. 'You're going to throw me through a window in a minute!'

'Aww, you worry too much!'

At every family gathering of this sort, there was always that one man who charmed everyone, who always seemed to have the kids gathered around him like the Pied Piper. It looked as though Noah had taken that accolade tonight, evidenced by the fact that when Libby got a moment to see where he was, she also saw that Scarlet had now managed to lose her parents and joined him and Olivia.

If she was honest, Libby could see why people – and in particular the trio of torment – gravitated towards him. Try as she might to deny it, there was something attractive about him and not just in a sexual or physical sense – it was something that shone from within, something almost spiritual. To meet him – as far as Libby could tell from his interactions at the wedding – was to instantly love him. He'd even managed to charm Rufus to some extent, a man who probably had every reason to hate him in light of his obvious jealousy. But conversations at the bar and borrowed bathroom facilities didn't lie – Rufus would never have accepted those offers from someone he truly disliked.

So if Noah was a magnet to everyone, maybe that was really all Libby was feeling? It would make sense, and the idea put her a little more at ease. Maybe there wasn't some primal, irresistible sexual chemistry; maybe she was simply drawn to him in the same way everyone else seemed to be, and maybe that was more OK than the alternative she'd been fretting about.

So if she danced with him now, there wouldn't be anything in it at all; it was just the same as Olivia and Scarlet dancing with him…

He caught her eye and grinned as he twirled both little girls – one on each arm – and she blushed at having been caught red-handed staring at him. Then he tilted his head to beckon her over to join them, but she nodded at Tomas to try and communicate that she might have a bit of trouble getting away, and so Noah danced Olivia and Scarlet across the floor towards them.

'Mind if we join you?' he shouted over the music.

'Noah!' Tomas yelled, instantly letting go of Libby to pull his friend into a drunken man-hug. 'You know I never told you how glad I am you flew all this way for me!'

'I think you might have done,' Noah replied wryly. 'Just a few times today. Seriously, man, as if I wouldn't. I'd never have missed your wedding.'

Olivia and Scarlet were now boogieing on their own, but they kept looking up expectantly at Noah as if they were waiting to get him back just as soon as Tomas had finished with him, like a couple of toddlers ready to pounce on the toy another child was currently playing with the moment they looked away.

'Want to dance with me?' Libby asked them.

'Yes!' Olivia said enthusiastically and looked instantly happier to have some adult attention once more. Scarlet seemed less certain about settling for what was clearly second best, but she shuffled her feet and smiled at Libby and tried to look grateful anyway.

A minute later, Tomas had drifted off and Noah was back with them, but the song was winding down. A few seconds later it faded and the DJ announced that he was going to slow things down with a trip to the nineties and began to play 'Eternal Flame' by The Bangles.

'Oh, I *love* this!' Libby cried, and she was just about to ask the girls if they wanted to do some kind of stadium-inspired candle-swaying dance when Noah, to her utter shock, took her by the hand.

'Mind if I cut in, girls?' he asked.

Olivia and Scarlet giggled and gave Libby a look that was a bit too knowing before clasping each other round the waist for an impromptu and rather strange waltz.

Libby gazed up at him. What was that about only the same sort of attraction everyone else felt for him? What was that about no chemistry? She could barely tear her eyes away from his. He gave her a smile that melted her.

'You don't mind, do you? It might be my last chance, so I figured why not seize it?'

'How very American of you,' she replied, still caught in his eyes.

'I thought so too.'

They began to sway. All the time her gaze was locked onto his and she hardly even noticed the music, except for her body instinctively moving to it. Then she was barely aware of dropping her head to rest on his chest, and she didn't even notice that his arms had travelled to hold her by the waist, and all the while they moved as one, slowly and rhythmically, the room fading away until there was only them in the universe of each other.

Libby closed her eyes. His chest was broad and warm. If she'd slept this close to him last night, this was what he would have smelt like – warm and safe and constant, but also dangerous and exciting and new.

The music bled into the cracks where the rest of her consciousness was filled entirely with him and the terrible but thrilling realisation of the lie she'd been telling herself for the last two days revealed itself at last. She didn't just like him because he was fun or generous or because he was the type of guy everyone liked. There was something deeper, something that had her trapped now as she rested her head on his chest, something that defied any logic or explanation or her attempts to treat it with caution. This was the kind of attraction that came only once in a lifetime, the kind of attraction that could turn into something so much bigger given the space to grow.

But that was the problem. There was no space to grow – not for them. In a few days he'd be flying back to California and there was a good chance she'd never see him again. All she could ever really have was this, right now, and perhaps the best she could hope for was to imprint this memory, to keep it safe so she could treasure this singular perfect moment with the one who got away.

She lifted her head to look up at him. She wanted to lock in the sight of him smiling down at her, those warm, sky-blue eyes that said so much of the man he was. He gave her a slightly quizzical look. His lips parted to speak. And then he paused, and the room seemed to pause, to hold its breath, waiting for something. Waiting for *her* to do something. Sensible, organised, predictable Libby. What could she do? What was that pause waiting for her to do?

She gave her answer. She did the thing the room would never expect.

She kissed him.

Libby had heard stories that told of a first kiss being like fireworks, but she'd never felt that, not even in her most passionate of moments with Rufus. Until now. It was like a hundred cannons going off inside her, like a supernova, like all the tension that had been building had burst into the open in one almighty explosion, like somersaulting through the air and plunging a thousand feet, like every possible sensation all happening at once.

Noah was the one to pull away, leaving her longing to bring his mouth back down to hers, but as she smiled up at him, he looked troubled.

'Libby, I…'

Her smile faded. He'd felt what she'd felt, surely? There was no way he couldn't have, right? There was no way she could have mistaken the fire she'd felt in him, the one that matched her own? She couldn't have got this wrong, could she?

But she saw regret in his eyes.

'I'm sorry,' she said. 'I didn't realise—'

'No, please don't be sorry. It's not that; I mean, you're amazing and, God, I've wanted to do that so badly since we first met, but…'

'But what?'

'Libby, I haven't been fair to you. There's something I need to tell—'

Libby jumped in shock as he was suddenly yanked away from her, clean off his feet, landing on the floor a few feet away.

'Bastard!'

In his place stood a furious Rufus. He looked straight through Libby, like she wasn't there, and then turned back to Noah, who was scrambling to his feet.

'Bastard!' Rufus repeated. 'I knew it!'

Noah looked dazed as he brushed himself down. 'Knew what? What's your problem?'

'You are!' Rufus roared.

He took a swing, but Noah ducked beneath his flying fist, wobbled and then righted himself, but he didn't hit back.

'What have I done to you?' he panted. But then he shot the briefest glance at Libby and it was like he'd suddenly pieced it all together.

'Rufus, don't be a dick,' Libby pleaded. 'You're making a fool of yourself.'

'You're the fool!' Rufus yelled, turning his fury on her now. 'This guy's playing you!'

'Rufus, I—'

'Buddy, stop…' Noah cut in. 'If you have a problem with me then let's go and talk about it like adults, somewhere quieter.'

Rufus glared at him. 'You'd love that, wouldn't you?'

'I'd love for us not to carry on making a scene.'

'More like you don't want your secret to get out so you can get your way with my girlfriend!'

'I'm not your girlfriend!' Libby yelled. 'Get it into your thick head, Rufus, we are no more! I will never, ever come back to you! You ruined things and you don't get to go again, not with me.'

Suddenly, for an awful moment Rufus looked as if he might actually burst into tears. 'Yeah,' he said, quieter now, 'I know I did, and I know we can't go back, but that doesn't mean I can't still love you.'

'But I don't love you; not anymore.'

'Because you love him?' Rufus flung an arm at Noah.

'Don't be stupid!' Libby said. 'Of course not – I've just met him!'

'Looked like it,' Rufus pouted. 'I suppose he's everything I wasn't?'

'Well, he hasn't cheated on me, so there's that,' Libby said impatiently.

'Oh, right…' Rufus turned to Noah. 'When were you going to tell her?'

Libby looked from one to the other. 'Tell me what?' she demanded.

'Not here,' Noah lowered his voice, and it seemed to Libby that he knew exactly what Rufus was talking about.

'Tell me what?' Libby repeated.

Noah made a move to lay a hand on Rufus's shoulder. 'If you've got a problem with me, let's go somewhere quiet and sort it out.'

Rufus shook him off, glaring at him. By now everyone had stopped dancing and the whole room was watching the drama unfold. Libby could feel everyone's curious eyes on her, and she wished it would stop.

'I'm not the only bad guy in town,' Rufus said, addressing Libby but also seeming to announce it to everyone there. 'And at least I'm not hiding a wife in California.'

Chapter Fifteen

Libby stared at Rufus. He didn't smile or look victorious or vindicated. He simply looked sad, like he knew he'd hurt and humiliated her but felt it a necessary evil.

'I know, you idiot,' Libby hissed. 'I'm not stupid!'

It was Rufus's turn to stare at her. 'But—'

'And while we're at it, tell me the truth… is your mum really ill?'

Rufus's mouth fell open. 'Who told you…?'

'You really do think I'm stupid, don't you? And that was seriously below the belt, Rufus, even for you.'

'I didn't mean… I only wanted to get you to listen—'

'Well, you've blown that now.'

'I only did it because I love—'

'Don't you dare!' she said. 'Don't you dare say that! You don't lie and manipulate people you love. Have you been hanging around here all this time when you said you were going home to see your mum? Have you been waiting for just the right moment to humiliate me? You've been intent on ruining this wedding for me ever since you found out you weren't welcome and, congratulations, you've finally succeeded.'

'That wasn't what—'

'And you know what?' Libby cut in. 'I felt sorry for you at first. I worried about you being alone here. I guess all the energy I spent on feeling guilty about that was wasted. So go home, Rufus, sleep well in the knowledge that you've made me look small and stupid in front of anyone whose opinion I ever valued.'

'Libby, you don't understand, I—'

'Go!' she shouted.

As Rufus walked away, Libby didn't dare take her eyes off him. What she'd just told him was a lie. She'd known, of course, that Noah was hiding something and that there had to be a skeleton or two; she'd even suspected maybe a girlfriend or a casual partner tucked away somewhere, but she'd never imagined a wife. She'd wanted to think better of him than that perhaps, and she'd wanted him to be available, and so perhaps it had been short-sighted on her part, because, now that she thought about it, the fact had been staring her in the face.

His failure to deny it told her it was all true, and if she looked at him now, she was afraid of what she might do or say. She had, indeed, been played – that much Rufus was dead right about. By Rufus and by Noah, and if she'd had trust issues before, they were going to be a thousand times worse now. But it wasn't all Noah's fault – she hadn't exactly discouraged his attention, and even though she'd intended to find out more about him, she perhaps hadn't tried as hard as she should because part of her hadn't wanted to know. The blame for all that was on her.

'If you don't mind,' she said, keeping her voice as steady as she could, 'I'm going to get a drink. I suddenly feel as if I really need one.'

'Libby, let me explain—'

'No need,' she said, already walking through the silent crowd. Even the music had stopped, allowing far more attention on her than she was happy with. 'No need at all; it's perfectly clear to me.'

She didn't look back, but she sensed him following. Then she heard Tomas's voice. 'Leave it for now,' he said. 'Give her some space; Willow will talk to her.'

And then, as if by magic, the one person Libby really needed was walking beside her.

'Come with me,' Willow said. 'The suite's free.'

'Not Noah's?'

'Of course not – mine.'

'It's fine, I don't need to go upstairs; I just need a stiff drink.'

'No, you need somewhere quiet to talk about what just happened. Besides, we have a minibar.'

'You want to talk about what just happened?' Libby turned to her. She ought to have been angrier, more upset, but she just felt weary and defeated. 'You mean how every man I ever meet makes a total fool of me? You mean the thing that just happened in front of pretty much everyone we know?'

Willow took her gently by the arm and steered her towards the orangery. 'You don't want to go upstairs, fine. This is not exactly private but it's the best alternative we're going to get.'

'And there's a bar,' Libby said. Right now she'd happily drink it dry; anything so she didn't have to think about how both Rufus and Noah had humiliated her.

Willow sat her down at a table near the window. Outside, the lights of the grounds made the snow sparkle. It was freezing over, but more beautiful for it, if only Libby could appreciate beauty in anything right now.

'Stay there,' Willow said.

'I don't need—'

'Stay there while I get you a drink,' Willow commanded.

Libby thought about arguing for less than a second before she nodded shortly and settled in the seat. She watched as her friend dashed to the bar, said something to the staff member on duty and then rushed back.

'He'll bring them over,' she said. 'Gin, right?'

Libby nodded. 'Gin's as good as anything. What about paying him? I've got some money in my bag but it's—'

'Don't worry, they're on our tab,' she replied, taking a seat across from Libby. 'I tried to tell you,' she continued without preamble. 'Every time I tried something happened to get in the way. Now I feel terrible that I didn't try harder.'

Libby let out a long sigh. 'Willow, it's not your fault. How could it be? I'm not a wet-behind-the-ears teenager – I knew something was up but I chose to ignore it. If it's anyone's fault, it's mine. I'm an idiot.'

'That's the thing,' Willow said. 'I know you've usually got your head screwed on so I didn't worry too much because I didn't think… well, after Rufus I didn't think…'

'That I'd get taken in like that again? That makes me more than an idiot – it makes me pathetic. But you knew he was on the guest list for the wedding?' Libby gave a rueful half-smile. 'You couldn't have warned me he'd be gorgeous, charming and very married before the wedding?'

'Well, I could have but I didn't expect you to go falling for him! To be honest, I hardly knew that much about him myself apart from him being an old friend of Tomas; he's never been on my radar really, so I never gave it a thought – he was just part of that little gang of old uni friends. Even Tomas isn't in touch with him a lot these days, and when he sent the invitation he doubted Noah would even come. Honestly, Lib, if either of us had seen this coming…'

'I know. I should have seen it coming,' Libby said.

Willow gave her a sympathetic look. 'For what it's worth, I don't think he's by any means *happily* married.'

Libby was about to reply when the barman came over with their drinks. Willow thanked him.

'I think that almost makes it worse,' Libby said when he'd gone out of earshot. 'So I'm like… what? An idle distraction? A dalliance? A bit of fun? What goes on tour stays on tour? He's not getting it at home so he takes the obvious clichéd route of seducing the chief bridesmaid at the wedding he's at?'

'I think that's a bit harsh,' Willow said. 'And if you're being honest, I think you know it too. From what I can tell he seems to have genuine feelings for you, and if he only wanted to sleep with you he could have tried it last night instead of giving up his suite to the girls and sleeping on a chair down here. Tomas says he's generally a good guy and I believe him. Even good guys mess up.'

'In light of recent events that's all a bit academic now, isn't it? We're certainly in no danger of getting it on now.'

Willow frowned slightly. 'Rufus had no right causing a scene like that.'

'I'm sorry.'

'Why are *you* sorry? He should be apologising for making a fuss at my wedding like that.'

'Well, I'm sorry that I made him.'

'You didn't, and that's beside the point. He had no right.'

'Well, Rufus does a lot of things he's no right doing. Rufus doesn't know how to be anything else – it's like he exists to screw up my life.'

She took her glass and knocked the drink back in one go. 'You know the worst thing about it all?'

Willow shook her head.

'I actually really bloody liked Noah. Like, *really* liked him, like it could have turned into... Oh, what's the point? Who was I kidding? Even without the wife in the closet, he still lives in California.'

Willow glanced up, distracted for a moment, and Libby followed her gaze to see Tomas striding across the orangery looking a great deal more sober than he had half an hour before.

'You're OK?' he asked Libby, who nodded. 'Rufus has gone – I saw him leave myself. I think he's finally realised the damage he's done.'

'I suppose we have to be thankful for small mercies,' Libby said wearily.

Tomas wouldn't meet her eyes as he shoved his hands into his pockets. 'I think Noah would like the chance to explain himself to you.'

'He doesn't need to,' Libby replied.

'No, but I think it would help him feel better and I think it's only fair.'

'Fair to him or to me?' she asked.

'Come on, Libby. He's honestly a good guy in a sticky situation. I didn't know what was going on back home with him, but he's just filled me in and it sounds... well, he'd kept it to himself I think because he's struggling with it.'

Tomas looked more awkward still. Perhaps he felt it wasn't his place to explain what Noah wanted to explain himself or was worried that stealing Noah's thunder would mean Libby would then feel she'd heard enough and refuse to hear any more from him.

'Just give him five minutes,' he pleaded. 'For me if for no other reason.'

Libby sighed. 'Only for you,' she said. 'Where is he?'

'Outside having a cigarette.'

'I didn't know he smoked,' Libby said, vaguely surprised.

Tomas gave a half-smile. 'I think, for tonight, he's making an exception. He used to at university; I guess you're never really an ex-smoker, are you?'

'I've never smoked so I wouldn't know; I'll take your word for it. Shall I go to him?'

'I'll get him to come inside and see you. Happy to stay in here?'

Libby gave the room a once-over. Apart from them, there was an elderly couple at a table close to the bar. Everyone else was presumably in the restarted disco, which they could hear from here.

'It's as good a place as any,' she said.

'Right…'

Tomas strode away again.

'I hope you don't mind,' Libby said to Willow, 'but when I've done with this chat I'm going to call a cab and go home. Tell your dad thanks for offering to take care of it but I don't want to hang around, and it's not fair to expect your parents to leave early just because I'm in a bad mood now.'

'I really wish I'd told you about Noah.'

'You tried; I can see that now. Even then, it wasn't your job to tell me; Noah should have done it. I think we both saw that kiss coming and I think even he can't deny that. It also explains why I was getting such mixed signals from him – he knew he was messing where he shouldn't and was probably feeling guilty. A bit of knowing he was straying where he shouldn't stray, the promise of forbidden fruit and all that.'

'But if I'd known you were falling so hard for him I'd have made the time to warn you.'

'I haven't fallen hard for him,' Libby said practically, though her tone fooled nobody, especially not Willow, who raised her eyebrows meaningfully. 'OK, maybe a little,' Libby sighed. 'But we've known each other less than two days – you can't really fall for someone properly in two days, can you?'

'It hasn't been a very normal two days though, has it? Extreme situations do strange things to our common sense.'

'Ah, well, that's where you're wrong…' Libby gave her friend a sad smile. 'Because, as we all know, I'm the world champion at common sense. It takes more than a couple of mad snow days to upset my apple cart like that.'

'I have to say, you're taking it well. I'd have freaked out.'

Libby shrugged. 'What's the point in freaking out? It doesn't change anything that's happened.'

She reached for her glass and then realised it was empty. She'd have asked for another one but she didn't want to give the impression that Willow was wrong, and she really was freaking out. The truth was, she was far from calm on the inside, but if her best friend didn't see that then she wouldn't get stressed and her own night might yet be salvaged. She'd already endured more wedding stress than others would endure in twenty weddings, and what she and Tomas deserved now was for any worries to disappear so they could get back to enjoying the rest of their celebrations.

Libby wouldn't be a part of those now, of course, and she was sorry for that, but no matter how much she might want to be there for Willow, she couldn't bring herself to stay after what had happened.

'Hey…'

Willow and Libby both looked up to see Noah approaching their table. Willow got up.

'I'll leave you to it,' she said. 'Don't forget to come and find me before you go, Lib.'

'Of course,' Libby said.

Willow gave Noah a brisk smile before leaving and then he took the seat she'd just vacated. Libby could still smell the cold of outside on him, as well as the cigarette he'd just smoked.

'I've been a jerk,' he said. 'I owe you the most grovelling apology anyone's ever given. I'm so sorry you had to find out about Michaela that way; I wanted to tell you a few times, but—'

'You didn't because you knew you had a shot at me?'

'God no… Do you really feel I think so little of you? I'm sorry if you do, and I guess that's on me. I didn't tell you because it's too painful and complicated, and I know they aren't good enough excuses but they're the only ones I have. I liked what we had – really liked it – and if I kept my mouth shut I could pretend that the possibility of something more was there, that I wouldn't have to go home and face the terrible mess I've left there.'

'I liked you too, but you should have been honest with me; knowing about your wife wouldn't have changed anything.'

'Are you sure about that?'

'If you'd explained it to me like you're doing now, maybe. I mean, I suppose I wouldn't have been quite so quick to kiss you, but the rest… I've loved spending time with you and that wouldn't have changed; it's just that the rules attached to it would have changed. I wouldn't have allowed myself to…' She sighed. 'You should have been honest, that's all.'

'I know, and I can't tell you how sorry I am.'

He did look truly sorry, but Libby couldn't allow herself to be swayed. This thing they'd started, whatever it was, had to stop, now more than ever.

'That guy,' he asked. 'Rufus? He's…?'

It was suddenly Libby's turn to squirm. Even she had to recognise that it was all very well lecturing Noah on honesty but she hadn't exactly been straight with him either, and that was partly why she couldn't be as angry as she might otherwise have been. It seemed they'd both been trying to forget uncomfortable truths during their time together, to pretend there were no strings, that they were free to have fun with no consequences. But in life, no matter what you did, there were always consequences, even if you didn't realise it.

'My ex,' she said. 'A recent, complicated, apparently not-ready-to-let-go ex. I guess if we're making admissions, I should have told you that at the start too.'

'Hmm, but I own it; I still win on the big fat lie-o-meter. At least he's an ex.'

'Yes, I suppose so. But you deserved some warning about what Rufus might do if he noticed us getting close.'

'Did you know what he might do?'

'Well, I knew he'd be pissed off, but I never thought…' She gave a tiny shrug. 'Just goes to show…'

'That emotions are a weird and unpredictable thing?'

'Exactly.'

'Listen… do you want me to get you a drink?'

'No, thanks, better not.' She gave him a small smile. 'I think perhaps alcohol has had its part to play in all this too so maybe I'll leave it alone if I'm at a wedding in future.'

'Libby, you have to believe that I never came to this wedding looking to score.'

'I do believe it.'

'I don't think you do. I never expected to meet anyone in that way, and especially someone like you. I tried so hard to ignore the attraction, but it was too difficult. And I guess there was a part of me that didn't want to. I felt like, if I threw this away, I might never find anything like it again and I didn't want that to happen. I didn't want my sham of a marriage to get in the way but it did. I suppose by being so determined, by using any means necessary not to throw it away, that's exactly what I've done.'

'You may think your marriage is a sham, but the fact is you *are* married. It's a big deal – it's not something you can ignore when it suits you. If you're so unhappy in it then maybe you should do something about that.'

'Don't you think I've tried? She's refusing to allow me to do anything about it, won't sign any papers, won't instruct a lawyer, won't even talk about divorce. She won't move out of our house either and I can't afford to, so even that's a problem.'

'But that's crazy? Who would want to cling on to someone who clearly doesn't want them? That sounds like torture!'

'She thinks if she ignores it, our rift will magically heal and we'll go back to the way we were. It won't, but until she accepts that then I'm stuck. I thought I could deal with that for as long as it takes but… then I met you. Now I know I really do have to do something about it.'

'How long has this been going on?'

'About six months.'

'And… I don't want to pry but was there anyone else involved?'

He hesitated. 'Does it matter?'

'Was it you? Did you cheat on her?'

'Would you believe me if I said it was her who cheated on me? I don't suppose I've done much to earn your trust so far.'

'She cheated on you?' Libby frowned. 'I'm sorry.'

'So you believe me?'

'If you're saying it now, then yes. What reason do you have to lie? It's not like there's anything between us now. What happened?'

'She says it was just one night, a moment of weakness with a colleague who decided he then wanted more, and when she wouldn't give it to him he came to me and spilt the beans, hoping that would swing it for him. It did, in a way, because for me the trust was gone, but the truth is, I'd probably been looking for a way out for a while. Things had been difficult, though she'd refused to talk about it – I realise now that's probably what drove her into the arms of another man.'

Libby blew out a long breath. There was something eerily familiar in the story he was telling. 'I don't know what to say.'

'It's a crazy situation. In my head I'm ready to move on, free of any attachment for Michaela and ready to love someone else, but legally and morally not free at all. It's confusing – I don't know where I stand.'

'Me neither.' She gave a slight smile. 'So, have we been having an affair then?'

'I'm not sure one kiss constitutes an affair. But then, I think we've established I'm no expert when it comes to this stuff.'

'Well, it was a bloody good kiss anyway.'

His grin was more than a little sheepish. 'It was. A nice memory to take with me.'

'Yes, I suppose that's what it is, a nice memory. It can't be anything else, can it?'

He held her gaze for a moment. 'I don't know,' he said finally. 'I guess that depends on you.'

Libby shook her head. 'That's where you're wrong. You're the one who's married. You're also the one living on the other side of the world. I think it depends on a lot more than just what I want.'

'But if all that was out of the way, would you... would we have a chance?'

'I honestly don't know, but those things aren't out of the way, are they? So I suppose we'll never find out. It was fun for a while though.'

'It was.'

Libby eyed her empty glass with another faint pang of regret. She'd said no more drinking, but it seemed like a stupid rule to set herself right now.

'Have one more drink with me,' he said. 'I don't want it to end yet and not like this.'

It was tempting and too easy to say yes. Libby didn't really want it to end either, but she knew ending it was the right thing to do. She shook her head.

'No, I don't think so. I'm sorry, Noah.'

He looked as disappointed as she felt. She was sorry about more than refusing his drink; she was sorry that they'd never make this work. She'd never been more sorry about anything in her life.

Chapter Sixteen

There were no hard feelings, but that didn't stop Libby from feeling wretched and lost as the taxi sped down the snow-steeped lanes with her in the back seat. It had cost her a small fortune, being Christmas night, more than she would have wanted to pay, but, in the end, she'd have paid whatever the driver demanded if it meant getting away from Lovage Hall. The air of the car was hot and dry and made her eyes sore and itchy. Or perhaps that was just down to the tears she was holding back. It had been one hell of a Christmas, and it wasn't even over yet.

Her parents would probably be getting ready for bed right now, so there was no point in taking a detour to call on them and try to make up for not being able to come for lunch, and she wasn't sure how much better a conversation with them would make her feel anyway. If anything it would probably make things worse. So she was heading home now, to her empty flat, to reflect on what might have been, what everyone involved did wrong and whether, as she pessimistically believed more and more as time went by, she'd just thrown away her one shot at the real thing. Or at least had it ruined by bad luck and mishandling.

She'd loved Rufus, of course, once, but it had never been like this. Rufus had never, in all the years they'd been together, made her feel like Noah had. Two days she'd known him, and already she felt his loss more keenly than anything she'd experienced after her split with Rufus. Different circumstances, yes, but the notion was strange and troubling just the same. Perhaps she only felt that way because now everything she'd ever had with Rufus was a tattered, messy web of lies and betrayal that she just couldn't see a way through. She was supposed to have had a child with Rufus, had almost married him. What did that say about the way it had turned out? If she'd had the baby after all, would things have been different?

But she'd lost the baby and that was a question she'd never have the answer to.

Her phone lit up with a call.

Rufus.

It was the third time he'd tried to get through since he'd left Lovage Hall, but she'd either been too busy or too fed up to take his call. Perhaps this time she ought to; perhaps, after all, it was the least he deserved from her. Despite all his mistakes and all his deceit, tonight, at least, he'd been the only one telling the truth.

She swiped to answer.

'Libby, hear me out…'

'I was going to – that's why I picked up.'

'Oh, right… Look, I'm sorry about hitting your boyfriend but you needed to know the truth. And I'm sorry I had to say it in front of everyone but there was no other way to do it. It's not really my fault.'

'So it's my fault? Because I didn't obsessively ask every wedding guest about him so I could dig up dirt? Then I guess I am guilty of that much. Hmm… so, grateful as I am for your assistance, I'm a grown-up and I would have sorted it out myself eventually. And while we're here, let's clear things up. First of all, he's not my boyfriend.

Secondly, you didn't hit him, because he ducked, and, thirdly, in giving me the truth you assumed I so badly needed to hear you also managed to humiliate me in front of a room full of wedding guests that I'll probably never be able to look in the eye again. So thanks for that. And lastly, you're a lying bastard capable of telling the most vile stories to get your own way. I phoned Kylie... there's nothing wrong with your mum, is there?'

There was silence on the other end of the line.

'Forget it,' Libby said. 'It's not even worth my energy.'

'I didn't mean to humiliate you; I was trying to help.'

'You didn't help; you did the exact opposite of helping.'

'I only did it because I couldn't stand to see him play you.'

'Again, it's kind of you to assume I'm that stupid. And in this scenario, it's alright for you to play me?'

'That's not what I meant. Lib, why are you making this so difficult?'

'Oh, do you think I should have made it easy for you?'

'No, but... I'm just trying to look out for you.'

'I don't need you to look out for me! We're over, done, kaput, dodo status. You have been relieved of your looking-out-for-me duties. I give you my blessing to move on and look out for someone else. If I screw up then it's my business and you no longer need to worry about it.'

'But I still love you!'

'That doesn't change anything for me. Today you've proved that I can never trust a word you say again and that you'll do anything to get what you want. It's over, Rufus – you need to accept that and let me go. Please... if you care like you say you do then you'll do that and move on. There's no point in being stuck like this forever, where neither of us can be happy.'

'You can't mean that.'

'Why on earth not? Say we got back together. It would only be because I felt sorry for you and you'd know that. How could you be happy with someone when you know they don't really want to be with you? And don't tell me that I could learn to feel something for you again, that we could get back to how we were, because we can't. Regardless of the reasons, you cheated on me. You were unfaithful and you were the one who left me for her.'

'I know, but I was confused; I didn't realise what—'

'It doesn't change a thing – not for me. I can't make myself feel differently about it no matter what you say now.'

'But it's OK for other men to lie to you?' he asked, and Libby heard his tone flip in an instant into something more savage and accusing. It seemed he hadn't believed her claim that she'd known about Noah's wife.

'If you're talking about Noah again then you're being ridiculous. How can what he did possibly compare to what you did? And if you think you're being clever, you're not – I told you I knew already.'

'But if you hadn't found out… if you'd carried on seeing him – would he have told you about his wife of his own accord? And if he didn't, that would have been the same as what I did, right?'

'He'd have told me,' Libby said, though she wasn't certain of that at all. 'He was trying to… he meant to.'

'Did he? Didn't look like he was trying very hard to me.'

'That's not the point – you had no right to interfere. How did you even know about it anyway?'

'All I had to do was ask a few people – wasn't hard.'

'You shouldn't have done that; it had nothing to do with you.'

He shouldn't have, but more to the point, he shouldn't have had to. Libby should have been the one asking around and it wouldn't have been hard to get the answers she needed. The truth was she'd known all along to ask more questions, and the bigger truth was that she hadn't because part of her hadn't wanted the answers. Noah might have hoodwinked her but only because she'd been so willing to let him. He'd been pretending, but so had she, and it had been fun and liberating for her, just like it had been for him. They'd both been trying to forget significant others who wouldn't let go, both looking for an hour's respite from that burden.

It was strange that it had taken Rufus to make her see that. She was also quite aware of the irony that it was probably the very last outcome her ex had hoped for. Right at this very moment, did she even care that Noah had a wife in California? Did she believe him when he said the marriage was like a dead man walking? Did it even matter what she believed?

'Why are you being so stubborn?' Rufus asked. 'What is he to you? You've only just met him.'

'I've only just met him, yes, but that's not the point. What I do now is up to me, my choices, my mistakes, and nothing to do with you.'

'Are you going to see him again?'

She let out an impatient sigh. 'Really? What do you think?'

'Sorry…'

At least his tone had lost its edge again. Now he just sounded tired and defeated, which wasn't that far from how she felt. That was one thing they still had in common at least.

'We're going round in circles,' she said. 'Let it go. Can't we just call a truce? I don't want to keep fighting with you forever; I just want closure. Can't I just have that please?'

'What does closure mean? You're never going to see me again?'

'It means we move on from this and next time we bump into each other for whatever reason – and we probably will – it won't be so weird. We can be civil, adult, not have to get into some mad standoff about something I do that you may or may not agree with. It means I live my life and you live yours and neither interferes with the other. It means we have respect and fondness for our time together, but we accept that those days are gone. I'll never stop being a friend if you need it but I can't ever be anything more. I think, deep down, you knew that even when you were saying you wanted to try again.'

There was a long pause, and for a brief moment Libby thought they'd been cut off. That would have been about typical for the sort of night she'd had. But then Rufus replied and she could hear the small, sad smile in his voice.

'You always did know me too well.'

'Not that well,' she began, and would have pointed out that she'd never seen his affair with Kylie coming but stopped herself. Closure applied to both of them, as did acceptance and forgiveness. It had been a rocky road but perhaps, at last, Libby thought with a creeping and cautious sense of hope, the end was in sight.

Chapter Seventeen

Because she didn't deal well with inactivity or a lack of structure to her day, Libby often looked forward to opening up the shop again after the Christmas break. Some years, if the holiday fell midweek, she took only Christmas Day off, having chosen to cover the last-minute Christmas Eve rush and then go back in again for the Boxing Day sale. She never minded; her colleagues had people they wanted to spend time with, and she often had nowhere in particular to be.

This year was no different. In fact, this year she had fewer reasons to spend Boxing Day at home than ever, and yet her heart just wasn't in it as she unlocked the shutters and lifted them to open up the shop for business.

She'd kept staffing as light as possible today. Her team were very good; most of them had worked at the store for years, if not decades, and they were fair to each other and the company. Usually – apart from Libby who often volunteered – whoever had worked the previous Boxing Day would take the next one off and the same went for Christmas Eve. Of course, nobody worked Christmas Day, though this morning, as she switched all the lights on, Libby half thought if she had it would have saved her a whole heap of trouble.

Stephen was the first colleague to arrive, stamping snow from his boots at the front door as Libby crossed the shop to let him in.

She locked the door again as he stepped over the threshold. Some customers were keen for bargains and no respecters of opening times; if the doors were open they'd come in whether the shop was open for business or not. It was better not to give them the choice until the tills were set up and all the stock was out.

'Hi, Stephen. Had a good Christmas?' Libby asked vaguely as he followed her through to the tiny staffroom. She switched on the kettle for him. Whoever was in first usually made the first cup of tea of the day and it was almost always Libby. She wasn't one of those bosses who thought her subordinates ought to do the mundane tasks like tea-making and she didn't expect to be waited on – she was happy to pitch in with everything, along with the rest.

'Lovely and quiet, what there was of it,' Stephen said.

Stephen had been working at the store when Libby had first arrived as a weekend sales assistant. When the manager's job had come up she'd expected him to take it and had been surprised to see him pass it up. He didn't want the responsibility, he'd said, and especially for only a few pence an hour pay rise, and part of Libby didn't blame him for that. It was a lot to take on if you weren't going to be much better off for it, financially speaking, especially if you weren't keen on the extra duties.

'How was your wedding?' he asked.

'Interesting,' she replied.

She reached for the tea caddy, and when he didn't offer a reply she looked up to see him raise questioning eyebrows.

'Long story,' she continued. 'In a nutshell, the wedding was fine until we all got snowed in at the venue and the power went off – it stayed off for most of the night and into Christmas Day. I slept on a chair in my dress and…'

There was so much more to tell, but it all felt huge and muddled and most of it, fond as she was of Stephen and as close as they were as long-term colleagues, wasn't for him to hear.

'Well, that's about the size of it,' she concluded. 'Willow and Tomas have gone home today and they're probably packing to fly off to Mexico for their honeymoon tomorrow. I only got home late last night so my Christmas definitely hasn't been relaxing or peaceful, and there certainly wasn't much of it.'

'Wow... that does sound eventful. You know, if you needed to take today off I'm sure we'd manage.'

'I know you would but I'm fine. I'd only be sitting on my own if I was home.'

'If I were you I'd go back to bed.'

'I could, but I doubt I'd sleep. I'd rather be busy here, take my mind off things.'

'Things...' Stephen said slowly. 'Any *things* you'd like to share?'

She replaced the lid of the caddy and popped it back onto the shelf, giving Stephen a brief smile. He was greying at the temples but still had a good head of hair, which was still quite dark for a man so close to retirement. His unruly mop and his little round glasses often made Libby reflect that if Harry Potter were a real person, by the time he got to pensionable age, he'd probably look a lot like Stephen.

'Thanks, but it's all a bit long and boring. We probably ought to get set up; if today is like any other Boxing Day sale we're going to be busy.'

'No problem. But don't forget that I'm here if you need a friendly ear.'

'I won't. Thanks, Stephen.'

There was a gentle tap at the outer door.

'That'll be Melanie,' Stephen said. 'I'll go.'

Libby smiled. 'Bound to be. She has a knack of arriving the second the kettle boils.'

'Yes, but the day she's here early enough to put it on we'll be throwing a party,' Stephen said, and Libby had to chuckle softly as he left the staffroom to let the third and final member of today's team in.

A moment later Libby heard two sets of footsteps coming back to the staffroom. She recognised both so well she could tell which was which. Stephen's were heavy and methodical, while Melanie's were uneven – she walked with a limp due to arthritis in one of her knees. Some days were better than others for poor Melanie, and Libby often wondered how she managed to keep working in a job that required so many hours on her feet, but when she'd once aired her thoughts to her colleague, Melanie had told her that, actually, it helped her to keep moving. Libby didn't really see how that could be the case, but if Melanie said it and she wanted to keep working, Libby wasn't going to argue. Melanie had been at the shop almost as long as Stephen and both knew their jobs inside-out – they were valuable members of staff and Libby really didn't want to lose either of them.

'Hi,' Libby said as Melanie came in. 'Good break?'

'Oh, lovely,' Melanie said cheerily. 'All the kids came home and Ethan brought his new girlfriend over.'

'This is the one you like?' Libby asked as she poured boiling water into three mugs.

'Oh, yes, he's still got her. She's beautiful and such a sweetie. I do hope he keeps her – I told him yesterday he'd have me to answer to if he doesn't.'

'So you had all the kids?' Libby handed Melanie a mug. 'All six? With their partners too?'

Melanie nodded.

'Blimey, you had your work cut out.'

'I had plenty of help so I didn't mind. It was really nice to have them in one room – now that they've all flown the nest and live all over the place it really doesn't happen very often at all.'

'I shouldn't imagine there are many rooms that can fit them all in,' Libby said, and Melanie laughed lightly.

'That's true. How was your break? The snow didn't affect the wedding too much, did it?'

'She got snowed in at Lovage Hall,' Stephen put in.

'Oh, that's terrible!' Melanie looked rather more horrified than the news warranted, but it didn't faze Libby, who was used to her dramatic reactions to often very undramatic events.

'It was a bit of a nuisance,' Libby said. 'Caused some headaches for the poor staff at the hotel, but at times it was actually quite fun.'

'I don't think I'd like it,' Melanie said emphatically. 'How long were you stuck for?'

'Until last night,' Libby said. 'Actually, I could have got away a little earlier but the wedding just sort of carried on – as we were a bit of a captive audience anyway – so I stayed for a while after the roads were clear again.'

'Oh,' Melanie said, 'I suppose it wasn't all bad then.'

Libby sipped her tea. There'd been plenty of drama and some stress, but Melanie was right – it hadn't been all bad. In fact, now that she thought about it, some of it had been very good, even the bits that, in hindsight, shouldn't have been. The time she'd spent with Willow and Tomas and the trio of torment, and Noah...

The beautiful wedding, the jokes, the drinking, the amazing food, the teamwork... that kiss...

She shook herself. It was all over now, and especially whatever it was she'd had with Noah – that was absolutely, definitely over. He'd probably be getting ready to fly back to California to resume his glamorous job in his glamorous home, and here she was, in a dingy backstreet tailors in a small northern town doing the same job she'd been doing since… Well, since forever. His life would go back to sunshine and sparkles in Tinseltown and hers would go back to tea with her old colleagues in a dusty shop selling suits and ties and terribly expensive shoes. She'd always been content with that, of course, but something had happened to her over the course of this Christmas – a growing sense of restlessness and a need for change. She couldn't put her finger on what that change needed to be or where it might come from, but suddenly her life didn't seem like enough as it was.

'Penny for them,' Stephen said, and Libby blinked, realising she'd been staring into her mug.

'Oh…' Libby said. 'Right, yes…'

'Are you sure you're alright?'

'I'm just tired, that's all.'

'Need a breather?'

'No, no… I'll drink this and then go and get the sale stock down from the store room.'

'Want a hand with that?' Stephen asked.

'That'd be good. It needs labelling up too – there wasn't time before the break – and if we can do that before we open the front door, all the better. I can't imagine we'll get very busy first thing, but you never know.'

'Hmm,' Melanie put in darkly, 'we say that every year and half of those we're proved wrong. Remember that time when that party of twelve wanted kilts for Hogmanay? It's not like there's a lot to choose from when it comes to kilts anyway, but they wanted very specific ones *and* they wanted them for sale prices. I mean, just because there's a sale on somewhere doesn't mean every scrap of stock is half price.'

'God, yes, they were a pain,' Libby agreed. 'If there was ever a time when I seriously considered quitting my job it was that Boxing Day morning.'

'And then they were somehow shocked when we couldn't sort them all out because we didn't have enough stock and we couldn't get more in time. Who keeps twelve Black Watch kilts in stock? We're not even in Scotland!'

'I've lost count of the times people have come in last minute for something like that and been shocked when there's no time to get it made for them,' Stephen agreed. 'Blokes are the worst culprits for that, and I say that as a reformed character in that regard myself. I used to be guilty of that all the time until I started to work here and realised just what a bad idea it is.'

Libby sipped at her drink. 'I wish more people would think about it. Still, it's not the worst thing we've ever dealt with and I expect there'll be plenty more like it in the years to come.'

'Ours is not to reason why…' Stephen said.

'Exactly.' Libby drank down to the bottom of her mug. It had been a bit too hot, but she was conscious that time wasn't on her side this morning; she'd got in later than she would have liked and ought to have been a lot more prepared for opening than she currently was. 'Right… time to get cracking.'

With three of them working together, it didn't take nearly as long to tag all the sale items as Libby had feared. Then they'd had the rather more physical task of taking it all down from the stockroom to the shop to hang on a display rail; formalwear was much heavier than it looked, especially in bulk. Libby had done her best to stay cheerful and had chatted with Stephen about this and that as they'd worked, but there wasn't a moment when there weren't dark thoughts in the back of her mind. Every time she walked those stairs between the stockroom and the shop it reminded her of the day she'd fallen down them and ended up losing her baby.

In the past she'd had to force herself to stop thinking about it, and she did her best to do exactly the same today. Dwelling on what couldn't be changed was painful and unproductive and wouldn't make the work she had to do any easier, but it seemed that having so much contact with Rufus over the preceding two days had brought those dark thoughts very much to the fore again.

She needed to focus on work, she told herself, especially as right now her job was pretty much the only constant, the only certainty in her life. And it wasn't the fault of the stairs that she fell, or the shop, or her job – it wasn't even hers really, though in more desperate moments she often blamed herself. It was nobody's fault – it was just bad luck. Terrible things happened to people who didn't deserve them and one had happened to her. Her luck was often fickle lately; though that was a whole other subject she really couldn't allow herself to think about now.

She was arranging the stock on the rail while Melanie was at the counter checking the float in the till and Stephen was getting rid of some packaging by dumping it into the bins out at the back when the shop door opened. She looked up, ready to greet the first customer of the day and slightly annoyed at herself for not being quite ready, and froze.

'A very good friend tells me this is the best place to buy a suit,' he said.

Libby hurriedly slid the linen jacket she was holding onto the rail and raced over, pulling him to one side.

'What on earth are you doing here?'

'Buying a suit.'

'No you're not!'

'Yes I am. You do sell suits, don't you?'

Libby pursed her lips. She was in no mood to play games. 'Fine – Melanie will measure you up.'

'I'm sure Melanie is perfectly lovely but I want you to do it.'

'Noah...' Libby began in a warning voice. 'What are you playing at?'

'I'm not playing at anything. I need something for an awards ceremony when I get home... can you recommend something?'

'You have a perfectly good suit – you wore it at the wedding.'

'Yes, but I want a different one. Even I can't pull off thrift-store chic at a posh award ceremony.'

He smiled down at her. He seemed infuriatingly relaxed, which was hardly fair when Libby's heart was beating like a drum machine at a rave.

'Fine,' she sighed. 'What do you have in mind? You must have some preference for colour or fabric I can use as a starting point.'

'Do you have something in sackcloth?'

She stared at him. 'What?'

'That is what you wear to say you're sorry, isn't it? Or am I getting mixed up with hair shirts?'

'I've already said you have nothing to apologise for,' she said in a low voice. 'There was a misunderstanding, but everything was out in the open before there was any real harm done. I'm not looking for an apology.'

'No, but that doesn't mean I don't owe you one.'

'We stopped it; nothing happened.'

'That's just it. Honestly, at the risk of sounding like a bastard, I didn't want to stop it. I wanted it to become something and I didn't care how wrong it was. And… I still do.'

'It's not possible.'

'Why not?'

'You know why!'

'There's an obstacle.'

'A bit more than an obstacle, I'd say. Your wife is not an *obstacle* – she's a person.'

'OK, that probably sounded way more ruthless than I meant it to.'

'It sounded horrible. If we'd ever got together, would you have talked about me like that one day?'

'God, of course not! Maybe it sounded horrible, but you don't know what it's been like with her the last few months… I'm sorry it sounded that way but you can't pass judgement; she's put me through hell. I'm struggling to see her as anything but an obstacle to the life I want.'

'I'm sorry, I know she has, but you still can't talk about her like that.'

'You're right; I'm sorry.'

'Do you hate her that much?'

'No… but I definitely don't love her.'

Libby gave him a crooked smile. 'I have to say that sounds horribly familiar.'

'Your ex? What happened with him? He left you alone last night, didn't he?'

'Oh, he called me so many times I was forced to pick up eventually. It was worth it though. I think finally I might have got through.'

'So you're free?'

'I hope so.'

'I wish I could say that.'

'Maybe you just have to try harder.'

'I know; I was thinking that myself this morning. I pretty much thought about it all night too. That's when I wasn't thinking about you.'

'You were thinking about me?'

'I couldn't fly home without seeing you, seeing if I could fix the mess I've made. Libby, tell me I'm wrong if you think so, but I feel as if we could have something. I'm right, aren't I? I'm not mistaken? You feel what I feel?'

'What can we have, Noah? You sound crazy.'

'I know, and I would have told myself that this time yesterday. I didn't even know I felt this way about you until you left Lovage Hall, and then it hit me all at once like running into a wall, just how much I missed you when you weren't there. Everything in that place made me think of you—'

'Noah…' she warned.

'I told Tomas everything and he said try. He told me to come and see you and it made sense. He told me where to find the shop – don't be mad at him; he knows me, knows this is serious, otherwise he wouldn't have done that.'

Libby glanced across to the counter. She could tell that even though Melanie was trying to look as if she was busy counting out notes and wasn't listening at all, she was.

'So, do you want this suit from the sale or are you happy to peruse the regular-priced stock?' she asked in a loud, clear voice, just for Melanie's benefit.

Noah frowned.

'You'll get more choice if you're willing to compromise on the price, of course,' Libby continued. 'Have you got a maximum budget? Do you need accessories? Tie, waistcoat... cummerbund?'

'That's it?' he asked, looking vaguely desperate. 'That's all I get?'

'You said you wanted a suit,' she said, and then lowered her voice. 'Another lie, I suppose?'

The jibe had come from nowhere. She hadn't meant it, and as soon as she'd uttered it she wished she could take it back.

'Low blow,' he said, looking genuinely hurt now, and for a second Libby wondered whether she'd tipped the scales and killed any affection he might have had for her. 'I thought we'd moved past that.'

'We had. I'm—'

'Look, I know I hurt and humiliated you, but I never meant to.'

'It wasn't just you. And I suppose I wasn't exactly forthcoming about Rufus, was I?'

'Well, I think Rufus was doing a dandy job of that all by himself,' Noah said, and Libby noticed the ghost of a smile now.

'He got there in the end, didn't he? Certainly made his presence known.'

'You think he'll really give up now?'

Libby shrugged. 'Who knows? I only know that it felt pretty final the way we left things last night. It felt like he'd finally accepted things were over.'

'I hope I have as much success with Michaela. I was going to talk to her when I got back, but I'm going to take a leaf out of your book and phone her later.'

Libby's eyes widened.

'You're sure you want to do that? You wouldn't rather wait until you got home?'

'It's been dragging on for too long and that's partly because I've let it. But I've realised I need to put my foot down and move things along.'

'Wow, that's... I don't know what to say. Good, I guess? I'm happy for you.'

'OK, so I'm going out on a limb here. I'm not telling you all this so you'll drop everything and come for a drink with me tonight – though I would love to take you out. I'm telling you because I realised that not sorting the situation and freeing myself is what ultimately screwed up my chances with you and I want you to know how much I regret that. It's time I grew a spine and you made me realise that. If the chance comes round again I won't mess it up.'

'I suppose that's one positive from the chaos then.'

'You think it was chaos?'

'Don't you?'

'Maybe. But some of it was pretty awesome chaos, right?'

'Are you referring to meeting me?'

'Could be.'

Libby couldn't help but smile. 'Well, it's the first time I've been called awesome chaos.'

'A smile, eh? Is that a crack in the armour?'

'No.'

'Am I making any progress at all?'

'No.'

'So I should leave right now?'

'You haven't bought your suit yet.'

'Hmm. Would you be very annoyed if I told you I didn't really need a suit?'

'I wouldn't be very surprised. I did have my suspicions.'

'I always said you were a smart cookie.'

Libby's smile faded. 'Noah, seriously, what are you doing here?'

'Seriously? I don't have a clue. What can I say to make things right? What can I say to convince you I'm worth a shot?'

'I don't know.'

'Me neither – that's the problem. I know there's nothing I can say to make you trust me after what I did. All I know is that I needed to see you and I couldn't fly home until I'd at least tried.'

'Tried what?'

'I don't even know that,' he said lamely. 'Something that would mean I wouldn't be flying home knowing I'd never see you again.'

Libby let out a sigh. 'If you don't know what to say then I can't tell you. We're just going round in circles and I have to work. You don't have to never see me again; I'm sure if you visit Tomas and Willow in the future our paths will probably cross again.'

'That's not really what I meant.'

'Yes, I know what you meant, but it's the best I can offer you.'

'Have a drink with me tonight,' he said.

'I'm busy.'

'No you're not – Tomas says you never go out.'

'Oh, did he? Wait till I see Tomas!'

'But that means you're free?'

'No, I'm not.'

'But you don't have plans?'

'I'm washing my hair.'

'Does anyone even use that as an excuse to stay in these days?'

'I do.'

'Your hair looks great – doesn't need washing.'

'God you're persistent!'

'I know – it's a Hollywood thing. You have to be persistent if you're going to make it.'

'You're not in Hollywood now. And just say, for argument's sake and not because I have any intentions of backing down at all, we did have that drink. What then? You're going home soon so what's the point?'

'Maybe I'll come back.'

'Yes, I expect you will… like next Christmas or to attend the next wedding.'

'Sooner than that… depending what I have to come back for.'

'What does that mean?'

'I'll tell you when we get that drink.'

'I never said I would come.'

'You never said you wouldn't either.'

Libby folded her arms. 'You're really annoying, you know that?'

'It's why you like me.'

'Cocky too.'

'Also why you like me. Come on, Libby. You already know we'll have a great time.'

He glanced towards the till, and it seemed he was now suddenly as aware of Melanie's eyes on him as Libby had been the whole time he'd been there. This was not a conversation she needed to be having right now, and no doubt Melanie would be angling for the low-down as soon as Noah had left.

'So shall I pick you up at eight?'

'At what point did I say yes?'

'You didn't exactly, but you did say you'd hear me out.'

'Did I?'

'Not in so many words, but I could see it in your eyes.' He gave her a crooked grin and she couldn't help returning it.

'You're hard work.'

'I like to think of it as tenacious.'

'You're really not taking no for an answer, are you?'

'Tell me truthfully: do you want me to take your no?'

She sighed. 'OK. I'm not sure what time I'll be packing up here – depends how busy it gets. Maybe I could make eight. If I'm running late though, I don't have your number. Come to think of it, you don't have mine and you don't know where I live.'

He raised his eyebrows, his grin spreading.

'Oh,' Libby said, her tone half exasperation and half amusement. 'I guess you asked Tomas that too. And he actually told you? I can't believe Willow would let him give that information out willy-nilly.'

'He hasn't exactly, not yet, so don't go all guns blazing. He said he'd give me the details if you said yes… So, I guess I have it covered, right? As you're saying yes?'

'OK,' Libby said, still trying to look serious but unable to prevent the feeling of excitement at the prospect of a drink with him, even though she knew very well it was probably going to land her in even more trouble. 'I suppose we can let Tomas make himself useful – so I'll see you tonight at eight.'

Chapter Eighteen

Noah arrived at eight on the dot. He was so impossibly punctual that Libby half wondered if he'd been waiting outside for the moment his watch would strike the exact time before knocking on her door. Still, she liked that he was keen, and yet had also learnt and retained enough knowledge of her habits to realise that presenting himself any earlier or any later than eight would throw her schedule right out and have her in a tizzy for at least the first hour of their drink.

She'd call it a date, but for now, she wasn't really sure what it was. She didn't know what she was hoping for, what it was respectable to hope for, whether going out with him tonight somehow made her 'the other woman' or what to think about any of it. She still wasn't convinced this was a good idea, but she was committed now and would see it through regardless. She just hoped it wasn't going to take her to a place she'd regret afterwards, but the attraction she still felt for him, despite everything that had happened between them, was so strong she was quite worried that, faced with a temptation she couldn't resist, that was precisely what would happen.

Her reaction to him as she opened the door didn't do much to assuage her worries. He looked good. In fact, he looked incredible. She'd loved the formal suit at the wedding, but he'd taken it down a notch, so he still looked slick and smart but in a low-key way, with a crisp, powder-blue cotton shirt, waistcoat (she'd always been a sucker for a man in a well-tailored waistcoat) with the last button left undone, exactly as it ought to be, and heavy woollen trousers to match. And whatever cologne he was wearing... it had to be laced with some kind of narcotic because it was making her feel strangely susceptible to being kissed... and maybe other things too.

'You look lovely,' he said, handing her some flowers. Hastily pro-cured, obviously, she told herself, and from goodness knew where on Boxing night. Cheap, petrol-station blooms or some such, no doubt. Terribly clichéd, of course. But still... he was trying, and she liked that he was trying. She held them to her nose and smiled.

'Thank you,' she said. 'I wasn't expecting a fuss.'

'I didn't think it was a fuss,' he said. 'I just thought it was courte-ous. Can't very well turn up empty-handed to... well, I can't, can I?'

He didn't call it a date either, though Libby assumed that wasn't because he was as confused as she was, but because he was trying to be tactful. He'd be well aware of her feelings on the situation, and she had to admit his playing it cool was a bit of a masterstroke.

'They go with your dress,' he said. Libby glanced absently down at her forest-green velvet frock. The flowers he'd brought were mostly white and cream, but she could sort of see what he meant.

'It's a lovely dress,' he continued. 'You look perfect.'

'I look like someone who didn't close up the shop until gone six, so didn't have much time to get ready and no warning that she might need a dress so had to get an old one out, but thank you for trying to make me feel good about it.'

'Sometimes our old faithfuls are just that for a reason. Classic looks never go out of style – you must know that better than anyone.'

She laughed. 'God you're good.'

'What do you mean?'

'You know exactly the right thing to say.'

'I'm not sure that's true but thank you.'

He did, and she had to wonder if it was a good thing. Did he just have a knack of saying the right thing, or did he cleverly devise it to get what he wanted? She didn't like the idea of the latter and he seemed so genuine that she decided she was going to refuse to believe it.

'I'll pop these in the sink,' she said. 'Just to keep them from drying out till I can arrange them in a vase later. Alright to hang on two ticks?'

'Of course.' He dug his hands in his pockets and gave her an easy smile. He looked a lot more relaxed than she felt, but it was hard to tell how much of a bluff that was.

She dashed back to the kitchen, filled the sink with a little water and stood the bouquet in it before going back to the front door.

'Nice neighbourhood,' he said.

'I'm sure...' Libby gave him a wry smile. 'Nicer than Hollywood?'

'I keep telling you I don't actually live in Hollywood. And this is very different, of course, but different can still be as nice.'

'I find it hard to believe anyone would swap it though.'

'That depends. I'm sure there could be some very compelling reasons to swap.'

'So...' Libby said, hastily changing the subject as she closed her front door behind her. 'Did you decide where we're going?'

'I had a few thoughts, but I wasn't sure if you'd want to eat or not.'

'I can always eat, but if you haven't booked a table anywhere we might struggle, being Boxing night and all.'

'Oh... I never thought about that.'

'Don't worry about it,' she said, feeling quite sorry for him because, the way his face fell, he obviously thought he was already failing at this date and they hadn't even started it yet. And then she reminded herself again that she didn't even know if it *was* a date. 'I'm not that hungry really and I'm sure if we can get in a pub somewhere I can get crisps from the bar.'

'Well, that's not usually the way I show a girl a good time, but...'

She gave him a reassuring smile. 'I'm happier that way than you might think. There's a nice pub a couple of streets away – the Anchor. Not very glamorous or trendy but a good atmosphere and likely to have a table because it doesn't get overly busy. Can you cope with rustic?'

'I think so,' he said with a lopsided grin that made him look more like his usual self again – at least, the version Libby was getting used to. 'Madame...' He went to the passenger side of the car he'd arrived in and unlocked it.

'I take it that's not your car,' Libby said.

'I didn't steal it if that's what you mean.'

'No, daft!' Libby smiled. 'I mean, did you hire it?'

'It's my dad's. He puts me on the insurance when I visit.'

'Ah. I thought it looked very sensible for you.'

'You're saying I couldn't pull off a sensible car?'

'Pretty much, yeah. The Anchor's not far – we could probably walk it.'

'Would you prefer to walk it?'

'It's a bit cold but the snow and frost look pretty, don't you think?'

'I agree but I'd have thought you'd seen enough snow these past couple of days.'

'True,' Libby said. 'I'd like the walk though; after the day I've had it will clear my head.'

'Then we'll walk.' He locked the car again and pocketed the key. 'Lead the way.'

'How was your day?' he asked as they began to make their way to the pub. The pavements were still glassy in places but most of the snow had been pushed away from the centre so that people could walk without slipping, and the sky had cleared, finally, which meant no more snow but a bitter frost to coat what was already there, so that it glistened, diamond hard, on rooftops and walls, and sugar-coated lamp posts and garden shrubs. The roads were quiet and almost every house was lit from within with families gathered in dining rooms and front rooms to continue the Christmas festivities. They'd only just started to walk and already Libby was feeling the cold, but there'd be a warm welcome in the pub, and all the more rewarding for the freezing journey to get there.

'Busy,' she said. 'But I'm sure you don't want to hear about that.'

'I don't mind if you want to tell me.'

'I can't say that I do, to be honest. It was just a regular busy day at the shop; nothing crazy or exciting happened.'

'Ah,' he said. 'Well, that's my way in gone.'

'Way in to what?'

'A conversation.'

'Surely we've got other things to talk about? You must have loads of conversation topics other than my job.'

'Yes, but women don't like the man to make everything about him, do they?'

She threw him a sideways look. 'Which self-help books have you been reading?'

He laughed. 'Everyone gets everything from self-help books in LA. That, or they get an overpriced therapist who sorts out problems they didn't even know they had until they got a therapist.'

'Is it really like that? I mean, you see it on films but…'

'It depends where you look really. The funny thing about LA is that there's the glamour you see on TV, but there's also enormous poverty and hardship. That's the side of it that gets me; I really struggle with it. I mean, some sections of the city have streets just lined with row upon row of tents where the homeless sleep. It's awful really.'

'God, I never knew that. You just imagine it's all shiny and everyone lives this impossibly gorgeous life.'

'That's all a sham,' he said. 'Nobody's life is that charmed, not really. Even the people who look like they've got it all are putting on a front.'

She paused. 'Why do I feel like we're talking about something very personal now?'

'That's one of the things I noticed about you straight away – you're nobody's fool. I like that.'

'Thank you. So I'm right?'

'You are. The good news is I think I'm finally getting somewhere with it.'

'Meaning?'

'I spoke to Michaela on the phone…'

'And…?'

'I laid it on the line. I think – at least I hope I did. We've finally reached an understanding when it comes to our marriage. I think she's realised that trying to hang on to me was never going to bring us back together – if anything it was always going to push us further apart.'

'So she's going to give you a divorce?'

'She says if I get things started she'll be willing to cooperate.' He shrugged. 'I don't really know what the change of heart is about. I think it's about more than me putting my foot down. Maybe the fact that I wouldn't allow her to come to the wedding with me and insisting she stayed home without me at Christmas finally made her see how serious I was. Maybe being home without me has made her realise she can cope far better than she thought she could.'

'I can't believe you asked her not to come to the wedding and she didn't just turn up anyway,' Libby said wryly.

'Oh, right, like your ex?' he asked. 'Yes, I think I won that one, didn't I?'

'It's going to be hard for you?'

'Financially, yes. But I'm ready for the rest – like, so totally ready. I'll have to find a new place to live and that's not going to be easy, especially on one income.'

'In California?'

'That's something else I've been thinking about. To be honest, I haven't had a lot of sleep with thinking about one thing or another. Maybe the divorce will be the first of many fresh starts. I know people in the UK who would give me work… Maybe I'll come home, see what happens. Who knows… maybe after tonight I'll have another reason to.'

'That sounds like a lot of sudden change,' she said, tactfully sidestepping a reply on the real crux of what he'd just said. A reason to come back to the UK after tonight? He could only mean her, but surely he wasn't expecting that much of their drink?

'It's not sudden,' he said. 'If I'm being honest with myself, coming home's been on my mind for a while but… well, for one reason or another I just haven't been able to grapple with the idea properly and I had no motivation to. It was just another problem for me to pretend I didn't have to deal with. And work is good too right now – I'm making a name for myself and making good connections and I was scared to leave all that behind. But when I think about it now, that seems silly – if I can make all those connections in LA then surely I can make them just as easily in the UK, if not more easily than out there. Failing that, I'm sure I can travel to jobs if I have to and still be based here if I really wanted it.'

The warm glow of the pub windows beckoned them as they turned the corner into Anchor Street, which was named after the pub, or perhaps the pub was named after the street – nobody really knew. It was unassuming – tucked into a thirties semi with leaded windows dressed with lace curtains, mock Tudor eaves, and only a swinging sign to tell anyone it was a pub at all – but it was always cosy and welcoming. They could hear music coming from within, muffled but unmistakeably 'Come On Eileen' by Dexys Midnight Runners.

Noah turned to Libby and grinned. 'They're playing our tune!'

'You do realise that if it's as loud as I think it might be in there, we're not going to get a lot of talking done.'

'I don't mind if you don't. We've got time, right? Have a bit of fun, a few drinks, save the talking for later.'

'I can live with that.'

Libby pushed the door open and was greeted by a blast of hop-scented heat. The music instantly swelled, and her previous suspicions were confirmed – it was very loud and very lively in here. At first glance she couldn't see a clear table at all, but there was a little gap at the bar where they could probably stand until something became available.

'Oh man!' Noah grinned. 'I haven't been in a proper pub like this for ages!'

'I'll get these in,' Libby said. 'I owe you at least twenty rounds!'

'One will do for now,' he said cheerily.

He looked excited to be there, which Libby couldn't help but smile at because to her the only place more mundane than this pub was her own flat. She loved it and she was comfortable here, but in exactly the same way as she was at home because she was there so often. It was nice to see it through someone else's eyes for a change and, as she glanced round at decor that was so familiar to her, she took a moment to appreciate it. The ceiling was covered in embossed paper with brass light fittings, and the floors were tiled in a rich terracotta stone; the bar top was teak but the side panels whitewashed, and photos of the pub at various points through its history and featuring various landlords adorned the walls.

The current landlord, Kelvin, came over to her. 'Alright, Libby,' he said amiably. 'What can I get you?'

'Oh, the usual for me and a pint of whatever you've got on tap for—'

It was then that she felt a light touch on her arm and turned to see Noah staring at the doorway, the excitement very much gone from his face. Instead, his forehead was crinkled into a frown.

'Houston... we may have a problem.'

She followed his gaze to see Rufus walk into the pub.

'He's got Kylie with him!' she said. She wasn't angry about that, only sad and disappointed that Kylie had let him talk her into taking him back. After everything that had gone on, she'd have hoped her cousin would have more sense and strength than that. But it wasn't Libby's choice, and nor was it really her business.

'What are we going to do?' Noah asked.

She turned back to him, her expression determined. She might have been sad to see Kylie with Rufus, but she wasn't going to let him get to her. 'We're going to have our drink, of course.'

'Won't it be a bit awkward?'

'If Rufus can be a grown-up about it then I can, so if we do get trouble it will be his doing. And he wouldn't dare, not when he has Kylie with him.'

Kelvin placed her drinks on the bar and she paid for them. 'There's space over by the skittles if you want to take your drinks over there out of the way,' he said, sending a meaningful glance at Rufus and then back at Libby again.

She gave him a tight smile. Good old Kelvin – he didn't miss a trick and he knew, like many in that pub did, all about her less-than-amicable split from Rufus.

'Thanks,' she said.

As she passed Noah's drink over to him, Kylie caught her eye and mouthed something. Perhaps it was 'sorry', but it was hard to tell. Then she leant into Rufus and said something, and he seemed to notice for the first time that Libby was in there. His gaze rested on her for a moment, awkward and almost apologetic too, but then he saw Noah and it settled into something far less forgiving.

'Just let him try and start something,' Libby muttered as she turned to find their spot by the skittles.

'We can leave if you want to,' Noah said. 'I'm sure we can find somewhere else to drink.'

'We've just got a round in,' Libby said. 'There's no way I'm leaving a perfectly good drink for him.'

'But you're really not OK with this,' Noah said. 'I can tell it's going to be weird.'

She lifted her glass to her lips and paused. Why wasn't she OK? What did it matter if Rufus was in there with Kylie? As far as she was concerned they'd finally put their relationship to bed. Maybe that was why he was with Kylie now? Maybe he'd gone straight to her once he'd realised there would never be a reconciliation with Libby, and maybe Kylie had been more forgiving than Libby ever could be. And if he'd got Kylie to give him another chance then good luck to them – Libby genuinely hoped right now that things would work out for them.

'You know what, it's actually OK,' she said.

Noah raised his eyebrows. 'Really?'

'Yes, really. I mean, what kind of date would it be if I had a problem with it?'

A slow smile spread across Noah's face. 'So we're on a date?'

'I think so,' Libby said carelessly. 'Don't you?'

'I wasn't sure… I hoped so.'

'Then let's not allow anything – or *anyone* – to spoil it.'

'I'm glad you feel like that but I meant what I said. If it's weird for you—'

'Is it weird for you?' she asked.

'I guess I'd be lying if I said it wasn't a little weird. I mean, we're having a date and your ex – the guy who very definitely has a problem with me – is staring at us while we try to make small talk. I hate to be the party pooper but…'

'Yeah, I get it,' Libby said. 'In some ways it's probably worse for you than it is for me. I can just get angry with the dickhead but you've got to be a bit more diplomatic, I suppose.'

'Diplomacy wasn't really on my mind, but a rerun of our fight isn't really appealing.'

'That was hardly a fight!' Libby said with a delicate laugh.

'It was to me!' he said with mock offence, and her smile spread, the anxiety she'd been feeling at Rufus's appearance rapidly draining from her. And the fact that Noah could put her at ease just like that, in the most stressful of situations, suddenly made her realise something very important. Not only was he stupidly attractive, funny and interesting, but he was good for her. Something in him reacted to something in her like the most perfectly complementary ingredients in a recipe, or two harmonious chemicals that mixed to create just the right conditions for something wonderful to happen. They were good together – it was obvious to her now. They were good together now, and they could be amazing together given time. Being at the wedding was one thing – jeopardy often forced the conditions for something to seem more than it was and she'd wondered if she'd feel the same pull to him on a normal night out doing normal things. She'd been scared to believe it was possible but now… there was no denying it. Was it enough to take a chance on?

One thing was certain, if she didn't she'd never find out and she was tired of living with regrets. So what if it was scary? So what if it was a risk? She might get hurt, but, then again, she might not. He might fly back to California tomorrow and never come back, but he wasn't likely to if he had something to come back for – he'd said as much himself. She looked at him – the winter-sky eyes that seemed to say that he knew her, that he somehow understood her in a way she couldn't explain, and she recalled that instant jolt of connection she'd felt the first time she'd seen him. It went against every instinct to stay safe she'd ever had, but in the end, why wouldn't she take a chance on something that powerful? Crazy, maybe, but maybe crazier to ignore it.

'You know what,' Libby said, 'you're right, we should probably leave.'

He nodded.

'You want to drink that first?' she asked as he put his pint down on a nearby table that had just been vacated.

'Don't worry; I can get another somewhere else. If you need to go then I'm OK with it.'

Libby finished her gin and put the glass down next to his. Then she followed as he made his way to the exit.

'So where do you want to go?' he asked as they stepped out into the frosty night and began to walk. 'This is your patch – anywhere else you can think of?'

'Home,' she said.

'Home?' he repeated.

She nodded.

'Oh,' he said, his voice laced with disappointment.

'Don't worry – you can come too.'

'You mean…?'

'Come back to mine. We'll have a few drinks and get to know each other a bit better.'

'That sounds amazing, but are you sure it's OK?'

'Why wouldn't it be?'

'Well, you know… it's your place and we hardly know each other.'

'Noah,' she said, laughing. 'Yes, that was kind of the point of you coming round. And, don't forget, we literally spent the night together at Lovage Hall.'

'Completely literally,' he replied with a grin. 'It wasn't quite the same.'

'No, but I'd say we probably know each other a lot better than most couples on a first date, so…'

'True.'

'And, you know, it feels like a good day to throw caution to the wind, doesn't it…?'

She stopped and pushed him up against a frosty lamp post and kissed him.

'Wow,' he murmured as she pulled away. His eyes were still closed and his lips wide with a soppy smile. It was so incredibly adorable that she had to kiss him again.

'We should…' he whispered as she drew away a second time and he opened his eyes to gaze down at her, 'get going.'

'We should,' she said. 'And, you know, we could spend another night together.'

'Could we?'

'Why not? You never know where it might lead.'

'Somewhere good, I hope,' he said softly as he smiled down at her. 'In fact, I know it will be somewhere good.'

'That's what I'm betting on.'

Lacing her fingers into his, she pulled him gently onto the pavement again and they began to walk. She was risking everything on this, but suddenly it didn't feel like a risk. As she looked at him walking beside her, his breath curling into the air and a broad smile on his lips, it felt like a dead cert. They were headed somewhere good, she was sure of it, and she couldn't wait to see where.

A Letter from Tilly

I want to say a huge thank you for choosing to read *My Best Friend's Wedding*. If you did enjoy it, and want to keep up to date with all my latest releases, just sign up at the following link. Your email address will never be shared and you can unsubscribe at any time.

www.bookouture.com/tilly-tennant

I'm so excited to share *My Best Friend's Wedding* with you. Of course, as I wrote about snow and twinkling Christmas lights the UK was in the midst of a spring heatwave, but that's a writer's life for you!

I hope you enjoyed *My Best Friend's Wedding* and if you did I would be very grateful if you could write a review. I'd love to hear what you think, and it makes such a difference helping new readers to discover one of my books for the first time.

I love hearing from my readers – you can get in touch on my Facebook page, through Twitter, Goodreads or my website.

Thanks,
Tilly

tillytennant
@TillyTenWriter
www.tillytennant.com

Acknowledgements

I say this every time I come to write acknowledgements for a new book, but it's true: the list of people who have offered help and encouragement on my writing journey so far really is endless, and it would take a novel in itself to mention them all. I'd try to list everyone here, regardless, but I know that I'd fail miserably and miss out someone who is really very important. I just want to say that my heartfelt gratitude goes out to each and every one of you, whose involvement, whether small or large, has been invaluable and appreciated more than I can express.

It goes without saying that my family bear the brunt of my authorly mood swings, but when the dust has settled I always appreciate their love, patience and support. The coronavirus pandemic has meant it has continued to be a strange and difficult time for pretty much everyone on the planet, and though our everyday freedoms have been curtailed, I'm seriously thankful to have my writing to escape into. My family and friends understand better than anyone how much I need that space and they love me enough to enable it, even when it puts them out. I have no words to express fully how grateful and blessed that makes me feel.

I also want to mention the many good friends I have made and since kept at Staffordshire University. It's been ten years since I graduated with a degree in English and creative writing but hardly a day goes by when I don't think fondly of my time there. Nowadays, I have to thank the remarkable team at Bookouture for their continued support, patience, and amazing publishing flair, particularly Lydia Vassar-Smith – my incredible and long-suffering editor – Kim Nash,

Noelle Holten, Sarah Hardy, Peta Nightingale, Alexandra Holmes and Jessie Botterill. I know I'll have forgotten someone else at Bookouture who I ought to be thanking, but I hope they'll forgive me. I hope at some point in the not-too-distant future people will be able to cram into a bar once again to celebrate together, so that our annual publisher bash can return and we can all enjoy a drink! Their belief, able assistance and encouragement mean the world to me. I truly believe I have the best team an author could ask for.

My friend, Kath Hickton, always gets an honourable mention for putting up with me since primary school, and Louise Coquio deserves a medal for getting me through university and suffering me ever since – likewise her lovely family. I also have to thank Mel Sherratt, who is as generous with her time and advice as she is talented, someone who is always there to cheer on her fellow authors. She did so much to help me in the early days of my career that I don't think I'll ever be able to thank her as much as she deserves. I'd also like to shout out to Holly Martin, Tracy Bloom, Emma Davies, Jack Croxall, Carol Wyer, Angie Marsons, Sue Watson and Jaimie Admans: not only brilliant authors in their own right but hugely supportive of others. My Bookouture colleagues are all incredible, of course, unfailing and generous in their support of fellow authors – life would be a lot duller without the gang!

I have to thank all the brilliant and dedicated book bloggers (there are so many of you, but you know who you are!) and readers, and anyone else who has championed my work, reviewed it, shared it, or simply told me that they liked it. Every one of those actions is priceless and you are all very special people. Some of you I am even proud to call friends now – and I'm looking at you in particular, Kerry Ann Parsons and Steph Lawrence!

Last but not least, I'd like to give a special mention to my lovely agent, Madeleine Milburn, and the team at the Madeleine Milburn Literary, TV & Film Agency, especially Liv Maidment and Rachel Yeoh, who always have my back.